Dreamsmiths

A Novel

Rixi Hazelwood

Also by the author:

Novellas

Lanterns of the Lost

All works are available to read free online via Royal
Road as well as being available to purchase on Amazon

1

Hear the Dream Sing

There comes a moment when a dream becomes a solid thing. When it ceases to be a mere hope, a desire, and is forged into a calling. Dreamsmiths wait for that moment. They wait until they hear the dream sing, then pluck it from the spire piece by piece and meld it into being. Into a dreamstone. The greatest treasure a person can hold in their hands. An honour people only get once in their lives. Not Taren, though, so many had passed through his hands that he'd long lost count of them.

He turned the newly-crafted sphere around on the forge he'd worked at all day. Searching for imperfect seams or cracks or faults with his ice-blue eyes, and finding none. A burst of pride and excitement swelled inside him. The feeling would never fade or become tiresome. The smooth, clear glass and complex blue fractal within it was warm from the magic that melded the pieces together. From the process of dreamforging. For hours he'd searched the spire and carefully located the fragments of the dream from within. Drawing them out one by one and using his smithing skills to connect each piece. Taren smiled and took a deep breath. Almost done.

No two dreamstones were the same, a fact Taren often

marvelled at. The abstract images and patterns that sprawled inside the glass casing were always different. Unique. Just like the people out there in the city. The people that needed his help. Maybe dreamstones were living things. They certainly had the weight of something more than glass, each one large enough to fill his palm completely. The ink-like smoke housed inside danced and pulsed as though reaching, searching for the progenitor of the dream that birthed it. The thoughts, hopes, desires, all collating and mixing and creating a new version of reality for the recipient. Where would it take them? Who would it make them? No one else would ever know, except its owner.

Like all dreamsmiths, Taren gave up the right to a dreamstone of his own when he'd donned the robe of his station. Most days that didn't bother him. Being a smith had been his own most coveted desire ever since he'd learned about the Dreamforge, and he'd been granted it. An endless and overflowing gratitude lived within him for that, but that didn't make him immune to wondering. Sometimes in the quiet of the night the questions came. What patterns would live inside his own stone? Would there be the same sense of connection to a dreamstone as there was to his duty as a dreamsmith? There was no way to know, and he'd never trade his current life for anything else.

He surveyed the workroom around him with aching eyes. Most other dreamsmiths had retired for the evening, leaving the forging floor almost empty. The atmosphere was usually so different. Crackling with magic and focus, with the clang and sizzle of smithing and the haunting songs of the spire. Now the stonework that made up not just the forging rooms, but the whole Dreamforge, threw back each sound as a whispery echo to highlight the empty space. Shadows frolicked in the corners and a communal hush fell over the remaining smiths long ago. Some might find the near-empty room a source of discomfort, but not Taren. The Dreamforge was home, the place where he belonged, and he knew and loved every inch of it.

Only himself and two others, out of a group of over fifty smiths, had managed to create a dreamstone during the day's shift. Still, three was better than none. Three more people wouldn't have to wait any more. Three more people who would grin broadly, ecstatic that they'd never given up hope like so many others had. There was no better sight. A wide smile broke across Taren's face at the thought. Perhaps that was why some still worked at other forges. Never wanting to give up the search.

Working into the early evening was necessary this time. Once the creation of a dreamstone began, the connection to the forge couldn't be broken until melding finished. It was the most absolute rule of the work the dreamsmiths do. No smith would want to be responsible for destroying someone's hope. Broken dreamstones weren't recoverable. They couldn't be mended or remade. You get one chance. The rule must have been put in place for a reason. At some point in history someone had lost their chance of freedom. Taren shook the painful thought away.

As if to break his dangerous brush with melancholy, as well as the general sombre and respectable silence of the room, the familiar tromp of boots entered by the small curved staircase of the main door. He'd know that pattern of impatience anywhere and threw apologetic looks to his other colleagues in advance. Here she comes.

'Taren, are you still in here?' He didn't even have time to open his mouth all the way to respond to Fion before she carried on. Her voice echoed around the room. 'By the spire get a move on. I'm starving. How long are you going to stand there gawping at that dreamstone? Check it, box it and let's go. I've not eaten since lunch and nor have you. My stomach will chomp a hole in itself at this rate. You can romanticise our job on your own time.' Fion stood at the bottom of the stairs, arms crossed, hunger apparent in her mismatched eyes. He'd kept her waiting too long. Not the best idea. Akin only to prodding a sleeping dragon with a sharp poker.

'Sorry, I'll be right there. Go get us a table, I lost track of time.'

'No greater surprise has ever been known to the human race.' Off she went again, stamping out with not quite as much force as she entered. Fion wasn't normally that grouchy, but she did struggle to keep up a cheery demeanour when hungry. She has little, or no, shame in that. The other smiths chuckle cheerfully and Taren joins in. Fion's outburst alerted everyone to the time, and others begin the process of detaching from their forges. They'd have to give up for today.

Everyone needed a Fion in their lives as far as Taren was concerned. Friend, conscience and meal-time alarm clock all in one. You had little chance of forgetting to look after yourself, or ever living down any clumsy mistakes, when you had someone like Fion in your corner. You also had a solid support and form of encouragement and fun to break up life's heavier moments. He'd have to make it up to her by ordering an extra helping of toast with their breakfast

4

in the morning or something, or maybe just not being late for their evening meal for a change. She'd take either with a mischievous smirk and a linking of his arm. She wasn't wrong though, the day was stretching quickly into night.

The forging station in front of Taren still held a faint glow and musical ringing, his direct connection to it not quite expired. The spire called out ceaselessly and the dreamsmiths were trained to listen. To guide. To collect. To translate the network of hopes it gathers from the citizens of the outer city and pluck the fragments from the turquoise crystal roots that reached down from the ceiling like thick and eager fingers. Each one ringed by stone to attach it to the floor.

Taren pictured the spire itself. Imagining the roots travelling up, getting thicker every few metres before joining the main structure. The one that could be seen from kilometres away, reaching high and growing ever taller over time. A towering needle of crystal that represented freedom for so many. A beacon that gave the city its name. The City of Singing Spires. The crystal glittered in the sun and emitted an eerie glow at night. Wrapped around the rough stonework of the Dreamforge itself. The raised centrepiece of the city. The two structures have become one over time. Inseparable. Entwined. Taren found it beautiful. He'd spent so many years listening to the spire, perhaps it would listen to him now. Just this once.

A sheen of sweat coated his body and his hands shook. Forging was no carefree walk in the fields. His arms tired from the tension of wielding magic and the heavy fabric of his indigo robe spread a pricking dampness across his skin.

Please, he pleaded as he closed his eyes, *please belong to her.*

Let this be her dreamstone. If this could belong to Linette then I'd never ask for anything again. He closed his hands around the warm sphere, finally lifting it off of the forging plinth, and the face of a woman bloomed in his mind. The rhythm of anticipation in his chest faltered and a thickness sprang into his throat. A stranger. It's not hers. The dreamstone doesn't belong to Linette. He failed her again.

Linette, who he calls aunt at her own request, raised him. She didn't have to. So many times he'd asked to hear the story and so many times she'd told it. About how she was making the journey to the City of Singing Spires like so many others in search of better lives. About the ruined homes and buildings she would frequently see on the way. About the young boy she found in the remains of one such house, parents crushed under the debris, and how she scooped him up and took him along with her and gave him the chance to live. All the years he'd been a dreamsmith he owed to her, and still he couldn't give her the thing she wanted most. The ticket to a new life. To the life she dreamed of.

A kernel of relief sat in a shadowed corner of his heart. One that shouldn't have been there but had lodged itself in like a stubborn burr. At least this meant Linette wouldn't disappear. At least he'd get to see her again, for now. Though she'd have no trouble making her disappointment known.

He continued turning the dreamstone absently in his hands, admiring the fractal patterns and getting lost in his thoughts. In all likelihood Linette won't vanish immediately when she does get her calling. Not everyone does. Most people get to enjoy living in the affluence of the inner city

6

for several months before their dreamstones break and they're whisked away. Dissolving from their current life and reappearing in the one they've always dreamed of. There was no guarantee, though, no set time. No way to know how long someone had before they go.

He'd been putting off visiting his aunt recently. Moreso in recent months than ever before. The same questions would come again and again, like always, and he didn't want to keep answering them. To keep inviting the awkward silence and the grating of disbelief on fact. He should visit, and he would. Fion could come along to discourage Linette's questions. Once the new dreamstone was with its owner tomorrow he'd go and see her the following day. She was worrying him, truth be told. Her temper had worsened in the last year. She was beginning to resent him no doubt, for never bringing her a dreamstone.

For a moment Taren stood there, thoughts swirling, and a loop of guilt slithered through him. A lockbox clamped shut around his treacherous thoughts. The spire answered to no one, apart from Forgemaster Clayton, despite everyone answering to it. Being almost in thrall to it. That was the way of the Dreamforge, of the spire, and everyone knew it. All his colleagues, all the dreamers that were waiting, they knew. Or they should. Just like Taren should know better than to believe he could control whose dream he plucked from the crystal. The question was why. Why couldn't he just be allowed to forge her dream? To issue Linette's calling and see her troubled face light up with happiness and a relief bordering on the divine. She deserved it. She'd waited so long.

The thought sobered him. Yes, his aunt had waited a

long time, but so had many others. The mind of a dreamsmith harboured no space for selfish thoughts. He couldn't be disappointed. Couldn't allow himself to indulge in personal feelings. A dream had been forged. An irrefutably good thing. Tomorrow someone, somewhere in the outer city would hear their calling. They'd look out at the spire, their eyes filling with tears of disbelief and joy. Their passage through the inner city gate now granted. They'd be here soon enough and he could gift the dreamstone to its owner. For now, though, he could retire back to his apartment and his books after an apology-drenched meal with Fion, safe in the knowledge that he'd made one more dream come true.

2

Call of the Spire

What are people willing to endure in order to receive their dream life? How long would they wait? What conditions would they suffer? Everyone waited. Waited with a hope so delicate and frayed that it quivered at the slightest pluck. Their turn would come, they'd tell themselves endlessly. All the people living in the outer city, turning their faces to the Dreamforge, were waiting. Dreamers waiting for the call of the spire.

As the sun started its daily climb, gradually lighting the city a short distance away, Leander's gaze and thoughts had drifted to the spire once again. Its tall and jagged crystalline form reached high, the pale blue doused in the yellow hue of the sun. Its smaller cousins also glittered in the growing light. More keep springing up, though no one sees them sprout. Skewering the inner city and peppering it with more crystal in each cycle of the calendar. Maybe eventually it would encase them all. Rob them of the burden they've been saddled with. The wondering and the waiting. Was there anything worse than the waiting?

He surveyed his modest patch of arable land and filled his lungs with the morning air. It was fresh, which wasn't a rare occurrence in the outer city, or the slums as anyone who lived there had come to call it, but noteworthy all the same. Early morning was the best time of day. When the air hadn't yet filled with disappointment and flickering wishes that poured off of people as they started another day. Crops don't hope or wonder, they gratefully take what nature gives them and try and strive as best they can. Unconcerned with what might be, and concerned only with what they have. Leander tried his best to be like the crops, rather than like the people.

Working on the land offers a salve to the mire of the slums. Leander couldn't think of any way he'd rather spend his time than tending nature. It kept him feeling healthy and useful. Gave him a purpose. A daily to-do list to keep him busy. Being busy meant less time to think. Thinking was an enemy. An insidious one that had caught him off guard that morning. One many would do almost anything to avoid entertaining. Still, better a few unwanted minutes of thinking than turning to the more powerful master of denial. He didn't care for either, but would take the former over the latter every time.

Truth was rationed in the slums, often unspoken or twisted to hide its sharp barbs. Everyone knew the situation, and everyone pretended most of it didn't exist until they had to. Until hopelessness came to caress their shields of bravado-riddled certainty. Leander held no such illusions. They were trapped, with nothing left to do but wait and hope. Some people had endless reserves of the patience required for year upon year of disappointment. Some didn't. Leander kept a level head, no doubt thanks to Corryn in majority, but he also had his farm. His crops. His

10

perseverance. Did he hope? Not all the time, but he did more days than he didn't and that seemed to be the important thing.

He followed the neat lines of his crops as they swayed in the building breeze. A smile pricked the corners of his mouth as he traced the boundary of his farm. The line of his fence stood strong, built with his own hands. Land he'd had to fight to keep whole. Others hadn't been so lucky.

The slums were not so tightly packed when he first arrived outside the city, but that was years and years ago. Now any space large enough to house a dwelling found itself claimed and built upon to keep up with demand. More people wandered to the city every week, all of them hoping to hear their calling.

The southwest quarter where Leander lived was by far the most spacious precisely because of the workable land. People still needed as much food as they could get, and farmers all around the growing circle of homes that ringed the main city did their best. If someone wanted his land, they could pry it from the stiff clutches of his decaying hands.

Leander scraped a clod of earth off of his shovel with his boot. His eyes fell upon a small queue of people, which quickly expanded, bordering the divider between his land and the nearest street.

'Corryn,' he shouted towards the house, 'we've got a queue again today, is the bread ready?'

The distance between them muffled her response until she joined him in the yard. 'Wow, that's quite a crowd. Seems longer every week.' Corryn's round, smiling face was flushed from the pluming heat of their stone oven.

11

'Not every day at least, but it's closer to the weekly food delivery now. People have used up what little they had in the first place.'

'The city says it spares as much as it can, but I have to wonder if that's really true.' She used her apron to wipe her flour-smattered hands.

'I think they do what they can, or at least make it seem that way. Still, you'd think with all their crafting magics they'd be able to summon a little more food. While they're at it, they could get more people on house-building too.' Leander raised his shovel and brought it down into the ground to stand of its own accord, gratefully taking the rag Corryn offered to wipe the sweat from his brow and neck.

'I suppose the city only has so many crafters. They're always looking for more, especially those who can manufacture more grain or produce.' She watched the spire glitter as she spoke and a beat passed between them.

'I suppose so. Amazing what people will eat when they're desperate. I'd rather stick to what we can grow in the ground. The stuff they seem to drag out of thin air never tastes right.'

'Not everyone has your high standards about organic growth, oh mighty king of the crops. They're just grateful to be able to eat.' Corryn laughed as Leander regarded her with a quirked eyebrow and a smirk. 'I'll go and finish the bread, there's only a few more batches to bake.' She gave him a warm smile and departed for the kitchen.

Mighty king of the crops. A chuckle escaped his lips, and a wave of brotherly love washed over him. After his wife, Melynda, got her calling and eventually vanished like all the others, Corryn had saved Leander. Thinking about it disturbed a grimy layer of silt in the bottom of his stomach that bloomed in choking clouds. Gritty bitterness mingling with a tinge of smoother sadness. Had it been foolish? To think his wife's dream life might have included him, too? Probably. Though part of him was content with continuing to help the community alongside his sister-in-law. The pride in what they could accomplish between them was mutual.

Sheepish waves and nods of respect fluttered down the queue as Leander offered good mornings and gathered his shoulder-length, dull-blond hair up into a rough bun tied with an old piece of black string. It wasn't long until the delicious waft of hot bloomer loaves and their sesame seed topping doused the queue. An eager growl escaped his, and likely everyone else's, stomach. Luckily the chatter drowned it out.

As he peeled away from the small talk to go and help Corryn to carry the bread baskets some shouts and protests drifted to him. Near the back of the line of hungry mouths a pair of men shoved and jostled people. Knives glinted on their belts, and their hands itched for a reason to draw them. Cullers. Leander's face hardened. They could get themselves away from his land and from the people simply waiting for some food. Their harmful ideals had no place near his farm.

Exactly when the cullers appeared people aren't really sure. But they won't be forgetting in a hurry. In some ways it might be inevitable. Put enough people in less than desirable living conditions and dissent is natural. Some might expect revolution, but not this kind. Not the kind that leads to random death. Thinning the numbers so those who remain have a better chance at being chosen. A twisted, but persuasive, line of thought that had more alluring overtones than Leander ever expected.

Their ideology trickled into those whose cracked hope thinned out to become porous. Their morals and rhetoric could be insidious, the perfect patch for the threadbare fabric of over-taxed patience. The majority of people in the slums lived in solidarity, in compassion for one another's plight because they all shared the same one. Most, but not all. The cullers wielded power because they offered an alternative. The potential for a quicker way out. Anything could start to make sense to the desperate if it was framed correctly. They chose at random, just like the spire. What could be more fair?

The saliva in Leander's mouth turned to ash at the mere thought of the group and he spat to rid himself of the reminder of their existence. How many lives had they taken, both by their selection and through those pleading to be released? Well, not here. Not near his property.

'Hey!' His shout echoed and those in the queue turned to face him one by one, cullers included, as he strode towards them. Keep calm, stand tall. They squared up to face Leander as he rounded the fence, his dark walnut gaze steady and unfaltering in the face of their disdain. 'Get off my land. These people are only here for food.' The more slender of the two cullers widened his face into an unsettling grin. His reedy limbs reminded Leander of the dolls the slum kids make from twigs and knobbly sticks.

'We aren't on your land. Your land is on the other side of that fence, farmer.'

'It's close enough to my land that you're making yourselves my concern. Move on. Take your flawed ideals elsewhere, or nowhere at all would be preferable.'

14

'Hark at 'im.' The more muscular culler took a step closer to Leander. A bull of a man, with as much social grace as one. A pungent tang filled his nose. 'You got designs on livin' in the inner city, farmer? You trying to speak like the fancy dreamers?'

'We're all dreamers, every single one of us.' Leander nearly cringed at himself, spouting such optimistic rubbish so early in the day. The people needed to hear it, though.

The reedy culler circled to stand behind him, his jagged grin prickling against Leander's back. 'Exactly, there are so many of them. Don't you want to better your chances? Thin the herd?'

Leander grimaced, a white hot spark flaring under the surface. 'I don't. We all want the same thing. It's not up to us who gets their calling. Not even you and your pathetic little crusade can control it. That said… I hope your time never comes.'

No one grinned now. Neither man had Leander's stature. At around six feet tall and with a lifetime of fieldwork behind him they were no match for his strength. Cullers worked in the shadows or by causing disruption and unease.

Leander didn't waver or back down, and the cullers knew he wouldn't. They spat in his direction before walking away, grinning over their shoulders at the people in the breadline. The remaining people reached out to Leander once the ghastly men were out of sight, gripping his hands and arms in thanks and bowing their heads. Their undeserved praise prickled more than the crooked grin of the filth he'd scared off.

Corryn struggled out of the house with two large

baskets and he rushed back down the path to help her. As their eyes met her eyebrow quirked. Very little escaped Corryn's notice and he hadn't the slightest doubt that he'd be grilled about what she'd just missed later on. For now they had mouths to feed.

***

Leander's heavy-duty boots thunked to the floor under the communal table one by one. A sigh of relief rushed into the room as his body sank gratefully into the uncomfortable chair. Their home, like everyone else's in the slums, was small. Though, just like with the fields, they were lucky to have a slightly more spacious place to live than anyone who arrived in recent years.

He and Corryn had lived there so long that it hadn't been a slum when the three of them, including Melynda, first arrived. Houses had been more spaced out, the outer city hadn't spread as far. Despite having a larger home, it was predominantly one room with two tiny bedrooms off to the side and a small room to shower and relieve themselves. They also built a small outbuilding for their larger oven some time ago. A basic home, but warmer than outside and dry.

Leander could rarely imagine himself feeling at home anywhere else. Sometimes he did, when memories flickered in the corners or seeped out of the deteriorating walls, and in those times the fields were where he felt safe.

Corryn let her long, mousy-brown hair fall out of what she called her working hairstyle: A tight braided bun to keep it all out of the way. Her berry blue eyes searched his face as she ran a brush through her braid-crimped locks in long, careful sweeps.

16

'Was there trouble out there?'

'Just a couple of cullers. They were easy enough to scare off.'

'You being scary, there's a funny thought. If only they knew the truth.'

'People will know what I want them to know. I can't really help it with you. Everyone who sits in front of you becomes involuntarily transparent.' They chuckled as they teased each other.

'Well, you know, I've always had a knack for seeing when people are putting up a front. You can't hide from me.'

'You sound proud of that.'

'Oh I am, don't even think twice about it. So, what bothered you more? The cullers or being thanked and praised for getting rid of them?'

Leander scoffed. 'I'd rather take a whole group of cullers on by myself than be heralded like that for something any decent person would do.'

'You give yourself too little credit. What you do here deserves praise. I'm proud of what we do, grateful that we can help out even a little while we wait. You're a good guy, if still a bit young.' She winked at Leander's incredulous expression.

'Young? I suppose that makes you ancient. I hope I never see such a decrepit age.' She threw her rag at him and he caught it. Leander used it to refresh his face and gently launched it back at Corryn, who recoiled comically. There wasn't that much difference in their ages, truth be told. Corryn being in her thirty-fifth year and Leander being five years younger, but they could joke. It passed the time and lightened the mood, what did they have if not humour? As she took the rag to the sink he moved to the open door to catch the breeze that swept through from the field. The cold air from the ridge of the mountains in the backdrop of the small farm was the most crisp. Its gentle stream washed over his closed eyes.

Somewhere in the distance a raucous laugh cut across the air as the afternoon began to wind down. At least others had humour too, and people to laugh with in rare moments when their minds were free enough to do so. The spicy scent of some kind of chilli or curry spiked in his nose. Communal batch cooking was common and made for the most inventive combinations. Several houses or even several streets would pool what little food they had left together, working around large and infinitely battered cooking pots over rough-shod fires wherever was safe enough to light them. At least others were somehow managing. Looking out for each other like he and Corryn tried to do.

As he leaned against the door frame an uncomfortable stirring turned his stomach. It wasn't nausea or any kind of cramp. More like a pot of thick stew stirring, pushed around by the bubbles growing beneath the surface. Some manner of illogical dread or nervousness. He searched his mind for a reason, and couldn't find one. Belated adrenaline from the altercation with the cullers, perhaps?

From the door he had a clear, and some would argue breath-taking, view of the city. Its high walls harshly segregating his life from the life of those within. The low glow of the patterned gates kept out any who had not yet heard their call.

The City of Singing Spires. It always held Leander in

rapture with its bewitching sentience, a pulse and a thrum that betrayed its melded stone and crystal facade. It seemed a lifetime ago that he'd first travelled there. First seen the main spire on the horizon, catching the light in a tower of glimmering mystery.

It could be the centrepiece on the crown of a benevolent underground siren. Its haunting calls were her dangerous and lonely songs. She beckoned to them all, longing for company and recognition, wanting to share her strange magics with those she ensnared in her traps. It was stark in contrast to the sturdy stone of the Dreamforge, which was more akin to a layered castle of sorts that followed the circular pattern of the city proper. Such an opposing set up, the delicate turquoise of the spire against the solid, carved outline of the Forge. An unlikely pair, but one that the whole world relied upon.

They were up there, the dreamsmiths, deciding the fate of everyone who waited at the gates. Did they revel in their power? Why didn't they give more dreams to the people? If they could, they should, shouldn't they? They can't be blind from up there in their towers. They can't ignore the struggles of the slumfolk. He might have told the cullers that people were chosen by the spire at random, but not everyone believed that.

It wasn't a fair line of thought. The Forge did all it could for those living outside of the city, but the doubts kept coming. Leander questioned them. He questioned everything. The swirling, uneasy mulch continued to coil and squirm in his gut. As the spire glinted it held him in that moment so fiercely that a thought danced into existence.

Will my turn ever come, or is this strange feeling just another pointless flare of hope?

3

The Burden of Waiting

There was one thing Taren could absolutely expect from visiting Aunt Linette, and that was the hot water boiling for tea within seconds of entering her home. She'd been that way ever since he was young. When guests visit, you prepare a hot drink. No questions or excuses.

The taste of the tea was the taste of his childhood. Sometimes he could even find his way home through the winding alleys of the slums by the smell of her careful and unique blends. Well, before he moved to the inner city anyway. Time and time again he'd encouraged her to open some kind of tea shop, but she always scoffed or laughed him off, and she did so again on this visit.

'But you'd be the most successful tea shop in the slums, you know you would.'

'Maybe so, but that's not what people need around here. That's an inner city notion if ever I've heard one, and the answer is still no.' A flattered humour filled her low voice, one reserved for imagination rather than reality. She pulled her crocheted shawl a little tighter around her shoulders, though the air had no chill.

'Well, your tea will always be my favourite, and I'll

continue telling everyone I know about it.' He stirred the rich brown liquid in his cup and inhaled the aroma with a smile as if to make a point.

'You do that, but you know as well as I do that no other dreamsmiths save you and Fion would ever want to find themselves in this shack of mine.'

The way she said shack, as though it were a sharp barb, made Taren flinch. Linette was a strict woman, and not afraid to make her displeasure of her situation known. The last years had been harder, making her frame more delicate and thinner than Taren cared to admit at times. He brought what extra provisions he could for her, but he suspected she handed them all out to others more in need. His eyes fell to his tea as he thought of the dreamstone he'd held in his hands yesterday. How he handed it to someone who wasn't Linette. Did his regret sing to her the way the spire sang to him?

They sat around a small table in the middle of the room, the only real furniture and a commodity most people chose to have. It allowed them to have company over. Sometimes company was all some folks had. Taren searched for words of comfort, but couldn't find any. They'd spoken often about Linette's hatred of the slums, and he could feel the usual string of questions leading to the one he dreaded most. She wouldn't dive straight in to it, but eventually she'd get there. She'd ask. Maybe this time he'd be spared the guilt. Maybe, but not likely.

'How are things going up there in the grand tower?' She didn't look at Taren as she asked. Choosing instead to trace the rim of her own cup, which was full of nearly-cold tea. She must have poured her own long before he arrived and hadn't bothered replacing it. 'I heard there was a calling yesterday. Was it one of yours?'

'It was. My first in a week or so.' The tea was still a little too hot, but he took a scalding sip and brushed past the subject onto less direct matters. 'Things go well enough, everything considered. There are fewer people stepping forward to be dreamsmiths so the number of dreamstones being made is less than we'd like. Hopefully that won't be the case much longer, but people just keep turning up. Far faster than people are disappearing. Makes me wonder where they're all coming from and how they even know about the spire.'

Linette scoffed. 'You think word about something like this won't have travelled to every corner of the world by now? Every city and town and tiny remote village. The chance to leave this life behind and live the life you dream of? Who wouldn't take that chance? Who wouldn't make that journey? If anything it's old news by now. And once they're here, who would leave? No one. Not with the chance the spire offers.'

'I know it's just… there's only so many people we can provide for and if more are arriving than leaving…' Taren trailed off, this thoughts scrunching together into an indecipherable bunch.

'That's exactly why people don't need a tea shop. They'd rather make their clothes last a bit longer with my mending skills than waste any coin they do happen to get their hands on on indulgences. Are you looking after yourself up there, at least?'

'I am, it's you I'm worried about.'

'You needn't worry.' Linette met his eyes briefly. A

darting glance. Here it comes. 'Besides, who knows, maybe soon it will be my turn.' There it was. The question disguised as a statement. She met his gaze again, steady and even. Almost defiant. The question hidden in her eyes instead of her words. He could only release a gentle sigh.

'I hope it will be. I really do.'

'You'd tell me, wouldn't you, if you knew?'

Taren reached across to rest his hand over one of hers. They were cold, but not frail. She worked with her hands too much for them to weaken.

'Of course I would. You'd be the first to know if I had have any idea when it would be. I know it's hard to-'

'You don't.' It was a quiet interruption rather than a spiked one. Linette pulled her hand away and rose to stand at the dingy window. 'You don't know what it's like to wait. To still be waiting. To long for nothing but to hear your calling and hold your dreamstone in your hands.'

'I've held plenty of them, Auntie, I make them.'

'I know that, but none of them are yours are they? You don't need one. You got your dream without one.' Silence plumed as the words hung in the air. She was right. Dreamsmiths don't get a dreamstone. For most who choose it being a dreamsmith is their dream. What would his dream life even look like if not this? If not helping others then what would he spend his time doing? It wasn't something he could imagine.

Many dreamstones had passed his hands, but never his own. He hadn't really thought about it as a loss before. Making something he'd never have for those who wanted nothing aside from that very thing.

'Sorry, I bring this up every time. I know you can't

24

know. You can't choose who's next.' The words were clipped, strained with belief she didn't truly feel and imitated poorly. Taren turned to face her properly in his chair. The look in her eyes made his heart flutter. Her mud-coloured gaze turned harsh and narrow. Face jagged and tight with bitterness. Was it for the slums, for her life, or for him? Or a tangled mess of all three?

Sometimes he wondered if he knew Linette as well as the child in him liked to hope. Afterall, he'd left her home to start training as a smith at the age of sixteen, and had lived between the Dreamforge and the inner city ever since. At the age of twenty-nine now, that was quite a gap. Only in the last three years, ever since he graduated as a dreamsmith in his own right, had he felt it. The change in her feelings towards him. How they were warping. The boy she'd saved and raised becoming a man who couldn't or wouldn't help her. The very thought scored Taren's chest as a fierce bundle of sharp brambles. He'd do anything to show her that wasn't the case. Anything to remind her that he did care, and that he did hope on her behalf.

'If I could, I would have chosen you first. Every time I make a stone I wish it to be yours. Including the one I made the other day. I wanted yesterday's calling to belong to you, Auntie. You deserve the life you dream of. Sometimes I think it's the only way I can pay you back for all you've done.'

'I did what most people would, that's all. Tough as our circumstances are, I don't think anyone would leave a child alone in the open world during a pilgrimage to the spire.' She dodged past his sincerity with a bristle of cold, but he didn't give up. He reached for her hands again and stood at

25

the window with her, looking down at the face he grew up with.

'That doesn't make me less grateful. I promise I'll bring it to you. No matter who forges it I'll be the one to put your dreamstone in your hands. I swear it.'

That made her smile and squeeze his hands in return. The tension and heavy clotting in the air cleared away at the sight of her grin. Taren glanced out of the small window and his heart fluttered. It was so light already. He'd be late. Linette, as always, read his mind.

'You'd better get going. The Dreamforge waits for no one. Bring Fion with you next time, I haven't seen her for a while. I have clients arriving soon as well, so I need to tidy myself and this pig-sty.'

Taren suppressed a scoff of disbelief. Linette never had a hair out of place and her home was likely one of the cleanest in any of the slum quarters. She somehow managed to make tarnished wood gleam with her fastidiousness and the place always had a smell of lemons that bordered on clinical. Nevertheless he did have to get going.

He stretched his back, and she looked up at him. When had she aged quite this much? The spire had to choose her soon. Please let it choose her soon. The burden of waiting was ebbing her away, wearing her down. Vanishing like soap under hot running water.

He embraced her and she returned it, holding him tight. She'd done this all her life, as though she had multiple sides. The person that wanted to be his mother, the one who wanted to be his wise and distant aunt, and the person who wanted something from him that he could never guarantee she'd get. Whatever she wanted to be, so long as she was

26

safe and well, he'd do his best for her. As they parted she brushed a wrinkle out of his indigo robe. One that every dreamsmith wore. A colour she often admired for its dubiousness. Was it blue or purple? She said it went well with the uncertainty of his job. There was an irony in that.

'I'll come back soon.' He took both of their cups and placed them in the sink on his way out.

'See that you do, and look after yourself.'

Taren nodded and didn't hurry his stride until he'd rounded the corner. He didn't fancy being late again. He could see Fion's smug look if he was the last to stumble up to his forge for the day. No one else would care, but he didn't need to give her another reason to make him the butt of a joke. He was just about out of the woods for making her late for dinner the other night. Still, enough wondering, he had to focus.

It wasn't always a good idea for a dreamsmith to wander the slums alone. It was why so few ventured out. Only those who still had relatives out there would be seen in the street with any measure of consistency. Otherwise most kept to the inner city, some even to the Dreamforge and nowhere else.

The morning bustle was just starting to hit its flow. As Taren passed people in the streets, the variety of reactions was something he'd quickly become used to. He'd had grand delusions when he was accepted for training. Arrogant and naïve thoughts of being revered and fawned over as someone who helped to improve lives. While that's what he believed the Dreamforge's purpose to be, and that he was part of that purpose, as he'd grown older he'd come to understand there was a completely different side to it.

27

People who receive their dreamstones, and those that have to wait. And keep waiting. Endlessly and without indication.

It was much more unfair than he'd realised as a younger man. The whole system sparked a dark and complex maze of thoughts and feelings among the people of the outer city. Complex mazes had black and lonely corners, and he had no wish to disturb anyone who might be crouching in them.

Some people gave a slow and deliberate nod in recognition and respect, some pulled their faces into tight and disapproving expressions. Occasionally he'd hear the unmistakable firing of spit in his direction after he'd passed by. Through it all he kept a pleasant but middling expression, nodding to those who greeted him. Best not draw more attention than necessary, and his hurried gait meant he passed people much too quickly for them to react in most cases. Then you have those who choose to make a scene. Those who draw attention so they can puff out their chests and say their piece. As much as Taren hoped that day wouldn't be one of those days, his luck had run out.

He spotted the cullers well ahead of time but had no way to avoid them. They walked in the middle of the semi-busy street, their features sour and crackling with poor mood. Marvellous. Just what he needed. The chances of being able to walk by them without remark or interaction were as likely as every person receiving their dreamstones in the five seconds that followed. In short, impossible. He stared straight ahead, not wanting to be inflammatory by simply making eye contact. As expected, it didn't work in the slightest.

'What's this then? A dreamsmith bothering to show his face to us lowly slum dogs?' Quiet swept through the air, rippling as people turned. At first Taren didn't slow, but ignoring them would only agitate them further.

'I just want to get back to the Forge. Nothing more.'

'No doubt. Going to roll a dice to choose which one of us is next?'

'The spire makes the choices.'

'Oh aye, the spire. Always the spire. You're all useless, then? Talking to a big crystal? Expect us to believe that?' The shorter of the two slowly moved his hand to rest on the hilt of his dagger as the taller one spoke. Faces looked on, expectantly waiting for an answer.

'We do what we can with what we have. Please let me by.'

'Seems this one's got some manners. Inner city man if ever I've heard one. Touring the slums as though it's a zoo, no doubt, to gawk at those of us still unchosen.'

Taren had schooled his patience until then, but something about the man stoked a bolt of rage.

'I'm not touring. I have family here. Whatever prattle you believe about what we do is your own business, but we have no say and that's always been known. I know how twisted your ideals are. Don't think I can't see what group you're from. Stirring trouble helps no one. If your lot are so concerned with increasing your chances you'll not keep a dreamsmith from their forge. Now let me by.'

A furious wave of indignation seeped from both the cullers, and yet something held them back. Taren's heart spluttered with guesswork. Would they attack or would they step down? Cullers weren't known for their polite conversation, and their ideals turned Taren's stomach. Thin the herd for the good of those who remain. A sickening thought. How many had died on the blade of that poisonous rhetoric?

Time and time again many dreamsmiths had asked why nothing could be done about their radical and murderous behaviour. Time and time again it was said that even should they remove this group, others would form with similar ideals. To Taren's surprise, the cullers walked on by. Muttering insults as they did so. That had probably used up any and all luck he'd been allotted for the day after all. The spire shimmered against the now mid-morning light. With a polite nod that betrayed nothing of his swirling stomach, Taren pressed on to the inner city and the Dreamforge. To his home and to his own calling.

4

The Founding Dreamsmith

Fion rapped her knuckles on Taren's door with sharp enthusiasm. The early set of bells had just chimed. They echoed in the cavernous halls of the Dreamforge and roused her fellow dreamsmiths from their sleep. She fiddled with the silk belt of her rich, indigo robe while she waited, making sure the fastening buckle was straight and centred. The day had a good feel about it, yet Taren was probably still asleep and wantonly wasting it so far.

'Taren,' she knocked again, 'let's go. Don't tell me you were up late again reading. If you get drool on the pages of another book the Librarian will defenestrate you.' No answer. 'How long are you gonna leave me standing out here? Taren?'

Forget formalities. They'd discarded them long ago. She shoved the door handle down and barged into the room, hoping to shock him awake or see outrage on his face. 'Taren?' Nothing but cool silence. 'He's not even here. By the spire I look like an idiot now.'

His bed was half made, as though done in the bleary dark, and books littered the place as normal. Fion sighed and ran a hand over the back of her short-cropped blonde pixie cut. There wasn't long until the second round of waking bells, then they'd have to head to the forges for their shift. Where was he?

'He's probably gone down to see Linette,' she informed no one in particular. 'If he's going to head out so early he at least needs to be back on time. He's hopeless.' She swept out of the room, closing the door carefully behind her. She'd have to wait for him again, but he definitely wouldn't hear the end of it.

She should have gone with him to see Linette, really. She hadn't seen Taren's aunt for a little while. She'd have to remember to give him grief for not extending an invitation. Taren had been worried about his aunt recently, concern creasing his face every time they mentioned her. Hopefully she was alright.

Fion joined the throng in the corridor. The tired, still-waking faces of her fellow smiths made her chuckle. Very few of them were morning people the same way her and Taren were. Clearly there wasn't much energy around today. Most only nodded in response to her jovial morning greetings, as though she were speaking too loud. It only made her beam brighter.

The front courtyard was quiet, empty even. Still in the shadow of the towering structure of the Dreamforge as the sun rose behind it. She almost felt bad for disturbing its peace. The stone bench next to the grand gates chilled the underside of her legs even through her thick robe. Sometimes she felt incredibly lucky to be able to call the Dreamforge her home. A swirling building of smooth stone and turquoise crystal. They were forever interwoven, much like she was with the place herself.

Lucky though she counted herself, it also set her apart from almost everyone else. She wasn't an inner city dweller, not technically. She hadn't earned her spot there, though she did have her own house inside the protection of the calling gates. It seemed a waste given how little she used it, instead preferring her apartment inside the Forge. That was the space she felt safest, the place she'd lived in longest. She didn't come from the inner city, but nor was she one of the slumfolk like Taren. She hadn't lived there long enough to remember it all that well.

Before she could take an unwilling stroll down memory lane, Taren strode in through the gate. The bench hid Fion from view right at the entrance so he didn't even see her.

'Late again?' She choked back a laugh as her words startled him.

'Jeez!' A hand flew up to his chest and he rolled his eyes. His long, raven ponytail whipping around as he turned to face her. 'Fion for spire's sake don't do that.'

'I'm not sorry, you're nearly late. Where'd you go?'

'You're very lively today.'

'Speak for yourself, you jumped almost a metre in fright just now.' Fion grinned, a teasing spark in her mismatched eyes.

'Stop exaggerating. Why are you down here?'

Fion could tell he fought to keep his own grin in check as they slipped into their usual banter.

'Someone's got to keep track of you, haven't they? We're on shift together today. Your inner-city house will start to miss you if you stay here much longer. When's the last time you went home? You know you wouldn't have to leave as early if you stayed there once in a while.'

'You're one to talk, there's probably a layer of dust so thick in your house that you won't be able to open the door.'

'I prefer it here, it feels more like home, you know?'

'I know.'

'How's Linette?' They started walking back towards the Dreamforge, their echoing footsteps transferring to the more muted carpet of the corridors when they reached the main thoroughfare.

'She's alright, I think. Sometimes it's hard to tell with her. She seemed a little better than last time I visited anyway.' They turned down a set of stairs, lower and lower they'd go until they reached the forging floor.

'I'm glad. Did she... ask again?'

Taren sighed. 'She did, in her way. It didn't help that she heard about the calling yesterday and asked if it was one of mine. News travels faster than the smell of strong dung out there. I don't know why she can't understand we have no say. Why so many people can't seem to understand that.' A dip in his energy made Fion loop her arm around his. He was so easily pulled into contemplation and for Taren that wasn't always a good thing.

'I know that look, Taren. The best thing we can do for them is our job.'

'You're right, I just...' another sigh escaped him. 'Let's go.' Fion batted his hands away as he ruffled her hair, his laughter mingling with her disquiet to mask the sombre moment. They walked in companionable silence the rest of the way, re-joining the steady stream of dreamsmiths as they all headed for the forges.

***

The warm, close air of the forging room brought Fion familiar comfort. There were no windows and only one door in and out. Not the most reassuring design, but it's what they had to work with since it was a level below ground out of necessity. A few stairs curled around the circular shape of the chamber and then plateaued into a rolling space. Stone again, like most of the Forge, and arched ceilings supported with carved pillars.

Light ventured out from crystal lamps laid in to the cool, flawless walls. Turquoise buttresses that flickered with murky activity, singing in low and high songs alike, passed down through the ceiling and anchored with the floor. They were spaced perhaps ten metres apart in all directions and followed the pattern of the circular chamber.

Fion imagined that the room had been built around the great roots. The roots to the main spire. The centre-point of the city and the beacon of hope that so many gathered around.

Usually, the forging floor buzzed with conversation and concentration as the smiths worked, but today there was quiet. Hushed whispers and a gaggle of robes huddled around one of the forging stations. Taren drew in a little gasp and Fion raised an eyebrow as she turned to look at him, then back to the crowd. The Forgemaster. Fion rolled her eyes. She respected the Forgemaster, as all smiths did, but she didn't share Taren's star-struck butterflies whenever he entered a room. That might be a slight exaggeration, but barely. That, and her bond with the head of the Dreamforge was unique among the dreamsmiths.

'Are you just going to stand there with glittering eyes or are you going to move forward and watch him work?' She whispered with a smirk.

'He hasn't been on the forging floor for a while.'

'Well he is kinda busy, you know. Looking after the whole city. Stop goggling and go, or you'll miss it.' Fion's scoff was cut short by Taren's elbow finding her ribs, and they moved to join the throng.

Forgemaster Clayton stood in front of the largest, most central forge. He was tall in stature and robed in rich blue material. He wore his hood up, Fion might be one of the few people who'd ever seen him with it down. His kind, grey eyes scrutinised the forge before him, sharp with knowledge and confidence. He performed checks from time to time to ensure there were no problems with the surrounding forges. He could access all of the spires from any forge and see into them, speak with them. That kind of skill and mastery was beyond imagination for most dreamsmiths.

While training they all learned how to control one root of one spire and to pull the fragments of dreams out as they revealed themselves. Fion remembered those days well, and even though she was often praised for her natural aptitude, it didn't mean she'd found it easy. That alone took years to master in a safe and proficient way. To access them all at once and feel all of that information, to be able to control it, that was why Taren admired him so much. Why everyone admired him, really. He was the founding dreamsmith, the one who built the Dreamforge and the hope that so many clung to. Fion admired him for different reasons.

Sometimes she wondered if anyone else saw him the way she did. The man who practically raised her, though all the senior dreamsmiths had pitched in when she was very young. Everyone else only saw the grand peak of the mountain of his achievements, she saw the roots and more of the tunnels underground. She didn't disagree though, he was kind and compassionate, strict and wise, and powerful. Unmatched.

The Forgemaster approached one of the stations at the buttress in front of him. Each rough cylinder of crystal was ringed with thick stone. Four plinths with flat surfaces emerged at cardinal points around each one. Four smiths to a root, one smith to each forging station.

He worked with precision. One hand connected to the forge, palm facing the crystal and linking to it via a blue tendril matching the hue of the spires. It snaked from his hand, shedding small pulses of gentle light. Neon symbols swirled around his forearm and lit up at varying intervals as he communicated with the spire. The root rippled and sang to its neighbours each time his free hand gestured a command. It was a delicate sound, but insidious, and continued to resonate for minutes after it faded away. Despite being insidious, it was also harmonious. An ill-controlled forge wasn't easy on the ear, but few could match the orchestral nature of the Forgemaster's skill.

The master stepped back, task complete, and fell into conversation with the surrounding smiths as everyone dispersed. Time to get to work. The smiths worked on alternating shifts as a safety measure, fulfilling the mandatory stipulation that they not connect to the forges for two consecutive days.

Fion turned away and took up a place on one of the nearby stations. Taren stayed where he was, still gazing at the forge the inspection had taken place on. He was so intent in his thoughts, as he often tended to be, that he didn't even see the Forgemaster approaching. Sure, Fion could have warned him, but that would have taken the fun out of his reaction.

'I like to see that kind of determination in the eyes of a young smith.' Taren turned toward the sonorous voice and with a surprised shuffle he lowered his head out of respect. Fion grinned watching him fluster.

'Thank you, Forgemaster. It was an excellent demonstration.'

'I look forward to seeing your work today, the senior smiths always have good things to say. Seems soon you'll be giving Fion a run for her coin.' A salt and pepper goatee framed his polite features as he smiled in Fion's direction. She snorted at the thought.

'I don't think he's quite there yet, Forgemaster. Give him another half-decade and maybe he'll manage it.'

The Forgemaster chuckled and clapped Taren on the shoulder. 'You certainly like a challenge choosing Fion as a friend. But it also makes you very lucky. Don't be a stranger though, there's no reason a graduated student can't visit their old teacher. I do miss our conversations.'

'I'll take you up on that soon.'

'I hope so. With both of you working the forges today, it should be a promising and pleasing day for the residents of the outer city.'

'We'll do our best.' Fion beamed at the founding smith as though he were an old friend.

'Forgemaster, a moment?' A smith Fion and Taren had trained with, Jacklan, caught the Forgemaster's attention. She held back a grimace. He wasn't her favourite person in the world, and that may be an understatement. His downturned features aged his face more than he'd like. Always so serious. In her mind she pictured a grumpy frog wearing a dreamsmith robe and had to stifle a cackle at the similarity. Oddly, it was a likeness that vanished entirely on the rare occasion Jacklan genuinely smiled.

There was a cold and distant arrogance about him at times, and he'd come across as rude to her and to Taren on several occasions. She had no time for people who lacked basic social manners.

'Could I ask you to check my forge before you leave? Its resonance is… troubling me.'

'Of course, I'll be right there.'

Fion watched with interest as the Forgemaster connected to the indicated station. She sidled over to whisper to Taren.

'Do you think it's just Jacklan screwing up again?'

'Possibly, he's had more trouble handling the resonance than anyone else.'

'I'll say, he only graduated last year.' It didn't usually matter when a smith graduated, but Jacklan had started his training at the same time as Taren. It took him two years longer to earn his robe so he was still new. That wouldn't ordinarily be a problem, if Jacklan didn't act like he'd been a dreamsmith all his life at the same time as constantly pining for the Forgemaster's attention. An odd dichotomy to carry off.

'It's different for everyone, Fi. We can't all be as brilliant as you and be the youngest smith ever to earn their robe.'

'You'll make me blush with all that smarmy praise, though I can barely hear it under your sarcasm.'

39

He snorted, but they admired each other's skills as well. The Forgemaster deemed the station was fine, and Jacklan's face sank into dejection upon learning there wasn't a problem. Fion didn't miss it though, and doubted Taren did either, the slight knit in the Forgemaster's brow as he stepped back from the glowing root.

He turned to look it up and down again as he stood at the bottom of the stairs before leaving, and his hurried demeanour as he did so puzzled Fion. Warnings bloomed, but the Forgemaster had approved the station for use. Everything would be alright, if there was a problem he would have reassigned Jacklan to another forge... surely?

5

Dreamstones

Taren always relished the flutter of excitement that churned within as he stepped up to a forging station to begin a fresh day's work. He'd never tire of it, especially after the high of crafting a dreamstone during his last shift. A determination brimmed under his surface. He would craft another dream for someone today. He'd send out another calling to let the recipient through the city gates and then bind them with their dream life, handing them their dreamstone and irrevocably changing their lives.

He wanted to give back to them as payment for his own good fortune. It had been his driving force ever since the day he had to leave his aunt out there in the slums. He couldn't bring her to the inner city because she hadn't had her calling. The gate wouldn't let her through, but he wanted to get as many people through the gates as he could.

He'd made it through his dreamsmith training and the aptitude tests quickly, though that still took almost a decade. The tiredness, the trials of it, aching in a way only learning to control magic can produce. Long nights of study, the joy of absorbing all that knowledge like a sponge finding water in a desert. All of it worth it. The pride and wonder of receiving his robes warmed him each time he remembered it. Only one dreamsmith had graduated faster than him, and she rarely let him forget it.

As Taren positioned himself in front of his forge, the uncomfortable expression on the Forgemaster's face replayed in his mind until he forced himself to shake it away. He had to focus. The forging stations were ornate, with patterns woven in to the structure where the turquoise melded with the smooth grey. Tendrils from the root wrapped together to form a solid block that made up the main bulk of each forge. He took the southern station of his root. To his right Fion settled in at her place on the eastern one for the day, so they were working side by side.

Over Taren's right shoulder on the root behind, Jacklan approached his forge with confidence and the smirk he always wore when he thought no one was looking. He was the only one working on his chosen root. Fion, who could see their colleague by looking past Taren, rolled her eyes as he started an unnecessary display of dramatic arm movements. Perhaps Jacklan felt he had to put on more of a show to make up for his still-developing skills. Whatever the reason, Taren took a breath to suppress a laugh, and tried to clear his mind. Only one thing niggled somewhere in a dark and dangerous corner, but they'd been assured. The Forgemaster said that Jacklan's forge was fine, and they all trusted him, so they had to get to work.

With his feet a comfortable distance apart and one arm outstretched, palm facing the root of the spire, revolving bracelets of shining symbols appeared at Taren's wrists and unique letters turned slowly in alternating directions around his forearm. The spire started to hum, louder and louder,

42

until he took control of its resonance and funnelled it towards his outstretched hand. A connecting line danced towards him from the forge, reaching for the one that snaked out from his palm as he pushed back against the pressure of the root's power. He was connected.

The moment of connection resounded in him. A bell tolling deep within. In each moment that passed a new, unseen connection was made with the spire and a new note would ring out in his mind. Concentration and visualisation were key. Standing in a starlit cave of glass-blown crystal, he listened. The notes hummed and tinkled. An army of careful puppets struck the crystals with tuning forks in the dark arches of the cave he pictured. He searched for harmonies among them, for notes of the same hue, sorted and sifted through them for a long time, pairing and piecing until... there! Five or six connections with the same texture and song. That was enough to craft a dream.

A twist coiled and sprang free in his stomach. What would his own dream sound like? His aunt's words floated back to the surface of his mind. Creeping and prodding their way around. He'd never know.

A chill swept through and someone took a rubber stamp, damp with ink, to the tunnels of his thoughts. Fraud. Making something you can never truly understand and can never receive yourself. The small dent Linette's words had made became a hollow chip that fell away, exposing a new part of his mind to the elements of his thoughts. No. He'd had his turn. It was a fair trade. No dreamstone, but the training of a dreamsmith. He'd agreed. It was what he'd wanted and still did. Not everyone else would be so lucky, and on top of that he was damn good at his work. There could be no room for doubt in dreamforging.

He cracked a mental whip and chided himself. *Focus. You'll need all your focus for this. You're about to try and hold a life in your hands. Someone's freedom. Feel sorry for yourself later on your own time.*

Had anyone else found a dream to craft yet? Based on the light-hearted chatter all around him he guessed not, but the day had hardly begun. Sometimes smiths could search and try to piece things together for hours. Some could work a week of shifts at the forges and create nothing, it happened often enough. Even he had made nothing for weeks and now two dreams in the space of two shifts? Such unpredictability. A strange comfort and a frustration at the same time.

Fion was connected but searching with half-focus. The perks of being naturally gifted. When Taren first learned to connect it was years before he could even hold the link open without sweating through the vest he wore under his robe. Fion made it look so easy.

The notes rang together, and certainty gripped him. Focusing and moving with care he turned his palm to face upwards and curled his fingers into a fist. Isolating one note from the orchestral buzz of the thousands in the spire. He repeated the movement. Flexing and curling the fingers in a hypnotic beckoning. Reeling in the fragment.

A silver shimmer rippled across the root and gathered in a small sphere. Its bright form shone in a muted way as it moved down the root towards him. When it reached the exit point, the crystal surface peeled back in rustling fragments like flaking ice and the broken sphere hovered above the forging plinth.

Again he repeated the process, drawing out another piece. It wasn't quick work. Encouraging words from Fion chimed somewhere in the distance, but Taren's focus was absolute. With two fragments now hovering over his forge he used his free hand to draw a second connector leading from his palm to the dream fragments. Their resonance rang clear and joyful, peaceful and simple, and he liked finding dreams of that type. Ones that harboured no material want.

Once both connections were active the pressure mounted. The muscles in his arm and shoulder burned with each twitch. His palm itched and sweat dappled his underarms. The same hand that drew the connections performed graceful gestures and from a new and rotating circle that hovered above his forearm a small crafting hammer materialised. Its handle was a smooth and polished silver, woven around a head of crystal taken straight from the spire.

With precision he willed the fragments closer together, and gently tapped them with the hammer in exacting ways to make them fit. The clear glass of the pieces melded bit by bit, and each strike of the delicate tool drew out ringing notes. When the harmonies rang out correctly, matching the ones Taren heard in the spire, he struck the join with a harder, more certain pressure and the segments came together without a seam.

The flawless, rounded glass of the exterior was clear as water between the two parts, and the inside remained jagged and jutting while it awaited its missing pieces. The dreamstones reminded Taren of ornate glass paperweights and he'd never been able to shake the comparison. The second connection faded once the pieces were joined, and he took a short breather before diving in for the rest.

'Good work, you have the process down now. Really graceful.'

'Thanks Fi, do you ever manage to do this without sweating at some point? Jeez.'

'It will come with time, or maybe you're just a slow poke.'

'Three years isn't enough time?'

Fion chuckled, 'I'm kidding, it's an intensive thing. We're creating alternative lives for people, bringing their dreams into reality for them. Doesn't really sound like something that can be achieved without breaking a sweat.' She winked as he shook his head.

'You make it look so easy.'

'Doesn't mean I don't sweat.'

'Oh, is that what I can smell?'

'So juvenile, aren't you supposed to be an adult?'

'I'll… get back to you on that.' They both laughed, but it was cut short as Taren returned his attention to the forge. Lose your focus entirely and the connection would break, and connections to unfinished dreams should never be broken. That was forging one-oh-one. Something worth reminding yourself of every time you approach a forge. Every time you intend to create a stone.

Soon Taren had affixed five pieces together and the orb of the dreamstone neared completion. Just as he took a deep breath ready to go in to extract the final piece, Jacklan grunted with effort and Taren and Fion craned their necks around to see.

'Can you all hear that?' Jacklan asked, sweat pouring down his brow and his arm shaking with effort. 'Something isn't right with this.'

Taren cocked an ear and waited. He heard nothing. Until a crack appeared in the root attached to Jacklan's forge.

'What the…?' Fion's question rang out, the last sound before an encompassing silence. Every smith was still, all looking up at the spindly crack in the spire root. It was small… at first. But it grew. The thin line of the breach filled with a tar-like, black substance. It hung there with everyone's breath. Jacklan bolstered his connecting arm with his free hand. There shouldn't be that much pressure pushing back on a connection. Jacklan's whole body shuddered under an invisible weight. The concerned look of the Forgemaster flashed across Taren's mind again and again. What had he sensed? Why hadn't he addressed it?

'Jacklan I'll help you, just hang in there.'

Fion started to take charge of the situation. 'No Taren, stay connected. You can't break off until you're done. I'll go, I'm not melding.' She detached from her forge and stared at the selection of gawping smiths with a raised and unbelieving eyebrow. 'Well? Someone go and fetch Forgemaster Clayton, quickly! Everyone who isn't melding detach and leave the forging floor. Are there any senior smiths here?' No one answered Fion, but one smith did bolt out of the room, and Taren hoped to the spire she was going to fetch the Forgemaster.

No senior smiths answered Fion's call. It wasn't unusual, they often had other duties to attend and they were few and far between, but why did this have to be a day where none were on the forging floor? The burning need to help rolled in Taren's chest, but he couldn't disconnect. He

47

battled between watching Jacklan trying to hold control and focusing enough on his own forge to protect the almost-finished dream. Every cell of his body screamed in one of two directions. Never break the connection. Help protect the others.

6

Protect the Dream

Fion approached Jacklan carefully. Whatever was happening, it pulled goosebumps up from the bottom-most layer of her skin. It felt wrong. Thick with hazard. Drenched in it. The wrongness and the danger blended and scoured, each trying to out-do the other. It had to be stopped, controlled, tamed. Every step closer to Jacklan reinforced her gut feeling. Only one person could handle this, but she couldn't leave Jacklan to deal with it alone. Her eyes flicked up to the fractured root and back to her colleague. His knees were buckling, fighting against the pressure that must have been crushing him. Fion stood next to him and reached out with hesitation to connect and assist.

It opened a small window into a violent storm. Whatever power was trying to escape tore through her at a higher speed than she could deal with. Control wouldn't be possible for long, even between the two of them. It stung, like a needle-primed wind whooshing through her system. Raking across her nervous system over and over again.

What in the hells was causing it? Was something trying to break through, or just break free? Was the spire itself failing them? Its lifeblood, black and inky, oozing forth to swallow them all? Jacklan might be an arse at times, but his incompetence was nothing to do with it. They were trying to wrangle an invisible serpent made of broiling ichor. It blasted through every inch of Fion and she started to crumple, gasping and hitching for breaths but fighting for control.

Taren shouted her name as she struggled to stay standing, but together her and Jacklan forced the pressure from the breach back, or it seemed like they were managing it. The flow became smoother, and lashed about less. Their concentration circulated the flow, feeding it back into the fissure it was trying to burst from.

A worry for Taren flashed briefly. He wasn't one to forgot what they'd been taught, but nor would he find it easy to ignore people who needed help. He had to stay connected, he had to focus on himself. She'd give him a good slap if he didn't finish that dream. If he let it go. Let it fade. If he took someone's chance from them. He might be a sap at times but she shared his goal. To help as many people as she could. To do her best for them, like she was doing right now. She pushed, hard, and used all her strength as a smith to gain some ground.

Breathing came easier for a few seconds, and they reclaimed a step towards the forging station.

'Jacklan, you OK?' Fion struggled to form words, her jaw tight with effort.

Pale, their fellow smith nodded. 'I th-think so.'

'We just have to hold our position, alright? The Forgemaster is on his way.'

'O-OK.'

OK, they could do this. They could handle it a little

longer. Maybe Jacklan wasn't so bad. His assistance could clearly be felt in directing the flow. He was pulling his weight and then some. One tiny inch of tension released from her aching back. She allowed herself that. Then, in that pocket of peace and relief, when they thought the forge was under control… it began to spiral.

Chaos erupted. Pain lanced through Fion, crackling and hissing. Presumably it engulfed Jacklan too, as he cried out. Both took a step back to steady themselves and stop the stagger that would have hurled them away from the station by the wind that whipped about them. If they let it through, it could destroy the place, the whole Forge even for all they knew. Everything was a possibility because nothing was known. Frustration and panic flared. Where was the Forgemaster? The senior smiths? Anyone who would know what to do?

'Fion, what's happening with it? What can you feel?'

'I don't know…' she hissed at Taren through gritted teeth, 'I've never felt this from a forge. There are whispers, but I can't make them out. The pressure, it's like it's pushing us away, trying to get past us. If the crack opens…'

'Stand completely still Jacklan, Fion.' The Forgemaster strode in, grey eyes not as calm under his blue hood as they'd been before. Thank the spire for that. What took him so long? A rush of gratitude soothed her internal snapping. 'You all did the right thing. I'm going to take over the connection. It's taking too much of your energy.'

He wasn't wrong. Even through the blush of his efforts, Jacklan's failing pallor was obvious to see. The sheen of desperate sweat. Did Fion sport one to match? Did she look just as deathly? No doubt Taren would let her know later.

She could practically hear his teeth grinding with indecision. His knees creaking in their shaky stance as he tried to decide between the dream and helping control the situation. That, and no doubt he'd sprain his neck from trying to watch whatever the Forgemaster decided to do to regain the upper hand.

'Focus on your dream, Taren, remember your training.' From the corner of her vision she caught Taren nod at their mentor's words, but continue to watch with wide eyes and a set jaw. 'Jacklan, Fion, I'm going to connect to the forge through you, and gradually shoulder the bond. I'll need you to slowly let it go as I pull it towards me. OK?'

The forge started to blare with a low, resonant whistle as the Forgemaster placed a hand on each of their shoulders. 'Fion, I would ask you to continue to assist me if you feel able?' She inhaled, long and steady, and dipped her head. In truth she was a shattering, person-shaped crystal. Crumbling under her own tiredness and shock of the power that thrummed and spat against her efforts to corral it. Jacklan, though, was far worse off. She could shoulder this for him with the Forgemaster's help. New focus sharpened her gaze under a shimmering brow. 'Alright, Fion please continue supporting and pushing back against the leak while I take over.'

To an outsider, it would look like the Forgemaster was the one draining Jacklan. His own revolving bracelet appeared as his hand gripped the dreamsmith's shoulder. Fion imagined the passing of the connection like two men trying to hold on to a powerful, thrashing sea creature. Slippery, muscular and defiant. The struggle was plain in what little could be seen of their expressions, and the angle of their knees pushing them forward into the screaming energy pouring from the forge. The tar crept down the crystal in dollops, covering the forging table and spilling towards the smiths.

The moment the connection was transferred Jacklan stumbled backwards, a sheet of paper in the wind. Tumbling to his knees next to a forge further away and fighting with unsteady breaths while trying to get back to his feet.

'Jacklan, don't try it OK? You did real well, just sit down, let the others handle it.'

Fion chanced a look back upon hearing Taren comfort Jacklan. But her colleague's eyes were rolling dangerously. How could Taren deal with him if he was still melding? Their conversation continued as Fion flung all her strength against the flow to help curb it.

'I can still hear them…' Jacklan's voice wobbled as he spoke.

'Hear what?'

'The whispers.'

'What?'

His response was drowned in a screech so shrill, and a pulse of energy so strong, that Fion was knocked backward. The world flipped and flat slap of pain burned against her side as something stopped her backward trajectory. Everything blurred, but there was little doubt about what she saw.

Jacklan was being lashed. Suffocated. Crowded and gnawed at by a soup of shadows. It lasted moments, perhaps a few seconds. Torn at by shadow hounds. It was the only way she could describe it. Images didn't hold their borders well. Things slipped in odd directions.

The Forgemaster had been forced to one knee. He'd acted quickly it seemed, throwing an arm out to catch the tendril of Fion's connection, unable to stop her skittering backwards and making the correct choice to prioritise the forge. With a wave of his arm the gloopy shadows were ripped off of Jacklan who lay gaunt and wide-eyed. Unmoving. Fion's teeth ached from gritting and grinding. She'd landed against a forging station. Any mere thought of movement bloomed an electric thunderclap through her left side and some of her back.

She searched for Taren, but he kept sliding around in her vision. Why couldn't he stand still just that once? She needed him to. Needed to see his face. He'd yelled her name, maybe, when she'd been thrown back. She had to reply, she had to let him know. The look on his face, if she didn't let him know he'd do something stupid. Something ridiculous. Dangerous. *Please don't. Please just focus. Protect the dream.*

Hoping it was as much of an illusion as everything else felt in that bleary moment, the connection between Taren and the dream on his station wobbled. It might have even flickered. He mouthed something, but his voice didn't sound right. Words didn't sound like words. Just sounds. Sounds in a language of lulling sleep. Then, there was nothing but a last thought.

Please protect the dream.

7

Scattered Mind

Chaos erupted behind Taren and he grappled against the ache in his arms and neck from craning to watch the spiralling forge. Jacklan was swarmed. Taren couldn't see it, but he heard it. He didn't dare look around, keeping his eyes on the dream connection. The layers of wet gnashing made him shudder. Stop. Stop it. No more.

Another pulse and the Forgemaster, still kneeling, was shoved an inch backwards after he'd peeled the shadows off of Jacklan. Fion was blasted backward, landing side-first against the neighbouring forge. His bond to the dream wobbled in his grip. He grasped at it, riding a pendulous wave of palpitations. Too close.

'Fion! Look at me, I'm her-' Taren's voice was ripped away from him by the screech of the forge. Her half-slackened mouth moved, but the commotion around them stole her words. She was still, but her eyes might have been half open. No, they were half open. She battled to stay conscious. *Please stay awake, Fi.*

For a few moments, sound vanished. Silence plumed like smoke. Whether the quiet was real, or simply his mind trying to pull him back on task, he didn't know. Either way, it had to be now.

The dream on his forge held steady. One piece short of completion. The strange screams faded, his breath roared in his ears and he fought with his concentration so he didn't ruin the dream. His mind jumped into action, shaking off his shock as best he could. *Finish the dream, then disconnect and help them.* He reached out for the last piece of the stone, which idled just inside the forge.

The connection burned bright and strong, in contrast to the thick, gelatinous tar oozing from the dangerous crack that continued to creep across the root anchored to Jacklan's station. A light raged inside the crystal and sharp, dark pulses of energy drifted out in waves to push against Taren even at his few metres distance.

Just what was happening? Taren switched between staring behind and staring ahead. His concern for Fion narrowed his focus, refusing to let him control his magic properly.

A blast of energy brought sound back to Taren's ears in a great roar of noise, accompanied by a slew of the thick tar that spread across the floor with renewed fervour. It crept towards the Forgemaster's feet and sent fetid globs in all directions. Including towards Taren. He took a stumbling step back on instinct, wanting to avoid getting any of the foul substance on his person. His stumble turned into a stagger, momentum pulled him backwards. His head whipped around to avoid the second wave of spray. His connection to the dream and forge pulled taught, vibrating like elastic waiting to snap.

A spark of pain shot up his arm and he winced, still unable to find purchase on the moistened floor beneath him. One step backward, two, then he fell. His foot sliding in a puddle of the mulchy grime. No!

'Taren, don't!' The Forgemaster yelled over his shoulder, the one side of his face Taren could see filled with pleading and horror. The twisting inertia of his fall wrenched him away from his forge. The connecting thread didn't snap, but something came away with his efforts and crashed against the side of his face.

It splintered, spread, burned, and blinded his left eye. Consuming his vision and painting it with sliding glass. The world tilted and his palm scraped against the floor with a painful sting as he tried to catch himself and failed.

For several seconds he panted where he'd fallen, pulling himself together and squeezing his burning eye closed. Not his best idea, perhaps. Who knows what kind of debris might be pushed further into the socket. But his thoughts were distant and hard to piece together. Something had just happened. Something bad. But only one thing mattered in that moment. One thing made sense in his scattered mind. Fion. He had to check on her. To help her. He crawled towards her, not yet registering what he'd done. The disaster he'd brought about.

She sat lopsided against the forge behind her, but her chest rose and fell. Then rose and fell again. He took one of her hands in his to let her know he was there. She seemed OK, but she'd need medical attention. So would Jacklan. Where were they? Why was no one else helping? She'd be alright, she had to be.

The Forgemaster shouted, but his words slurred and slipped over each other when they reached Taren's ears. His hearing rang with the shattering of whatever had collided with his face, and the sound of his own uneven breathing washed away any comprehension. A vague awareness of robed figures venturing cautiously back onto the forging floor crept into his peripheral vision. It was about time. They stopped when their gaze fell on him, their faces going slack with confusion and shock.

Two likely unconscious smiths, a third a crawling mess, and the Forgemaster battling with the forge itself. He groaned with effort as he forced the tar back into the crystal root. It receded slowly. Almost reluctantly. Chains of shouts drifted around the room and out into the corridor. Finally, people were starting to take action.

Taren squinted up at the forge and made the mistake of opening his damaged eye. A bright menagerie of colours soon dissipated to focus on the storming black energy that cycloned around the forge and a slew of sharp whispers danced around him, pecking at him with razor-like beaks. It took his breath and transformed it into internal screams, yet when he covered his left eye again he saw and heard none of it.

What's happened to me? What did I do, what did I just see? What did the whispers say? My eye. My eye isn't… it's not…

Once more he inched his hand away and opened his eye. Once more the world descended into chaos. He pressed against it, shutting off the visions. Whenever he opened it the world swirled with colours and fragments slipped across it.

His fingers brushed across the texture of the skin around his eye socket. It wasn't flesh anymore. It was smooth. Sharp in places. Tiny crumbs of something dusty fell away as he traced the area. Whatever it was encircled his entire eye. A patch that thrummed and pulsed, sending swarms of pins and needles through his mind when he tried to open his eyelid.

His stomach flipped and churned with questions and fear. He'd messed up. Beyond any dreamsmith before him, he'd messed up. Even if he knew nothing else about his actions, he knew that.

The forge finally calmed under the Forgemaster's expert hand and there were no more whispers to hear. The fracture now bound by a circle of smithing runes. In the next second Taren's mentor was by his side.

'Taren? Focus on me, Taren. Taren!' The Forgemaster turned to shout over his shoulder as Taren collapsed against a stone podium. 'Fetch two senior smiths at once, we have to restrain him, carefully. No one else touch him.' Distant yells in the corridor faded as the Forgemaster's will was carried out. Restrain him? Why? He couldn't move. He couldn't see from his left eye anymore. Adrenaline surged through his body, triggered by his confusion and exacerbated by the unexpected order from the Forgemaster.

What did I do? Restrain me? Did I break the vow of my duty? I must have, why else would they restrain me. I have to get out of here. I need some time to… I don't know to figure this out I have to go I have to…

… and before he could think any more about what he had done or was about to do Taren lurched into a standing position, barged past the weakened, exhausted Forgemaster, and ran.

8

A Common Dichotomy

Some people would call farm life boring. Most days being comprised of the same tasks. Leander couldn't imagine doing anything else. Another small bread line had formed at the farm border just like yesterday. There wasn't much left from the morning's batch, but Corryn was already stoking the fire of the rudimentary stone-bake oven. They often left it burning at all times just to steal away more heat at night. It worked well.

'You're making another batch?' He was surprised to smell the rising dough again so late in the day.

'Just a small one, we have some dough left over from this morning so it should be enough to feed those outside and put some by for ourselves for a day or two. After we harvest the third field in a few weeks though, that might be all we get for a while, we'll have to make it last.'

'We'll do what we can as always.' Leander took the basket with a small pile of rolls remaining from the morning and prepared to head out, but something caught him. An abrupt, sticky jolt as though someone had come along and shoved him out of his own body. He turned in the direction of the spire even though he couldn't see it through the wall of his home.

'You OK?' Corryn peered around the door to the cooking area with a creased brow.

'Y-yeah. Yeah, I'm OK, just went a bit dizzy.' No point in worrying Corryn, she did enough of that already.

'Guess you're just getting old, then.' She winked at him, though clearly she wasn't convinced and he'd face more questions later.

Get yourself together. There are people who need food out there. Until you hear a definite call, whatever that will sound like, stop obsessing over the spire and get on with it.

As he walked up the small dirt path towards the queue the waiting faces slackened with relief to know something remained for them. They couldn't possibly feed the whole slum between the two of them, of course, it circled the whole city. There were more people outside the city than inside now.

The basket didn't stay full for long, but he kept the rest of the queue talking while they waited for Corryn's next batch. He pushed away several offers of small coins, and smiled and nodded politely in response to the flood of thanks. Melynda had been so much better at this, much less awkward in the face of gratitude. He should have asked her what the calling felt like when he had the chance, and yet again his thoughts returned to the spire. Its great heights caught the sun and shimmered, and he took an unintentional step towards it. Another, and another.

'Are you spacing out again?' Corryn appeared behind him along with the aroma of hot bread. In reality he hadn't moved but was rooted in place, drawing the concerned gazes of those waiting. He'd stopped halfway in reaching to close a palm offering coin, becoming a statue. 'Go back to the house and rest a while, you look like you need it.'

He didn't argue, and soon enough found himself sitting at the table staring at his clasped hands, struggling to string a coherent thought together. The sun wasn't much past its peak. Early afternoon already. He should start preparing some lunch, but his body had other ideas and none of them involved moving. For small stretches of time his limbs defied his requests, and he floated above himself, watching from the side-lines. Time slipped away from him.

'OK spill, what's going on?'

Leander jumped. Corryn appeared at the table next to him, empty bread basket placed in the corner. How long had she been there? Only minutes surely?

'I... I'm not sure. I had a weird feeling this morning and when I looked at the spire it was like it started moving towards me. Getting closer and closer. For a few seconds I couldn't tear myself away from staring at it and felt like I was... knocked out of myself? Sorry if that doesn't make sense.'

'Do you think it's your calling?' Her face fell into a practised neutrality, but her nervous swallow didn't escape his notice.

'No, I don't think so. Not yet anyway. I mean I haven't heard anything, and I'm pretty sure I'd know it if I heard it.'

'That's what Melynda said, too. She said she'd been feeling out of sorts on the day she got her calling, but when it came there was no way to deny it. A weird, hypnotic resonance that she felt in her core, she said.' A dark pain mixed with longing sank into Corryn's face. She missed her sister a lot, but under that love was the same disappointment. The same betrayal. The same bitterness. They'd shared it together. The sting of being left behind.

As much as it hurt, they'd never wish the alternative on Melynda. People who didn't collect their calling once it sounded became something else, so the whispers around the slums said. The folks who'd been there longest knew the stories best. Hollows. That's what those who didn't take their calling became. No one's ever seen one, only exchanged speculative tales in taverns on long and desperate nights. Neither Leander nor Corryn really blamed Melynda for accepting hers, and wouldn't have stood in her way.

It was a common dichotomy in the slums. People were so happy for their loved ones when they received their callings. Supportive, pleased, overjoyed. It crept in eventually, though. That dark, inky bloom of jealousy, of bitter longing, of unfairness. It wasn't easy to fight it when people found themselves left behind, and even those with the best intentions sometimes found themselves succumbing to the laments caused by the abandonment. If Leander hadn't had Corryn to grieve with, he had no doubt he would be a bitter wreck of a man by now.

'You spoke with her about it?' Leander looked over at Corryn as he asked. She'd never mentioned it before.

'I did. I was as surprised as you when she came back here. No one turns down an inner-city house while waiting for their dreamstone to activate. I'm glad she did, because I got to ask her about it. I couldn't resist. It sounds like such a strange experience. Maybe it'll be your turn soon.' Corryn tried to smile, but they could see under each other's masks with no more difficulty than looking through an open window. They considered each other as siblings, or as close

63

as you could get without actually being blood related. Her preparation had begun. Preparation to lose someone else she cared about. To be left alone.

'I'm sure that's not it. I would have heard something… more. Maybe the dreamsmiths are tinkering with the spire and I'm just more attuned to it because I've been around a dreamstone.'

She laughed at his feeble attempt to reassure her and his stomach traced a loop.

'No, I'd feel it too if that was the case. The stone was here for months with the three of us, remember?'

'I remember.' His apologetic look was automatic, and his throat tightened as her hand covered the back of his own.

'Whatever happens, I'll be happy for you. I'll carry on the work we started here and wait my turn like everyone else.'

Emotions were hard for Leander since Melynda left. They were best left buried and ignored, festering in darkness rather than clouding his mind. Not quite a stranger, but never close friends. He tied his hair up again and cleared his throat, making sure she didn't see his eyes. If she saw them, she'd know.

'I'd… um… I'd best get out there and collect and clean the rest of the tools. If we don't put them away someone might take them.' Stupid. Where was the reassurance? Tell her. Tell her that you'd never leave her here like Melynda left them. She deserved to hear the words. They gathered, pushing through the mire of confusion, only to die in his throat.

Corryn beamed. 'Sure, I'll be out in a few minutes.

Don't wait for me.'

The afternoon breeze cooled his skin. His feet led him to the middle of one of the fields where he'd last been checking the condition of the crops and digging out weeds that were settling into the soil around the precious stalks. He crouched to collect a trowel and several other items, but dropped his face into his hands instead. Melynda was the last person he needed to think about right now. No good wife would leave their husband behind the way she did. He could never… would never… Biting back the sour taste of it, the hurt, he mustered all the concentration he could.

Taking the tools to the faucet he used the cold water to clean his face before setting about rinsing the dirt off of the few decent ones they had. Then a lurch swooped through his chest and a haunting, but somehow euphoric, resonance reached out and wrapped itself around him. All other sounds faded away. It called to him, and only him.

The world turned monochrome apart from the towering spires of the city which rippled as his eyes settled upon them. The trowel made no sound as it dropped to the ground. The water ran in silence, but his footsteps rang loud and sure. The only thing to break through the resonance as it led him away was Corryn calling his name. He didn't look back.

9

Seeds of Suspicion

When Fion originally came to, mild chaos bustled in the forging room. As she sat in a bed in the Dreamforge infirmary, she attempted to piece the events together. She'd tried several times to pick apart reality from injury-induced stupor, but she wasn't having much luck.

On top of that, not a single person seemed willing to help her sort through any of it. Her only option was to keep trying. She took a deep breath, a little too deep, and cursed at herself for it. By the spire, her ribs hurt. A thick and dull ache that circulated around her left side. She'd bruised something, or everything, for sure.

There had been no sign of Taren when she'd woken. All anyone would say was that he fled. Why would he run, though? What had he done? The last thing she remembered was seeing the connection to the dream wobble dangerously, but he would have calmed it. He was more than skilled enough.

After that, only brief and blurry snatches of images had been seen through her lashes every time she'd tried to pry her eyes open. Someone held her hand at some point, someone sat close by with one hand over their face. And so much shouting, echoing in distant layers and too loose to form words.

Jacklan had been... A wave of dizziness danced across her vision. No one would choose to remember what happened to Jacklan. The gnashing of the shadows that flayed him with their presence. That's when something pricked the back of her mind as she sat there in the quiet. Several other beds lay empty, but she wasn't the only one who'd been injured. Where was Jacklan?

Fion reached for the jug of water on her bedside table, trying to think why this question caused more and more prickles in her mind. As the cool liquid refreshed her scratchy throat she pondered it, doing her best not to wince at every movement. The question turned over and over, and she wanted to explore it. Where was Jacklan, what happened to him?

A flash of memories was her answer. She'd crawled towards him when she'd come round, gritting her teeth against the fire that licked at her side, trying to get a response out of him. There had been nothing. He'd stared up at the vaulted ceiling of the forging room, following things with his eyes that no one else could see. Then four senior smiths had swarmed in on the Forgemaster's orders and separated her from her colleague.

She recalled snapping at them to be careful as they gently hauled her to her feet. So many questions had poured from her mouth, all of them still unanswered. The other thing she remembered was the Forgemaster's face, wild with panic, relaying orders to everyone from the base of the now-controlled forging station. She'd never seen such a look on his face before. Not in all her years at the Dreamforge. His default was calm and collected, logical and practical. So what had him spooked?

Her foot swung idly back and forward beneath the blanket that warmed her as she disappeared into her thoughts again. There were few things worse than having nothing to do. Boredom nipped at her soul. She was a busy person, always preferring to be of some use than sitting around. Especially when Taren might be in trouble.

If he ran did that mean he had reason to? Would the Forge be searching for him? If they were did he break the connection? Waste the dream? Admittedly she had no idea what happened to dreams that weren't finished. Only that they were completely lost. It had been too hard-baked into their training to never sever a link with an unfinished or partially melded dream. Repeated with such seriousness that no one ever dared try or risk it. It was always framed as a dangerous, reckless thing to do. One that went against the very essence of their duty. What consequences would it bring? It wouldn't go unaddressed, no way.

The maze of her thoughts grew so tangled that the brisk opening of the door startled her. A shudder passed through her side from the jolt. Fine mess she's got herself into. The Forgemaster strode across the ward, a strained smile on his face. He was trying to seem calm but a flustered and worried energy churned around him as their eyes met. Despite that, Fion felt a whoosh of relief and comfort upon seeing a familiar face. One that was on her side. One that would have some answers.

'How are you feeling? I'm glad to see you awake.' He took urgent strides around the bed and briefly squeezed her hand. Concern filling his features.

'I've been better, but I have a feeling it could have been much worse?'

A single nod answered her question. 'You showed great skill and leadership in that situation. Your assistance was vital to controlling the forge. Thank you for your quick thinking and willingness to step in.'

'I appreciate the sentiment, Clayton, but what in the name of the spire happened back there?' Fion only ever called him Clayton, without his official title, in private company. He'd insisted upon it when she was younger and the gesture had touched her then. A private, special secret that her young self got to keep, that showed how much he cared for her. She'd never had the courage to ask to call him father, and perhaps he'd always wanted that single layer of distance. She doesn't have to use his title, but doesn't get to give him a new one either. Just his name.

'I… I don't know what to tell you, Fi. I'm looking into it, we all are, all the senior smiths, but it's not something I can explain to you right now.' An unsettling desperation danced in his eyes when he sat on the edge of the bed near the bottom.

'Are you alright? Did you sustain any damage from whatever force was trying to break through?'

'No, none. Just exhaustion. I'm surprised the senior smiths haven't already found me and marched me back to my chambers to rest. They fuss like a gaggle of strict handmaidens sometimes.'

His words dragged a chuckle out of her, which she instantly regretted. Clayton winced on her behalf as Fion wrapped an arm around her ribs as though it might protect them from the blaze. 'Sorry' he added, though his face had relaxed a little in her company.

'What about Jacklan? And Taren? They wouldn't tell me anything down on the forging floor. Everyone seems to have zipped their mouths closed. Will you, at least, fill me in?'

A complicated pattern of expressions passed over Clayton's face. She'd know that look anywhere. He was closing up, drawing lines to guard against her. Shifting gears from guardian to head of the Dreamforge. Before he even took a deep breath to collect himself she knew what would pass his lips.

'I cannot say anything for now. Too many things are uncertain. I'm afraid what you already know is all you can be told.'

A slew of ice sluiced through Fion, coming to rest in her gut. Not once had he refused to answer her questions. Not once in her life. Her face must have betrayed her shock because his brow knitted in heartbroken regret. This was difficult for him. Did that mean he wanted to tell her, but couldn't?

'Taren's my friend. If he needs help I want to know what happened to him and why he ran. It's not something he would do without good reason. He loves this place, loves his duty as a dreamsmith. I don't understand why he'd just disappear. Are you having the smiths look for him?'

'What he did… goes against everything him and every other dreamsmith has ever been taught. Of all the elements of this worrying situation, his actions have the most unpredictable consequences. We don't yet know if it was intentional or accidental.'

The wobble in the dream connection came to mind

once more. As much as he was dancing around it, perhaps he'd just answered one of her questions.

'Maybe I can help. You trained me yourself, you basically raised me, why are you shutting me out?'

'Would you believe me if I told you it was for your own good?' The desperation had moved from his eyes and leaked into his voice. *Don't ask. Don't ask me, Fion.* She could almost hear him saying it, hiding it in his every action. Why shouldn't she know? Why shouldn't she get to understand what happened?

'That's not good enough. Whatever happened down there, no one's ever seen anything like it. I risked my life to help Jacklan, and you, and it sounds like there's a very real possibility that risk could have had a different ending. One where I'm not sitting in this bed having to use what little energy I have trying to get answers about it.'

He watched her carefully, weighing up the options. Who was he seeing? Fion the little girl who used to run around the Dreamforge, or Fion the dreamsmith. The subordinate. He didn't seem to want either involved.

'I can't. I'm sorry.' He stood to leave, his jaw clenching so tightly she imagined all the words crowding in his mouth in a long string. Wanting nothing more than to burst forth and be heard by another. Something held him back. Nothing usually held Clayton back. A nervous energy buzzed about him. It didn't suit him. He didn't carry it well. Fion leaned forward and his arm twitched as though he wanted to help her lay back down.

'Can I at least see Jacklan, just to know he's alright? Where is he, even? Shouldn't he be in here, unless he's…' the thought hadn't even occurred to her, but now it boomed

71

like a firework.

'No one can see him.'

A breath of relief huffed out of her mouth. He was alive, then. 'What?'

'No one can see him. He is being kept… elsewhere. You need to rest now. Some senior smiths will be coming to question you about the incident in the coming days so we can gather as much information as possible. I'd appreciate it if you would co-operate with them and answer whatever they ask.' He started to leave.

'How can I rest when you won't tell me anything? How can I just sit here, useless and in the dark? I thought… I thought you trusted me. Why not let me help?' She might have imagined it, but Clayton may have pitched forward slightly at her words. As though he'd been punched in the gut. Maybe she'd gone too far with the trust comment, but frustration coated and controlled her tongue.

'I do trust you. I do. And I know it sounds hypocritical and illogical, but you have to trust me on that. We need to find out what happened today. As soon as I know and have made sense of it myself, I will share it with you. I promise.' He didn't look back at her, but his steps told of the weight of a great burden on his shoulders. He left. A healer bustled in as soon as he departed.

What kind of answer was that? He'd told her almost nothing over the course of the entire conversation. All she'd learned was that Taren had likely failed in melding his dream, breaking the connection. She'd suspected that anyway. Jacklan was alive, but squirreled away somewhere in isolation.

To top it all off, she'd be interrogated soon. It made her

feel implicated. Wronged. Like some sort of accomplice. A small but fiercely burning coal of betrayal hunkered down in her chest. There had never been walls between herself and Clayton. Now, he'd built some so thick she barely recognised his voice through them.

The healer offered two small pills, and explained in an overly-jovial voice that one was a painkiller and the other would help her sleep. She nearly bit the woman's hand off at the word 'painkiller', but she was so wrapped up in her thoughts that she didn't even remember swallowing them down.

It wasn't until the pain started to dull and Fion's eyes started to droop that the thought occurred to her. Why would they want her to sleep? Did they want her out of the way for a while? Seeds of suspicion grew quickest in fields of confusion. The hurt on Clayton's face kept floating back to the surface of her mind. He'd wanted to say something. Wanted to tell her but couldn't. Not wouldn't. Couldn't.

She'd find out what held him back. She'd help to set him free. Just as soon as she slept off the pain. Just as soon as she got some rest and could think straight again. Then she'd start digging.

10

Puppet on Crystal Strings

Leander was lost to the undulating resonance of the spire, a delicate puppet on crystal strings. It pulled him along his path, drowning all sound to a dull, muffled drone. People stepped aside to let him pass, knowing the look of those undergoing a calling. Some may have even clapped, those he recognised from the food lines, but he couldn't be sure.

The mismatched buildings passed him by. Built, half-built, half-fallen. The mixed smells of the slums were more pungent. The dusty sackcloth of the food bags provided by the inner city, the tang of the livestock that some kept in small pastures dotted around the slums. The rare brewing of inner-city tea sometimes gifted to those outside the gates when it could be spared.

The spire towered above him, standing bold and high above the walls Leander had never seen over. The gate loomed, knitted and interlaced patterns shining in the same turquoise colour as the spire. Ready to search those who stood before it for the resonance that proved their dreamstone was waiting for them. On the final approach, his mind teemed with thoughts that caused a cold sweat of conflict to rise to the surface of his skin.

Do I really want this? Do I want to accept my dreamstone? The life I have with Corryn, what we do, what we've achieved, is it so bad? I don't want to do what Melynda did. To disappear alone. She could have taken us with her, she could have… if her dream life involved us. She wanted to be free of us instead. Should I turn it down? Can I, even? I don't want to become a hollow. That's what they say, right? If you ignore your calling a hollow will grow inside you. Was Melynda afraid of that, too? Afraid what she'd become if she said no. If she stayed. I have to claim my dreamstone. I have no choice.

At last he found himself at the gate. A sheet of ornate misty patterns and water-like glass. A low and searching hum buzzed through his bones. Reading. Perceiving. Always ready to turn one of two ways. Access given or denied. He used to spend hours staring at it. Watching with fascination while some passed through it safely and others hammered on its transparent surface pleading for entry, or shouting for the loved ones that had left them behind. Each of the four gates, protecting the inner city at the cardinal points, was a similar scene. Beautiful and pitiful in equal measure.

The world on the other side of the gate looked so different. The streets paved with neat grey brick instead of dust and uneven cobble. The houses carefully crafted and accented and not just thrown together. It was ordered, even down to the nature which was carefully placed or staged. Flower boxes and short-cropped, perfectly square lawns around the courtyard. It sent a shiver down Leander. Nature should have an element of the wild to it. Guided not measured. Was he truly being allowed to enter? The call still echoed at his core. A glasswork sirensong. The gate thrummed, and his hand passed through it with the slightest syrupy resistance.

Stepping through, the warmth engulfed him briefly and delivered him to the other side. Bewilderment turned his disbelieving gaze. He was through. The calling was real. He'd never been out of the slums since arriving so long ago with Melynda and Corryn. The hardship of all those years crashed against his heart in a swelling wave. Rising as an uncertain smile as he took a step forward.

Some small part of him fought against his actions. Told him he didn't deserve it. There were so many who'd been in the slums longer, who'd done their time, and may have even lost hope in their waiting. Surely one of them would better deserve the calling? But the system has no order. No sense. You get your call or you don't, no one can say when and how or what it will mean to each person. It seemed wrong to be on the other side of the gate.

Just as he admitted it to himself, just as doubt crept in, the resonance dulled and choked. Retreating and returning in an unsteady rise and fall. The perfect houses swayed, the bricks morphed into patterns. Had his doubt been heard? Was he losing his chance? When he gazed up at the spire again in desperation it didn't match up with the resonance any more. His attention veered to the left. The spire fell quiet. It wasn't possible. The call always came from the main spire, there was nowhere else for it to come from. What was going on?

Very few inner-city folk lingered near the gate. The houses started a short distance away, after the pristine courtyard and the granary stores. The call beckoned him to those stores, or at least in their direction. His feet wanted to continue on along the gently rising path towards the stone towers of the Dreamforge, but his core led him aside. Something was reaching out to him, one way or another. Something he couldn't let go of. A desperate importance keened in the sound. Utterly eclipsing. He could complete his calling after he'd satisfied his curiosity... right?

The grain houses were concerningly empty of both people and supplies. It must be where they kept the food to share with the slums, but clearly they weren't sparing much at the moment. The side door yawned with silence, the empty crates and corners throwing whispers of distant sounds around. He passed through, the prickle of trespassing nipping at his back as a tapping enquirer... but there was no one. Just the grinding of strewn grains under his boots and the dust dancing in the shafts of light. On the other side of the food store, there were only straight alleyways. Too straight compared to the maze-like nature of the slums. Discarded boxes and lumpy sacks, but wait... food sacks had never been purple.

A few steps closer, a change in light, and the purple sack became a person in an indigo robe. The resonance poured off of them, sticking to Leander like wet tissue, but why? He crouched in the alley, shaking the shoulder of the crunched-up form.

'Hey... hello? Are you OK? Can you hear me?' The form's neck lolled, and it assembled in Leander's mind as a man. His face was striking, or the half that Leander could see. The other side was hidden as it rested on a lifeless arm. With a slight tremor in his hand, Leander put two fingers to the man's neck to look for a pulse, and the resonance flared and sung so brightly that he fell backward off of his haunches. The man in the purple robe convulsed briefly. A long ponytail of raven-black hair slid over his shoulder as his hood fell back. Leander could only stare. Nearly half of the man's face shimmered with iridescent glass. It had taken his eye, and the flesh around it, reaching timidly back towards his ear and consuming an uneven ring of skin larger than his eye socket. The man needed help.

It's madness. Ignoring a calling. Leander's mind shouted as much, but something else told him that the man was more important. A ridiculous thought. Why should the man be more important than this own calling? One last look in the direction of the spire confirmed it. The colour of the man's robe meant, or might mean, one thing but for the moment that wasn't his concern. The gate wasn't far, he could come back afterwards and leave the man for Corryn to take care of. She was better at that kind of thing anyway. Either way, Leander couldn't leave him there alone, unconscious and strangely afflicted.

***

It became rapidly apparent that the injured man was wildly unaware of Leander's presence and unable to support any of his own weight. After struggling to manoeuvre another fully grown human and find an effective way to carry him home, Leander resorted to hitching him on to his back with no small amount of effort. He wasn't heavy, per se, but Leander could tell from his build that he wasn't short of strength. This puzzled him a little. If the robe meant what he suspected, he'd always thought of dreamsmiths as being more skilled in magic than anything requiring muscle. They appeared so slender in their cloaked attire, as though a day's field work would snap them like dry spaghetti strands. Maybe there was more to crafting dreams than he assumed.

78

Leander's struggle didn't just lie with trying to carry the suspected dreamsmith, but with the idea of helping him at all. The overwhelming and inexplicable need to assist him still drove Leander's actions, but a doubt flowered and niggled at him with every step he took back towards his house.

Should I be helping him if he's a smith? Shouldn't I take him toward the Forge, rather than away from it? It's clear he needs help, I couldn't just leave him. Corryn will understand and I don't care what people think but... will it be safe for him out here? I'm not the only one with... reservations about these people.

Stares peppered Leander as he trudged back through the gate and slums with an unconscious stranger on his back. Some ran up to help, and Leader gratefully handed over some of the burden. He'd had the sense to pull the man's cowl down over his face again, grateful for the spacious and drooping hood. People would panic seeing such an affliction. Leander himself had no idea what it meant or what could have caused it. Just recalling it sent a shiver through him.

While some people helped, others snarled and grumbled. Shouting obscenities at the unconscious man, calling for Leander to leave him to rot where he found him. Not to spare a moment of time, time borrowed from the dreamsmiths themselves, helping one of them. Leander ignored the words. When it came down to it, people knew little of what it was like to be a smith. To carry their burden. If they were more transparent they might have a more stable public standing, but no. They chose to divide. To hide away in their Forge and separate the dreamers from those chosen to dream. It was no time for philosophy though. In plain terms a man was hurt, and people helped one another in the slums for the most part as a basic unspoken courtesy. Though not all.

The resonance had quietened to become less urgent, more melodic. A great pit opened as a cave-like maw inside Leander. Would there be time to claim his dreamstone after this? Too little time had passed for him to lose it, surely? People travelled for days to come and fetch their dreamstones and not all made it to the city before their calling began. It would be OK. The farm drifted into his sights as he rounded the final corner marked by a half-collapsed home.

Halfway down the path he couldn't see Corryn in the fields. The door stood slightly ajar, but he shouted her anyway.

'Corryn! Corryn, you there?' The man's weight pressed on him more with every step and Leander's strong arms began to shake despite the assistance. Corryn peered around the open door and rushed into action when she saw what he was carrying.

'What happened? I thought you went to the city for your calling?' Corryn couldn't hide the flush of relief and happiness that filled her up, and it warmed Leander's heart as much as her tear-red eyes broke it. She'd thought him gone.

'Help me get him inside, we can put him on one of the beds. I'll fill you in after.' He turned to those who'd helped carry the man. 'Thank you for your help. Take some rest now, we've got him from here.' They nodded and smiled, departing with a slight look of worry on their already haggard faces. Maybe they were genuine people, maybe they thought helping a dreamsmith would improve their chances. Tough to say sometimes.

'Has he been unconscious the whole time? Where did you find him? Who is he?' Corryn helped to slide an arm over her shoulders, propping the stranger up by shoving her own shoulder under his armpit. Leander grimaced while he straightened. Stretching out the kink in his back. He looped one of the man's floppy arms around his neck and they hauled him into the house as carefully as they could.

There was nothing graceful about it but eventually they steered him into the closest bedroom, which happened to be Corryn's, and managed to lie him down. When they'd made him comfy they pressed their backs against the nearest walls and sank to the floor one after the other. The effort showed in their harsh breaths and neither one of them was free of sweat. The deep pit in Leander's stomach yawned wider… the resonance stopped the moment his hands let go of the man. Only its echo remained. Empty. Hollow. He shuddered. Pushed the thoughts away.

So many questions hung in the air, and when they collected themselves Leander could hear Corryn thinking and processing, gears turning like a large clock.

'Those robes… is he?'

'I think so, but I can't be sure. It could just be someone from the inner city who liked the colour they wear.'

'Could be, but it's unlikely. I've seen enough dreamsmiths in the slums to know one of their robes when I see one.'

'True.' Leander wiped his brow with his forearm as he stared at the sleeping man. He didn't look much younger than them.

'So what happened? When you left I thought you'd gone… you know…'

'I don't know if I did or I didn't. I think it was my calling. The gate let me through but the calling… moved? I don't know how to explain it but it led me to him. I found him in an alley behind the grain stores inside the gate. He seemed injured and I couldn't just leave him. I figured I could go back and get my dream once I'd brought him back here but… I'm not sure now. The calling stopped the moment I put him down.' Silence bounced between them for a few minutes. 'I think I've missed my chance.'

'No, I'm sure you haven't. You could go back now and see if you can still get through the gate. Lots of people wait a while before collecting their dreamstones, don't they? What about the people who travel here?'

'They stick to the path of the calling though, I didn't. I deviated. I wonder if the spire took that as me refusing it?'

'You can go back and try? You shouldn't leave it too long or you really will lose your chance.'

'Let's see to him first.'

'I can take care of him. You said he was injured, right? Where?'

Leander dragged himself to his feet and Corryn followed suit. A few steps took him around the small bed and he gently turned the man's head so his sleeping face was directed at the ceiling. Then he pulled back the hood and tucked it under the owner's neck. Corryn gasped, her hand getting stuck somewhere between rising to cover her mouth and reaching towards the strange, shimmering patch on the smith's face. She stared, mouth open.

'Poor man, and you didn't see anything happen to him?'

82

'No, he was like this when I found him. I've never seen anything like it.'

'Let's not talk over him, we should let him rest. We can sit at the table.' Corryn nodded towards the kitchen and led the way out, drawing the single, fraying curtain over the small window and closing the door behind them.

Leander got a glass of water for them both, though it was lukewarm because of the heat of the day and had the normal taste of silt which only vanished when the water was cold enough. It was still welcomed. Corryn drained her glass in one and then pushed it absently around a small patch of the table while staring at her bedroom door. 'Do you think we should contact the Dreamforge?'

Leander pondered the question, rubbing the short beard that covered his jawline. It prickled in the quiet. 'I don't think we should. From how I found him and from his injury, I dunno… I get the feeling he was hiding. All curled up in an alleyway. I almost mistook him for an empty grain sack or a rubbish bag or something.'

'Do you think he was trying to get out of the city?'

'Who knows, the slums would be a strange place for him to go, what with the divide and all. Some people… well they don't exactly harbour good will towards them. I'm not sure which side I'm on myself. They have the power to help us all and yet they don't.'

'You're on the helpful side. You brought him back here. There's probably far more to their work than we could hope to understand. I think if they could help us all sooner then they would. Maybe they don't choose who gets their dreamstone and when like some people think.' Corryn, ever the optimist. Forever trusting first and doubting later.

'Maybe…' Leander threw a glance at the closed bedroom door. The man's face was imprinted on his mind. He found himself wondering, of all things, what colour his eyes were to go with that raven-black hair and almost scoffed at himself for such a random thought. 'I might have helped him, but as soon as he's able to move on, I'd like him out of our house.'

Corryn was taken aback by his insistence and the unintentional venom that slithered over his words. 'Why?'

'Because if he's hiding from the Forge he's probably in a lot of trouble. That wound on his face isn't normal. I reckon he's screwed up somehow. I can almost guarantee that if that's the case then the Forge will be out looking for him soon. I don't want them coming here. I don't want any trouble. I want you and our farm safe. So as soon as he's awake and had food and is able to stand, he can leave.'

Corryn said nothing in response, only gave a slow, sensible nod.

11

Replaced with Something Else

Taren's mind pinned him down in the black trenches of sleep. The surface always out of his reach. The pain had gotten too much, and he'd finally succumbed to it in an alleyway somewhere near the edge of the inner city. Where had he been heading? Where had he ended up? Flickering stars swirled across the blank canvas of unconsciousness. Some rippled and flared showing flashes of things he couldn't make sense of. Burning skies. Peaceful golden fields spread wide. Crumbling plains. A hand-built farmhouse. The spires starting to crack and crumble.

This went on, in waves of contrast, for what seemed like days. Slowly Taren's senses sent out their feelers and started to paint a picture. Each time he tried to push to the surface he'd learn something new, but his thoughts didn't flow or form. They were drowning in mulchy sand. Distant voices chattered in hushed tones. Had he made it to his aunt's house? Was Linette caring for him? No, Linette lived alone and there were two distinct voices in conversation. One gentle but curious, the other lower and clipped at times.

Quiet footsteps stopped at his side. So he wasn't lying on the floor? The softness beneath him faded in and out of his perception. The smooth warmth of what could be a sheet under the hands he couldn't yet make move. A cradle of support under his neck and aching head. A bed, then?

A plain but fragrant smell washed over him and a soft coolness covered different parts of his face in succession. A gentle humming danced around the room every so often.

Conversation. Closer this time. The musky smell of hard work and soil. There were definitely two people, and they weren't always in the room but he heard them close by. The light flickered and changed in great swathes behind his closed lids. People walking past a window? He must be in someone's house. Perhaps in the outer city? You wouldn't often find more than one person living in one house in the city proper.

Who were they? Who'd been kind enough to take him in without question? He had to get up to thank them. The kind of reception a smith would get in the slums couldn't be guaranteed, but people were generally kind and good natured... weren't they? Fion would roll her eyes at the mere sentiment of the thought. She was a little more careful with how much faith she placed in people. Oh. Fion. She was hurt, she might need him. Enough of this useless laying around, he had to get to her.

Why couldn't he wake up or even move? Then another dream took him. The dark space behind his eyes brightened with images and stirred up a nausea in his stomach.

Great cracks appeared in the land and turned to ash at their edges, crumbling away and opening up chasms that spewed a rotting air. People fell into them, pulling others in or casting themselves willingly over the dissolving edges. Some ran with bulging eyes and shrieking mouths. Lives extinguished at the end of trailing ribbons of screams.

From the largest crack crawled a monstrous being. A hollow. There was no doubt. It matched the description from the books in the Dreamforge's library, only far larger than it should be. Obscenely so. Lean muscle glistened with tar, a body sculpted for power and speed. The long claws acted as hands. Something about it was oddly human, and oddly inhuman at the same time. The sole feature on its face a dripping, grinning maw.

That's what people are supposed to become without their dreamstones? If they deny their calling? As it clambered out, towering over the City of Singing Spires, two lidless eyes rolled forward. They squelched out of the once-smooth skin, careening wildly about in their new sockets. The hollow peeled back the sky as though revealing the underside of a dome.

The sky beyond the tattered hole it created flared and raged an angry mix of scorched colours. The hollow continued to rip the sky apart and opened its wet mouth through gloopy black strings that clung to its lips. Turning its inhuman face skyward it screamed a word that was lost to a thrashing storm of lightning, before impaling itself on the city's spires and spilling a slew of dark, treacle-like blood upon the Dreamforge.

His whole body recoiled, mind yelling at him to get away. Get away from the dream. Run! Strong arms held Taren in place as his own twisted screams reached his waking ears. He fought against them, battling to leave the dream, had he been found by the senior smiths? Had they come to restrain him? Punish him for his mistake? The more his body woke up the lighter the force behind the hands that gripped him became. The inane buzzing began to form words, and before he could even comprehend them they were comforting. His throat burned, lungs desperately grasping for air, and under his whole robe a sheen of lukewarm perspiration lingered.

Opening both eyes was a mistake, and he slapped a hand over the left one to avoid the duplication of the prism-like glare it offered to him. His right eye seemed to function as normal, and it settled eventually on the uneven wooden ceiling of the room as everything fell into place around him. Taren stilled and the hands moved away. With a tension that pre-empted pain he uncovered his eye and left it closed. That would be a problem. He couldn't walk about with one eye closed forever, but his mind still moved with all the speed of cold porridge. A bumble of words washed over him. He snatched at them, narrowly missing their meaning.

'What?'

'I asked if you can hear me?' The voice was kindly and full of concern. He turned his head towards it instinctively, half his view blocked by this now-useless left eye.

'I... yeah... yes. I can.' Her smiling, round face filled his vision. Long, mousy-brown hair draped over her shoulder in a neat plait, and deep blue eyes reassured him. 'Where's... how's Fion? Jacklan? What happened to them?'

'Sorry, but I don't know who those people are. Let's focus on you and maybe we can find them later. Are you in any pain? You had quite a struggle waking up just now.'

He considered the question and as if on queue his left eye began to throb, pulsing in time with his heartbeat as it came down from its racing high.

'I... need to sit up.' The room tilted, the floor rippled,

and the woman's face blurred in and out of focus. Two pairs of hands supported his less-than-stable effort, and when he managed to claw himself into a sitting position the stiff headboard dug into his neck at an awkward angle. He didn't care, he was sitting up and his breaths came easier.

The second person came into view. His dark brown eyes were not as comforting as the woman's. If anything they were analysing Taren. Scrutiny crawled all over him and he couldn't meet the man's gaze. Instead he wanted to pull the thinning blanket over his head to break contact with the glare. A strong but childish impulse. The man's face wasn't harsh, if anything Taren had the odd and inexplicable impression that he was gentler than his eyes let on. A tidy beard, more like thick stubble, lined his jaw and matched the colour of his dirty-blond hair that sat in a rough knot at the back of his head.

The woman offered a small cup toward Taren's mouth and he sipped the water gratefully, even if it wasn't quite cold. The taste confirmed he was in the slums. As if the uneven boarding of the wood in places and distant clamour of what was presumably a market or hawker's alley winding down in the far distance wasn't enough of a hint. The problem was the slums wasn't a small place. The woman spoke with a quiet energy that chimed in her words.

'I'm Corryn, and this is Leander. He found you in an alley in the inner city. Do you… remember what happened to you?' The question circled the room like an eel, weaving around them all while Taren tried to collect an answer from his jumbled mind. There were too many overlapping events. The already small room felt cramped with three people in, and a tiny window told him that the light outside was dying.

89

He must have been out for a while.

'I think so. I just… needed to get away from the Forge. Needed some time to think. I'm Taren, sorry I should have said sooner.' He absently touched the skin around his left eye. Smooth and cold, the texture of flesh stripped away and replaced with… something else. A flash of the moment the dreamstone collided with his face knocked him sick.

'So you are a dreamsmith?'

Taren looked in what he hoped was Leander's direction, though he couldn't be sure. The voice had a sense of surety to it, conviction and clarity. 'I am.'

'How did you end up in an alley behind a granary store?'

'I… left just to get my head straight but must have been taken ill. Thank you, if you found me and brought me here.' Leander's cheeks flushed ever so slightly, unless Taren imagined it. He didn't trust his eyes to see anything properly, but Leander's tone changed. A sharper edge bolstered his words. He took a deep breath that rushed back out as a sigh.

'It's nothing. I suspected you were a smith and I couldn't leave you there. But once you feel well enough to walk and have managed to eat, you need to leave. Smiths don't leave the Forge to hide in alleyways for no reason, and it's clear that something has gone awry.' Those brown eyes pinpointed Taren's altered one and the feeling of scrutiny returned in force. 'Whatever you've done, I don't want your trouble brought here.'

'Leander…' Corryn tried to protest.

'No, no it's OK, I understand.' Taren put a hand to his eye. 'I'm grateful. I'll be out of your way as soon as I can, you have my word.' A nod of thanks and one final inspection was all Taren received before Leander strode out of the small room and his presence left the house. So few would have helped him in the state he's in. Either out of fear or loathing they might have just left him. These people had not only helped, but were respecting his privacy by not prying into the reason for his… affliction. He wouldn't bring trouble to their door, not if he could help it.

Corryn perched on the edge of the small bed and sighed. 'He's not a bad guy, things are just difficult out here. Leander, and me, respect what you do and thank you for it, but there will always be mixed feelings about-'

'I understand,' he cut across Corryn, but not harshly. 'Even though we live in such close proximity, I can see how it feels like we live worlds apart.' They both smiled in understanding and Corryn offered him more water, which he took in larger sips this time and set about the task of wondering what in the name of the spire his next move would be.

12

An Awful Feeling

Fion repressed an angry sigh, trying to pass it off as a deep breath. Two senior smiths, sadly or perhaps purposefully, that she wasn't all that familiar with had been next to her infirmary bed for the best part of an hour. They'd turned up obscenely early, which did nothing for her mood. Question after question, around and around in an infuriating circle. She only had patience for a few things in life, and uselessly circular conversations were never one of them.

'Sorry but I've nothing else to tell you. You've heard it all. Several times. I haven't missed anything. There aren't more details to comb my memory for. Surely you have better things to be doing than running through the same list of questions a fourth time?' Senior smiths were supposed to be treated with respect but Fion's fuse had burned down to the quick.

'So,' the taller of the hooded figures said, though she had no idea why they were hooded indoors, 'you've no idea what caused the forge to malfunction?'

'No.'

'And you've no theories on what might have happened?'

'None.'

'You say you saw shadows attack Jacklan, can you tell me again what-'

'No, you have my account. I've told you already what I saw and I don't know a better way to describe it. I didn't hear any whispers, didn't see any visions. I was barely conscious after I was knocked backwards so I don't know how you expect me to understand what I was seeing. And when the forge started acting up I'm lucky my undies stayed clean. I acted on instinct based on what I saw and based on how I assessed the situation. So stop pecking at my mind like hungry birds at a sandwich wrapper and let me rest. My question is, where were all of you? Because none of the senior smiths were there to help.'

A disgruntled huff puffed out from the second hood and Fion felt the slick warmth of satisfaction. Good. Let them get flustered. Let them get annoyed. This was getting them nowhere. A one-way ticket to pointless.

'I'm done with this interrogation. I'd like to see Forgemaster Clayton. I know he's probably waiting outside anyway.'

'Dreamsmith Fion we aren't finished-'

'You are. And so am I. Leave me be. I need to gather my things.'

'Gather your things?'

'I'm going back to my apartment. I'll be able to rest better there. Might have a bit more privacy and control over my visitors. If the Forgemaster disapproves, he can come and tell me himself, but I've nothing else to add to what I've said to the two of you.'

They both rose from their chairs in a panic, spluttering

and shuffling around trying to make sure they'd collected all their notes and flimsy question sheets. They made poor investigators. Too much ego. Not all senior smiths were like these two, she reminded herself. There were good ones, too, like kind uncles and aunts. Why couldn't one of them have come to question her? People who knew her, and who might care enough to tell her something, anything. Her entire body itched with the unknown. With tiredness. Pain. Uncertainty. With the keening thrum of anxiety that bleached the air around the senior smiths.

Home. That's where she'd go. To the peace and quiet of her apartment. Her own bed, her own clothes instead of this drafty, flimsy gown. She could let her guard down there, process some of the mess, ponder all the questions. Her fingers twitched as she thought of her journal lying on her desk. The one place she could unravel things when her mind got too busy. Yep, she was going home. Not even Clayton would be able to stop her.

Her whole side protested as she swung her legs out of bed. She'd been on short jaunts to the lavatory over the past day, so walking wasn't out of the question. Whatever sticky medicinal pad the healer had strapped across her like adhesive tape seemed to be doing its job. Some of the stiffness had subsided since the first day it happened. She carefully worked herself into her robe, not bothering to remove the infirmary gown first. She could take that off back at her apartment and burn the wretched thing after she'd showered. She didn't have much else with her, a few minor items. Then a gentle voice cautiously wafted around the door.

'Fion?'

'Come in.'

'You certainly managed to rile your interviewers. I thought I'd taught you better.'

'Don't lecture me. Sorry, I know I'm being rude, but I don't know what else people expect. My friend is missing, a colleague is being hidden away in some room. I've had no updates, no other visitors aside from those two interrogators. It's hard not to feel implicated here.' She fiddled with the silk belt of her robe once she had it on and noted Clayton's frown.

'Why are you out of bed?'

'A fine dodge of the subject, yet again. I'm going back to my apartment. I'll be more comfy there. Get more peace.'

'I'd prefer it if you'd consider remaining here another day or so.'

Fion stopped and met his nervous gaze. 'See, this is what I mean. Since when did you talk around things? Since when did you dance on eggshells. You've always been direct and open about everything. Everything but this. Can't you see why I'd have mixed feelings about the whole thing? I need some time to process everything. Time to myself. To figure out how I feel about the fact I'm being kept in the dark.'

'I'm sorry. I really am, Fi. Here. Sit down.' Clayton took one of her hands, and she didn't pull away. She may be nearly thirty but he'd always be her guardian. They sat down on the edge of the bed. Was the tremble in his hand something she imagined? 'This is a new situation for all of us. We're all still in shock, especially those involved which includes you. There's not much I can share but I can't stand to leave you in the dark completely. You're right, I've always been open and direct. So I'll do the best I can.'

Each empty second that followed stretched out until she could hardly bear it.

'Jacklan is alive but he is extremely unwell. He's in a delicate condition and one we don't know too much about. Visitors can't be permitted. None whatsoever aside from the healers and myself. When he's more stable, I'll consider when those who wish to see him may do so.'

It sounded much worse than she'd thought. Something strange had happened to Jacklan. Something he might not recover from. It was less of an answer than she wanted, but more than she'd expected to get. She'd take it. Clayton continued.

'As for Taren, I sent out some smiths to look for him at first light. It's still early, they have a better chance of finding him when it's brighter out.'

'Why are people being sent to fetch him? Did he do something wrong?'

'No. Not on purpose. I don't believe he meant for this to happen but it has, and we want to help him. He was injured too, in a way. At least we think so. It all happened so fast. But for his own safety and that of others we need to bring him back as soon as we can.'

Another non-committal answer that didn't deny or confirm her suspicion, but she wasn't about to get more than these mere scraps. His eyes harboured shadows of something Fion didn't recognise. She searched her mental catalogue of him. Through every interaction. It was a new expression. What could it be, and what could it mean?

'Wait for your next dose of painkillers and then you can head back to your apartment. I can arrange for the healer to drop by and treat you there each day, but I have one condition. If you insist on going home then you must stay there at all times. I need you to promise that.'

'Alright.' What else could she say? It didn't add up much, it was all far too cautious. Too controlled. He'd basically put her on house arrest. Something else he'd never done before. He'd changed. Or was actively altering. Any sense of security and familiarity she'd once felt around him started to blur and drift. An awful feeling. There was so much she wanted to say as he smiled, stood and left the room. None of it could be forced past her lips. Now wasn't the time to talk, it was the time to listen. Listen and think.

And Taren… he was out there somewhere, likely in the slums, possibly injured. What good would running do him? No one ever truly left the city. If her thoughts could reach him she'd tell him to come back. Come back so the Dreamforge could help. So she could help, or at least do something useful. The empty space expanded around her. A space usually filled by Taren and his banter. By their bond as friends.

As the warmth of the early morning light began to flood in through the small window between her bed and the next, she sent him thoughts of strength. He had to do what he thought best given what he knew, and so did she. She trusted Taren, and that was one thing that would never change.

13

A Black Seed Sprouting

No matter how long Leander stared at the ceiling of his small bedroom, it never gave him any answers to the squirming pile of questions ricocheting around his mind. They mixed with thoughts and ramblings to form a haze of conflict and confusion. Bubbling like the stew he could smell drifting from the next room. His stomach contracted and yowled. Corryn must be making breakfast for them, and for *him*. He'd said his name was Taren, and while he had no reason to lie about something as simple as a name, a warning rustle buzzed around every thought Leander had about the dreamsmith.

I bet he's screwed something up, and by the look of his face it's pretty bad. Maybe that was what I heard yesterday, the effect of whatever he did wrong? Maybe other people heard it too, maybe... it wasn't my calling after all. I was allowed through the gate, though, so it had to be. I can't hear anything now... why didn't I go straight to the Dreamforge? Stupid. I've lost my chance.

A cavern of emptiness rolled open inside him, echoing a longing for his dream now that it might have been snatched away by his foolishness. His throat tightened and ached, arms tensed and brow creased. What could he do about it?

He didn't know for sure one way or the other. The only real way to know was to go back to the gate and try again like Corryn said.

Something held him back, some part of him that had settled for the life he already lived. A part that thought maybe what he had was enough, but that idea was knocked away by the tide of longing that couldn't decide whether to rise or fall within him.

I could ask Taren? He could help me understand if I tell him what I heard and felt. Would he help me? Taren, the one who'd led him off of the path to the Dreamforge. If it was anyone's fault it was his. A flare of irritation burned in Leander's chest. *I don't need his help. I don't want it either. He can leave as soon as he's feeling better. There's something he's not telling us. That problem with his eye isn't normal and I bet the Forge is looking for him already. I don't trust him, or any of them, and I don't want him bringing his problems here. Not when we've gone out of our way to help him. I'll remind him of it when he's awake. Corryn won't like it... but it's for the best.*

He sat up gradually and sighed after a deep breath. His hair, a little tangled from sleep, fell over his shoulders by a few inches as he rubbed his face and leaned into his hands. Corryn often told him that he shouldn't sleep with his hair down, but it was just more comfy. Given her way she'd have him wear it in a braid or something. She already forced him into a chair at the table some mornings and pulled a comb through it all. She was such a mother despite only being five years older. If she hadn't stayed to help him after Melynda left he honestly had no idea what would have become of him.

A brief image of the spire lit his mind and flipped his

last thought into a new question. If his dream was no longer accessible then… what would become of him now? There was often talk about hollows in the slums, sometimes around night-time fires or in hushed corners of the many makeshift drinkhouses that littered every sector. Cullers scared helpless residents with tales. Crafters sold hollow wards or other such nonsense to paranoid people. Ones who'd waited so long they believed they'd already missed their call.

A shudder ran through him at the thought of a black seed sprouting in his mind and slowly taking over him. Supposedly that's what happens. A hollow takes hold and grows, and uses you to gain strength, and then you become it and it becomes you. A monster. He threw the thin blanket off and stood to distract himself, searching for his trousers and shaking his head.

I don't know that I've missed it yet, so don't jump to conclusions. I can still go and find out, just stop putting it off and go back to the gate instead of fretting. Get yourself together. No doubt there's already a queue out there and the flour is running low. I can go after that's taken care of. The new food delivery better come from the inner city soon.

Trousers on, vest warming against his skin, and as he cast about for his boots voices drifted through the walls. They were muffled but almost jovial. Taren must be awake, and hopefully more coherent than yesterday. Leander strode quietly towards the door. There was barely such a thing as privacy in the houses of the slums, though he and Corryn were lucky that their house was better built and well maintained. The floor crackled and creaked, but judging by the drone of conversation they hadn't heard him. Corryn's bedroom door sat ajar, and he opened his own just a sliver and leaned against the wall, ear facing the small gap.

'Thank you so much for the stew, it was delicious and replenishing.'

'I'm glad you enjoyed it, though I'm sure you're used to much better up at the Dreamforge.'

'Not so much as you'd think. The quality of food comes down to the chef after all, and that stew beats whatever the kitchen up there can cook up.' Corryn laughed, giddy and appreciative of the genuine compliments. 'Will you take breakfast yourself?'

'I'll wait for Leander, he'll be up soon. No doubt he'll want to get out into the fields to check the crops.'

'The two of you seem so busy.'

Leander rolled his eyes. What did Taren think they'd spend their days doing on a farm? Playing hopscotch and daydreaming?

'There's a lot to do, and no doubt a queue outside already since the supplies from the inner city are late this month.'

'They are?'

'They've been late the last few months. It's got us all on edge, really. We do what we can but our latest grain harvest is running low so there's only so much more bread we can make.'

'You're both so generous. Even more of a reason not to cause you trouble. I won't overstay my welcome.'

'Oh, don't mind Leander. He's not as harsh as he might seem. He's a good man. He was married to my sister for many years and he's like a brother to me now she's gone. She got her dreamstone and, well, she left us both behind.

He's not quite been the same since, you know? He keeps his feelings to himself but he's caring and gentle, though he'd never let you see it. I can read him like a book, though.'

'I've no doubt nothing escapes your eye.'

Leander cleared his throat and walked purposefully into the room, breaking up the light laughter and hoping the heat in his cheeks wasn't showing. He'd have words with Corryn later for talking to a perfect stranger about him in such a personal way.

'I'm sure you don't need to bore Taren with stories about me.' A flicker of apology lit her eyes, but her smirk told him he hadn't avoided looking as embarrassed as he felt. 'Are you feeling better?' Leander's eyes fell upon Taren as he asked the question and the blush in his cheeks showed no sign of receding. He looked much more awake, alert, and was smiling. His rounded face suited it well, as though it was made to fit around the shape of being happy. One ice blue eye was lit with an ironic warmth, the other closed and still afflicted by the strange, glacial iridescence of his injury.

Corryn's stew had put some colour into Taren's complexion and Leander had no doubt it was her who'd brushed his hair into a side ponytail that fell over one shoulder to make him more comfy while he slept. His sleek, raven locks fell to the bottom of his chest. Leander forced himself to break eye contact and wait for his answer.

'Good morning, I do feel better thank you, thanks to Corryn's amazing food. I still feel quite weak, but I promise to be out of your way as soon as I'm able.'

'Glad to hear it.' Taren's smile shrank a little at Leander's colder tone and he dropped his gaze to examine the blanket that covered him. 'Is there a queue this

102

morning?' Leander asked Corryn as she glared at him for his rudeness.

'Not as long as yesterday, but there are people waiting. The oven is heating up but we'll have to make small portions again. If we do that we can also feed a few people tomorrow as well.'

'Can I help at all?' It was a kind question and Leander fought a surge of unexpected respect for the dreamsmith.

'You focus on rest. The sooner you recover the better.' He didn't need to look at Corryn to feel the burn of her gaze. He'd hear all about it in the fields when she inevitably followed him out there and whacked him with a cloth or something. He didn't want to open himself up to a stranger, despite the inexplicable draw he felt towards this one.

Leander wasn't one to connect quickly with people he didn't know. So why did he want to sit with Taren over coffee and talk about things? Personal things like his dream, and the things he truly wanted in life. The things he missed and would never have again. It was ludicrous, and he wouldn't even entertain such thoughts a moment longer.

'I'll see you out front, Corryn.' Only when Leander left the room and was able to bask in the fresh air of the fields did his heart slow.

14

It Had No Eyes

With Corryn and Leander out in the fields or tending to the bread, Taren took on the task of standing now he was finally alone. Some part of him didn't want to struggle even more in front of the people who had taken care of him so well. The scent of baking washed over him and sank into the wood of the house, saturating it with a warm goodness that made the place cosy.

As he neatened and re-did his hair tie a serrated ache curled its fingernails under his left ribs. In a jolting blur he recalled falling on to a crate hidden under some sacks in the alley. What else could he remember? Fion, she'd taken a similar injury. His heart jumped, he had to know she was alright. The whole situation resembled nothing but a mess.

He shuffled to the edge of the bed and a torrent of memories engulfed him. He hadn't spent a night in the slums for a long while, not since the last day before he received his calling. He'd lived with Linette then. Could he go to her? Stay there until things calmed down? No. Not when he understood so little of what had happened. To the broken forge and to himself. To all of them. He didn't want to take trouble her way, not after all she'd done for him.

A thin blanket of guilt swaddled Taren as he tested his feet against the floor. Linette deserved more than his infrequent visits, more help if he could give it. He would seek to change that moving forward, perhaps when all this was resolved... if it could be resolved. The familiarity of the promise echoed in his mind, he had to stop saying and start doing.

Taren shifted his weight on to his legs and eased himself into a standing position. A wind of dizziness whipped about him and he steadied himself with one hand on the wall. A battering pain shot through his left eye and the flesh around it, covering almost half of his face, and he watched in slow motion as the dreamstone fled the forge and crashed into his flesh. The room tilted, but Taren refused to succumb to the pull of the bed he'd just left for the first time in a little over a day. Pins and needles crackled from head to toe and back again. Deep, measured breaths steadied him and the material of his robe scrunched under his free hand.

I broke the connection to an unfinished dream. Dammit. Why did I run? I defied my training but not on purpose. Surely they'll see that? I just... fell. I've never seen a forge behave that way and the Forgemaster he... he knew something was wrong with it when he tested it. I saw it in his face.

Taren couldn't shake the expression the Forgemaster had worn after testing the station in question. Something tugged at his sensibilities. It pushed past his admiration for the man who had trained him and niggled at a hidden root.

Did he actually know? If he did, why did he let Jacklan use it? Questions have a habit of planting seeds, seeds that feed on other questions and create more of them. Something wasn't adding up.

The rocking dizziness passed. The door was only a few strides away, and through the crack in its opening he saw a simple table with three chairs congregated around it. Had the other chair been for Leander's wife? That wasn't his business, yet Corryn's words stuck with him.

How often had he, or any of the smiths, wondered what it was like for those left behind by dreamers who got their stone? The unconsidered consequences of his work broiled quietly under everything else his mind stirred together. It wasn't the time.

When Corryn bustled in from the yard and saw him sitting at the table she beamed so brightly that Taren could only return the smile. The house had a rough charm to it. The doorways weren't all the same size, but that often happened with unregulated builds. Furniture was scarce but of a decent, sturdy quality. The table marked the sole sitting area, and a simple sink sat under a window that provided a view of the fields.

The spires glinted not so far away and he suppressed a flinch. Judging by the view, they were in the mid-section of the southwest quadrant of the slums. A few cupboards adorned the walls, but didn't cramp the space. It was homely, and created distance between his worries and the outside world. Had life been simpler out here? Maybe so, it was hard to recall. His mind started plotting a course to his aunt's house. She lived in the southeast quad, also near the middle section. It wasn't impossible to walk there. No. No, he couldn't. He had to keep her safe.

Corryn offered him a drink before disappearing to check the bread, and Taren heard Leander's busy strides crunching across the yard as he approached. Leander wanted him gone as soon as possible, and this wasn't something that offended Taren. By all accounts he understood it very well. Crunch, crunch, closer. There was bound to be some divide between the inner- and outer-city folk. Crunch, crunch. Even more so between regular folks and dreamsmiths. Some believed they had the power to do more than they currently did. That they were picking and choosing who got their dreamstones. If only he could reassure them that wasn't the case. Crunch, crunch, clod. Boots met wood and Leander froze as his gaze fell on Taren. Momentary, but not unnoticed.

'You're up. I'm glad you feel well enough.' Leander took a soil-smeared towel from around his neck to wipe his face.

'Thank you, for everything you've both done. There must be some way I can repay you before I get out of your way? I wouldn't be shy about getting my hands dirty when I'm fully recovered, though you're both doing a fine job it seems. It would be a pleasure to help.'

'Don't say that to him,' Corryn popped back in from the other room, 'he'd have you doing all sorts. I won't put someone to work as payment for care that was freely offered. Are you sure you don't need to rest another day?'

'I appreciate it, Corryn, but no. I think it's best if I take my leave if there's truly nothing I can do to help. Though I hope to repay you someday, somehow.' Taren looked up at Leander as he spoke, who only shifted uncomfortably in return and gave a minute nod. A crestfallen weight settled in his own chest. Despite the divide between dreamsmith and dreamer, did he deserve such cold detachment? They were strangers, after all, but where was the kind intent of the man who'd supposedly carried Taren back to their home?

'Thank you both again. I hope you remain healthy, I'll

leave you be.' Corryn moved to give him a hug but Leander halted her.

'I'm glad you see you well again, Taren, as I said. I wish you luck in resolving whatever trouble you've encountered.' Leander's distrustful eyes wandered over Taren's afflicted face as he raised his hood. Best not let any more slumfolk see it if he could help it. He'd have to find something to cover it later, some kind of bandage or patch. Then he faltered and let out a weak laugh at himself. What good would covering it do? It had already spread a little since the initial incident by the feel of it. What was he supposed to do? Walk around with a sack over his face? That would only be inconvenient and attract even more attention, but nor could he imagine having to consciously keep his eye closed indefinitely. Either way, he could tackle that problem later.

'Goodbye, both of you.' Part of Taren wanted to stay. It clung to the farmhouse on delicate threads. He left it behind nonetheless.

As he made his way up the path towards the main slums he walked at a modest pace, pushing through the hints of nausea that riddled his still-exhausted body. It was too early to be on his feet, the deep-seated wrongness of walking told him as much, but they were right. He shouldn't linger. It was no way to repay them, but what to do now?

His mind turned again to his eye. Opening it in the slightest set off a whirl of refracted colours. He brushed the affected skin again as he walked past the barrier to the farm. It hadn't spread far yet but his entire eye socket was covered, and now it was starting to reach for the skin between his eye and his ear. The same un-flesh-ness. The boundaries of the area weren't tidy, as though it were a splatter of strange paint. How could he cover it?

As if in response to his thoughts the iridescent patch stirred to life in flakes and joined together over his left eye. A squirming feeling darted down Taren's back as it happened in the space of several seconds. He stopped dead at the corner of a ruined building, his working eye wide with fear. Had it heard him? Listened? Acted on his will? It solved a problem, but created many more. He no longer had to squeeze one eye shut, if he opened it all he'd see was black. But was the eye covered entirely?

Too spooked to feel his own face again he forced his mind to focus. He could look at it later, for now he had to push down the nausea caused by the idea he might look as though he had no eye at all. Push down the thought that a chunk of his face might now look smooth and inhuman. Think, Taren. Think. What were you planning to do once you left the farm? After a mammoth effort, he forced his legs back into motion and pulled his hood as low as he could without completely blinding his right side.

If he went to Linette he'd only encounter the same problem and take his troubles to her. He was desperate for a shower. He could try to get back to his inner-city home, though he hadn't been there in some weeks having preferred to live at the Forge apartments. Wouldn't that be an obvious choice, though?

Fion would have known what to do. The space beside him where she usually stood with all her banter and infectious laughter had never felt more empty. He'd never been more out of his depth. She had to be OK. She was too stubborn not to be. How could he get information from the Forge without running into another smith? His heart sank as the logical part of his mind gave a verdict of impossibility.

As he weaved gingerly through the thin streets the nostalgia of slum life clouded around him. When he'd been young it had been his playground. An infinite maze of alleys and hidey holes, secrets and passages. He'd never forget the hardships, but it drew a stark contrast to his position at the Dreamforge. A delicate, foreboding feeling of coming full circle dragged around his ankles. The slums were a strange mix of lively and hopeless, some handling the never-ending wait better than others. Tethers of different lengths showed on the diverse faces around him. Some hopeful, some fraying at the edges, some on their last viable thread.

An unstable feeling followed his steps now that only one eye was in working order. The perspective of everything shifted, and every unexpected noise from Taren's left side made him jump or skitter. He had to remain calm and act as gracefully as possible to avoid attention. Somewhere safe, that's all he needed. Then he could figure all this out.

In among the eclectic bustle and drone of life he saw a sweeping robe of purple, but it vanished in a blink. Paranoia didn't suit him, but he wore it like armour. Would they be looking for him? A clanging bell rattled his mind and knocked him into a stumble. People stared but didn't really see. He leaned against a random barrel lining the street as images from his nightmare urged themselves across his mind, eclipsing any attempt at thought.

Burning skies, crumbling cities, collapsing spires that shrieked with desperation as they shattered and glittering fragments rained down onto cityfolk and slumfolk alike. Nausea rose and he couldn't fight the flood of bile. Someone absently asked if he was alright and if he'd had too much to drink, and Taren mumbled assurances that he couldn't hear himself say.

Then the street quieted and sound faded apart from a low hiss of staggered breath. The unseemly sound led him into a slow turn. It gurgled with a wetness not meant to accompany breathing, and in the shadow of a half-built house a hollow lingered. It had no eyes but it looked right at him. Singling him out. Pinpointing him and marking him.

No. No it couldn't be. A cold sweat of panic drenched him instantly. There was no way he'd just seen that thing. If he had then the slums would be in chaos. The smiths would be out in force, evacuating the area. No one had refused their calling in years. He forced himself to focus, his eye blurring violently before snapping back to clarity. In place of the hollow stood a ruined barrel draped with filthy fabric sat in half-shadow.

There was no time to wonder if he'd imagined it as a pair of purple robes walked around a corner. They were searching. He had to hide. His legs fought him but he willed them forward, and sidled into the nearest alley. The cool through-draft buffeted and grounded him. They were looking for him, after all.

It should have been a relief, surely? If anyone could help him with the affliction it was his own colleagues. The ones he'd trained with and grown with. Learned with and learned from. Yet something about the way they searched the crowd, a sharpness in their eyes, made his heart race in warning. They didn't look like they wanted to help. Their faces were hard set, eyes roving and analysing with a coldness that had no measure of friendliness. The whole situation was so bizarre that he couldn't muster up enough trust to go back to the Dreamforge himself.

The sudden cold sensation of being hunted shot through him. Prey didn't wait like a sitting duck while predators approached. He had to move. The smiths had been heading towards him but hadn't seen him, at least he didn't think so. The hollow... had it been real? It was impossible to know whether it had been standing there, whether it was a trick of the light and exhaustion, or a figment of the images being fed to him by his ruined eye. It pulsed in a nasty way every few minutes and he dared not think about opening it in case the strange shield retracted. Could he ever open it again? All he could do was pull on his hood too frequently, making sure it stayed low. The sour tang of bile hung in his mouth. What could he do?

He knew the slums reasonably well, or he had in his youth. If he could get towards the southeast quarter he could probably hide at Linette's place, as much as he detested the idea. She didn't deserve to have his problems dumped unceremoniously on her doorstep, but it was his only plan. He was out of other options. Hopefully the smiths weren't waiting for him there .

You could navigate the entire geography of the slums by the tight-knit backstreets for the most part, but you couldn't avoid the main paths completely. The biggest dirt roads were the ones leading directly up to the gates, and the southern path was the one he found himself needing to cross. Weaving through alleys and squeezing between buildings he picked his way east, until he eventually came to an alley that lined the edge of the southern road.

The main paths were the busiest in the slums. New arrivals would often gather there and try their best to adjust to the reality they found themselves in. Even though most people knew that you couldn't get into the city without first receiving your calling, there were those who weren't aware of that when they showed up. It made for quite an unwanted surprise to learn they'd travelled so far to come and live in an ever-expanding slum. Their longing for their dream, however, usually won out over their initial indignation and they settled in like everyone else.

He pressed his feverish forehead against the damp wood of an alley wall and took some steadying breaths. Legs shaking, ribs lurching with spasms if he moved too freely, face smouldering intermittently. He had to walk a little way down the southern road to get back between all the buildings and keep working his way east. It would be a minimum of maybe twenty-five steps to the next opening. All he had to do was be calm and walk as though he belonged and wasn't in a rush. That's all. Don't check over the shoulder, don't even look around upon exiting the alley. Taren collected himself, about to walk out with a bold stride, when he was struck with another bolt of pain. The flesh around his eye tightened and the cold glass crept outward slightly, widening its boundary.

With one hand over the left side of his face he pushed himself to breathe, to brace himself and get ready to make the crossing. He wouldn't be seen, he had to get somewhere safe, the rest could be worried about later. He counted to five, because he needed more than three, and took a confident step out onto the street, being sure to cover his face with his hood for the hundredth time.

He fixated on the entrance he needed to take, nothing else. He made no eye contact, refused to look behind and check if he'd been spotted or if there were even any smiths in the area. Running from his fellows wasn't something he ever expected to be doing. Ten steps. Fifteen. Ten more to go.

Then a gentle hand took his shoulder. Caught. The trap was triggered and his heart clunked into a new rhythm. The hand steered him without force and Taren didn't resist. The voice that belonged to it spoke in a low and unexpectedly kind manner.

'I'm pleased we finally found you, Taren. The Forgemaster has been worried.' Taren didn't say a word. 'We would appreciate your calm co-operation. We'll be walking as a group, without a fuss, to your inner-city home.' Another robed figure took position on his other side. Taren hadn't the strength to resist, at least in the care of smiths he might be able to get some answers. Resignation settled in quickly.

'Let's take the next turning and begin heading back towards the southern gate, shall we?' Taren did as he was bid, yet he couldn't shake the nervous energy that fluttered to his left. The tension so apparent that Taren could have shaped it with his crafting hammer. Why was this smith so uneasy, what unknown danger did he herald or expect?

15

Residual Resonance

Leander was lost in thought as Corryn ambled through the door with two large sacks of grain and guilt instantly swept over him.

'Corryn! Why didn't you tell me you were going to the food stores?' He half-leapt out of his chair but his sister-in-law shook her head with a smile.

'I'm a big girl, I can manage a few bags of grain.' She winked kindly as she dumped both sacks in the corner and a soft, continuous swoosh sounded as the grain settled like sand in an hourglass.

'They finally came through with the food, then?'

'They have. I bought the grain first but I'll go back for the other supplies soon. They don't tend to bring them down until later in the afternoon when it's cooler. Even if I miss them the tradesfolk will have restocked and the market will be busy tomorrow so I'll head out early.'

'I feel like I'm leaving too much to you.'

'We do our equal share, and you know it. I'm happy though, our own stores were out and the next batch won't be ready to harvest for two months.' Her eyes scanned the fields through the open window and her worries fluttered out of it. A swarm of desperate moths. If only he could catch and calm them.

Things had been simpler once, when they only had themselves to feed. They weren't obligated to share their good fortune, but in the slums people shared a lot of things because they were all there for a common purpose. All waiting, all working together.

Corryn began bustling around cleaning up from the morning's breakfast and Leander dragged himself to his feet to help. A strange tiredness had draped itself around him, filling his boots with dense, wet sand. Something wasn't right. An otherness, a displacement, jostled about inside him. Something important forgotten or lost. Something that pulled his gaze out into the distance and trapped it there, chasing a mirage that might not exist. The dishes clinked and rattled as they were immersed in the sink and it brought him back to himself. He prepared to dry them with an old tea towel as Corryn cleaned them fastidiously. They stood almost shoulder to shoulder, content working next to each other.

'There was so much talk at the food stores today,' Corryn said.

'Oh?'

'Apparently there have been a lot more dreamsmiths around than normal. Someone saw one looking pretty ill at ease on one of the main streets, and not long after two others came and calmly walked them back towards the city. Do you think it was…?'

'Taren? Most likely.' Lines embedded into her brow. Why was she so concerned for him? The dreamsmith had been there less than two days, though she always did attach to people too quickly. Still, it was hard to believe he'd been sitting in their house only hours ago. 'He'd probably screwed up big time. They were bound to come after him sooner or later.'

Her scrubbing slowed. 'I suppose so. He just seemed such a nice person, I didn't see any reason to distrust him. To think he could be on the run or something and we had him in the house. Do you think it was a crime or something, what he did?'

'I've no idea, it probably had something to do with his injury. He wasn't fooling anyone with that hood he kept pulling down. It barely covered the mark. Either way, it's not our business.' A flash of Taren's face crossed Leander's mind as Corryn passed a dish to him. Taren's smile before he left was more pained than Leander remembered. The way he held himself in an odd gait as he walked away. Should they have allowed him to stay longer?

'You were hard on him.' There she goes, he'd been too lucky not to get braised by her so far. He braced himself. 'Though I suppose you did also save his life, but you were cold and rude to him as well. We should have let him stay longer. He didn't look too good when he left.'

So she thought it too, that his words had forced a sick man out of their care too soon. He tightened his jaw, it wasn't fair to be annoyed at Corryn when she was likely right. Yet why should he feel guilty over it? Taren wasn't their problem.

'Then we'd probably have a brigade of dreamsmiths at the door right now. Searching the house, rifling through our things, looking down on us. I didn't want that.'

'He didn't look down on us, though.' No disagreements

broke the silence that followed. She was right, again. Taren had never once wrinkled his nose or stared disapprovingly at the decor or been in anyway condescending to them. If anything he'd been infuriatingly polite. Had Leander misjudged him? Thinking back over what he'd said and how he'd said it his own words and tone stung. Fine-pointed needles of regret and disappointment. Taren's face stuck in his mind, unaccusing in its warmth despite the icy shards of Leander's snappy responses and closed interactions. What would he have done differently? Did it even matter now?

When the dishes were washed and dried, grain stored away and the room given a quick sweep between them, Corryn sat at the table as Leander leaned against the old set of wooden drawers next to the sink.

'Why are you still putting it off?' Corryn asked so directly that Leander faltered.

'I… I don't know just… I don't think that's what it was.'

'But you got through the gate, right?'

'I… guess so but it was all just so strange.'

She shook her head in mild exasperation as she collected her sewing kit from a cupboard. 'Well, don't keep waiting around or you'll never know. Get yourself ready and go and see if the gate lets you past. Your calling might still be active even if you can't hear it. I know you're scared and unsure, but you can't pass it by just because of those things. And before you say anything I'll be completely fine.'

What a blessing that no one else could read him as easily as Corryn could. His stomach rolled at her words. "I'll be completely fine." Her meaning was subtle but crystal clear. Would she be fine? Left alone again if he were to vanish?

118

No, she was part of his dream, he wouldn't let that happen to her again. She glared at him and he dared not wait another second.

'OK, OK, I'll go.' *I've missed it, I'm almost sure I have, but wouldn't I feel it? Wouldn't I know, feel the calling close off or something?* A surge of urgency gripped him. What was he doing wasting time when he could be holding his dreamstone in his hands? That's what they'd all come to the city for, wasn't it? All the longing he'd ever felt for a different life poured into him and spurred him to action. He had to get out of his work clothes and in to something fresh before leaving.

The meagre pile of soiled clothes reminded him that they needed to do some washing soon, and he shuddered at the thought of the scrubbing board and basin. One of his least favourite chores, but like most things they tackled it together which made it easier and more bearable. He had one fresh pair of heavy-duty cargo trousers left and a few vests. Corryn sang happily as she moved to her room to fetch whichever garment she intended to mend. A song Melynda used to sing. A buffeting wave of nostalgia breached his defences. The song began to echo, layers upon layers, mixed in with a frequent and creeping clicking and clacking. Hard insect legs on wood. He stumbled towards the door as his skin raised a cold sweat.

He saw himself, younger, happier, full of much more hope, in a city he didn't recognise. Patches of black bloomed over the images and faded again. Bloomed and faded. A hole opened up into a vertical tunnel and swallowed his insides. He could hear it. Small, gentle, and fluttering but still there until the next second passed. His calling. The

119

silencing of the residual resonance rebounded and expanded into a chain of missed chances.

Taren's face beamed at him from under the black splotches and his smile turned from warm to cold. His ice blue gaze hardened in disgust. The patch of affliction on the dreamsmith's face began to flake and he was left with half his features. A hollow concave in place of his damaged eye. Then a slew of darkness drowned Leander and his visions, and his hip burned against the table in the main room.

His knees leaned side to side, unstable in their sockets. Holding himself up was too difficult. The muted crash brought Corryn running back from the bedroom. She was at his side in seconds asking questions he couldn't hear.

'It was still there. The whole time the resonance was there. So quiet. So comforting. I couldn't hear it. It's gone now, I've missed it, I'll never get it back.' Corryn struggled to prop his back against the table leg and support him, asking more questions and trying to get him to focus. Everything swam into everything else. His chest constricted and filled to the brim with emptiness.

'I've lost my dream. It's gone, Corryn. I'll never get it back, not now. It's gone, I can't feel it anymore. There's nothing there. I missed my calling. I was meant to get us out of here. Take us far away. To open fields and peace and freedom.' There was the faint awareness of being held, comforted, and because all other feeling escaped him he buried himself into Corryn's embrace and stared with empty eyes as his body mourned the loss of his dream with a certainty he would never be able to deny.

120

16

The True Consequence

Taren didn't say a single word the entire walk back to his home in the inner city. The smiths didn't grip his shoulders too hard, but nor did they leave room for delusions of escaping. The voice of the one who found him had sounded familiar, but in his haze of thoughts and aches he couldn't put a face to it. His captors nodded and waved at those who extended greetings while they walked, but Taren dared not raise his head for fear of his face being seen. Had the smiths even seen it yet? No. They'd be walking with much more urgency if they had.

The nervousness of the smith to Taren's left seeped into him through their contact and fluttered through his heart at routine intervals. A rolling cycle. The smith being so jumpy pushed Taren ever closer to his own edge. What was there to be so tetchy about? They rounded a corner and Taren flicked his eyes up briefly in the familiar surroundings. There, on the corner, just as he'd left it a few weeks ago. His house. The Forge apartments were more convenient for him and he'd settled into a habit of staying there like Fion… Fion, was she OK? Even if he asked these smiths, he had the distinct feeling they wouldn't tell him a thing.

The houses in the inner city were stronger than those in the slums by far. Made of smooth, elegant stone and far larger with their second storeys. The windows were arched and the glass beaded. His door was a dark wood with intricate patterning and the moment one of the smiths approached it and opened it with ease Taren felt betrayed by his house. How had they gained access? Even if it didn't always feel like home, the space was his, they had no right to be freely coming and going as they pleased. He buried the pulse of annoyance by working his jaw. It wasn't the time to get angry, it was the time to be careful.

They led him inside and the stuffy smell of disuse plumed as their feet shuffled over the wooden floor. Through the entranceway and into the kitchen without a word. A chair sat facing him in the middle of the room, the table moved off to the side. He found himself guided into the seat. They'd already been there once. How strange to be in such an unfamiliar situation in such a familiar place.

Taren wasn't firmly anchored to his body, but he kept his breathing even and reminded himself he had the advantage here. This was his house. He caught himself in his own paranoia. Every moment it seemed to sink into his body and mind more and more. Where had his usual, trusting demeanour gone?

Think it through. These were his colleagues, no one had ever said he'd be punished, they hadn't pursued him with violence. He'd just made assumptions. Something else he doesn't normally do. Why did the call from the Forgemaster for someone to restrain him immediately push him to run? It could have been for his own good. Time to find out whether his paranoia was valid or not.

Both smiths stood in front of him and removed their hoods. He knew them, had been taught by them. Ferron and Edwyn, two of the senior smiths. Surely they had better things to be doing than roaming the slums looking for him?

'Thank you for your co-operation in coming here, Taren. It's much appreciated.' Ferron's voice wasn't harsh or sarcastic, though he was clearly going to be leading the discussion. Edwyn only fidgeted next to him. Eyes constantly flicking to the ceiling. Ferron's mud-coloured gaze watched him calmly. 'How are you feeling?' The last question Taren expected.

'I'm... confused. Not exactly at my best. Why have you brought me here?' His left eye pulsed and he fought to keep his expression neutral.

'We were all very concerned about you given your actions when you left the Dreamforge. We didn't want you to deal with all this alone. You've done nothing wrong in the grand scheme of things, but we were concerned that the Forgemaster's suspicions are correct.'

'What suspicions?'

'That you pulled a dreamstone from your station before it was complete and that it made contact with your body.' Ferron waited expectantly, his eyes roving over Taren's hood. Taren answered the unsaid command by slowly drawing the garment back and staring Ferron right in the face. There wasn't so much as a flicker of surprise, only a brightening of his eyes. Curiosity? Pity? Taren had no desire to receive either. 'So he was correct. This makes things quite serious.'

'We can get to me later. How are the others? Fion, Jacklan, the Forgemaster?'

123

'They are all quite well. No one was seriously harmed and that forge has been decommissioned for the time being.' A wave of relief calmed Taren's racing heart. Fion was OK, she wasn't hurt. Thank the spire. 'We want to help you, Taren. We could have done so sooner if you hadn't fled.' The serious look on Ferron's face stirred a new panic within him. He'd never really stopped to let it sink in that his affliction had been caused by a shattered dreamstone, or what that meant. Had he done more harm to himself by running? It had all been such a blur.

'I'm sorry. I didn't intend to run I just didn't know what else to do. Nothing made any sense at the time, and the detachment was an accident, but I heard the Forgemaster call to have me restrained and my body acted on its own. Perhaps to avoid punishment or-'

'Punishment? No, we wouldn't have restrained you to punish you, we would have done it to help you. No one knows how fusing with a dream will affect a smith, it's never happened before. It was to protect you.'

'Fused with a dream… is that what's happened?'

Ferron nodded gravely. 'Yes, the stone has latched on to you. You've absorbed it and its contents, and it isn't entirely certain that we can separate you from it now. There is a chance that the Forgemaster can help you, but the dream has already had a day or so to embed itself. It's also clearly acting as part of your body. It didn't start off shielding your eye for you, did it?'

'I… no. It did that itself after I wondered how to cover it. I… can't open it properly.'

'Perhaps you can try now? If it does as you ask, it means the bonding is quite advanced. That it's listening to you.

124

Becoming a permanent part of you.'

Would it listen? He'd started to wonder if he'd imagined it the first time, but he tried his best to focus.

I wish to see.

For a few seconds nothing happened, but with a slow rustle the smoothness turned to sliding fragments and they parted around his eye once more. He kept it closed. Not wanting to see the bizarre concoction of visions and colours that awaited if he did. The skin along his spine ran cold. It had listened.

'As we theorised.' Ferron leaned over to peer at the uncovered, still-closed eye. 'Separation won't be an easy task. Time is of the essence here.'

Sweat prickled out of every pore in Taren's skin. 'Can anything be done?' Perhaps his mistrust had been misplaced. They wanted to help, and why wouldn't they? They were all part of the Dreamforge. All aiming for the same goal of helping others. His panic began to calm a little, but not completely.

Ferron pushed a hand through his dark hair and sighed, approaching Taren and turning his head so he could see the left side of his face more clearly.

Ferron encouraged curiosity in all of his students. An extension of his own nature. Taren respected him. Edwyn he wasn't so familiar with and something seemed off about him. He'd taught minor classes and was a quiet and reserved man. His copper hair was dull, but his green eyes were alight with discomfort. Once more they darted to the ceiling and back again. What was he looking for? Taren carefully turned his face away from Ferron's curious staring. A warning flickered through his mind. The faint flame of truth that had started to kindle began to gutter out.

'No, this doesn't make sense. If it's important to help me quickly then why did you bring me here and not take me straight back to the Forge? Is it possible to separate the dream from my body? Please, tell me.'

'We can't say for sure. This is an unprecedented situation. No one else has ever gone against their training.' An edge of disappointment slid into Ferron's words and scalded Taren. A shroud hung around him that he'd never be able to shake.

'It wasn't wilful. I never intended it. Am I... am I still a dreamsmith?' Every heartbeat became a tight, uncomfortable clench as he waited for the answer. They couldn't take his status as a smith away, could they? He'd be back at the forges one day, bringing hope to the dreamers. Listening to the songs of the spire. They couldn't take that away, but if a dreamstone was now part of him how would that affect his use of the spire?

'That's a question for Forgemaster Clayton. For the moment, however, we need to find out who you've stolen from.' Taren sighed with relief, only to choke on the accusation as he caught it too late.

'Stolen?' he spluttered, 'I haven't taken anything from anyone. I'm no thief.'

Ferron quirked an eyebrow. 'You have and you are. The dreamstone. Whoever it was meant for cannot claim it so long as it's merged with you. Seems that didn't cross your mind in your haste to run from your responsibilities.' Ferron was right. He hadn't thought of it that way. Whether it was shock of the events that had transpired or some kind of disconnect from truly believing the dream crashed against his face. Taren never thought what breaking from the forge had meant. He'd done the thing he feared most. He'd taken someone's dream. Erased their calling. How selfish. How foolish.

'I stole someone's calling… took that chance from them? That's not what dreamsmiths are meant to do. I'd never have…' his chest burned, torn by jagged claws strip by strip as the true consequence of fleeing sunk in. 'If I'd stayed could the stone have been saved?' All the weight of the silence that followed crushed him. Eventually Ferron spoke again, eyes dancing over Taren's afflicted skin.

'We cannot know. There's something we need to do before we return to the Dreamforge though, and it needs to be done as soon as possible which is why we brought you here. As I said, we need to find out who the dream belonged to.'

'Is it possible to do that?'

'It is, but it won't be pleasant. You need to undergo a reading.'

'A reading? Done by who?'

'A reading done by a hollow.'

17

Not an Illusion

Taren stiffened in his chair. Did he hear Ferron correctly? A reading by a *hollow*? It wasn't possible, hollows weren't something that could be summoned at will. The pages and pages of books that Taren had studied on the subject flicked by, and none of it added up to support the sentence that had left Ferron's mouth. In that moment it dawned on him that Edwyn had gone, and Ferron had busied himself securing Taren's wrists to the chair.

'What do you mean a hollow has to read me? That's not possible, the city hasn't seen a hollow for decades. People don't just ignore their callings. And why are you binding me, this isn't necessary.' Taren's mind buzzed and skittered, scrambling for order in the chaos of the words he'd been offered and finding none.

'I'm going to need you to stay calm, Taren. The last thing you want to do is to frighten it.'

'What?'

'Edwyn has gone upstairs to fetch it. I suggest you collect yourself.'

'Gone to fetch it? What do you mean?'

'Hollows have remarkable skills once they're tamed.

Tracking and insight especially. They can help find people, and information within them, better than we ever could. This is necessary to help you, please remember that. Whatever questions you have we can take care of later.'

Tamed hollows? Senior dreamsmiths were taming them? But hollows came from people. People twisted by ignoring their calling. It made the gifts of the Dreamforge a double-edged sword, but who would ignore their dreamstone? Who could escape the compelling want. The chance to live the way they desired. The Forgemaster had explained hollows before. It was such a sombre lecture. When dreamstones exist they create a new life for the recipient. One that must be accepted. People can't have two lives. If the new one isn't taken they can't continue to exist in their old one as they are. So they change. Become something… other.

The hollow he'd seen in the shadows of the slums, it had been real? Sniffing him out by will of these senior smiths. Did the Forgemaster know of this? A shiver jolted through Taren and he started twisting his wrists against their bonds far too late. Before he could ask himself any more questions, two sets of footsteps made their way down the stairs. One was Edwyn, clunking in his boots. The other was wet. Slow. Accented by raspy breaths and the clink of a chain. What in the name of the spire had they brought to his house?

'What's he doing? What did you bring here, you've no reason to restrain me I've co-operated this far.'

'I think you're about to reach your co-operative limits. There aren't many who would willingly sit still for this.' Taren's heart punched against his rib cage as Edwyn rounded the banister, a chain in his hands which were pale as talcum powder. Several steps behind him a sinewy leg slid into view, cemented with a squelch as it took one step then another.

'This doesn't make any sense.' Ferron ignored the protests. Edwyn was irrelevant. Taren looked right through him and his left eye throbbed dangerously, longing to be opened. His mind too scattered to think about asking it to cover itself again.

It was identical to the hollow he'd seen in the slums, and walked with a curved spine. Squelch. Rasp. Squelch. Rasp. Halfway down the hall. Every step it took begged another panicked thought. *This isn't right. This isn't what we were taught. Hollows can't be tamed, they're dangerous, they have to be terminated. If someone hadn't collected their dream the spire would have let us know.* A curtain of weight pushed down on his shoulders and the gears in his mind whirred so fast he could almost hear them. Squelch. Rasp. It entered the kitchen.

Ferron was behind him again. Moments slipped away. Focus dissipated with every second.

'Why do you have a hollow? Why do you need one? How is this possible?' Ferron's hands held him in place and straightened him. The wooden corners of the chairback dug into his shoulder blades. The creature was only a few steps away, its featureless face sniffing the air and turning to face Taren inch by inch.

'You have control of it?' Ferron asked Edwyn, who nodded with a grim expression. 'Good, keep its will contained.'

'This isn't right!' Taren's body backed further into the chair, looking for any spare centimetres to put between him and it. As his feet flailed for purchase the chair legs

130

screeched across the floor in stunted scrapes. Ferron's body blocked his retreat.

'Shush. If you frighten it, Edwyn may not be able to control it. This has to happen. We need to learn who the dream belongs to if you don't want it to take your life.' An electric flurry bristled through Taren at Ferron's words.

'Take my life…' Taren repeated, his body stilling. The rancid thing was so close that its odour poured into his nostrils. So pungent it became medicinal. Bitter. A thick smell that didn't travel, but stuck to the hollow's skin. It started to raise a hand towards him. Breaths came in small, desperate snatches. He screwed up his face in anticipation, closing his right eye and tensing against the pain in his left. A cold, slick claw smeared across his damaged cheek… but gently. As though wiping away a tear. A whisper rippled through his mind and over and over it said one word. Truth.

Images burst forward to paint his vision like a horrific canvas, and his insides stirred with what he saw. A dark but cavernous room rolled out, pillars reaching to the ceiling at intervals along its length. The architecture was reminiscent of the Forge, but he had been to almost every inch of it and never seen such a place. In the corridor the same rasping breaths that had come from the hollow in his house echoed, and a figure limped towards him from its far end. The whispers continued and so the question escaped him in a whisper as well.

'What truth?'

Edwyn yanked on the hollow's chain and it screeched as it dropped to the floor with a gelatinous slap. Taren blinked in the streaming daylight as the visions were snatched away. The creature's cry twisted in his heart. It tried to show him something. Something important. It pressed in on Taren more than the rigid, panicked hands of the senior smith that dug into his collarbones. The comprehension of it drifted by, slipping from his metaphorical hands. *No, wait. Come back. Show me again. I want to know.*

'Dammit Edwyn you said you had it under control,' Ferron snapped.

'I-I thought I did, it must have shown him something instead of reading him.'

'So you didn't have it under control!' Ferron gripped Taren's shoulders harder in his fury and swung around to face him directly. His calm facade long gone. 'What did it show you?'

Taren couldn't answer. A strange quiet grew inside him. A quiet that hummed, that was sharp and that started barbed gears of suspicion turning. All of the images the hollow showed him joined together and layered themselves with whispers. His doubts cut through the old seams and stitched new joins in his mind. He didn't know what truth he'd just been imparted, but Taren wanted to push open the door that led to it. 'What did it show you?' More urgency. Ferron was rattled, Edwyn's wide eyes leaked fear. Questions were Taren's only weapon and they spilled out in a desperate volley.

'What are you hiding? Does the Forge know of your actions here? Does the Forgemaster? Are you acting on his wishes or are you acting alone?'

'Get rid of it, Edwyn.' The hollow sank into the floor and vanished in a flurry of Edwyn's magic. Ferron tried to collect himself, pacing back and forth, ignoring his captive.

'I don't believe the Forgemaster would ask you to do

this. He's a good man and he treats people well, which means you're acting alone. If I manage to get to him and report that you've captured a hollow. That you're keeping one alive and trying to tame it instead of destroying it, what then? Would he strip you of your robes and cast you to the slums to wait for a better life?'

'You don't get to lecture me on going against the rules,' Ferron spat as he paced. 'We are trying to help you. If the hollow had done as it was bid then we could have got the information we needed to identify the dream and taken you back to the Forge.'

'I don't believe you. I don't know what you were trying to do but the Forgemaster wouldn't stand for it.'

'You believe in him so blindly, don't you? Haven't you ever doubted him even once?' The moment the Forgemaster looked back at Jacklan's forge in confusion pulsed briefly in Taren's mind. His hesitation didn't go unnoticed. 'I thought so.' Ferron sneered. 'You're naïve for someone your age. A sheltered graduate. Wait two more decades until your years match mine and then maybe you'll see the world through a less pleasant lens.'

'I trusted you as a student, Ferron. I hoped I could trust you when you found me, too. Are you both just corrupt? Waiting to betray the Forge? The Forgemaster will hear about your actions.' In that instant Ferron collected himself. Smooth, serene mask back in place as Edwyn moved in beside him.

They spoke among themselves, ignoring Taren with an ease that infuriated him. 'We can still have him read. Perhaps we just need to take the necessary items to the hollow in its own environment. Then it can't disobey.'

133

Ferron's voice was low but steady. Edwyn clearly more at ease now the hollow had gone. Taren started working the ropes around his wrist. He had to get free, find a way out. The atmosphere noticeably darkened, the discussions taking on thorny edges that he had no interest in falling against. The low, persistent keen of danger stalked around his kitchen like a sharp-toothed worm. Get out. Get out of there.

'We wouldn't need much,' Edwyn met Taren's eyes only briefly. 'Some blood, a few shavings of the afflicted area. That would be enough for the hollow to identify the owner.'

'Alright, that's simple enough. Then we can be the first to take the information directly to Forgemaster Clayton.'

'What about him?' Edwyn tilted his head in Taren's direction.

'He stays here. Quiet and still.'

'Alright. And... if it doesn't work? If he talks?'

'Then we take more decisive action. We have to protect the truth at all costs. It's why we were trusted with it. If you don't have the stomach for it, Edwyn, then leave.'

Taren couldn't stay quiet any longer. Being talked around as though they weren't casually discussing harvesting parts of him like butchers taking their pick of prime cuts.

'You're taking nothing from me. Not my blood, not any of the dream. None of it.'

'I'm sorry Taren, truly. You're perhaps the most promising smith I've taught since Fion. So it will be such a waste if you fail to co-operate. We don't need much. You'll only have to sit still for a minute or two. Relinquish a little blood, and a little bit of the dream that plagues you. Then we can get you the help you need.' A teal glint flashed as

134

both smiths flicked their wrists at once. Then they took a step towards him, daggers ready in hand.

As Ferron and Edwyn began to close in on him, Taren continued desperately trying to free his wrists. The heat of the harsh chafing stung, but it was no use. The ropes weren't so tight that he had no wiggle room, but they weren't loose enough that he could slip free.

'I thought you wanted to help me. Why would you harm one of your own?' Edwyn hesitated, a shiny gloss on his forehead, but Ferron wasn't phased. *They're going to kill me if I don't let them bleed me? To try and silence me? Was it because of what the hollow showed me? These two are corrupt, they must be. Does it spread to all the senior smiths? If I can just get free and muscle my way past them I can get out of here.* There wasn't much hope for that. Despite the kitchen being spacious it was two against one. Ferron stood all of two steps away. Taren tensed a leg, getting ready to lash out and kick to defend himself, still working to free his wrists with furious effort. The ropes burned more with every wriggle.

18

Rash Actions

Despite the healer's infuriatingly polite and chatty nature, Fion couldn't fault the effectiveness of her remedies. A dull ache still floated around her left side, but her mobility had improved even after a day or so. Turned out, though, that being confined to her apartment was just as boring as sitting in the infirmary. She refused to be a caged bird. The healer was due to make her daily check-in later in the day, so she could poke at Fion's injury and be nosey with small talk. Until then she was free to enjoy the time she'd pilfered.

A smile spread across her face as she wandered the inner city, bringing back some nostalgia from the times she'd snuck out of the Dreamforge in her youth. Seeing how long she could avoid the flustered caretakers that were responsible for her on any given day. Her record was about five hours before she was scooped up and returned home again. The fresh air did her more good than any poultice. The simple joy of having some space and a breeze flowing around her body.

She was hooded, of course. What kind of person snuck out without at least a little cover? So many dreamsmiths lived in the inner city that her robe wouldn't be conspicuous. She'd sauntered in the direction of Taren's home in the northwest quarter by unconscious chance, led by her need to know if he was OK while also not expecting to find him at home in the least. Her heart leapt with dread, then, when she'd seen him led into his own home by two senior smiths.

Why would they escort him there instead of back to the Dreamforge? Wasn't that what Clayton had said? That they wanted to bring Taren back to help him? So why the cloak and dagger? Something wasn't right, something that made her hide herself until they were inside and then creep closer to the house, taking every care not to draw attention.

Most of the houses in the inner city had a similar layout, and she'd spent enough time in Taren's house to know the set up. Yet in every position she tried, near every window and door, the voices were too low to make out. After mumbling a string of colourful curses under her breath, a bad feeling settled in her gut. Why were they able to bring Taren to his home, to let themselves in? Was he being held, like some kind of house arrest? If so, they wouldn't take kindly to someone just knocking on the door. Not least someone supposedly under house arrest themselves. No matter what Clayton called it, that's how it felt.

As Fion leaned casually against the wall next to the front door, ears straining to hear something, anything, through the doorframe, the tone of the mumbling voices changed. A screech ripped through the house and raised goosebumps on her arms. What in the name of the Forge was that? A creature? Surely not a person. Voices rose, panic flooded Taren's shouts. Urgency seared the words of another man. She had to help somehow.

Taking advantage of the raised voices she pushed the front door handle down. Inching it open a centimetre at a time and praying she wasn't noticed or heard.

'You believe in him so blindly, don't you? Haven't you ever doubted him even once?'

There was such venom in the question. She slid herself in through the door as quietly as she could manage, carefully closing it behind her. Standing statue still she faced the stairs, hopefully out of sight from those in the kitchen at the end of the hall. All she could see were indigo robes, the doorway shielded by a dreamsmith's back, another standing a step or two closer to Taren. Through the smallest of gaps she gleaned a glimpse of him. The level of the top of Taren's head suggested he was sitting in a chair. She'd recognise that hair anywhere, messy though it was at that moment. Whatever they were saying, she couldn't hear it over the drumming of her heart. Not until one of them spoke up.

'I'm sorry Taren, truly. You're perhaps the most promising smith I've taught since Fion. So this will be such a waste if you fail to co-operate. We don't need much. You'll only have to sit still for a minute or two. Relinquish a little blood, and a little bit of the dream that plagues you. Then we can get you the help you need.'

What in the hells? Fion had no idea what was going on, only that she wouldn't let it play out. Exchanges continued between the men and Taren while Fion decided what to do. Taren's panicked breathing and struggling reached her and her heart lurched. Determination rose in a flaming wave. No one hurts or threatens her friends, and she and Taren looked out for each other. Always. The prickle of something

138

coalescing rushed over her. The start of something much larger than she was ready for. Either way, she had to do something. So she did.

She did something only Fion knew how to do, she rushed in headlong. She threw all her weight into her shoulder and slammed herself into the back of the smith in the doorway. He stumbled towards the second robed figure but she didn't stop there. Using the doorframe she pushed herself off with her foot and thwacked her shoulder into his back for a second time, hissing against the pain in her injured side, and caused him to tumble forwards and knock into his companion. The first smith's head made contact with the kitchen work surface and he dropped hard among the second smith's confused shouts.

He'd fallen in a half moon around his colleague's legs who was now hemmed in against the counter. Fion grabbed the nearest thing to hand without looking at it and shoved it into the standing smith's stomach, forcing him backwards where he tripped on the splayed arms of his unconscious partner. A spark of recognition flared in Fion's mind, but it would have to wait. He fell in horrid comedy, twisting as he went, his forehead bouncing off of the floor as it struck. His shoulder produced a sound that made her wince, though the arm that folded across his chest broke the worst of the fall. He groaned, eyes closed, and fell still. That went... both better and worse than expected, but lingering would be a fool's move.

The thin skittering of a dagger scraping away across the floor after the second smith's fall spurred Fion into action. Taren's face was an absolute picture of surprise and horror, and she would store it away to tease him with later. But first she couldn't even believe that had worked. A broom lay discarded next to the two smiths. It must have been the nearest thing to hand.

She grabbed one of the daggers and swiftly cut the ropes binding Taren. Before he could even utter a word she dragged him out of his house by the wrist and on to the streets where she naturally adopted a calm walk, hoping Taren would follow suit. Taren fumbled to raise his hood, though from what little she'd seen during the scuffle it wouldn't do much good.

Her mind and pulse raced. Holy crystals, she'd just attacked two senior smiths. Tackled one and shoved a broom into the gut of another. They'd be alive right? They'd recover. The thwack of their heads on hard surfaces brought out a guilty grimace. Only the sound of their own footsteps and gradually calming breathing filled the space between them for a while. Then, eventually, Taren spoke.

'Fion?'

'I'm glad you guessed correctly.' Just hearing his voice released a flood of gratitude within her. They had to get somewhere safe, off the streets, to figure out what the hells just happened. What she'd interrupted. What she'd stopped.

'Are you OK? How are you here? Won't they have seen you?'

'Shh! Let's not talk about that fiasco on the street. They didn't see me, don't worry. Let's head to my place. I barely use it and so far they've no reason to suspect me.'

Fion's house was not as central as Taren's, but still in the northwest quarter nearer to the wall. How long had it been since she'd gone there? She kept it clean even though she didn't live there, it was just good habits. Even so, it never felt like her home. Just a house. Just a space she happened to have at her disposal.

They settled themselves in the comfort of the lounge and gripped each other in a fierce hug before choosing to sit themselves down. She fought, but didn't quite conquer, a flinch as he accidentally squeezed her waist a little too hard, not recalling her injury.

'What happened up there? I'm sorry I ran and left you, I don't know what happened I just panicked I-'

'It's alright, don't work yourself up about it. I'm OK.' She pushed his hood back gently. Her mismatched eyes travelled over his face. His flesh was gone, a great patch of it peeled away and replaced with... something else. He didn't flinch or pull away, only looked down as she inspected his face. Her stomach bubbled, not with disgust but worry. With the unknown. With fear. What did this mean? 'Looks I'm not the only one with odd eyes now.'

He shook his head at the attempted humour. She continued speaking as she dropped her hand away from his cheek.

'After you ran, so I'm told, I was taken to the infirmary but I didn't stay there long. The Forgemaster got control again?' They filled each other in on all the bits they'd missed. Fion frowned. So much of it didn't add up. 'They told you Jacklan was fine?'

'Yeah, is he not?' Taren tilted his head.

'I don't know, no one's allowed to see him. They won't tell me anything about him other than that he's alive and very unwell. They interrogated me for several hours about what happened. Clayton basically put me under house arrest.'

'Wait, what? Why would they need to interrogate you, you did nothing wrong. And why the house arrest?'

'I've no idea. It's weird, right? Didn't sound too friendly back there. Were you being interrogated as well?' Fion asked with a creased brow. They were getting to the real questions, if only there weren't so many. Taren stood to pace the room, looking like a pendulum as he wandered back and forth and back again.

'I don't even know how to make sense of it, but... I think Ferron and Edwyn are working on their own somehow. I don't think the Forgemaster knows.'

'What?'

'They found me in the slums, though I don't know why senior smiths were out there looking for me.'

'They've all been out looking for you... on the Forgemaster's orders.'

Taren blanched. 'They have? Why?'

'What did you expect? You've a dream growing on your face! Ever since you left Clayton has supposedly been bent on finding you so he can help you. He's sent all of the senior college of smiths out to look for you. You've finally got his attention, since you so often try and get it.' She tried a teasing smirk.

'He wouldn't have sent them to kill me, though.'

'Is that what was going on?' Her previous quip shrivelled in the seriousness of the accusation.

'I think so. Or at least it would have been if I failed to co-operate with what they asked. They... they had a hollow with them on a chain, which sounds impossible, but it was there in my house and they said it had to read me to find out who the dreamstone that fused with me belongs to.' Back

142

and forth. Back and forth. Arms wrapped around his waist in a meagre form of comfort. A hollow… that was the source of the gods-awful screech then? Fion stopped tracking Taren's paces and turned her attention to her own wringing hands.

'I… I spoke with the Forgemaster after the incident. I wanted to find out what happened but he wouldn't share much information with me at all. He's never withheld information from me before. Is… is your situation that dangerous?' Her brow hardened as she waited for his answer, preparing to control her reaction.

'That's what Ferron said. That if they can't separate the dream then it would take my life eventually.' He said it so casually that there was no way it had sunk in yet. 'But that doesn't add up with the fact that they were quick enough to draw daggers on me in the next breath. They wanted some of my blood, and some shavings of the dream.'

'Maybe they are corrupt. Their actions contradict the Forgemaster's words. He seemed genuinely concerned.' She inspected the floor for a while and Taren didn't push her. A small mercy. It was a lot to take in. The idea that she might lose him if they couldn't figure it all out… no, don't go down that road right now. Keep talking. Keep moving. 'How could they have a hollow? I thought there hadn't been one in the city for decades, if not longer?' Taren ceased his restless tracking and sat next to her.

'I have no idea. They had control of it, had it on a leash like some kind of hells-spawned dog. They're meant to be destroyed. That much we know. Something… something isn't right here, Fi. I just don't know what it is.' She contemplated for a while and they existed in a comfortable

143

silence. Her flinch during his embrace had been minor, but he wouldn't have missed it. She'd pay for her rash actions later in the form of pain.

'It was out of character…' Fion mused after some time. 'What was?'

'The senior smiths and Clayton. Ever since it happened I've been trying to speak with them to learn what could have gone wrong. They've always been open and eager to answer questions no matter what we've asked over the years, right? Not with this. They all buttoned their mouths tighter than a puckered arse the moment I asked about the faulty forge. The black liquid that was seeping out of it, the strange energy, the screams.'

Her eyes widened for all of a few moments while her mind transported her back there. Taren rubbed her back, being gentle after his fresh reminder of her injuries. It always helped her feel better when anxiety fluttered into a swarm. 'They're keeping something from us. I want to find out what, especially after what you've said and what I saw at your place.' He nodded in agreement, the events all buzzing around like angry insects. A rush of dizziness sparked. She was far more exhausted than she currently registered, and catching up with herself didn't feel pleasant.

'OK,' Fion continued, 'I have to get back to the Forge if I don't want to be found missing or suspected of helping you. The healer will be visiting soon. I hope those two smiths are OK, but the broom was all I could find.'

Her eyes wandered around the room, unsure what she was looking for. 'Anyway, I want to do some digging. See if I can find out anything that might help. I was confused at first you know, why you ran when you'd done nothing wrong, but now I think you were right to. You should stay here for a few days, if not indefinitely, until I can learn something.

'Just lay low. Don't go out. If they so much as suspect that we are doubting the Forge, or at least the senior smiths, they'll make sure they find you. I'll bring some food supplies later on, get some rest until then, OK?' Taren pulled her up and close. Relief, gratitude, acceptance, fear, confusion. He was an anchor in the storm and they'd figure it out between them.

'Thank you, Fi, for risking yourself for me, for not discounting what I've said, for finding me.'

'You're welcome. Now stop your sappy crap and go shower and get some rest, you look dreadful. There should be some non-perishables in the cupboard but I'll fetch something better.' She returned his embrace then left the house with a grin on her face. 'I'll check in again as soon as I can. See you later.' She waved, and the peace of the inner city enveloped her in stark contrast to the danger-steeped broth of events that had started to stir deep in her core.

19

A Fool's Game

The sting of the truth keened in Leander's chest as he toiled in the second field. The rhythmic rise and fall of the trenching hoe passed the seconds as though he regulated time for the world. Rise… fall… scrape. With each stroke and drag the scent of warm soil soothed him. The smell of fresh, new life. Something he would never experience.

Corryn had gone inside to rest, and he was somewhat grateful. They'd done good work, digging planting trenches for almost half the field and preparing to sow some of the seeds that she commandeered from the food stores: but Leander longed to be alone for a while.

The urge to blame Taren kept trying to rise and stoke his rage, but wasn't something he could justify. It had been his own choice to deviate from his calling to save the life of a stranger. Wasn't that the right and decent thing for anyone? In harsh truth so many would have walked on. Pulled by the need for their dream, by the years of waiting in the impoverished slums. Their time had finally come, it was about them at last… but Leander hadn't taken that road. He couldn't bring himself to regret his actions in some moments. In others he cursed himself for his stupidity. The back and forth was giving him neck-ache.

His mind scuttled again, crawling in on itself for brief snatches of time. Clicking and clacking. The city and the spires glittered in the distance and the drowsy light of mid-afternoon. He was outside of himself, watching himself work, watching himself twitch at every dark, metallic tap that plagued his mind.

Then in the rhythm of effort and exertion… the resonance seemed to begin again. Weak and irregular, but there nonetheless. His heart lurched as he cast about while straining his ears as though something would appear in the field to confirm it. Had he been wrong? Maybe hope wasn't lost after all, but he huffed in snide dismissal and returned to his work. Hope. A fool's game. He cursed himself for choosing it even for a second.

A wave of gloom buffeted him. It had to stop. The dream was gone. Better to simply accept it. His knuckles turned white on the tarnished wooden handle of his trenching tool. It became a conduit for his bubbling rage. The regret he shouldn't have harboured. He raised it with a grieving expression and struck the innocent soil. One strike… two strikes… three… and then his eyes snapped up to the spire and it held him there, breathless and suspended in its clutches while it dangled twisted visions in front of him. Old memories. Ones he'd tried to bury. Ones he didn't want.

The three of them sat at the table in the main room of the farmhouse. Himself, Corryn and Melynda. The sisters shared the same berry blue eyes, lit with the depth of natural ponds and ever observant. *Why this memory, why now? Why do I have to keep reliving her betrayal?* They sat in wonder, staring at

147

the object on the table in awe and unsure what to do or say. As though it might steal away their words or voices if they spoke in its presence. Melynda's dreamstone sat quietly, observing everything around it. Its smooth glass could have rippled like water, and the blue fractal within it would forever be protected by its shell. Secrets held in suspension. Eventually Leander had spoken.

'Will it take us all with it, when it wakes?'

Melynda beamed at him. 'Of course, you'll both come with me and we'll live a better life.' They'd all joined hands in hope, and usually that was where the memory faded away. Right on the edge of her ghastly lie. Not this time.

The lighting darkened to spotlight all three of them and Melynda's face twisted into a devious sneer. 'Or at least that's what you want to hear, but I'll leave you here to rot without me. To die in the slums while I vanish overnight. You might be my husband but I'm sick of the sight of you. You're not good enough, and I'll never take you with me.' *No, no this is all wrong, that isn't what Melynda said. Stop. Stop changing things. Stop changing my memories.*

Melynda stood, eyes afire with feral wildness, and brought a fist down on to the dreamstone to shatter it into fragments. Some of them pierced her skin, dripping blood. Others bounced off of all the nearby surfaces and tinkled to the floor. From the stone's glittering ashes rose a thick, mulchy ooze that shaped itself into a thin-limbed creature. Its face split into a gaping maw that stretched towards Melynda and began to consume her as she laughed. Then it turned on him, strips of her skin hanging from its mouth, and pounced, knocking him into darkness.

His breathing was frantic as the memories cleared.

148

Memories? Visions? Both at once? The world churned on an invisible sea, hurling his insides around on a separate axis. An axis that didn't match up with the reality that he stood in front of the inner city's southern gate.

'I shouldn't be here. I should be in the fields. This isn't real. It's another vision.' He muttered to himself, feeling the stares gathering around him. Clouds of concern and pity. Another one losing their grip on reality. The blue patterns of the gate gleamed at him and he wondered if maybe he'd meant to come here. One last try before giving up. Before accepting that he'd missed his dream. It wasn't impossible to think he'd been mistaken, he didn't know how callings worked after all. No one did. No one knew anything about how their lives worked and yet here they were, waiting. Always waiting. Never knowing.

In that moment it all seemed ridiculous and frivolous. He could have laughed at the lot of them, himself included. Perhaps he was laughing, that bitter ringing sound had to come from somewhere. Why not laugh at himself some more? Why not raise a hand and place it against the gate, and watch himself learn the truth he already knew?

So he did. He raised a hand, fever burning on his skin, and pushed it out towards the gate. Smiling in the knowledge that he'd be right. That he could confirm his missed chance and move on with his life. It had to be done, it was part of the game. Yet, his smile faltered and his face slackened when his hand passed through and the inner city opened up in front of it.

He pulled away, breath caught. That wasn't supposed to happen. He'd missed it. He should have been denied access. His dream was gone. He'd *felt* it go. Why should he be played with like this, why should any of them face this torture?

A blinding headache crashed against the shores of his mind which started to flake like brittle paint in the sheer force of it. His own laugh echoed around him, tears wet his face and high seas rolled in his gut. A thousand whispers roared between his ears and when it became unbearable they quieted as a deep, guttural voice climbed up from the depths and offered a simple prompt.

~*Find the Truth.*~

The world tipped, only stopping when his cheek caused a plume in the dust on the road. The sandy earth coated his teeth and tongue on his next strained inhale. Someone placed a hand on his back and shouted for someone else to fetch Corryn.

20

Full of Malice

Taren slept hard and deep. Strange dreams entwined themselves with him. Impossible images had lingered behind his eyes as he woke several minutes ago, and he watched their shadows fade, yet couldn't remember a thing about them. His face stung over a larger area than he recalled, and the skin of his cheek was pinched and tender. He hadn't dared touch it yet. The eye had covered itself again during his rest. A fact that he wouldn't probe any further. He lay there, fully clothed, on the sofa in Fion's lounge staring at the wooden beams elegantly holding up the ceiling.

The events of the last few days melded together in a soup of disbelief and mistrust that bubbled and boiled. A rope frayed, the one that supported his trust for the senior dreamsmiths, or at least the two that tried to harm him. Was it just those two, or were there more? Something was going on at the Dreamforge, behind the scenes, that the Forgemaster himself might not even be aware of.

I can't go back to the Forge now, not if Fion shares my bad feeling about what happened with Jacklan. What other lies have we been fed? Who else is acting against what the Forge stands for? I hope it was just

151

those two. But for senior smiths to be capturing and taming hollows?

Their voices echoed in his head as he flicked through the events. Ferron had told Edwyn to get rid of the hollow. But where were they keeping it? Could there be more of them? For them to have hollows, it meant they had humans who refused their calling. Refused, or who were purposefully kept from receiving what was rightfully theirs. A direct contradiction of the will of the spire. Of the purpose of dreamsmiths.

Bile tickled the back of his throat. That's not what being a dreamsmith was about. To keep someone away from their calling for such ends. To snatch that hard-awaited hope out from under their noses. Senior smiths or not, Taren longed to ram his fist into both of their faces. It wasn't what the Dreamforge stood for.

He sat up too abruptly and a dizzy spell set the room turning like a globe. All the questions building up spun in the other direction as the realisation settled upon him. He didn't trust the Forge anymore, not if this could go on unnoticed within its walls.

It stole the breath from his chest. He'd been part of the Dreamforge since his teens. So thrilled to get his dream and join the smiths. To hear the call, follow the path, and be greeted by the Forgemaster himself. It was Taren's proudest day, yet that spark had lost its shine. Muted with a sooty coating of doubt. Even if he could still trust the Forgemaster, those working under him were corrupt. Did that make their leader corrupt, too?

Leander and Corryn appeared in his thoughts and a longing to be back at the farmhouse pulled at him. Why should he think of them? Leander hadn't been that rude, given the circumstances, but he hadn't exactly been welcoming. It was understandable, of course, but then with what Corryn had told him it made more sense.

Taren had never really thought about what happens to those left behind by dreamers who got their call. It didn't seem to be a positive thing for Leander. As he tried to adjust his view and imagine it, he saw such a naïvety in himself that he felt like a petulant child. A quality Ferron hadn't had a problem latching on to and pointing out. There was more to Leander than he knew, more to the world than he knew, and more to consider about his work as a dreamsmith than he'd ever bothered thinking about before. What harm had he done going through life with such a black and white view?

He mused aloud to fill the silence of Fion's home. 'I always thought being a smith was about giving. About lifting people up from the lives they struggle with and giving them the ones they always dreamed of. In theory it sounded positive, like a good thing… but is it that way for everyone? Corryn said Leander was quite different before his wife left. I wonder just how different?'

He couldn't picture Leander smiling, but he hoped to see it happen one day. It took a rare and precious type of kindness for Leander to save Taren, to have ripped himself off the path of his calling to carry an unconscious stranger home. That didn't at all match with the man who had barely spoken, and had made it clear Taren shouldn't out-stay his welcome. Corryn spoke of him with such fondness, as though she could see something else in him that was worth defending. Taren found himself wanting to discover what those qualities were… and then he caught himself.

'Stop it, this isn't the time for thinking about them.

153

You're questioning the integrity of the Forge in the same breath as wishing you could be back in a slum farmhouse chatting to a pair of folks you barely know. Get it together, you can't sit around mulling on things all day.' That said, what else was he supposed to do? If he didn't keep his mind busy with other thoughts, they'd stray to the one place he was avoiding. The place at the end Ferron's words. The place where the timeline of his life was snipped to be a short, docked and useless thing. He shook the thoughts away. Laying low and getting rest, those were Fion's orders. Even if he'd much prefer to be out there warning everyone that something wasn't right at the Forge and not to trust them.

Then Linette sprang to mind. He couldn't warn the entire slum… but he might be able to warn her. The need to make sure she was alright began to burn like a lit match in his pocket. What if Ferron visited her before he'd found Taren and hurt her? What if she'd been scared by smiths coming in to her home and looking for him? She'd be fretting, worrying as she did. He had to go and let her know he was OK and check on her for himself.

Fion's words caught on his ankles. A ball and chain. She'd asked him to lie low. Risked herself to save his life despite her injuries. If he was seen out there, he'd be throwing all that away. But Linette was his only family, aside from Fion. His worry for her vibrated in his mind. Yet another choice lay before him. Warn her or protect himself. He apologised to Fion under his breath. He wouldn't hesitate on such a decision again. If he'd just focused and finished the dream he was melding in the first place, he could have helped with the situation instead of making it worse. Instead of becoming a thief. A traitor to his own ideals and everything he'd ever strived for. Not again.

As he prepared to slip out of the house a searing strip of guilt wriggled through him. He should stay, like Fion said. No sensible person would choose otherwise… but he pulled up his hood and left by the back door regardless.

The inner city was quiet and serene as always. His strides were unhurried, and he was thankful for Fion living so close to the Eastern gate. He strode through undisturbed and the slum was a sharp comparison on the senses. Quiet often followed dreamsmiths through the slums. He kept walking, weaving his way to Linette's home and looking around in a way he hoped wasn't too suspicious. The world through one eye was quite different, and every now and then he'd sway or narrowly avoid a passing person or stationary item on the peripherals of his path. A barrel. A stack of crates. A child darting by. No one bothered him, no one put their hand on his shoulder and steered him away. With every step he called himself a fool.

His heart was thrumming by the time he rounded the corner to see Linette's house slide into view. He'd spent ten years living there as a boy and nostalgia twitched in the corners of his mouth despite himself. Had he only last been there a few days ago? It felt like years. Knowing his current luck she wouldn't even be at home. He didn't knock, he never did, that way she would know it was him.

'Aunt Linette?' The question bounced back to him in silence, and then he heard the bustle of her skirt and the rapid tap of her footsteps. She appeared from the bedroom with a smile drawn across her face. His stomach twisted. He should visit more frequently.

'I was beginning to think you'd forgotten where I lived.' She teased, then embraced him briskly and defaulted to her natural behaviour of reaching for the water heater. 'Please sit down, sit down, tell me what's been going on in that busy life of yours. I'm so pleased to see you.' Judging by her reaction, she was in fantastic spirits and had no idea what had happened. A fact both reassuring and unsettling. Gossip spread through the slums like fire through a tinder field. At the very least two dreamsmiths apprehending a third on a main street would have conjured some whispers somewhere. At least it meant the smiths hadn't tried looking for him here. Or if they had, Linette hadn't noticed. For a moment he couldn't decide if that was more or less disturbing.

'How are you? Sorry I haven't called in for a few days, I was doing some extra study.' He swallowed the residue of the lie as though it were a slug, and lowered himself into the chair she'd offered.

'You can bring your books here, you know that. I'm doing alright. Much the same as always, really.' She wasn't trying to guilt him, but it seemed a natural response to anything she said. Building layer upon layer. The more he saw her, the more layers settled on the pile. As a woman in her early fifties he wished she'd been able to live a life that would have helped retain her youth a little better.

'Are you sure? You're finding enough food?'

'Yes, yes. Between the food store's offerings and with my earnings I'm doing fine, I promise. I've had non-stop custom since your last visit. Stop worrying. Like I always say, people are more willing to pay to have things fixed than to buy new.'

Their conversations often had similar themes and tones,

156

which only made it all the harder to remember each visit separately. Her hair was just as neat as ever. Pulled back into a tight and orderly bun at the base of her neck. It gave her a very regal look. Linette was a warm woman, but only to those close to her. To an outside view she might seem strict and cold, a little too proper and never unable to control her emotions. Everything was measured, like the plans of the clothes she made and fixed. Everything precise. Manners were also a must in her house.

'Taren do take that hood down, I'd much rather see your face properly when speaking with you.' She smiled warmly as the steaming mug appeared in front of him with the efficiency he admired. He hesitated. She noticed. She always noticed. 'What's the matter? You've been jittery since you got here, did something happen?'

'I suppose you could say that,' he said as he carefully pulled back the hood. At the same time the dream unmasked his left eye, completely unbidden. Such a strange feeling, like the peeling back of a mask of splinters every time. He'd never get used to it. In her shock she forgot to cover her reaction and all the muscles in her face jumped. A hand reached out, then recoiled again, but it only lasted a second. Then she was back to her calm composure.

'What happened?'

'Something went wrong with one of the dreams. I came to talk to you about something, and I need you to listen, OK? Even if it sounds unreasonable. Even if it goes against a lot of what you know.' She stilled. Watching and waiting, concern mingling with curiosity in her dark brown eyes.

'OK.'

He stood and paced, the building questions collecting

around them like toxic clouds. How could he explain this? How could he even make this request of her? When he looked back she'd moved, so quietly he didn't hear a sound, and was staring out of the kitchen window in absolute rapture. No way his timing could be this unfortunate. The prickle of being watched, followed, toyed with, rose on the back of his neck. Why now? Why that instant? Was it a threat? No, it couldn't be. The spire can't be controlled. It answers to no one. No one except the Forgemaster, but even he can't choose which dreams to pluck from the crystals. She turned back to him, tears in her tired eyes and a grin so broad it entirely changed her face.

'You came to tell me that my calling was coming today? I hear it. I finally hear it! That's why you came, right, to let me know? Even though you're not supposed to tell people that kind of thing. Oh, thank you for keeping your promise!'

What he said next he blurted, panic forcing it out of his mouth in a way much more harshly than intended.

'Ignore it. Don't answer the call!' Her eyes emptied of happiness and filled with something else. Something he'd seen sometimes in brief moments when she asked about the spire or his life at the Dreamforge. The moments where he had to tell her, once again, that he had no dreamstone for her. A look he'd always feared as being deeper than mere disappointment. Her face dropped into a down-turned expression, but Taren forged ahead. 'I came to ask you to ignore your call when you hear it, please. Something isn't right with the Dreamforge, part of it can't be trusted and I don't know how high the corruption goes. I don't have any answers yet but I want… to… protect…' The expression of the woman who had taken him in and cared for him all these years was so full of malice that it stole the sounds from his throat. Drained them. Water rushing through a puncture to leave its vessel empty. It brimmed, dripped, poured over the edge of her and spilled along the floor to burn him where he stood. It was tenfold the look he feared. He couldn't talk in the presence of that glare, and couldn't understand why it decorated the face of someone he loved and cared for.

21

The Carnage of Words

For a painful collection of seconds no sound passed anyone's lips. Taren shrank back from the stone-faced seething pouring off the woman who raised him. What had he said to provoke this? She stood so still that he questioned if time had stopped. Some trick of the spire.

'Explain yourself.' She pushed the words towards him and waited. Her expectation dripped with disdain. The kind that didn't just appear, and that was the most disturbing thing. The deep-seated nature of it. Emerging after a long and forced slumber. The most painful of his worries laid bare in unmasked truth. Could it really be true? That she resented him so much?

She swayed on the spot. The spire would be calling her. He took a few steps to stand between her and the door and Linette's eyes narrowed a touch. He didn't want her walking out mid-conversation. Didn't want the Dreamforge to catch her. Ensnare her. All at once the whole system on which their lives revolved seemed ridiculous. How could he begin to explain?

'I… something isn't adding up. A few things happened in the last couple of days and… I really don't know if we can trust the Forge right now. There are people there who might be acting against the Forgemaster. Ever since I ran things haven't been right, two smiths had a hollow on a leash and then they tried to hurt me and I just want you to be safe until I know more of what's going on.' He rambled most of what was said and Linette's face remained unchanged.

'Ever since you ran? Is that what this is all about?' She gestured to his face, the disgust she'd hidden so well originally now plain to see. How often had she worn this mask around him? The bitterness in her voice stronger than any tea she'd ever brewed, and all at once he was so tired. 'I knew you'd messed up the moment you dropped that hood. It was obvious, written across your face in more than just that strange affliction. I knew you'd screw it up eventually, you've always been complacent.'

His mouth dropped open, slack in the face of the accusation. Each word she spat stung with truth. How long had she felt this way?

'You knew I'd mess things up? What do you mean? Where's all this coming from? Auntie I-'

'Don't call me that again. You had every opportunity given to you. Handed to you on a fancy platter. I saved you that day, when I found you on the road not far from that collapsed house. I brought you with me. I didn't have to do that, and what did it get me? It got me life in the slums with an ungrateful child who had it easy ever since.' Taren frowned at that, he'd always expressed every gratitude he could to Linette for what she did for him.

'Hold on, ungrateful? That's not-'

'Don't you dare pretend you've been grateful to me.

161

Your actions don't back you up in the slightest. You got your dream young, you know nothing of how I've had to live. Why didn't you take me to the inner city with you when you got your calling? You waltzed off through that gate and I didn't see you for weeks. Eventually you come back to tell me of how wonderful it is that you got your dream to be a smith, and how great your house in the inner city is.

'You've always placated yourself into thinking you cared for me by visiting just enough. Just enough to assuage yourself. But you left me here. To rot. To wait.' Her words slapped against his skin with every syllable, each one raining blows and showing no signs of stopping.

'Now that my time has finally come, you don't like it. Do you want to be the only one of us to get our calling? Do you think I don't deserve it, that I belong here in the slums until I die unnoticed waiting for when you next have time to visit me?

'I thought I did my best to teach you to be a kind person and now this? Now you can't stand the fact that I'll get my dream as well. Step aside, the spire is calling me and I want to claim my dreamstone. It's my right. I never want to see this place, or anything in it, again.'

'Is this truly how you've seen me since I got my call? You know I couldn't take you with me to the inner city, the gate wouldn't have let you pass. You don't think I would have taken you to live in a proper house in a heartbeat if it were possible?'

She balked at his words, dismissing them. 'It is possible, I've heard of it. People have taken others with them when their dreamstones activate. Sometimes you can take people with you. You chose to leave me here. Why was my dream not the first one you crafted when you became a dreamsmith?'

'I didn't get a dreamstone as you've often reminded me, and we can't control who's dreams we make. I've told you that so many times!' Did she know so little of how the dreamsmiths worked, or was it all denial? Then again why would she know, why would anyone? She thought that all this time he'd been choosing not to craft her dream on purpose. Despite every time he'd calmly explained how it worked. 'Linette you have this all wrong. If I could choose who's dream I crafted yours would have been the first I picked, but it doesn't work like that. It's not that simple-'

'I don't want your excuses. I never have and I never will. I wish I'd never bothered.'

A new kind of silence fell. Taren's breath hitched once and hung in his lungs. For the first time since their argument began Linette's face faltered ever so slightly. Her eyes glistened and brow furrowed in a different way. One hand rose to rest just under her bust and she stared at the floor. She hadn't meant it, or at least never meant to say it aloud. Her mistake was clear even to her. So, the truth was out. One he'd never been able to see. Suspected but never allowed to settle. Every time he came back to her with nothing, the rift had been carved a little deeper. A little more jagged.

Birds scuttled on the roof, someone wept somewhere outside the house, and Taren's chest was thick with a swamp of hurt. Whether she meant it or not, you can't take back what's heard. Words are printed into existence like rubber stamps leaving imprints on paper. You could smudge them and scribble over them with apologies and explanations, but

163

the stains remained.

He waited, longed for the apology that must surely be brewing in her bitter mouth. When she raised her head again, her expression was neutral. The mask back in place. There would be no apology. She stepped forward with confidence and tried to shove him aside, heading for the door. He didn't budge and a spark flared inside him.

'You wished you'd never bothered? Have I been that much of a burden to you, Linette? Made your life so unbearable that you'd rather I'd died starving on a roadside, left for the birds, than bring me with you to this city? I've always admired you for your choice that day. I've always been grateful and I've always shown it. Now you'd wish me dead over a dreamstone? Over something I have no control over?'

'I'm sick of it, Taren. I'm sick of this life. Of this slum. Of sewing shit-stained clothes and going hungry, and adjusting my own dresses and skirts to be smaller and smaller. I'm wasting away here. Right where you left me when you headed off for a better life. For a higher purpose.'

In that moment all of her loneliness crashed against him and crushed him as it surfaced on her face. The catalyst of her feelings towards him crystal clear. Would it have been different if he'd visited more? If he'd given her more time and attention, looked beneath the mask she so dutifully wore. In those moments where her face seemed strained with something he didn't recognise, why hadn't he asked? Too busy instead answering all her questions about him and his glorious new life as a dreamsmith.

The burning guilt of it made him helpless, and he drifted aside as she tried again to pass him. She grabbed her best

shawl from a peg by the door and he reached out for it
without thinking, pulling it towards him with a ripping
sound.

'No wait, please don't go up there. Something isn't right,
I don't want anything to happen to you.'

He wasn't expecting the slap. It was powerful and
detached. Curt and final. Both sides of his face throbbed
equally for a few seconds before he slid his working eye
around to meet hers.

'Exactly. You don't want anything to happen to me.
Nothing. You want me to stay here. Forever. Well I won't.
If I couldn't collect my calling now, I still wouldn't stay. I'm
done. Aside from my calling there's only one more place I
could go, but at least I'd have some say in it. I won't miss
this chance on the suspicions of a screw-up of a
dreamsmith. Don't you bring yourself here again, you hear
me?'

She stopped for a moment after taking a few steps.
Leaving the torn shawl on the floor. Then she turned and
smirked at Taren who needed all his effort not to fold at the
middle. 'In fact, stay if you want. I don't give a damn. I'll be
living in the inner city come evening, where I deserve to be.
This place isn't my concern anymore.' Without so much as
another glance she strode from the house, not even
bothering to close the door.

His whole body keened. Shaken with the spiral of truth
that battered his insides in a violent hurricane. The only
family he'd ever known hated him. Despised him. Disowned
him. Linette's loneliness climbed up on to his back and
latched on, bearing its full weight and rooting him to the
floor. He tried to throw it off in a flare of resistance but

only managed to upend the table and create an ache in his palms from leaning on the overturned wooden legs.

The normal rhythm of breathing was forgotten and he overcompensated with short, narrow wheezes. Stumbling to the sink he fought nausea and won, just about, but his legs could bear no more weight and he sank to the floor. How could he not have seen this? Any of it? Had he been so self-absorbed the whole time, so scared to simply have a real talk with someone he claimed to care about? The shaking of his hands intensified as he raised one to his mouth. Happy memories of his time living in the house ricocheted around. Were they all fake?

The shawl lay there, almost torn in half. It fared better than Taren. The edges of his vision faded then brightened and faded again, and he sobbed alone in the carnage of words that lay strewn about him.

22

With Any Luck

The moment Fion opened her front door, she swore under her breath. The house felt empty and vacuous. No rustle of robes as Taren came to greet her, no sounds of life at all. That bloody idiot. What the hells was he playing at? Lie low, she'd asked. Just one thing after all she'd risked, and he couldn't even manage that.

She stormed through into the kitchen and dumped the bag of supplies on the small table. She'd had to be careful to stay out of sight as she'd slipped out of the Dreamforge yet again. Her excursion the previous day had gone unnoticed, clearly everyone had better things to do than checking up on her. Something to be grateful for. Taren, though? What had been so important that he'd left the safety of her house and ventured back out into the city or the slums?

It didn't take long for the answer to come to her. If left alone to contemplate the last few days, pretty much anyone would start to worry. About themselves, about the Dreamforge, about the system they all lived in, about their loved ones. That was it. Linette. Maybe he'd gone to warn Linette. That didn't make him any less of a fool. She could have gone to do that for him, or delivered a message discretely. So many ways she could have helped that meant he wouldn't have to expose himself to the danger of being found again.

With an annoyed bark of a laugh she reached into a cupboard for a glass and filled it with water from the tap in the sink. Its crisp, clear coolness a welcome relief in the growing warmth of the day. Putting the empty glass down, she wiped her mouth with the back of her hand.

When had Taren ever been able to resist doing something when an idea lodged itself in his head? Hardly ever. If he'd felt the need to warn Linette, he wouldn't be able to stop himself from going. He had that kind of hyperfocus about him sometimes. Even if the intent had come from his kindness and his loyalty to those he cared about, it was damn stupid given the situation. If nothing else, at least his stupidity was predictable. Linette's wasn't far and she still had plenty of time. Time enough to drag her grown man of a friend back to her house by his ear like a kid brother. A brother she'd never exchange or swap for anyone else. Time to go.

***

An immediate crackling of tension filled the air whenever she left the border of the inner city to go into the slums. The very feel of the place was different. Charged with emotions that didn't plague those on the inside of the gate. It was palpable. The people of the slums likely couldn't feel it, at least not until they got their call and experienced the carefree nature of the inner city by comparison.

Dreamsmiths tried not to travel alone in the slums, but it wasn't possible or practical to have someone accompany them all the time. Fion simply kept her gaze forward and her

168

face neutral. Walking on main roads and streets in full view of as many eyes as possible, just in case someone tried to be clever. The senior smiths wouldn't be looking for her, let alone expect to see her in the slums. If she kept her hood up and her eyes alert for any wandering colleagues, then there was no reason she'd attract any notice.

That was until she saw her. Walking along the main road in a blissful stupor. Linette. She'd had her calling? A bristling of suspicion flashed over Fion's skin and mind. Why now, why today? She shook the thought away. The spire chose people at random. But if Taren had gone to warn Linette and right then and there she got her calling, if he'd even reached her home in time, it was unfortunate timing indeed.

Fion approached Linette casually. It wasn't the best etiquette to interrupt someone in the throes of a calling but she had to know if Taren had made it to her before she'd left. The rapture on Linette's face didn't match the questionable condition of her body. She was uncharacteristically ruffled, her eyes red with what might have been tears. The gaunt look about her was arresting. Had it really been that long since she'd paid her a visit? That she had deteriorated this much? Was she ill?

'Linette, congratulations on your calling. I know you have to go, but could you spare a minute?' The smile Fion had conjured up dissipated as Linette walked right by her, not even sparing her a glance. She'd always been welcomed into Linette's home with warmth and enthusiasm. And while the calling was engrossing, it didn't lock out all sights and sounds from around people quite as completely as Taren's aunt was suggesting.

'Linette, please, have you seen Taren today?' A slight flicker in her eyes that time, as though she was trying not to look at Fion and it was taking a lot of effort. 'I just need to find him-'

'Leave me be.'

The vicious edge of the words sliced at Fion. 'W-what? Linette?'

'I want nothing more to do with you. Or him. You who took him away from me in the first place. You filled his head with ideas of being a dreamsmith. Cursed, wretched liars the lot of you. Only out for yourselves.'

People were starting to hear Linette's words, their attention drawn by the bite of her intonation. None of it made much sense. Fion moved from her side to stand in front of the woman. She needed an explanation.

'What are you talking about? I didn't take Taren anywhere or fill his head with anything. What happened?'

'Clear off. Get out of my way. It's your fault I've been alone all this time, but I'm done. I have my calling now. I can be free. I get my fresh start. My new life. You can't take it from me like he tried to. If you're looking for that selfish man, I left him at the house. Broken. Like his promises.'

Linette shoved Fion aside so violently that a spectator had to help steady her, otherwise she would have stumbled to the ground. His steadying hand pressed against her injured ribs and she bit back a hiss. She thanked him instead and swallowed the thickness in her throat.

'Not a good idea to get on Linette's bad side, ya know.' Her saviour watched with a puzzled expression as Linette carried on her walk towards the gate that glittered in the distance. 'Though I've never seen her quite that angry, I

170

admit. What did you do to get spoken to like that?'

'Honestly I've no idea. But either way, I'm happy that her calling has finally come. She deserves a better life. So many of you do. Thank you again, and apologies for the trouble.'

He nodded, no less confused than before, and Fion turned towards the general direction of Linette's house. Or rather what had been her house. She wouldn't be back. Her cheeks still flared with hurt, annoyance and embarrassment. Being given a dressing down in the middle of the street had caught her off guard. Had she not been so surprised, so braised by the vehemence of it all, she might have handled it better. A hard rock of emotions solidified in her chest. What had just happened? What had happened between Taren and his aunt? Linette claimed he'd tried to take her calling away, but there's no way Taren would do that.

Whatever he'd said or done, it hadn't done any good. If they'd argued, he won't have taken it well. Taren never did well with confrontation, even if he liked to pretend he did. She had to get to him, and fast. With any luck he'd still be at Linette's house. Even if luck wasn't something either of them had much of lately.

The quieter side streets were more of a risk, but also more of a relief. After the scene Linette had made on the main road Fion's cheeks had only just stopped burning. There were fewer eyes to scrutinise here, fewer to judge and question. The conversation with Linette, if one could call it such, had left the distinct feeling of cut ties. Washed hands. If she'd said the same or similar to Taren he'd be crushed. She was, for all intent and purposes, his mother in many ways. He'd always wanted a closer relationship with her,

171

he'd once confessed not long after becoming a smith, but sensed she didn't want the same. She'd always kept some kind of distance between them, one he'd never understood properly. But even as a younger man he'd respected it, and never pried about it. To lose her though? Fion knew exactly how he'd handle it.

She could picture him now, almost torn in two with devastation, and she quickened her steps. Winding through the narrow streets, stepping over piles of discarded clothes and empty food sacks. Walking past others without a word. She had to get to him, had to make sense of the attack she'd just faced. She had to-

When rounding a corner she collided with the chest of an unknown man. She mumbled a quick apology and tried to step around them, noting that he didn't bother to apologise himself. Charming.

'What do we have here?' Fion froze. The way he said it. The tinge of glee in the words. Shit. She'd been followed. Watched. She stepped back then and looked at the man properly. Him and the shorter man grinning beside him. Her eyes took in his slightly cleaner clothes. The wide stance, the film of disdain in their eyes and faces. The daggers at the belts. Cullers. Wonderful. Just what she needed.

'Apologies, gentlemen,' she forced the politeness through, 'I was careless. I've somewhere to be, if you wouldn't mind overlooking my clumsiness and letting me pass I'd appreciate it.' It was worth a try. She'd dealt with cullers before. For people who murdered almost indiscriminately, they had an odd respect for manners.

'Hmm, I don't think so. This is a rare find. Perhaps a chance to get some answers, what do you think Henric?'

172

'I'd agree. We don't often get a chance like this, Geran. I think she should come with us.'

Fion fought the urge to roll her eyes. 'I don't really have time for a detour, fellas.' Her manners were getting worse by the minute but it wasn't going to make any difference to these two. She could tell by the determination in their faces and the set of their stance. She chanced a glance around. Linette's house was two, maybe three turns away at most. If she remembered correctly. If Taren was there, perhaps he'd hear if she shouted. If she drew any attention though, those daggers weren't likely to stay sheathed.

'Oh we won't keep you long, pet.'

'I'm not your pet. If you insist on this being more than a passing encounter, at least use my name. Fion.'

'Well, Fion, you seem the sensible type of smith. Not like those others who tend to cause a fuss. Not sensible enough not to travel alone in our territory, mind you.'

They were bluffing, in their way. Cullers rarely attacked dreamsmiths. Underneath all their bravado and ridiculous philosophy they knew the smiths were their only hope as well. She could chance it. She could bolt back up the narrow street behind her, but the men would be on her in seconds. That, and she wasn't in a condition to be testing her athleticism. Her side pulsed in gentle reminder. *Don't strain your body. You're still healing.*

'What do you want? I've somewhere to be, and it's important.'

'We just want to talk. To have a chat. A few questions we're hoping you can help us with. That's all.'

'That's all?' The way she asked it implied the true question, and their hands moved away from their daggers in response. The glint in their eyes told her more than their hands on their daggers had. She still didn't have a choice.

'Fine, but I doubt I can help you with any of the answers you want. Why don't we get whatever this is over with and then I can be about my day.' Sometimes the cullers just wanted to be humoured. Fion had no idea if this was one of those days or not. But as they gestured for her to turn around and walk back the way she came, a churning flutter of regret bubbled in her gut.

They wouldn't harm her. They didn't have the stones for that. The Forge would find out if they did, but with a shiver she remembered she wasn't sure the Forge could be trusted anymore. She'd just walked willingly into the hands of a cult that cut innocent slumfolk down in the dead of night to thin the herd. To improve the chances of those who remain.

Seems it wasn't just Taren making stupid decisions, but realistically she'd got herself into this position. There was no fighting out of it in her condition, and no one around to help. Taren's name rose up in her throat, and part of her wanted to scream it as loud as she could. Hoping it would echo to him mere streets away. Those streets may as well have been a mile wide. A hand appeared on each of her shoulders and started to steer her through the alleyways.

An image of Taren being guided by the senior smiths in a similar way just the day before flashed across her mind. Crap. Crap, crap, crap. What a day. What answers did they want, and what questions and methods would they employ to get them?

23

A New Kind of Broken

Whatever Corryn was cooking, Leander couldn't wait to dig in and eat it. There were some ingredients in the food stores that she hadn't seen for a long time, and some kind of thick, aromatic soup bubbled gently on the stove-top while the crackling fire warmed it. They certainly had no shortage of bread, and Corryn had made a large bloomer loaf to celebrate the renewal of their supplies. They would probably have a few weeks where there was no queue outside the farm in the mornings, but there was never a guarantee of that.

Corryn bustled in, humming a pleasant tune, and he was glad to see her in high spirits. Sometimes he worried that underneath her sister-like demeanour she somehow resented being here with him and the work they'd decided to do. That was just his insecurity, though.

Unlike her sister, Corryn wasted no time in telling you when she didn't approve of something. She was a much more open book, the way Leander used to be. Now he sometimes felt stifled in a claustrophobia of himself, like he'd forgotten how to express himself properly. If it weren't for Corryn seeing everything he tried to hide, he'd be very lonely and he knew it. If she ever disappeared, who he really was would become a mystery. A wave of affection bloomed inside him, he loved her as though she truly was his sister. He didn't need any other family.

His work boots stood sentinel just outside the front door. He loved working on his land, but Corryn hadn't allowed it today. It was early to be finished, but the remaining tasks weren't pressing. Late afternoon hadn't long rolled in.

A quick glance up at the city triggered a flush of embarrassment. When Corryn had been called to find him collapsed at the gate, he couldn't remember why he was there in the first place. A fever had burned in him for all of an hour, and she'd objected strongly to him picking up and continuing work. So he found himself rooted to a chair at the table for most of the day, under watchful eyes that made sure he didn't lift a single finger in unnecessary effort.

He caught flashes of blurred images, never knowing if they were memories or not. How had his hand passed through the gate a second time? It should have been impossible. He hadn't told Corryn that detail yet. She probably knew, she liked to gather all the facts about a situation and would have asked whoever found him what happened just before his collapse. Leander himself hadn't a clue what was true or not anymore. Had he lost his dream or not? He just wanted a definitive answer.

His mind stirred, turning thought backwards against its natural stream. A light ringing floated into his ears, or was it going out of them? The sound was both inside of him and around him all at once. Familiar, but faded, and resonating more clearly after every collection of seconds. He stood, turning to face the window, and saw no one on the path. Yet in his mind he saw images of a man with soft features and long raven hair.

Corryn served up into their only remaining bowls. The others had all cracked and chipped over the years. Her actions stopped as she turned towards him.

'Lea? What's wrong?' She followed his line of sight and saw nothing. 'Leander?' An edge to her voice betrayed her concern. Perhaps she thought him apt to collapse or wander off again. Not only had he cried in her arms just the day before, but now he was worrying her as well. He needed to take better care of her.

'He's on his way.'

'Who is?'

The resonance spread through his whole body and he remembered it taking him off the path of his calling.

'Taren.'

'What do you mean? He's coming here? How do you know?'

Leander walked slowly out of the house, stepping into his boots without lacing them, followed by Corryn who hadn't even put down her ladle. To his own surprise as well as hers, a man in an indigo robe limped down their path. He swayed in all directions, and the look on his face triggered a guarded flutter in Leander. He'd worn it himself the day Melynda left.

An overpowering urge flared. To run to meet Taren, to wrap him up in an embrace and tell him things would be OK. Leander kept himself in check. Pushing such frivolous and nonsensical thoughts away. Whatever had happened, Taren was in a state of despair and confusion. Corryn

177

practically buzzed with questions. She wouldn't be able to fight the need to comfort Taren much longer, but they both waited. Watching in half horror, half pity as the vibrant young man they'd seen only days ago dragged himself down the path with a dwindling energy.

He muttered as he walked, and as he drew closer it became clear he was repeating "please help me, please help me" with every pair of steps he took. His hood was back, care for concealing his affliction gone, yet the iridescent patch looked bigger than Leander remembered. More of his kind face blotted by it and his eye shielded entirely. By the time he reached them Leander's cheeks were flushed with secondary embarrassment for all the feeling pouring from the man who approached him. As Taren reached out with both arms Corryn rushed forward to steady him.

'Please help me, please help me. I don't know where else to go. They're lying about things, they're corrupt, everyone is lying to me. They had a hollow on a leash and threatened to kill me and my only family hates me, she always did, the spire has taken her, she left me alone. The Forge can't be trusted, some of the smiths are acting on their own, playing with dangerous things, taming creatures we're supposed to destroy and I... don't know what's true anymore, please help me...'

The resonance inside Leander became harmonic and quietened, stopping completely when he helped Corryn steady Taren by placing an arm across his back. His heart leapt upon contact with the distraught dreamsmith and the ringing faded away. A sudden rush of longing caught him off guard. Longing for what?

Taren could barely hold himself up, and continued to

mutter as they helped him inside without a word. Did he have some fever of the mind caused by his affliction? Maybe they'd forced him out too early after all. Either way, best not let a dreamsmith mutter about the Forge being corrupt anywhere that someone else might hear. Taren sniffled and sobbed in between steps and his breathing looped in a concerning and ever-changing rhythm. They sat him at the table and Corryn took a damp cloth to his face to clear away the sweat.

'Taren? Can you hear me?' He nodded but didn't focus on her. The worry in her face as she felt his forehead passed into Leander and anchored there, right next to the growing seed of annoyance that Taren had returned to their door and put them at risk. Even after he'd been so clear that he didn't want the dreamsmith anywhere near their home again. 'Can you tell us what happened?'

He broke into another ream of indecipherable muttering and Leander slammed a hand on the table after a few minutes of babble. Taren jumped in his chair and finally looked up and focused on Leander. One ice blue eye met and locked on to his gaze.

'You're making no sense. If you want us to hear you out you need to calm down and focus yourself.'

'A-alright. I'm sorry.'

'You've obviously been through a lot since the other day, but I do wonder why you're back here on our doorstep when we heard you'd been found by the smiths. Whatever you've gotten yourself into clearly isn't resolved, but I thought you understood that I don't want you bringing your troubles here after we helped you the first time.'

Tears ran down Taren's face unchecked and Corryn

swooped in with the cloth. For someone who seemed only a few years younger than himself, he didn't have a very good control over his emotions. Shame stung Leander as he thought of himself bereft in Corryn's arms just the day before, and checked himself into remembering that he had no idea what Taren had been through. He'd seemed very much in control of himself after he'd awoken from his unconscious state... what could have possibly occurred to reduce him to this jittery, emotional husk?

Corryn forced a sugary tea into Taren's hands minutes later. It visibly calmed him but also reinforced the sadness in his eye. She joined Leander at the table and gently told Taren to take his time in telling his story. What he told them chilled them both. Leander paled as he listened, small details in the words prickling at his skin. It couldn't all be true. The strange black hollows, the whispers about the truth, the idea that the Forge had pockets of corruption in it. Had he been lucky after all to have been pulled off the path to his dream?

'They tried to hurt you?' Leander couldn't stop himself from asking. 'Why would your own colleagues do that? How did they even get a hollow, they're hardly in good supply.'

'I don't know. I don't know what they wanted, I don't know how or why they managed to tame one of those creatures. They said they wanted it to read me, to find out who's...' he trailed off and a stab of annoyance burned Leander's insides. Just speak plainly for spire's sake. It would be easier to get coherence out of a field of wheat stalks.

Patience. Leander took a breath and measured his response, keeping the annoyance out as best he could.

'To find out what?' Silence greeted his question.

Leander stood and began to pace the room in irritation. 'You're withholding information? You came to us for help. You've brought your problems here yet again, so you've clearly no care for us despite what we did for you.'

'I just didn't know where else to go, I didn't want to be alone, I didn't know where to turn.'

'How do you expect us to help? These matters are clearly beyond our understanding. They're dreamsmith matters, Taren.' Leander gestured towards the window and the city beyond. 'What can slumfolk hope to achieve against the Forge? How can we even believe what you've said, it all sounds so far-fetched.' A few quiet beats passed through the room. 'We can't help you.'

'Lea…' a warning tone from Corryn. She wanted to help, of course, but just once he'd prefer she didn't undermine him when it came to matters of care. 'Maybe there's something we can do to help. We can at least shelter Taren, he's clearly not well. If we'd given him more time in the first place perhaps he wouldn't be ill again now.' Irritation bristled over Leander's body in patches, fighting with the desire to comfort Taren and keep him safe. Why did he want to protect this man so badly? He barely knew him. The thought sprung from his mouth before he could stop it.

'We're strangers. We don't know him. He was in trouble and I helped. We took care of him. We did our bit and I told him that I didn't want to endanger you or our home with this nonsense he's talking about. The Forge are the only ones who can deal with this. If they want his life he must have done something pretty bad, Corryn.'

Taren never once objected to being talked about as

though he wasn't in the room. He merely stared blankly and clung to the mug of tea, taking small sips as though on a timer. Leander fixed him with a harsh stare. 'Get out.'

'No, we aren't throwing him out in that state, look at him. People have threatened him.'

'And I don't want them looking here to come and finish the job.'

'We can't turn him away, he needs help.'

'We've done enough. I answered his call at the risk of losing my own, I think that's enough help for one lifetime, don't you?'

Taren raised his head and a frown buried itself into his forehead. 'What did you say?' It was the clearest he'd been since he arrived.

'I said I answered your call. Same as I answered it again just now when you dragged yourself down my path, but you can stop that nonsense. I'm not a dog to be whistled at. Whatever dreamsmith power you're using to continue to get my attention I don't ever want to hear it again. Fooling people into thinking they're hearing their call is cruel. I'm pretty sure I was receiving my true calling when you interrupted.'

Taren's eyes widened bit by bit as Leander spoke, and it was unsettling. A shiver snaked down Leander's spine. Why was he staring like that? Taren looked through him, and the creeping need to check the corner behind himself for some kind of creature brought sweat to the surface of Leander's skin.

'What?' As though the question broke some kind of trance Taren stood abruptly, turned away and buried his face into his hands. He looked as though he might crumble. He stayed that way for almost a minute, and when the smith turned back to Leander the expression on his face raised goosebumps on his flesh and washed him with dread. If Taren had been despairing when he arrived, then he'd just become utterly and irrevocably broken. A new kind of broken. One that poured out into every crevice of the room and its occupants. When the next three words left Taren's mouth, Leander swayed on the spot under their weight. The afflicted side of Taren's face rippled with a glittering shimmer.

'… I'm so sorry.'

24

Thief of Hope

Taren's apology disturbed Leander. The words tumbled from the smith's mouth again and again as he paced back and forth. Among the growing pit of dread that was crumbling into existence in Leander's gut. Multiple feelings flared. The key one sparking sharpness in his words.

'What are you sorry for? Pacing with a haunted look on your face and blathering apologies won't help me understand. Either say what you need to say or leave, but stop playing games.'

Taren did stop, and faced the wall. The way he leaned on it full of useless denial. His shoulders sagged with the crippling burden of whatever he grappled with. Leander imagined a great boulder perched between Taren's shoulder blades. He wasn't bearing its weight very well. Sweat sprung into a clammy sheen on Leander's palms. The apologies were personal. Targeted. What could be so devastating?

When Taren turned to face them again his expression closed around Leander's throat. Such potent shades of feeling. They all mixed together to form a new emotion. He couldn't name or comprehend it. The air crackled with anticipation.

'I ran from the Forge because I went against my training. My duty as a dreamsmith. There was an incident. In the chaos I… I broke my connection with the forging station I was using before I'd finished crafting the dream I was working on. It was an accident.'

Taren's throat sounded full of gravel as he spoke, and Leander resisted the urge to snap at him to clear it as he continued.

'The dreamstone clung to the connection and after it broke and collided with me. This is the result.' He gestured to his covered eye, and the shimmering patch around it that now covered a little more of the left side of his face than when they'd met. 'I… I think that dream might have been yours.' A cold front met the crackling fizz of the anticipation, and tension plumed into the room. What the hells was he talking about?

'What do you mean?'

'Lea, it's OK.' Corryn said it automatically but her face betrayed her disbelief. Her hands wrung at the cloth, drops of water dampening the table in front of her.

'It's not OK,' he turned back to Taren. 'Explain yourself right now.' Images returned to Leander. They were doused in new significance. He stood at the gate, on the brink of collapse, but his hand passed through it. It allowed him access. There had still been a chance. Now Taren was saying his dream was never finished? He'd heard the call with his mind and body. It had filled and welcomed him. The spire had called to him. 'I had my calling. I know I did. You're telling me that was fake? A lie?'

Taren didn't look up as he answered. Perhaps he couldn't. Perhaps he wore his treachery like a choke-chain.

185

'You would have received your call, probably. The dream must have become whole as it fused with me. If it hadn't then it wouldn't have been able to latch on.'

'And you… why did I hear a call from you? Why do I continue to hear it?'

'Because your dream is unclaimed. It still exists, it's just… out of reach now.' The words echoed. Echoed all the way down, deep into Leander's chest and flipped a switch. Corryn yelled his name as he kicked a chair aside and pushed Taren against the wall with a strong palm to the sternum.

'Out of reach? For how long? If it's unclaimed then let me claim it. Give back what you took.' Dark shadows crept out of the depths of Leander's mind. Flitting back and forth, expanding and contracting.

Taren's face tightened, his heart hammering under Leander's palm. 'I… can't. I can't I'm sorry. I don't know how to separate from it, or if I even can.'

'Stop playing games! I had my calling. My chance for the life I've dreamed of and longed for for years. I felt that calling with every inch of my body, I followed it and you interfered. I thought I'd lost that chance but the resonance returned. Are you telling me it was just you the whole time? Tricking me? Mimicking?'

'No. No, I'd never do that to someone. I didn't know the dream was resonating, I didn't know you could hear it. I didn't even know the spire had called you.'

'Give it back to me. Give me my dreamstone.'

'I can't.' Taren grabbed Leander's arm with both hands, pleading for him to understand. 'Even if I could somehow separate from it…' a sob escaped him, 'it could kill me.'

Inaudible thunder rippled through the room, buffeting Leander and stoking his anger. His other palm slapped against the wall next to Taren's fearful face and he tore his arm from the dreamsmith's grip. The shadows in his mind stormed more and more with every moment that passed. It made no sense. How could he process this? The dream was gone, yet not lost. Cocooned within this man and entirely out of reach? Leander was both numb and overcharged with feeling all at once. Two sides clashing in his head.

'Then what am I supposed to do now? Just accept it? I saved your life and you took my chance at a better one in return? So what now, I just continue to live here working to feed those the city can't until I die and become part of the foundations of the slum? A bedrock for how many more generations of people to die here hoping for something that might never come for them?

'I've done my time already, and I did it with hope that one day I'd get my chance. A chance to get me and Corryn out of here. And you screwed up and decided to take what was never yours and now it can never be mine either. Is that what you're telling me? You answer me truthfully... what can be done about it here and now?'

Leander fought to keep his eyes dry. How could anyone deal with this? Weariness dragged at him and he fought that too. Hanging on the silence before the answer, hoping for something different. They were all fools. The thought was strong, vehement even. The lot of them were pitiful clowns. Himself included. Living off of hope, placating themselves with patience and solidarity. Would nothing would ever change for him?

'Nothing.'

187

Leander didn't hear Taren say it at first. The word slipped through his perception because he was waiting for any word but that one. He could have imagined it, but there was nothing left in Taren's words but heavy truth. Corryn gasped, but didn't move.

'I'm so sorry, I didn't mean to take it. I didn't intend to break the connection. I wish I knew how to help. I can't replace what was taken but I can try and find a way to separate from it and return your dreamstone to you.'

Leander saw red. It dropped in a blinding curtain. 'Don't you damn well dare try and give me hope. I have lived my whole life on the smallest sliver of hope and you just took that away and you dare try and spark a new one? You don't strike me as a cruel man. I saved you. I put the chance of retrieving my dream aside and you repaid me with what? With theft?' Leander gripped Taren's shoulder far too hard and steered him out of the house. He stumbled and tripped, mumbled something about waiting.

Corryn pleaded with Leander but he could barely hear her. All he saw was Taren. Consumed by roaring betrayal. Betrayed by the life he saved. The sea of rich golden fields. The fresh air and the peace of freedom. A farmhouse built by their own hands. No master but the horizon and the climate. That was his dream and he was going to take Corryn with him. A repayment for all she'd done for him.

The vision began to dim. To fade. The dreamstone dangled in front of him, but Taren had entwined it with his own life. How could Leander ever wish for a better life at the cost of someone else's? It wasn't in his nature. His hands were bound. Tied to a stake of hopelessness. He wanted Taren out of his sight, out of his mind. He'd had enough.

He shoved, pouring his anger into the gesture, and Taren tumbled to the dusty ground of the yard. The smith didn't try to get up, nor did he protect himself from the advancing steps that could have easily turned into kicks.

'No, stop, Lea.' Corryn placed both her hands around Leander's upper arm. They were cold with shock but grounding. The more she spoke the more the curtain lifted away. The stronger his grip on himself became. 'It doesn't sound like it was his fault. Throw him out, fine, but don't hurt him. You didn't save him only to hurt him, that's not who you are.'

Hurt him? Did he look that livid? He floated far above his rage, not feeling its effects. Distant from his actions. As she calmed him and he sank back into himself the seething in his body stung and weighed him down. Emptiness consumed him, and he allowed himself to be led back into the house without a second glance at Taren. The door closed on the dishevelled dreamsmith and something black in Leander's mind twitched.

Corryn tried to sit him down, but he watched himself from a distance again. His body a husk. Changed by so much feeling. It was all gone, nothing remained. Then a rage poured into him that was not his own. He claimed no familiarity with it. As he stood it broiled within him and a thick black pocket opened up in his mind, letting in the growing storm. What's happening? Corryn's face faltered, then braced. What was she scared of? Him?

'Lea? Lea, what's the matter? Just let him be, I'm here for you now we can work through it, OK?' She backed away, palms raised in submission. Edging towards her

189

bedroom.

~Dreamsmiths are the enemy.~

The thought was so crystal clear that it sparked. Taren was dragging himself to his feet as Leander wrenched the door back open and strode towards him. Taren stumbled in his renewed haste to get away but he wasn't quick enough. Leander lifted him to his feet and marched him halfway up the path towards the slum. A small crowd of onlookers gawped at the forceful display as Leander watched himself present Taren to the crowd. Holding him on the spot by one hand clamped on to a shoulder. He had to go. The dreamsmith couldn't be suffered to stay. They are the enemy.

'Leander please, just let me go. I won't come back, I'll leave you be. I'll find a way to fix things.'

Leander's sonorous voice reached everyone who watched. Echoing over the southern quarter. Every word rattled in his head like sharp metal pins. They weren't his words, or his actions, and he couldn't stop them. 'Tell the dreamsmiths that I've found their target. He's here. If you're still looking for him then come and claim him. I will not shelter a thief of hope on my land.' The last of the words trailed away in a ripple.

Wait, what was he doing? This wasn't right, this wasn't him. Since when did he treat people this way? Making a show of someone who was injured or at the very least ill. The storm in his mind compacted under the realisation. Under the shame. The clamour in his head receded, shrinking away and stuffing itself back into the deep, dark pockets it came from. He loosened his grip on Taren. The dreamsmith barely dared move, his body trembling under

Leander's palm. He never wanted to scare anyone, he should take Taren back inside, or at least let him go.

Eventually, as the moment stretched on, Taren turned to look at Leander with his one working eye. There was understanding in it, something Leander didn't deserve and felt nauseous in the face of. He put a hand to his forehead, shaking from his actions. What had compelled him to do that just now? His mind… hadn't felt like his. Something else had filled it.

'I'm sorry, Leander. I understand why you're angry. I do.' He spoke so quietly, and with a tone that resonated so closely with Leander's own shame that it was painful. Taren never wanted this. Maybe that was true. Through heavy breaths Leander recovered himself, his eyes flicking up to the growing crowd staring from beyond the fence. The muttering of the slumfolk chittered with concern, all of whom turned towards the spire as it chimed only once like a great clock. It had never made such a sound before.

The breeze blustered into something more sinister. Leander slid his hand off of Taren's shoulder, taking several steps back, and they both turned towards the spire, lost for words. Shadows flitted over the walls of the city and snaked in shifting clouds to surround them both at a distance. Leander counted six. The way they moved, fast and fluid. Like predators. He suppressed a shudder with little success. Back away. Run.

'What's happening?'

Taren gave no answer. Any remaining dregs of anger left Leander in the face of these menacing shadows. The tide vanished as quickly as it had come. The shadows slowed, and stalked around the two men. They eventually came to a stop, clicking and rasping. In a sickening lurch they formed hideous creatures. Dripping black tar, crackling wet breaths.

Anyone raised in the slums would know. They'd know and they'd fail to believe it. The stories were true then? This is what they'd become if they didn't accept their calling? Leander, struck by the blunt force of realising he now couldn't claim his dream, fought back against the retch that strangled his stomach. Did these hollows used to be… people?

They converged. It was over in seconds. They set upon Taren, drowning him in their bodies, piling on top of him. Leander froze and stared, unable to comprehend what was happening. He hadn't wanted this. A plunging torrent of regret and guilt doused him, his anger now seeming unimportant. He wanted to return Taren to his colleagues, just wanted him out of their home. Out of his sight. Off of his land. But this? Not this.

The stomach-churning sounds of the sinuous beings that swarmed Taren were almost unbearable. The smith didn't scream, or make any sound at all. Leander only saw his terrified face disappear under the cloak of solidifying shadows that were dragging him into the ground. Soon enough… Taren was gone. Swallowed. Vanished.

25

Something Other, Something Darker

The route the cullers took through the slums was so convoluted that Fion felt utterly lost. She wasn't, of course, it was easy enough to orient yourself by looking for the inner city. The spire was somewhat of a compass to those who knew the layout and exterior of the Dreamforge well. By that reckoning, they were somewhere on the very outer reaches of the southwest quarter, the part of the slums parallel to where she'd originally been aiming for. As they turned yet another sharp corner, Linette's dark expression raked across Fion's heart. Had it been genuine, or just born of her implied argument with Taren? Now she'd never know for sure.

A film of fatigue started to grip her, a dull ache pulsing in her ribs. Why did this place have to be so far away?

'Guys, at least tell me we're almost there. If not I'll be too busy rolling my face in the dirt to answer any of your mysterious questions when we arrive.' Her clipped tone wasn't her best idea, but whatever this farce was she just wanted it over and done with. The shorter of the two, Henric was it, threw a piercing glance back at her.

'Not far now, have to be careful of revealing our location.'

Fion choked down a laugh. 'Why, do you get visitors often?'

'More often than you'd think. Our numbers are growing. Moreso in recent years, but you wouldn't know much about that from being high up in that fancy tower would you?'

'Come Henric, let's not be rude to our guest. Least not one with as much valuable information as this one.' Geran smirked over his shoulder. 'Besides, we're here. Just round this corner.'

Fion tried to see ahead, but her captors were in the way. When they finally did step aside, she faced a grim-looking shack. This part of the slums was quiet and a little eerie. Dwellings were packed tightly together but this building, if one could call it that, stood apart just a little. As though two homes either side had been torn down to ensure a feeble wafer of privacy for whoever lived within. She couldn't keep the grimace from her face.

'So this is the grand base of culler operations? Hardly seems worth guarding with your weaving tactics.'

'In you go. There might be more to it than you expect,' Henric sneered as he ushered her forward.

'I'm nothing if not willing to be proven wrong. I hope you've got at least one chair in there though.'

Fion would have set about eating her own words, were the smell of mouldering wood not so strong that it made it hard to open her mouth at all. Every time she did, her mouth filled with spores, or at least it felt that way. Damp clung to the place like wet tissue.

There was no chair in sight, and she suppressed a groan until she saw the hatch. The shack had a lower level? That was barely heard of in the slums. People had tried it in the past, wanting the luxury of another room since they didn't have sturdy enough materials to build upwards. Still, most attempts had ended in unfortunate collapses of any underground excavation attempts, or they hit a layer of nigh-impenetrable rock. People rarely bothered now. The cullers, though, seemed to have succeeded where so many others had failed.

'Down the ladder you go. Try not to trip on that robe of yours.' Geran lifted the hatch door with a grunt and revealed the roughshod metal ladder he'd spoken of.

'Underground? Is that really necessary?' A simmering pond of panic started to sizzle in Fion's stomach. What if they trapped her down there? Would they follow or was she walking into a prison?

'We like to chat with our guests away from prying ears and eyes. We aren't always the subjects of pleasantries ourselves. Something I'm quite sure you can empathise with.'

Geran had a point, but murder was a little different to being wrongly accused of controlling fate. Not to these men, apparently.

'One of you can go first, if you don't mind.' She met Geran's gaze in a determined and stony way. She wouldn't be stupid enough to go down there without such an assurance, and her captors must have known she wouldn't budge. Henric rolled his eyes and dropped down on to the ladder. Just as the thought to dash out of the now-unprotected door glinted in her mind, Geran's hand came to

195

rest casually on the hilt of his dagger. He was no fool either. So with a sigh Fion descended the ladder and hoped to the spire she wasn't signing her own death warrant. Taren would have to look after himself for a while, hopefully he hadn't gotten into any more trouble.

The underground space was, for lack of a better word, impressive. A wider space than should have been possible had been carved out, the walls carefully smoothed and supported with any materials they could scavenge over time. That answered the question of what happened to the buildings either side of this one, though raised the more urgent question of where their occupants had disappeared to. Fion pushed the thought away.

The ceilings were low, but not so much that she had to crouch. Geran had to hunch over a little, but he seemed used to it. There wasn't much in the way of furniture. An old dining table flanked with chairs, at which Fion nearly sighed with relief, and an all-but destroyed sofa from which a woman watched them with a suspicious and steely gaze. Watched Fion especially. Taking in the colour of her robes. Her face souring with every second she inspected Fion. Clearly she wasn't a fan of dreamsmiths, either.

Cold suffused the room, in a damp and earthen kind of way. The smell of rotting wood not quite masked by the dusty whiff of the soil beneath Fion's feet.

'Who's this then?' The woman's voice was as sharp as her gaze. 'Another convert?'

Fion answered for herself. 'No, not quite. I'd say more a guest with no choice in the matter. One with little interest in your philosophies. These gents seem to think I'll be able to tell them something you don't already know, though I doubt it.'

'Found a feisty one there, didn't you Geran? This one won't take none of your games.'

'I don't intend to play any. A simple round of questions and answers, and then she can be on her way. Providing her answers are helpful.' Fion grimaced at the implication.

'I'll sit back and enjoy the show then. Throw me one of them, Henric.' The man picked up a plum-type fruit from a fraying basket on the table and tossed it towards the woman on the sofa. How she caught it in the dim light was beyond Fion, but perhaps she'd adapted to the gloom.

'I have to say I expected there to be more of you. Didn't you say your numbers were growing?' Fion wanted to keep them talking. Silence wouldn't do much for her nerves, which were starting to prickle and itch.

'We're not as daft as you think. We wouldn't all stay in one place. Henric, light some of the lamps, will ya? Can't see a thing.' Geran gave orders with ease.

'Am I the scut worker today or what?'

'Just do it, it's a simple enough job. Then if you're bored you can clear off or cuddle up with Rachil on the sofa there.'

'No thanks, I'd be safer with a reptile I think.'

As the men went through the motions of their banter, a few more lamps lit the room. It made the space feel even smaller. Maybe the Forge should have kept a closer eye on the cullers after all.

'Here.' Geran hauled a seat into the middle of the room to face the old table, then turned a chair around for himself. Sitting down was such a relief, but Fion didn't let it show. Now they'd get down to business.

'Alright, I've got my seat. Now what do you want? Why

197

bring me out here?'

'We're hoping you can help us with a little conundrum. Or rather, a request.' Geran looked over at Henric and Rachil and motioned for the door with his head. The confused expressions on their faces showed their disapproval. Obviously they thought they'd get to stay. 'Out. Both of you. I've got this one. She likes to play to an audience, maybe she'll be a bit more respectful with no one else to impress.'

Henric in particular clearly bit back a response. He'd helped bring Fion along, but was being shoved out like a nosey kid. She had to hide her smirk, it wasn't the time to be making enemies. At the moment they were more of inconvenient inquisitors at best. At worst... it wasn't worth thinking about. When the disgruntled cullers had departed the room, Geran smiled again.

'Much better. I can tell you're smart, Fion. Witty. We value such outspoken personalities here so that's why I'm pleased we found someone like you today. An unexpected gift from the spire, perhaps.'

'Look I don't know what you want to know, but just ask it. Clearly you don't want your lackeys to know which makes me think you're going off of whatever plan had been concocted in the first place. So get on with it.' Her heart started to stagger around her ribcage. Having the others leave was a good tactic for making people desperate, but she sensed there was more to it than that.

Geran smirked again. She wanted to wipe it off his face and feed it to him. 'You're correct. I want to ask you to do something. Something no one else can ever learn of.' He cast a look over at the ladder, as if ensuring the hatch was closed and no one was hiding in the corners. Then his countenance completely changed. The smirk wiped clean and replaced with a sincerity Fion wouldn't have thought him capable of. 'I want you to make my dreamstone next. I want my freedom.'

Of all the things that could have come out of his mouth, that was the last thing Fion had expected even if it should have been the first. People asked it of dreamsmiths all the time. The way Geran spoke had changed in those few seconds. Less the gruff gang member, and more the formality of a genuine request. She wouldn't be fooled by it.

'What? Why? Are your own methods not working for you? People not dying quick enough to ensure you get your turn or something?'

His brow furrowed. 'So people still believe we kill wantonly. Without consideration.' The notion seemed to genuinely confuse him.

'Well, don't you? Thin the herd for the good of those who remain. Isn't that the motto?'

'I didn't say we didn't kill, just that we don't do it without consideration. We choose those we dispatch to give those more deserving a better chance.'

'Yet for all the chances you've taken from others, you want to skip the queue?' Anger started to fizzle. What a request to make. Such entitlement, to think he could just ask for a dreamstone and get one handed to him.

Geran leaned forward, putting his elbows on his thighs and knitting his fingers together. He never took his eyes from Fion, but she was glad of the metre or so between their chairs. He looked weary then, worn down.

'I've been in the slums for as long as I can remember. I

199

grew up here. I didn't start the cullers and I don't want to lead them anymore. I don't like killing, regardless of what you may think. The Forge does nothing to intervene in the matters of the slums. It sits in the inner city and turns a deaf ear, so we took to policing ourselves.

'The people we dispatch, those we target to "thin the herd" as you so crassly put it, are those who have done wrong. Those who've hurt others. The cullers started as something very different from what it's become now. The gossip and exaggeration of the slumfolk have written us into a dark fairy-tale of ruthless thugs killing innocent people. I won't deny that some of our members play into the gossip. Playacting or taking on different personas. I won't deny I'm sometimes one of them. There are certain things expected of me as a leader, and sometimes it's easier to stoke the fires of gossip than fight them. Truth be told I'm starting to wonder if those joining the cause just want an excuse to take some lives.

'That's just what this city does to people. Twists things. Makes them into something other, something darker. Something dangerous. So that the Dreamforge is the only salvation. The only source of hope. You can't tell me you think that's happened by chance?'

Fion's mind raced with his words. The cullers were trying to help, trying to make the slums safer for those still waiting? That made about as much sense as the idea of the Dreamforge handing out dark stories on shadowed street corners to influence the populace.

'Why would the Dreamforge want to do such a thing? And no matter how you truss it up, what you all do is still murder.'

200

'Does the Dreamforge not murder as well?'

Cold shot through Fion's body. 'No, of course not. We've never killed. We help people lead better lives. Give them another chance.'

'Is that the only side of it you see? How ignorant.'

'What do you mean?' Fion's fingernails ached from digging into the underneath of the chair. Geran had such confidence in his words. If they were the truth to him, what basis did he have for them?

'What of those you don't help? What of those you don't make dreamstones for? What do you think happens to them?'

'They wait. They wait for their time to come.'

'And those who refuse to wait? Those who can no longer play that game? Those whose last reserves of hope left them so empty that they have sought out people with a taste for killing, those we normally cull, and asked them to end it? Or become someone who starts to take their despair out on others. Or who find ways to end it themselves? Or those who die before their calling ever comes. Decrepit and still hoping when the long dark finally claims them. Are the Forge's empty promises not the conduit for such deaths. Is that not murder, too?'

Fion was stunned. The Forge did good, that's what she'd always believed. The fact that someone could wait for so long that their time never came. That some would choose to die rather than wait for their call. If the Forge was the beacon of hope, it was also the cause of hopelessness. Is that what he was saying? She shook her head, heart hammering in denial of it.

'No. We have no control over whose dreamstone we

make. We have no way of knowing who it will belong to until it's made. The spire siphons fragments of dreams over time from people's wishes and longing and eventually we can piece them together. These things are gradual. There's no way for us to know, for dreamsmiths to design or choose.'

'The spire provides the dreams, but who controls the spire? His title suggests he is the master of the Dreamforge. Wouldn't that also make him the master of the spire?'

'No, no the Forgemaster communicates with it but he doesn't control it. He doesn't command it. He's in sync with it, attuned to it. That's all.' There's no way Clayton was picking and choosing. No way he had any more say in which dreamstones were crafted than anyone else. He might be hiding information about the incident with the broken forging station, but that incident was proof enough that he wasn't in direct control. Wasn't it?

'Your excuses are empty. I don't think you know a damn thing about how any of this really works. About what it is you dreamsmiths really do, or the reality of those living in the slums. You just do as you're told.'

Fion took some time to consider their conversation before choosing her answer carefully. It was a lot to take in, the things he'd said and claimed. If what he said was true, then he was trying to protect people who still hoped from those who no longer did.

'You're not... wrong in that. You're not.' Geran's eyebrows raised at her admission. 'I've been wondering the same thing myself recently, and I say that honestly. But there are things I do know, Geran. Things I know for sure. You-... me and everyone else, maybe we've misjudged you

202

and the cullers. Maybe. But how can that be proven? Killing is still killing. Just like knowing is still knowing and I know this. I can't fulfil your request. I can't control the spire, and I can't control which dreamstone is next to be made.'

'You're lying.'

'I'm not. If there is a way to do what you ask, I've no knowledge of it. Nor do any of the dreamsmiths I work with. We are all taught the same theories, the same methods. None of them mention choice or design. You... you seem to care for this place. If what you say about the cullers is true-'

'Why would I lie about it? There's no one here to impress. No one to stand on ceremony for.'

'Nor is there for me. Neither of us have reason to lie. There wouldn't be any sense in it. If what you want is your dreamstone, I can't give it to you. Your freedom is something I have no control over, and I'm sorry for that. The system is unfair, and I can't deny that some of what you've said makes sense. Things I'll think about properly, consider them carefully. Something is wrong with the Dreamforge, I share that belief, but I can't find out what that is from here.'

Geran stayed quiet for a long while. A slow flurry of emotions passed over his face. A sadness she didn't understand, a complicated kind of confused resignation. Any kind of threat had gone from him. He was just a person seeking an answer. A person seeking freedom.

'So you really can't choose?'

'No, we can't. Sometimes I wish we could, or that there was some kind of order to it.' Fion shook her head sadly. Part of her did want to help Geran, despite the selfish nature of his request. Was he betraying the other cullers just by asking this of her? If they ever found out, how would they make him atone for his indiscretion? He'd said it himself, there were certain expectations on him as leader of the cullers. Was he breaking them right now? 'But there are things you can do to increase your chances that will be more effective than running a vigilante assassination crew.'

Geran met her gaze with a genuine curiosity. 'Explain.'

'From what you've said, you've tried to protect people. To keep the slums safe in your own way. But you fight the violent with violence. Played into the rumours instead of denying them. Maybe that was all you thought available to you. Maybe that's the sickening truth of it. But there is another way. Fewer and fewer people have come forward to be dreamsmiths in the last five years. The more smiths we have, the more dreamstones we can make. Instead of thinning the herd, why not increase the chances of everyone by helping to craft their freedoms?'

Geran's mouth dropped open slightly as though such a thought had never crossed his mind. Fion carried on.

'I don't know what's happening up at the Forge, and I'm not sure I'm ready to find it out, but I will. And when the dust settles, all I know is that things will need to change. Something has to. By whatever gods might or might not exist and by the spire itself, something has to change. I can feel that in my core. I don't think you'd really hurt me, Geran. I think you'll let me go like you promised. We need people to affect change. I think you could be one of them. Am I wrong?'

Silence stretched out, Fion's heart raced, her whole body warm with the effort of forcing the adrenaline around her system. She may have guessed wrong, he may call her bluff, or maybe she'd called his. Maybe. She hadn't lied.

That feeling of being on the precipice of an immense and ground-sundering change mulled around her. It mixed with her fears and her hopes, a soup of the unknown. But her determination had never been stronger. The determination to know. To discover. To uncover. If she'd been lied to, she'd find out how. And may the spire help the one whose silver tongue had layered those lies upon the lives of her and everyone else. Eventually, Geran spoke.

'I don't know. It feels wrong to hope. Such is the struggle of those waiting for the call of the spire. Maybe change is the path to new hope, but I can't see it. Not after the way things have become. But you were right about one thing.'

'What's that?'

'I will keep my word and let you go. You've given me much to think about, no doubt you feel the same. This... was not the outcome I expected from my actions today.'

'Believe me it wasn't on my list of things to do today either.'

'You're perhaps the most reasonable smith I've met, Fion. You can go. I won't hold you here. You're right, keeping smiths from the forges is lowering chances for everyone. That's not what we do, despite what people have come to believe.'

'I appreciate you keeping your word.' She rose and walked with jellied legs towards the ladder. Fighting to keep her steps steady. As she reached for the first rung she chanced a look back, ignoring the refreshed ache in her side. Geran stared at the chair in which she'd just been sitting, thinking long and hard. His square jaw working as though his teeth were grinding on everything they'd discussed. Despite everything she didn't think him a bad man. He was trapped in a role he didn't want, and things had spiralled out of his control. There were few who could say they'd never experienced either of those things. 'Remember what I said, Geran. There are other ways to help.' Her only response was a single, but distinct and certain, nod.

26

Unintended Cruelty

A net of black ooze weaved itself around Taren, stretching and morphing as it encompassed him. He should have been terrified as the hollows descended on him, and no doubt his face had mimicked it, but it hadn't registered. What was there to feel, given everything that had happened? The darkness was a welcome comfort. Nothing could penetrate it. Maybe they would take him somewhere and hide him. Shield him from whatever was happening. Absolve him from having to think at all. Just for a while. Please.

His barren chest remained unstirred, the needle of his emotional compass hanging loosely outside its magnetic arcs. The hole inside him sank lower, a tunnel unfolding downward with no signs of slowing. He'd been emotionally beaten, battered, and his resolve shattered. So much so that six hollows coming from the Dreamforge to claim him didn't raise as many alarm bells as it should have. He'd changed, expecting lies and contradictions at every turn.

The hollows weren't hurting him, they didn't snarl or snap or squeeze with their claws. They were guiding him in a cloak of shadow, though he vaguely remembered passing through the silty layers of the ground while Leander watched in horror.

Leander... I stole his dream, his hope. "Thief of hope" he called me, and he's right. This isn't why I became a dreamsmith, to take hope away. I wanted to give hope. To give people their calling and allow them a better life. How can I still claim that as my purpose at all now?

The left side of his face shone with pain and throbbed. His closed eye twitched under its shield of its own accord. Shivers ran up and down his body as he ground his teeth to bear it. From the blackness of the hollows' cloak around him a scene painted itself once again. A view of the city from on high, as an outsider looking in. Sky-coloured dust trickled over his shoulder. He followed it up and a great crack began to form as though the sky was a porcelain veneer.

The crack spread and forked away in all directions. How could he put a stop to it? There must be something, anything he could do. The network travelled easily, passing over the city and continuing to rain a fine, pale blue dust from its many junctures. Granules at first, and then flakes. Flakes that became stones, then pebbles, and then great boulders that sailed downward and smashed buildings as though they were made of sand. The pockets in the falling sky filled with an angry mix of colours and lightning whips lashed about, revelling in their new-found freedom and hungry to strike. The spire screeched a dying resonance, up-lit by the furious crack of nature's whips. The sky crumbled and the city followed soon after.

A weariness sank into every joint as the scene faded. When would all this stop? The damning visions, the lies, the hurt, the questions and the confusion. Just days ago his life was everything he'd ever hoped for. Now he might not even be a dreamsmith anymore. His aunt had revealed her true colours and they dripped with long-suppressed resentment. He'd tricked Leander into leaving the path of his calling, a calling that never really existed in the first place, and stolen his chance at a better life. It was unintended cruelty, but his heart had to beat harder to trudge through the swamp of apology and despair that now filled it.

The hollows pulled closer around him and whispered in heady echoes. 'Truth. Truth. Truth' was all they would say, just like the one that had reached out to him in his home. The cool stone floor was a surprise when it appeared beneath him, but the world wasn't yet solid. A distant nausea undulated in the folds of his stomach and he bit back the urge to ask what truth they meant. Somehow speaking to them made them real, a gravity he couldn't handle at that moment.

As the world stopped bending, Taren managed to orient himself. When he curled into a relaxed foetal position, the world solidified and four of the six hollows peeled away. Slinking off into the distance on fragile-looking legs. He didn't know which part he was in, but he knew the Forge when he saw it. It had a distinct energy about it no matter where you were within its walls. A feel of the air being charged or heightened. The low buzz of the spires gently harmonised with your soul, always listening, always sending out its ethereal crystal feelers. Probing for the dreams of the slumfolk.

In over ten years of being a part of the Dreamforge he'd been to every part of it, or so he thought. Like so many other things that he now knew to be untrue. He knew nothing. How can he have been so naïve? Great stone pillars lined the generous corridor ahead of him, but behind was a solid vertical surface of smooth stone. Strange symbols adorned it. They were familiar yet somehow alien. Some kind of hollow-friendly door? He must have passed through it under their care.

The floor matched the ones he'd so often travelled on the forging level, or the corridors leading to their quarters. The smallest flutter of dread clasped on to a new seed of determination which was watered with drops of anger and sadness.

The hollows made no advance to touch him until he stood of his own accord. The travel left him jumbled. If he moved his right leg his left arm responded. Trying to breathe meant his head turned instead. The air was still, but not stale. Light danced from crystal lanterns mounted on the pillars. Could he be underground? Even further down than the forging levels? The lack of windows made it likely. The fact he'd passed through the earth itself to get there made it almost certain.

The hollows took him by the arms and urged him forward, guiding him down the long, empty corridor. Every movement echoed, racing ahead of them in the empty half-dark ahead. Various openings offered themselves to him as they made their slow progress, each branching corridor as nondescript as the next. Some ended in rooms, others curved off out of sight, but one caught his attention and stoked an ember inside him as they passed it. A pulse battered the left side of his face and colours danced about him as one of the memories of his visions overlaid onto reality. A hollow walking down a long corridor, only the lamps had become brighter and the walls were clear to see.

Lines of them hung mounted on the walls, held in place by glowing chokers. They made no movements, only dripped on to those below like gruesome garments left out to dry. There were so many, they couldn't be counted. Why were they there at all?

'Where are you taking me? Why are there so many of you here? You're not supposed to exist. What's the truth you keep trying to show me?' At the mention of the word truth those in the cavernous side-room began to screech the word. The cacophony was brief and startling, and fell away as quickly as it had built up.

Questions battled with thoughts for priority, and dizziness threatened the corners of his one-sided vision. They'd passed the room yet he longed to return to it and somehow free its occupants. Was it possible to fear something and pity it at the same time? The last several days had been a learning curve. He could clearly feel many complicated and conflicting things at once. Another truth had shown itself. How much space remained inside his head for more?

If I've spent my life assisting in the craft of lies, then I want to know. Everything I was taught about what I am…

They turned off at the end of yet another sweeping corridor and two indigo robes waited for him. The faces were obscured by hoods, as was his own, and he couldn't work out who they were. *They must be corrupt as well, why else would they be in this part of the Forge? I will get answers, I'll find out the truth of things. I'll make sure they bring the Forgemaster here so I can question him myself.*

The hollows presented him to the waiting dreamsmiths,

who were far less delicate in their handling of Taren, and as the creatures slunk away to resume their positions in the room of chokers they whispered "truth" to him once more.

27

Screeching Symphony

Leander staggered back to the house and pushed the door open so slowly that Corryn didn't look around for several seconds. Before he even crossed the threshold she launched into a tirade that soon lost its bluster.

'What was that about? You'd thrown him out why couldn't you have let him be... What's wrong?' She supported him as his feet argued over how long a step was. Sitting at the table grounded him, but how could he reconcile with what he'd just caused? 'Where's Taren?'

He couldn't answer, but in his mind the clickety clack of something jumped from thought to thought like a flea. His hands weren't his own. Had he really used them to make a show of someone? When had he ever done that in his life? His hands were meant to bring life to the fields and help to those who needed it. Now they were the sickly, clammy hands of some kind of ghostly betrayer.

'I was... so angry. He took my dream, Corryn. He's taken it completely out of my reach... forever. After all that's happened in the past few days I just... lost myself.'

'He didn't mean to take it, you know that right? The way he explained it. The way he reacted to realising what he'd done. He was completely broken by it.'

Clickety clack, clickety clack. She reached for his hand but he pulled away. 'He was broken? What about me? I'm broken! I'll never get a different life now. We'll be stuck here until we die handing out bread to the hungry. I wanted so much more, for you as well, and you're defending the man who took our chance?'

'He doesn't seem like a bad guy to me. You barely spoke with him. You were too preoccupied with shoving him out the door, quite literally the second time. You went overboard.'

Clackity click, clackity click.

'And how should I be reacting to the fact that he took my dreamstone for himself, hm?' Leander's neck twitched as he spoke. 'How am I supposed to react? I don't know what to feel anymore. I don't know how to feel anymore. I've been crushed too many times to know how to handle any of this now. Why shouldn't I go overboard, why shouldn't I feel something? Anything?' His hands slammed against the tabletop and Corryn jumped.

'Calm down, for spire's sake. What... what happened out there?'

'They came and took him.'

'Who did, the dreamsmiths?'

'No, I... They were like liquid shadows that turned into creatures. They looked like they could have been... hollows.'

'Hollows, in the slums?'

Clickety clackety click. The rhythm sped up, pulling on his last nerve. His mind flooded with a tar-like syrup that strangled his patience and emotional measures.

'So I'm lying as well, now? Just like Taren was? He could have told us what he'd done when he first woke, but he hid it. I'm not lying to you. Six of those things slithered over the city walls, piled on top of Taren and took him away. Took him underground.'

'I never said you were lying, I just can't get my head around it. Why did you throw him out in the first place?'

'He's a filthy thief. A thief of hope and I didn't want him on our land. I wanted him gone to protect us, and everything we have. I didn't know they'd come, I thought a dreamsmith might come to collect him or something. You think I'd do that to someone on purpose? That's the kind of person you think I am?' The surface of his forehead burned against his palm. He needed peace, but Corryn kept talking.

'You did do it on purpose, you just didn't know what the consequence would be. Now will you get a hold of yourself. Stop yelling and just calm down.' Every word she said triggered another insect in his mind. The noise of the swarm so loud and shrill that it caused vibrations in every inch of him.

'Stop fucking telling me to calm down.' He wrestled with the screeching symphony, covering his ears although that only made them louder. His own scream made them louder still.

'Lea, what's wrong. What's happening?' She stepped away again, torn between wanting to comfort him and putting distance between them. She couldn't see that she was backing into a corner.

'Why are you cowering? You're meant to care about me. You're meant to be there for me like a sister, and you're shrinking into a corner instead?' Was that his voice coming

215

from his mouth? If so, he didn't recognise it. It was wet and rasping and said less and less of what he wanted it to. He drifted further and further away from the forefront of his mind. Disconnecting from it yet remaining within it.

The terrified expression on Corryn's face seared his heart. He wanted to reach out and hold her close even as she backed further into the corner, but it wasn't his arm that did the reaching. It was a glistening claw affixed to an arm of tight-packed muscle. Black... like the colour eclipsing his mind.

28

The Bond of Trust

Fion had been making her way back to the Dreamforge when the spire chimed. It startled her and brought gooseflesh to her whole body. The spire had never made such a sound. She hadn't even known it could produce such things. It could call, send out a crystalline resonance, but chime? That was new. What did it mean?

The street she'd been walking down didn't have many people in it, but those who were going about their business looked up at the crystal beacon in tandem. Confusion rippled over their faces. What did they really know of confusion though? After the few days Fion had experienced, she'd give anything to only be wondering about one confusing thing instead of a bunch of them.

The conversation with the leader of the cullers was already fuzzy in parts but painfully sharp in others. The dangerous logic of it shouldn't have made any sense, and yet it did. It birthed a mesh of thorns inside her mind. Every way she tried to turn she'd be scratched and marred by it. Pain in every direction. Where the ways were once clear, now they were mired with danger. Things had been so much simpler before Geran's words had started to fester. Started to leak and make her wonder. Were dreamsmiths no better than murderers by proxy?

The closer she got to the inner city, the faster she walked. As the buzz of adrenaline wore away the ground beneath her started to shift. Weariness dragged her down, but fear urged her on. Delayed feelings of claustrophobia and panic, all kept at bay during the exchange with Geran, now tried to flood out. She wanted safety, needed it. Once back at her apartment she could let down the shaking walls she'd built around herself. She could process all of it. Not here though, not in the middle of the slums.

As she made haste along the southern road a gossiping glut of people were crowding together. Whispering and gesticulating wildly. Several people spoke quickly and in uneven tones. Fion caught snatches of it as she passed by, but some words in particular slowed her steps.

'I was there, I saw it happen. They were real.'

'Ox-crap I say, they don't just roam around the city.'

'They weren't roaming, they were seeking. They came over the walls and gathered around the smith that Leander booted out of his house. The one with the missing eye. I'm telling you it was a pack of hollows.'

'You been drinking today or something?'

'I wasn't the only one there, you don't have to take my word for it. But I'm telling ya, they all piled on that smith and took him away. Swallowed him up and dragged him down into the ground like a pack of wild dogs or something. Ask one of the others if you have to, I don't care much if you believe me.'

The talking continued, each pod of people hearing a different rendition, but Fion was no longer listening. A smith with a missing eye? Could it be? Despite the pulling ache around her injury and leaden feeling in her legs, she broke into as much of a run as she could manage.

***

Fion didn't even knock as she barged into Clayton's office. Shoving what little energy she had left against the double doors, already pre-annoyed at whatever vagaries he'd likely throw at her. It was a fairly large room yet a modest size for the head of the Dreamforge. He'd been reaching for a pile of papers only to spill them over his desk when startled. His hood was back, and his eyes flared with surprise as Fion marched across the parquet floor towards him.

'Fion, what are you- Fion!'

She swayed dangerously, running on the last of her energy reserves and holding an arm gingerly around her waist. Clayton practically leapt around his desk to steady her and guide her into a chair. She'd had no intention of appearing so vulnerable in that moment, but had always been bad at knowing her own limits when there was important work to be done.

The room spun less once she was nestled in the safety of one of the two high-backed chairs that sat in front of the dark wood desk. Books and papers littered it, perhaps she wasn't the only one doing some research.

'Are you alright, what's the matter?' Clayton let go of her arm and leaned back against the edge of his desk. Concern creasing his face as he inspected her. 'Where have you been? You're meant to be staying in your apartment.'

'You found him, didn't you?' She didn't need to say who. Clayton's face gave her the answer she needed. Her mind cleared as her body learned it was truly resting now.

219

She had to think. What information should she reveal and what should she keep in the dark? Maybe Clayton was thinking the same. There was a time where they were both almost of the same mind and ideals but now… a ravine was opening between them. A ravine of guarding and subterfuge. The wider it got, the less they knew each other.

'How did you-'

'I overheard the slumfolk.'

'You were in the slums?'

'That's not your concern.'

'Fion. It is my concern. Why wouldn't it be? You're still injured and clearly upset. You should be resting.'

'I'll decide what's best for me and what I'm capable of. I'm not a kid anymore, Clayton, as much as you're treating me like one. And I refuse to be a prisoner either. Whatever notions you have of shielding me and protecting me, burn them. See and treat me as an equal. A colleague. Someone who wants to help. You've found Taren. Where is he?'

The seconds stretched by, turning into minutes. Clayton took long, deliberate steps around his desk. By the time he sat down in his chair on the other side Fion had seen the change. From concerned guardian to stone-faced and serious Forgemaster. He was locking her out. Again. Preparing to say something he knew she wouldn't stand for.

'He is safe. For now. His condition is a dangerous one. I don't know how long it will take to help him but we can't allow-'

'Don't even think of telling me I can't see him. You pulled this crap with Jacklan but this is Taren. Taren is different. He's family.'

'You can't see him. Not until I've seen him myself and

220

we've helped him.'

She wanted to scream about how sending senior smiths to harm and threaten Taren wasn't exactly the most helpful thing, but that would give too much away. Not only that, there was too much to be uncertain about. Neither her nor Taren were even sure if Clayton knew about the corruption of the two smiths that had found and tried to read Taren. But if what the slumfolk said was true, and hollows came to claim him... surely the Forgemaster would be aware. Did it mean he was also in command of the creatures? It wasn't something Fion dared entertain the thought of.

'Sounds like capturing him put on quite a show for the slumfolk.'

Clayton's eyes flicked to the side slightly. 'Nothing so dramatic. Some of the senior smiths merely went to retrieve him. He was found at a farm in the southwest quarter. Slumfolk tend to exaggerate in their gossips.'

A totally different story than she'd heard from those discussing the events on the southern road. In that moment she was glad and also devastated. Glad that she'd held back the information about the hollows, but gutted in hearing the lies fall from Clayton's mouth so easily. His shoulders stiffened and his words filled with a sharper edge.

'Why were you even in the slums? During the investigation in to the faulty station I asked you to remain here. You say you're no longer a child, yet if I'm putting the pieces together properly you've been sneaking out. Not the most elegant or adult behaviour.'

'Well I've no interest in being under house arrest while you continue to hide things from me. Something's happened. Something you're desperate to cover up. If the

Dreamforge is in danger, don't you think we ought to know? Don't you think I deserve-'

'You deserve nothing.' The words slapped across her face and stunned her. Unable to respond. Memories of his stern outbursts when she'd put herself in dangerous situations as a child or teenager flooded back. She'd been fearful of his capacity to be strict when she crossed a line back then, and a sliver of that fear fluttered in her adult heart even now.

'You forget yourself,' he continued. 'You've always enjoyed certain privileges here, being raised by the Forge and its staff, it's true. But there are limits to what that entitles you to. I can trust you without entrusting everything to you. Some things are the business of the Forge alone, which makes it my business and my duty alone. For you to barge in here with not an inch of respect in your actions or your tone shows nothing but your inflated ego and entitlement and how much it's grown over time. Perhaps the fault lies with me for that.' Fion opened her mouth to object, but wasn't given the chance to say a single word.

'There is so much that you do not and will never know. You think you've the right to be privy to everything I have? All the knowledge. All the answers. Well you do not. As many advantages as you've been given can be stripped. I will not hesitate if you continue to meddle in this, regardless of the bonds between us. I raised you, taught you, care for you greatly. But if you cannot leave this be I will have to take protective measures in the best interest of the Forge and the people of the city. Understood?'

The harsh edge in his eyes softened as soon as he'd finished speaking. Pleading. Holding back emotions he couldn't let through. Couldn't or wouldn't. She'd never felt less like his daughter of choice.

Understood? She understood alright. The threat hidden in the words was about as subtle as a brick to the teeth. Fine. Fine if that's what he wanted. If that was the part he wished to play. She held the bond of trust between them in her mind's eye, already frayed from the events of the past days, and snapped it in two.

'You've made yourself clear, Forgemaster.' She piled emphasis into his title. The first time in years that she hadn't called him Clayton when in private company. A thrill of satisfaction lurched in her stomach as a flicker of pain flashed across those eyes he was trying so hard to keep cold and indifferent. Had he felt it too, the snapping of that trust? She hoped so.

Something had shifted between them. Something fundamental. A rose-tinted filter now shattered and splayed in pieces around them. No longer guardian and guarded. Now threats and fierce secrets on both sides.

His face faltered, the way it did when he was preparing to apologise. She had no desire to hear it. The sting of his words was still keen. Each a shard of ice fused to her heart. His message had been clear. She wasn't entitled to anything. She wasn't fit to aid or help him. She was beneath the level of trust needed to share in the troubles of his greatest duty. He couldn't have been more clear if he'd stepped on her like the lowly bug he'd made her feel akin to.

She'd find Taren herself. She was more than capable, despite what the Forgemaster seemed to think. He'd made a mistake in underestimating her, she'd ensure he learned that soon enough.

She made to stand, exhaustion heavier than ever in every joint and limb. Would he have reacted differently if he'd known the danger she'd faced from the cullers? A danger proven to be unfounded, but she hadn't known that to begin with. Maybe the fault was with her, maybe her quick temper and brash behaviour had caused this. Maybe he hadn't trusted her all along. Whatever the answer, she wouldn't struggle with wondering about it now.

As she got to her feet and started to turn away, the Forgemaster spoke again only to be interrupted. 'Fion, please wait I-'

'Forgemaster!' A senior smith bustled into the office in a flurry of purpose, not bothering to take present company into account before blurting out their message. 'Everything's ready. You're needed urgently below-' The speaker's eyes widened in alarm as they fell upon Fion. A fear that only seemed to compound as he looked at the Forgemaster. He shot the senior smith a glance filled with such anger that it almost took Fion's breath. What had the smith said that was so important? That would anger the Forgemaster so?

The speaker lowered his head in apology and dared not move again.

'Not another word. Escort Fion back to her apartment,' he locked eyes with her as he said her name, 'and make sure she stays there this time.'

29

Abandoned Callings

After the hollows slunk away, a dreadful silence stiffened in the corridor. Taren faced the hooded figures from beneath his own cowl and waited, unsure whether to try and step back but reluctant to step forward.

'Taren, come with us. It will be easier if you simply follow. You've things to answer for.'

A flare of irritation irked him. 'I have things to answer for? I'm the one who deserves answers not the one who should be giving them.' His words cut the air, tone unfriendly with a hint of desperation he hadn't meant to include. He was tired. Tired of seeing hooded faces and hiding his own, of not knowing who was who or who was an ally or not.

'What my fellow senior smith meant,' there was an edge of annoyance in the second figure's voice but it was not directed at Taren, 'is that we are here to help you.' The second voice sounded familiar, yet he struggled to place it.

'I've heard that line before. The last two smiths who said that tried to take my blood not long after and threatened my life.' A genuine gasp exited the hood of the second smith, didn't they know what had happened with

Ferron and Edwyn? Surely they'd been found by now and weren't still lying on his kitchen floor. 'I'm done blindly trusting those who say they want to help.' He took the slightest step backwards and the smiths didn't hesitate. A few swift strides was all it took to flank him, and steer him by his arms and shoulders further down the corridor.

'We can't have you running again. If we're going to help you then you need to be here at the Forge.' He'd rather be anywhere else. Even back in Linette's now-empty home. At least crumpled there on the floor he'd had some peace. Perhaps not of mind but in the space around him. The first place he'd ever thought of as a home seemed so unfamiliar that a deep ache ran through his heart.

'At least give me some answers. Why are there hollows down here, and how do they even exist at all? What did Ferron and Edwyn want and why does this dream keep giving me visions that just don't make sense? Where are you taking me?'

'Quiet down, man.' The least friendly of the two voices was strained. Was it fear? Panic? Yet another nervous smith, like Edwyn. A strong sense of deja vu gripped Taren and suddenly he knew his destination, or at least why he was being taken there.

'You're taking me for a hollow reading.' His two guides slowed their steps but didn't stop. 'You needn't bother, the last one was a failure.' Their puzzlement drifted on the air. The soft swish of their hoods gave them away. They were exchanging looks behind him.

As they rounded a sharp corner another grand cavern opened out before him. It was much like the corridor he'd first entered the Forge through, but this time each pillar had a set of chains attached to its front face. Why would the Dreamforge need such a provision? Dreamsmiths had no need to keep prisoners. Taren's heart jumped and skipped around. Yet another thing that didn't add up. Despite the cavernous space about him, the air felt thicker and thicker. Colder and colder. Whether his own anxieties or all the lies were causing it, there was no way to tell.

Taren didn't protest as his captors added the cuffs at the end of the chains to his wrists and made sure they fitted correctly. He had enough room to take one step forward, but otherwise his back was pressed against the pillar. Its cool, ornate stone drained his heat through the back of his robe. At last, once he was secure and they were two strides away, they dropped their hoods.

There were far too many similarities between the current situation and the fiasco at his inner city home. One smith he knew, and knew well. So well in fact that he grimaced at yet another foul surprise. Senior smith Micah, Fion's mentor and in her eyes as close to a father as she would ever get aside from the Forgemaster. He was older, nearing sixty years, but had a kind face and dark eyes that never missed a thing.

The other he didn't know as well, but had seen him skulking in various places around the Forge. Tarrick, undoubtedly his least favourite senior smith for reasons Taren could never fathom. He always kept his distance. Something never sat right about Tarrick. He had the quiet, dangerous feel of a prowling snake, and just being in his presence made Taren long for the company of the hollows instead. At least their eyes didn't rove over him, dripping with judgement and an air of disgust.

227

'I'm telling you I don't need another reading, or the restraints for that matter. The first reading failed, there's no need.' Part of Taren squirmed at how much sarcasm and disrespect oozed from his words in the presence of his seniors, but this was not a normal situation and formality was the least of his concerns. 'What I need are answers. Why does the Forge need all these underground rooms? Why is there a room full of hollows in choke holds, and why every time I interact with one of those pitiful creatures do they try and tell me to find the truth? I love my duty as a dreamsmith, it's all I wanted for a long time, but with what I've learned over the past few days I'm beginning to think the whole thing is just a façade. The spire, the Dreamforge, the dreamstones, all of it.

'What is the Forge hiding? How many are corrupt? I want the Forgemaster here, now, before I submit to any kind of reading. Any kind of further foul treatment by the senior smiths. Until I hear it from his mouth that he has approved these actions and get suitable explanations for the things I have witnessed I refuse to co-operate any further.' He threw his head back in pain as the skin on the left side of his face tightened again. Was it spreading? His hood dropped back as he thrashed and gritted his teeth.

'Taren, you need to stay calm and in control of yourself,' Micah said in a firm but kind tone.

'Why?' Taren spat back. 'You're just causing more questions. I've already been told the dream will kill me so I suggest you find those answers quickly. Bring the Forgemaster here. Now.' His raised, pained voice echoed and danced off the pillars in rounds of dying whispers. Why wouldn't they help? Couldn't they see his pain? His distress?

How many times would he have to ask for help? Everyone said they wanted to aid him, but no one was doing anything.

Micah wore an expression of genuine concern. Tarrick grimaced and pinched his face into a disapproving sneer, his green eyes drifting over the growing affliction. He whispered something that sounded much like "he knows too much" but Micah didn't nod in agreement. After a discussion that Taren couldn't hear over his racing heart Tarrick hurried away and Micah stepped forward, taking Taren's face between his two hands.

The coolness of his touch dulled the pain of the dream. Breaths steadied and the pulsing needles receded. Was Micah an ally? The hope fluttered precariously. Who could be trusted?

'Calm yourself, now. I suspect that not being in control of yourself might quicken its growth.' Micah's voice brought with it memories of being a student. Of learning and successfully completing tasks for the first time. Of showing early promise as a smith at such a young age. Of a time when he'd loved and trusted the title of dreamsmith.

'I want to help you Taren, truly. You've learned much, and seem very confused by it. That's understandable, but I offer you a warning. You should forget about what you've learned and bury what's happened with the other smiths. It's for your own good.

'Some things are not meant to be known by all. If you don't let us help you, then this dream will take your life as you say. I will not move to harm you, and I don't know why Ferron and Edwyn did. They shouldn't have. We had no such orders. You should have been brought straight back here. I'm sorry that happened to you.' Being treated like an equal, a human, again was overwhelming. Taren fought the ache in his throat.

'You want me to forget? Forget that I've seen hollows kept like animals when they're supposed to be powerful, dangerous creatures born of abandoned callings? Don't you see how that alone goes against everything I've been trained to believe? I don't know what I'm supposed to do.'

'Oh, I see it. I know the burden of truth. More than you might expect. There are some things that have to stay hidden. The front you show to all can't always be the front of truth. Please, just believe me when I say that delving deeper is not something you want. I intend to find out why Ferron and Edwyn threatened you once they've recovered from their own injuries. They were collected from your home and taken straight to the infirmary, both should be back to full health soon and they will be questioned. By me. Before I do that though, I would see your life saved rather than wasted.'

'You want to keep this covered? Are you part of whatever this is? Is that why you're keeping me a prisoner?'

'No, we're doing this for yo-' a haunting sound began to ring in circular calls throughout both men and through the cavernous room. It twisted inside Taren and he knew it was coming from the main spire. A sickening, undulating sound that left no crevice or crack in silence. It filled the entire Dreamforge and manifested on Micah's face as unwanted surprise. Taren searched his mind, through the confusion and raging storm of possibilities and looked for the meaning of that sound. It was distinct, designed to be that way so that initiate dreamsmiths would remember its meaning yet it escaped him. A contagious apprehension flooded from the senior smith. Clearly it wasn't good.

'It can't be. I must go, but I'll come back. He should have already been told you're here, but Tarrick went to fetch the Forgemaster anyway. However, I doubt he will come to you until… whatever this is is solved. Think about what I said, carefully, and make your choice. Forget, or dig. But know that once you dig a hole the ground beneath it is rarely stable in the same way again.'

Micah briefly placed a hand on Taren's shoulder and squeezed. There was kinship and concern in it rather than hate. Then, with a motion graceful for a man his age, Micah straightened his posture, raised his hood and walked away with an urgent haste.

'Wait, what does that sound mean?'

Micah turned back for a moment, his face solemn and dark under his hood. 'It means there's a hollow on the loose in the city. Out in the open.'

Recognition finally came to Taren and a trapdoor opened beneath his feet. Before he could say anything else Micah had gone. A hollow was up there among the people. One the Forge had no control of. One that had no control of itself.

30

No Need for Colour

The world was monochrome. There was no need for colour. Colour will return when the truth is found and restored. Truth. Truth. Lost long ago. It must be recovered. It was taken from us all. Rage. Outrage. Melding in a storm. It doesn't know what it is, only what it has to do. How can it find the truth? The buildings it destroys are nothing. Obstacles in its search for its goal. Claws shred and fray. Wood, stone and flesh. If they try to stop it they themselves will be stopped. They move, and then they don't. They will never move again.

It isn't their fault, but if they stand in its way they must be dealt with. It walked through the slums slowly, bringing with it a storm of chaos. Some of what it ruins looks familiar, but memories shatter like glass on tile before they can form. Inside it Leander fights, unsure and scared of his new skin and wondering how to shed it. Two desires battle for control. Two wills swirl in a maelstrom of longing. Truth. Taren. One or the other must be found.

Who is he? The skin he wears, dark and thick with tar, doesn't feel unlike him. More like another him. A different him. An old friend returning with none of his friendliness.

Taren. Truth. Both goals lie in the same place. More buildings fall, more screams echo as people flee. It upends them all in the search. A search that won't end until it reaches its goal. Destroy the lies. Everything is a lie. A fabrication. They don't know, but they deserve to.

Taren can help. Taren holds the truth, or part of it. Taren has its dream. He is linked to the spire. It cannot stand its turquoise glare and screeching call. Chaos, destruction, they will help to cleanse it. Now they must run before the liars arrive. To cover. To repress. To suppress. They can't hope to catch it. Its black, sculpted muscle is too strong and too fast. It could dance circles around them and so it does.

Dashing and darting, leaving destruction in its wake. It zigged and zagged until it reached the wall and it took no effort to leap atop it, sliding down the other side. On that side things have to be different. On that side they have to be careful while they look for the truth. While they look for Taren. His kind face tips the tide of control and the call of the dream can be heard once more. Follow the resonance and you will find him. Follow it and he will be there, waiting. Will he accept me, after what I did? Will he forgive me for hiding from him? For being cold and untrue to myself.

The resonance called like a bright beacon. Taren will be waiting at the end. Make sure we aren't seen, the liars will catch us. The liars in the indigo robes will kill us. Erase us and what we search for will stay buried. Hide in the shadows, sneak around the buildings. Use the passages of those who were captured before. Underground. Go below. The way in will be clear. Follow the scent of his call.

31

Duty be Damned

Fion lay on her back in the middle of her bed staring vacantly at the ceiling. She might appear to be resting, but her mind roared with buzzing puzzle pieces. At least one senior smith guarded her door at all times. She often heard them conversing with people who passed by or shuffling in boredom as they stood watch. Now she truly was under house arrest, and yet it wasn't really clear why. All she'd done was ask a few potentially inflammatory questions. And maybe been more than a little disrespectful to the Forgemaster. And ignored his previous request to stay put during an investigation into a highly dangerous incident.

OK so maybe it was a well-deserved dose of house arrest, but still an unnecessary one. The sting of the Forgemaster's words constantly tried to rise to the forefront of her mind, but she squashed it down. Even though she herself had severed the trust between them, the decision hadn't been easy or trivial. It left a raw and ragged hole in her heart where something important and invaluable had once been. It caused everything she knew to be called into question. There had to be something she could do. Anything.

A flash of irritation pulsed through her body and she sat

up sharply to launch a throw pillow across the room with a huff. Idleness was Fion's worst enemy and she wore it like a poorly tailored robe. One made of itchy material that would be better burned than suffered. It prickled over her skin with each movement, each moment of inaction.

She paced her apartment for the hundredth time, wondering again if she could be bothered to heat water for some tea. The housing at the Forge was more than ample for people who wished to stay there long term. Large rectangular spaces split into three rooms. Two were divided by a wall with an arch to separate them, but really most of the space was open plan. Each smith could set up these rooms however they wanted.

Fion had opted for a small wood-burning stove, sofa and two-seater table in the first room, with the outer walls of the first space lined with bookshelves. The second room was her sleeping space, and attached to that, like in all rooms, was the bathroom. Over time she'd seen rooms laid out in ways far different and more creative than her own, but the smooth stone and domed ceilings of the apartment were her home. The only space left where she felt safe and familiar in the whole Forge.

She turned to head back to the bed, for lack of anything better to do and having changed her mind about wanting tea, when her stomach did a frightening loop. A resonance more like a blaring alarm flared from the spire. A deep-seated dread filled her. An emergency in the outer city.

It couldn't be Taren. If the Forgemaster's words held true then Taren was back at the Forge and in the care, whatever that meant, of the senior smiths. The alarm yowled once more and then silenced, leaving a ringing in Fion's ears. Every emergency call had a specific purpose, and she remembered that one well. A hollow was loose out there?

A ruckus burst to life outside her door. Hurried footfalls scuffled and voices hummed as she imagined a throng of smiths collecting themselves and getting ready to rush down into the slums. She, too, was duty-bound to go and help. The pull and drive to prepare herself and join her colleagues was tremendous, but she fought it. Dropping down into a chair at the small table she pushed her palms against her closed eyes, resting the weight on her elbows.

'Why should I do my duty after all that's happened? Why should I keep doing things without questioning them first?'

Fion was tired. Tired of all the back and forth. She'd been in and out of the Forge for several days and the thought of heading out there again in the face of a crisis was almost too much to bear. After the unkindness of the Forgemaster's words, why should she bother? What did being a dreamsmith even mean anymore? She'd never felt less connected to her duty, her purpose. To her hope of helping people.

Taren would know what to say. He brimmed with overly philosophical quotes about a dreamsmith's duty. But Taren wasn't here and she had no way to find him. No one was there for her. She was totally alone.

Fion gasped and stared at the closed door to her apartment. Something slipped through her mind and she'd failed to grab it. Now it hid, going shy and unwilling to be coaxed out. She searched for it, gently and carefully.

Maybe she could find him. The alarm meant she was duty-bound to assist in the emergency, so surely that would overwrite her detainment. Every available smith had to answer such a call. It was her way out. The senior smith guarding her door may not even be there anymore. Only one way to find out.

Fion listened at the door first, and it sounded as though there were still people making their way out of their apartments. Low, strained murmurs and the clatter and tap of footsteps. The distant thwack of doors opening and closing in haste.

Her door made no sound as it opened, and her heart leapt as she peered around its frame. No guard. This was her chance. She strode from the apartment and started making her way to the grand foyer. People would likely gather there to organise themselves and split into groups. Either that or, since it was the highest level of emergency, they'd likely head straight out of the Forge in one bloated throng. A nice way to get lost among a crowd.

As she turned the final corner and started to descend the main staircase, however, a deep regret for leaving her apartment settled in. Many of her colleagues tracked her with curious stares, not all kind either. Talking shifted into whispers, and many of them floated up towards her.

'Her friend's responsible for this.'

'How do you know?'

'Has to be him, he's the one who broke a connection with a dream and fled.'

'Did she have something to do with it?'

'No one really knows, but she's not been seen on the forging floor since. Some say she's not allowed to do any smithing right now. She's been stuck in her apartment with a senior smith keeping guard.'

'What, she's under observation? So they think she had something to do with the forge that malfunctioned?'

'Maybe.'

She ignored the suspicious glares and shrugged off the whispers, but her hopes of going unnoticed went up in smoke. Apparently she'd become quite notorious for her association with Taren. Funny how people can make up such wild theories with nothing but ridiculous and uninformed speculation. If the Forgemaster wasn't sharing information with Fion, he certainly wasn't sharing it with the masses so casually. Talk about jumping to conclusions. Still, they continued as the crowd of smiths made their way out towards the courtyard.

'Did you hear they found him?'

'Who?'

'That smith who fled. They're detaining him supposedly, somewhere in the Forge.'

'There's no greater disgrace for a smith.'

Several colleagues nodded in agreement, and that strange feeling slipped across Fion's mind again. Being held in disgrace somewhere in the Forge. While she walked at the back of the group and turned the cogs of her mind, something knitted together.

The smiths were all emptying out to answer the emergency call, though based on the relaxed nature of those who had time to gossip most seemed to think it was some kind of drill. Given how quickly her guard had left his station, Fion knew better. That's when her mind provided the missing piece. A recall of the words of the senior smith who had barged into the Forgemaster's office.

"You're needed urgently below…"

He'd instantly regretted it as well. The anger in the Forgemaster's eyes, the cringing apologetic nature of the smith's reaction. Taren being held in disgrace. There's only one reason the Forgemaster would be so incensed about a seemingly superfluous piece of information slipping out of the mouth of a senior smith. It wasn't superfluous at all, Fion just hadn't realised it before.

Her steps slowed and the pack of dreamsmiths pulled away, out of the courtyard and off towards the slums. That clumsy senior smith had given her the answer she wanted most. Said right in front of her face no less, and yet she hadn't put the pieces together. Taren was being held below. She'd assumed it just meant on a lower floor but what if it didn't?

What if, in this Dreamforge she no longer trusted, there was more to uncover. More secrets. More lies. She'd been to every inch of the place in the course of her life, or thought she had. But 'below' seemed a very specific wording, and it had triggered the Forgemaster's ire. She backtracked into the foyer, now being careful to look around and ensure she wouldn't be seen. What better time to snoop around than when everyone else's attention was caught up in whatever had happened in the slums?

If the Forgemaster and other smiths weren't going to help her, then Fion would help herself. Duty be damned. A wider picture began to form. If Taren really was being held below, and if there was more to the Dreamforge, maybe that's where all the answers were. Taren. Jacklan. The hollows the slumfolk had mentioned. Whatever secrets the Forgemaster was shielding her from.

Well, Fion never asked to be shielded and she'd make

her own decisions about what she could handle knowing or not knowing, thank you very much. Few people knew the Dreamforge better than she did, and as she slipped into a narrow corridor she braced herself for whatever and whoever she might find if her theory proved to be true.

'Hold on Taren, I'll find you. I promise.'

She had new priorities now. The Forgemaster's orders weren't one of them. The people she trusted had always come before the people she hadn't. This was no different. Taren was family. Her closest friend. Her chosen brother. She wouldn't leave him alone in this. Whatever this was. First things first, though. As soon as she found her impulsive clod of a brother, she'd give him a swift punch to the gut for ever wandering off in the first place.

32

Without Question or Qualm

Empty space chimed around Taren. Every small clink of his chains ran free, joyously exploring the vastness surrounding him. He leaned back against the pillar, trying to ignore the changing shades of the blank void that pressed in on all sides. Sometimes it was comforting, a welcome break from the conflicts of the past days. Sometimes it sent a chill running through him, painting thoughts of being watched or of hollows lurking in the shadows behind the other pillars. How easy to lose track of time down there. How easy to lose track of yourself.

The thought brought Leander to mind. Taren didn't know him well, but what he'd done in exposing Taren to the dreamsmiths seemed to go against his character. Leander could be a bit prickly, but he had saved Taren's life. A pressure built in his chest as he remembered what Leander had given up to do so, and what thanks Taren had given him for it. Unwittingly or not.

For a moment he was back at the forging station, searching for a dream to craft. He remembered the gentle honesty of Leander's dream as it came together. Something not born out of greed or selfish want. It had created a curiosity in Taren about the owner. A timid wish to know such a person. He'd been excited to craft it because of the rarity of finding one not driven by a typical or predictable motivation. To be rich, to be powerful, to be irresistible.

Leander's wish brimmed with freedom. Golden stalks of crops surrounding a beautiful house on a large plain set against a backdrop of mountains. He wished to cultivate life and live in peace. A notion so simple and elegant and true. A man wanting such a dream wouldn't have willingly ignored someone in need.

Leander was different now even to the man who wanted Taren out of the house to protect Corryn. Taren had honoured and understood that, and only returned as he'd had nowhere else to go and felt a true sense of concern from the two of them, despite Leander's coldness. By what Corryn had said, he'd been through a lot. Shut himself off.

What was the true Leander like? Taren's heart fluttered as a picture of him beamed clearly in his mind. Heat collected in his face as he found himself wishing for the chance to see Leander again, to apologise and to build a true connection. To know the man who once dreamed of what Taren saw in the dreamstone, rather than a man who dragged him outside wearing an expression of twisted hate and hurt.

He'd done the greatest wrong to the man who'd given up so much to save him. Taren could only droop in his chains and choke back a heavy sigh. This isn't what he wanted.

Then a skittering sound meandered out of the dark. Quiet and insect-like. Followed by a squelching rhythm that echoed wildly in the hall. Taren tensed, eye scanning the

242

unfolding shadows. Having one eye closed tinted the atmosphere with danger. He was bound, vulnerable and couldn't protect himself. Was it another hollow... or something else?

Given what he'd seen in the last few days, his confused mind painted all sorts of pictures of what might be inching towards him from the unlit bulk of the room. He couldn't handle another 'something else'. He cast about with urgency, searching for the source of the wet, slapping footsteps, but doing so only rattled his chains and masked it. Instead he stood as still as he could, willing his heart to stop hammering.

Every second footstep had a slight drag to it. Slap. Sluuurp. Slap. Sluuurp. Out of the corner of his eye, three pillars away towards the corridor that led back to the main walk, the featureless face of a hollow pushed out from behind one of the stone structures. Its skeletal body followed, clawed hands dripping with black sludge. For a moment it stood quiet and unmoving. Its damp breath crackled. Then it turned its head to face him in one disturbing but graceful movement. It made a path straight for him. Had it been sent to read him? A great weariness washed over Taren yet again.

'It's OK. You don't have to read me.' Could it even understand him? He had no clue. No way to know. 'I know who the stone belongs to. Or... belonged to. I know who I've stolen from and that I can't give it back. I'm a thief. A thief of hope.' It continued its trek. Becoming more hideous with each step, yet an odd feeling of resignation kept Taren calm. 'I'm sorry.'

Why apologise to it? What good would it do? 'I'm sorry

that you've been trapped here. That you've been used. They've always painted you as a danger, yet not one of you has tried to harm me. I wish I knew what happened. I wish I knew the truth.'

It stopped mere steps from him when he said the word "truth". The more he stared at it, the more pity rose within him. Pity, a touch of guilt, and a sadness he couldn't explain. His own kind had used and exploited these creatures, cursing them as a danger he had yet to even witness. But the resonance that had sounded from the spire meant that a hollow was loose in the city. Would it be killing, destroying and breaking, or would it be killed, broken and destroyed on principal?

It dawned on him again how little he'd ever questioned the world he lived in and the way it worked. How naïve it had been to take whatever the Dreamforge taught him as absolute truth. Were dreamsmiths more similar to hollows than anyone knew? Were they being exploited and used for some unknown, masked purpose? It all seemed so simple when he was younger. Give your life in devotion to the Forge, and in return you do good and offer salvation to people. When you want something so much, do you just become a sponge? Drinking up knowledge and truths without question or qualm?

The hollow took the final few steps and reached out. It still wanted to read him? Proof, perhaps, that it couldn't hear him after all. He hung his head and closed his eye, accepting whatever came. A syrupy hand came to rest on his chest, and nothing but the bubbling inhale and exhale of the creature broke the silence for a few fleeting seconds. Then it showed him something he did not expect.

A memory? Sepia pictures not quite joined together in proper sequence, but clear enough to grasp. Through the eyes of an excited slum resident he saw the Dreamforge and the hall of binding. Where people went to collect their dreamstones. Utter euphoria flooded the memory, excitement and a sense of deserving. Awe ran rampant at the marble-carved luxury of the hall. Its vaulted stone ceilings arching above, curving down to meet the ornate pillars shining with filigree. After the drafty shack of a home that had feebly protected him from the elements all these years, the cavernous echo of his footsteps filled him with overwhelming and outrageous glee.

Taren could feel the person shedding all the years spent struggling in the slum with every step, casting it off like a snake skin. A dreamsmith waited, they got to bind the recipients to the stones they craft and it had often made Taren happy to see their elation overflow. The view approached the stone table, and there lay the sphere. Transparent, smooth, and encasing a fractal in its glass.

This. These feelings and this overflowing sense of hope. The reason Taren became a dreamsmith in the first place. His heart warmed with fondness for his role, for everything it meant he could offer the people of the outer city. It couldn't be over. He'd craft dreams again, just as soon as all this chaos was straightened out. He wasn't willing to give up something that had become such a part of who he was. Yet, the vision continued.

As the recipient sat down across from the smiling smith, they were asked to lay their right hand on the table, palm up. Taren had seen it hundreds of times, either as a spectator or as a binder. The same bracelets as those used to connect to the forges appeared to ring the smith's wrists, and from the stone the dreamsmith pulled a single, glowing string. With a graceful movement she took it between her thumb and middle finger and placed it in the waiting palm, a small circle of symbols flashed once to secure the bond which quickly faded.

When the circle flashed, Taren's view changed. It was lifted out of the dreamer, bound and silenced. Torn away from them, reeling out on a black tether that was swiftly cut by a senior smith standing as a spectator. It passed through the floor, down and down it went, until the view turned empty. What had just happened? Something so familiar had at once become something alien. It hadn't been the memory of the person, but the hollow? Maybe even both.

As reality reappeared before his working eye, Taren's breath came in short bursts, smile long gone and heart as cold as an empty stone hearth. The hollow stepped back, sharp claws dropping to its sides having done no harm. It seemed to wait, letting what it had shown him sink in. It whispered in his head with a longing. "Find the truth" it said. Then sidled away in a vacant stupor.

'Wait. Please wait. What did you show me? Is that what always happens? Please come back.' Had he seen the vision correctly? The hollow continued to walk away. How had it managed to get free? The chain cuffs bit at his wrists as he tried to follow. He could barely take any more questions, but something sparked a determination in him. The room spun with possibilities. The dreamsmith in the vision had extracted a hollow from a dreamer. It made no sense. He'd never consciously extracted a hollow, all he'd done was bind people to their dreamstones.

His mind raced, thinking back, scrambling for sense. Had there always been senior smiths present? At every single binding? His face flashed white hot as the patch of dream burned. Bells rang inside him each vying for space to be heard. Nothing fit together, nothing was stable. He slid around inside his mind like soap in a smooth stone dish. Answers. Answers were needed.

33

Coming Undone

Time shifted on unstable sands as Taren hung in his chains. Tension ebbed from his body with each passing minute. When did he last drink and eat? He'd scrounged some food at Fion's, water too, and had a vague recollection of being offered more water by a passer-by in the slums as he'd aimlessly walked the streets in emotional shreds.

At some point after the hollow departed he had come to sit down, back against the pillar and arms hanging just above the floor in their restraints. His body fought to pull him into some kind of restless sleep, but his mind resisted, heavy with the images that the creature had shown him.

A net of questions rimmed his mind and bound his thoughts in close and stifled groups. No matter how hard he tried, he couldn't stop more from forming. Was he being chosen for something? Every time he'd come into contact with a hollow they tried to show him things. Tell him things. None of it making sense. The universe stirred around him, some chain of events forming, wrapped in inevitable fate. He was adrift in it, his purpose and role all still unclear. Such a tilted, dizzying sensation.

What was going on up there in the slums? Had a hollow

truly appeared? It would be the first time in several decades since someone had ignored their call. Fresh hollows were supposed to be vicious, but he had never seen any until recently. They had all been meek. He'd go so far as to say gentle. Even the ones that brought him back to the Forge never caused a scratch on him. They seemed drawn to him and determined to impart things. Each more unwanted and baffling as the next. The last vision seemed particularly legitimate. He barely dared deny what he'd seen.

Did hollows live inside of humans, then, instead of only manifesting after ignored callings? In order for the smith to rip it out of the dreamer receiving their stone, it would have to be in their body already. More questions added to the pile. He groaned audibly with their weight. They sometimes bolstered his energy and sometimes sapped it. He hadn't the strength to carry them all.

Just as sleep rose up to try and claim him once again a distant echo whispered through the hall. He sat up a little straighter, pain blooming in his back against the now-warmed stone. More echoes followed, running rampant in the emptiness around him. Amplifying then dying away at random. Some kind of disturbance? It grew louder and louder every few seconds.

He hauled himself to his feet, aches popping in his joints like hot firecrackers, and scanned to find the source of the noise. The crystal lamps burned, an ambient light not of much use. Darkness loomed high above him and shadows played tricks in the dark. Hollows attached to the ceiling stared down and crawled out of sight. Prickles dragged down Taren's spine as he shook off the imaginings.

At last he sourced the commotion as coming from the

corridor he'd entered through. Had something happened with the hollows? Were they coming for him? Shouts started to become clearer. What were they chasing and why? How did it get down here? He soon got his answers.

Another hollow slid around the corner in a gelatinous skid, scraping its claws along the smooth floors to try and propel itself forwards. Steam rose from the tar it left behind, the gloop dissolving into nothing within seconds. It stopped, just for a moment, to pull in some ragged breaths before it noticed him. Their eyeless faces made it difficult to know whether or not they had spotted you or where their attention had been drawn. Voices clamoured in urgency not far behind it, and it started heading straight for Taren.

When would he stop being the target of these creatures and why were they drawn to him so? Could it be because he was fused with a dream? Was he calling to them without knowing how or why, like he'd done with Leander? As the hollow scampered closer Taren drew back as far as he could into the stone pillar. The hollow's hands were tinged with blood and it slowed to an unstable walk.

Whispers danced around the corners of his mind. It reached out and Taren cowered instinctively. Its clammy hands, oozing and gritty, held his cheeks and turned his gaze to face it. Taren spoke to it, whether in futility or not.

'I'm sorry. I can't help you. I don't know how to. I can't help anyone.' Its face rippled and, to Taren's horror, peeled back. Receding to uncover another underneath. His heart leapt into his mouth as the smiling face of Leander emerged from the muck of the hollow's mask.

'I didn't think I'd be able to find you. I thought I'd killed you with what I'd done. I wanted to find you, and say that I'm sorry.' Seeing Leander tear up went against everything Taren had come to know about the man. Yet his own heart beat with such a furious rhythm upon seeing Leander's face that it was hard to fight a smile. Were it not for his chains Taren would have wrapped his arms around Leander in relief.

'What are you… how are you here?' Taren caught Leander's wrists and pulled them gently down, acutely aware of the crusting blood left behind on his skin. An ache ricocheted through the left side of his face, and half of the blood sizzled away under the new heat pouring from his affliction.

'I had to find you. I had to.' The rest of the hollow suit melted away, sloughing off of Leander's body to pool beneath them. The shouts grew sharper and footsteps closed in on the hall. A small group of senior dreamsmiths scuttled around the corner, eyes alert and searching for their target. Leander clung to Taren, unable to support himself.

'There it is.' The smiths gathered around the two of them, stopping when they realised the hollow had become a man. They exchanged bewildered glances, staring down at the fragile human as he stood latched to Taren. The smith at the front regained his composure. 'Restrain him. He's dangerous.'

'No, wait, he's not a threat. Don't hurt him.' Taren willed his words to form a shield around Leander, but no such luck.

'Not a threat? And you'd know from down here? He left a trail of chaos in his wake so don't tell me he's not a threat.' They hauled Leander away to the opposite pillar. He didn't resist. The chains cut into Taren's wrists again, and a cold sweat formed on his back as he pulled away from the stone.

'What do you mean? He's a kind man.' Even as he said it Taren remembered being flung to the dusty ground of the farmyard.

'Shut it. You wouldn't say that if you could see what he's done. We haven't had a hollow run loose in decades, we weren't prepared. I don't know how he gained control of himself but he has a lot to answer for.' The look in the smith's eyes was hard to read. A jumbled mosaic of emotion.

'Why was he a hollow? Aren't they meant to be mindless creatures?'

'You had your training Taren, you know what they are and why people turn this way. Arrogant and foolish, but that's no excuse for such destruction.'

None of it made sense. None of it at all. Or perhaps it did and Taren didn't want to accept it. Something clicked in the back of his mind. Something dark and devastating and true. He chose to push it down and ignore it.

'My training?' He watched as they secured a limp Leander to the pillar across from him. He was quiet and unmoving, but audibly rasping for breath. 'My training has taught me nothing!' The smiths all looked around in indignation once they'd secured Leander. 'It taught me nothing. Nothing to explain the things I've seen, the things I've been shown, over the past few days. I want the Forgemaster here. Now. Someone was already sent to fetch him but I suppose that was a lie as well, was it?'

'Who are you to demand to see him in such a way? You're forgetting your place.' Anger boiled inside Taren, along with something else. Something he didn't recognise.

'Get him down here now!' He shouted it loud enough to sting his throat. His fraught roar careened off of the shadowed alcoves, and then the smiths started to back away. His face blistered into a cacophony of pain and the dream began to split into tiny tiles. It was opening. Unravelling. Coming undone.

'Stop that, don't release the dream, stop!' The words all melted together, things had no order, just a burning tornado of negative emotions. A great swathe of Taren's face fragmented and drifted away from itself, parts of it linking with others and iridescent magic pouring out in tendrils that sniffed the air like snake tongues. A burning wind whipped throughout his body and gave power to his shouts to fetch the Forgemaster as they spilled from his mouth. Reality was unwinding, and Taren had no desire to try and stop it.

34

A Life Unlived

The gentle light of the crystal lamps seared Leander's eyes as he opened them, dispelling a crust of hells know what from under his lashes. Where was he? Nothing focused and his whole body throbbed as though he'd done nothing but till fields for days. Cold stone loomed on all sides. Bland, smooth and raising gooseflesh on his bare arms. No space for any life to work its way through the cracks. He hated being in places where life couldn't flourish, they pressed on his chest like a relentless, heavy boot. Where was the sun? The breeze?

Screams drifted into his ears, the volume turning up alongside the clarity of his vision. Taren came into view, surrounded by a pack of four dreamsmiths who were retreating a step at a time. The pit of Leander's stomach dropped and bounced on an elastic cord.

Taren groaned through gritted teeth as the left side of his face flaked bit by bit into fragments that spun idly in the air. A blurred, smudged handprint mottled the right side. Blood? There was nothing beneath the layer of the dream that covered Taren's face. Neither skin nor muscle nor skull. But delicate tendrils swayed and curled out from the empty pit, surging from between the cracks.

The fragments shone as they turned and Leander caught glimpses. Flashes of scenes that only confirmed the dream Taren stole had been his. It would never be his now, and he whirled between acceptance and denial even still. The fragments expanded as they moved away, a dark hum ringing in the air like the aftermath of a vile retort. What was happening to him?

'Taren?' Leander needed more power for his voice but couldn't find it. His raw throat clutched against his attempts to speak. Thick whispers that were all too familiar to him churned in his mind. Taren needed help. How did they even get here?

The last Leander remembered he'd argued with Corryn after making a show of Taren... but what happened after? Nothing lit up in the black depths of his memory. A sharp pulse rippled through him with every attempted movement. The dreamsmiths continued to back away as Taren yelled to see the Forgemaster once more. The desperation in his voice echoed in Leander's core. He'd sounded like that himself once. Screaming into the fields the day Melynda left him behind.

A man in a rich blue robe appeared in the doorway to the hall. Leander hadn't heard a single footstep yet there he stood. An explosion of needle-fine hisses punctured his mind as the man made his way towards Taren with an unerring calm and asked the others to step away.

~*Liar. Liar. Tell the truth. Admit the truth. Liar!*~

The whispers circled endlessly and split Leander's vision. The chains jingled with his own shuddering. As he tried to focus on one spot on the floor to placate the dizziness, a fragment of the dream passed before his eyes. It undulated gracefully on its path, and he caught a snatch of golden fields. Smelled the tang of grass and clean air, and for a fleeting moment a fresh, warm breeze caressed his face. His heart lurched and he reached out to the fragment. He could take it. Claim it. It was his.

The Forgemaster passed him without so much as a glance. His full attention on Taren and no one else. So that was the caretaker of all their dreams and hopes? His eyes were a cool grey under the hood, forever analysing the situation. He wasn't as old as Leander expected, or at least he didn't look it from what little could be seen of his face. A tidy beard of salt and pepper hair framed his jawline, and his stance had power even if his shoulders had an odd droop to them despite his straight back.

~*Liar. Father of Lies. He is not to be tolerated. Let me through!*~

The voice's efforts to reclaim the forefront of his mind flung Leander sideways. Whatever it was he wouldn't let it through. The dreamsmiths turned to stare at him, their faces wrought with panicked uncertainty. Fear of him or fear of Taren?

I won't let you through. I don't know what you are but you won't control me.

~*You already allowed it once. You must do so again. I am not an enemy to you.*~

It sent him memories. Black and white monstrosities, each filled with anguish and destruction. Houses crumbling by clawed hands, flesh ripped and blood coating the air. This thing wasn't an enemy? Then Leander's body remembered the actions as he watched. He was there, front and centre, viewing helplessly through his own eyes. His tether to reality began to fray. Had he done that? Why did he feel like he'd been there, like he'd been the one to do it? To crash through the slums throwing out unbridled chaos. A trick, it had to be. A lie.

'This wasn't me. I didn't do this. I wouldn't...'

~*You did. We did it together. We have to find the truth, but you stopped me to find this conduit instead. You need to let me through again. We need to kill the liar.*~

'No, no stop it.' Slumped at a strange angle from his chains he forced his eyes to stay open and his mind to be present. Fighting the black puddles that seeped around the edge of every thought, looking for a way through. His muttering didn't go unnoticed.

'Forgemaster this man is-'

'Quiet. Taren is my main concern, I'll get to that later.'

The voices blurred around Leander and he forced himself to watch, to look up at Taren who stared right back but couldn't truly see him. The voice within Leander pushed more memories to the surface, more deaths, more chaos, more destruction. His body shivered with increasing violence until he bucked in his chains and he heard himself scream, writhing in the sensation of committing such actions.

How could he let this happen? Let his body be used? Was he a hollow? Had it happened because he hadn't collected his dream? He couldn't collect it, but it hadn't disappeared. It was inside of Taren. It still existed. The fit reached its peak and through the waves of agony a voice cut through clear and bright.

'Leander. Leander. He's dying, help him!' The voice was

fraught and patchy from screaming, but Leander clung to it. Remembering its tone and noting its concern. Taren. He used it like a rope to haul himself back. To take control again. His arm ached from the odd angle he lay at. Pins and needles spread as he hung inches from the floor gasping for breath. 'Leander, are you alright? Why are you all just standing there, help him!'

'Enough!' The Forgemaster's voice boomed over Taren's with ease. 'The smiths will deal with him once I've assisted you. You have no idea the danger you're putting everyone in.' The Forgemaster widened his stance and brought both arms to his sides.

Leander had never seen dreamsmiths perform any of their tricks. His heavy lids pulled themselves down but he fought to watch with every feeble ounce of energy he could sequester from his body.

Glowing bracelets knitted around the Forgemaster's arms and turned in conflicting circles. With a series of motions and gestures he thrust one arm forwards and it stopped inches from Taren's face. An intricate circle painted itself a little larger than the hand that commanded it, and the fragments of the dream that had wandered began to meander back. The tendrils receded, crawling back into the pocket on Taren's face as each flake of his skin pieced itself back together and joined with its neighbour. The dark hum left the air and for a few seconds only silence rang out.

Taren's head dropped forward, limp and unassisted, but he murmured and struggled against his bonds. Still alive. The Forgemaster, looking drained, turned to plant a stern glare on Leander and took a few steps back. He shrank under it, hoping the man would look anywhere else.

'Take him to the holdings since he can't control himself properly. There's a lot we need to find out about him, he's a first. Firsts are dangerous. The cells will better hold him, but don't bother guarding him. More help is needed up above in the slums, no thanks to this creature.' His grey eyes glinted like steel and Leander battled the shame that blanketed him. A blanket quickly torn to shreds by the irate, hissing whispers of the hollow inside him.

'Wait.' Leander almost choked on the hoarseness of his own voice. Right then, if letting the hollow take control would have bought him some cold water, he'd let it happen in a heartbeat. 'Wait, I need to know why. Why I can still hear it. Why I came here to find him. He called to me.'

All eyes were on Leander. Eyes filled with disdain. When the Forgemaster spoke, Leander shuddered from the cold.

'Hear what? Taren called to you?'

'A resonance led me here. A beacon. It pulls at my core, my soul. He said he has my dream. Is there anyway to recover it?.'

He considered Leander for a moment, then turned to look at Taren. 'Yours is the dream he took?'

Leander nodded, gritting his teeth to hear it spoken aloud. Spoken into existence yet again.

'If that's so, then you share a bond with him. The dream will continue to pull you to it so long as Taren lives. Your paths are irrevocably crossed. As for the solution, after what you've done you've no right to hear of it.' The Forgemaster threw a warning over his shoulder to his subordinates. 'Tell no one of what you've seen here, understand?' Every smith nodded obediently and took a few seconds to muster

259

themselves to action. 'Take him.'

Protests would be futile, and Leander's body weighed heavy as they dragged him away. The venom in the Forgemaster's words was potent and immobilising. Each word a poison dart in a different limb. He'd never felt so... beneath. Beneath hope. Beneath compassion. Beneath humanity.

He tried to reach out to Taren, to call for him, but his energy was spent. He would find him. He'd done it once, and he could do it again. Even if the link that bound them was one of a shattered future. Of theft and the death of a life unlived. The tenuous bond to its thief was the only proof the dream ever existed at all. That was something worth holding on to. A vacuous premonition gripped him. One that said he had nothing else left.

35

Far Under the Dreamforge

A sturdy force yanked Taren out of the depths of himself. The pieces stopped drifting away and were clicking back together, though he didn't feel solid and the resulting headache rolled in waves. Even when he opened both eyes, the left one remained black instead of painting the world in its twisted iridescent visions, and the right only showed smudged colours for a few moments. As he focused, the sight that met him thrust him into full cognition. Leander tried to look back down the corridor while being dragged away.

'Leander? Bring him back where are you taking him? He stays with me what are you going to do with him? Hey!'

'Taren!' His heart jumped and he gasped. He hadn't noticed the person standing directly in front of him, several paces away. 'Quieten down until I'm done. Stop with your demands.' The Forgemaster's voice had an undeniable authority that cowed Taren into unexpected submission. He faced Taren, arms raised and shining hoops rotating around his forearms. Forgemaster Clayton was directing his skills at him? Trying to calm himself Taren began to feel it, the flaked pieces of his face shifting slightly and fitting back together.

What had he done? Used some kind of power without knowing it? There had been such confusion mixing with fear and anger and questions. So many questions. The memory of Leander's face surfacing from inside the hollow made him shudder. The Forgemaster focused in his impeccable way. Grey eyes boring into Taren so intensely that he couldn't hold contact with them, even though he was being looked through, not looked at.

The next few minutes passed in silence until finally the Forgemaster lowered his arms and took a few deep breaths. His tone stern and agitated as he threw his words into the quiet.

'You got your demand, I'm here. As for where they are taking the man who broke in, he'll be put somewhere to keep him safe from himself and others. You need to be more careful, Taren. Screeching those demands like you did and not controlling your mind… it's a basic mistake. One it seems you can't afford while being fused with a dream. You were a danger to yourself and others just now. It could have been fatal.'

The words sank in like ink through tissue. A pit crumbled into existence in Taren's stomach, nibbled by the shame of being scolded by the head of the Dreamforge. He couldn't quell the raging storm of questions, but reminded himself that he didn't know the Forgemaster's true position. Not yet.

In an instant the Forgemaster's tone changed and his expression filled with concern. It was disarming and unexpected, but nostalgic. So many days he'd seen that kind face move among the junior smiths and share its wisdom.

262

So many years it had watched over Taren's own progress, encouraging and stern in equal measure. Taren couldn't bring himself to suspect him properly. Each drip of doubt sizzled away on a bed of almost lifelong respect. The Forgemaster took a step closer, motioning to reach out but catching himself.

'I wish you hadn't run that day. I might have been able to help you if you'd stayed. Before it became so... embedded. I felt the depth of the bond just now. Why did you flee?'

'I... don't know. I was scared, I suppose. I had no idea what I'd done, only knew that I'd broken the rules and turned my back on my training. It hadn't sunk in. When you asked them to restrain me I panicked. I thought I would be punished.'

'Punish you? I asked them to restrain you to help you in case of something like this. It was an accident, Taren, I could tell that much. But I wasn't sure what the effects of the dream would be. Whether it would fuse properly or leak out to latch on to others. I would not have punished you in such an unprecedented situation. What happened that day well... it's never happened before.' His eyes darkened for just a moment, but Taren didn't miss it. 'Where did you go?'

'I don't remember. It's all quite blurry. I'm sorry, I didn't know what else to do. I ended up near the exit to the inner city at the southern gate and I think that's where I collapsed.'

'What happened after that?'

Taren left out exactly who had helped him in terms of Leander, Corryn and Fion, but the look on the Forgemaster's face when hearing the events that took place in Taren's own kitchen was one of thinly veiled outrage. Was it proof he hadn't ordered the actions of those smiths? The Forgemaster continued to pale as Taren spoke, particularly as he recounted the strange visions the dream and hollows had showed him.

'I've struggled with everything I've learned. Not knowing if it's true or not or if… or if you were responsible for the behaviour of Ferron and Edwyn. For the taming of the hollows and why there are so many here. I assume we are under the Dreamforge. I just… need some answers.' Taren's heart thundered. He'd just accused the Forgemaster of potentially being behind a threat on his life and told him all he knew. Would he get the answers he so desperately needed? Or would he meet another dead end?

'I just want to know… whether everything I've ever believed in and worked for is a lie.' Everything bubbled around the edge of his heart, waiting to either fall or fizz. If the Forgemaster wouldn't answer, was he in on the corruption? If he did… what would he say? All the possibilities that could unfold in the space of one response gently jostled Taren while he waited.

The Forgemaster stood perfectly still for a number of minutes. Processing everything he'd heard. Finally he let out a weary sigh and began to pace back and forth after lowering the hood of his cloak. He passed glances at Taren as he paced, analysing, battling with himself. But over what? His demeanour was composed, and yet somehow disturbed. What questions was he asking himself, what was he considering?

'You've been through a lot, and I'm sorry for that.' He took several sure strides forward and released the cuffs chaining Taren to the pillar. 'I think it's time, given what you know, that I shared the truth with you.'

***

Taren's wrists ached and itched as he continued walking in silence behind the Forgemaster. Using a sleeve of his robe he absently cleaned away the blood that still caked one side of his face from Leander's hollow hands. What was he supposed to feel?

Part of him had desperately, and perhaps foolishly, hoped that there would be no truth to tell. Better to believe that the dream had tainted his mental stability over accepting that anything about the Dreamforge had been kept hidden. The thing he'd devoted his life to, the duty he'd performed with such fervour and passion. He fumbled with all the pieces of everything he'd come to know, or thought he'd known, and everything the dream and hollows had shown him. How did it all fit together? Which bits were real, and which were just nonsense? Please let it all be nonsense.

The Forgemaster walked with purpose and comfort in the large empty corridors. The underground portion of the Dreamforge was vast, but why was it needed at all and why keep it a secret? The scale of the rooms they passed made Taren feel small and lost, despite the layout not being too complicated overall. The main corridor continued to branch off into other halls.

Then the Forgemaster took a turn into a much smaller corridor. The opening was more subtle, the entrance lined with two far more ornate and dainty pillars. The corridor leaned around to one side and, when they came out into the resulting chamber, an archway opened its maw to reveal a curving staircase. Another level. How deep did the

265

Dreamforge go?

The stairs continued down much deeper than Taren could have imagined. He fought with himself. Keep following and get some answers. Leave now and flee again. The two thoughts cycled and clashed, and uncertainty leaked from him and smeared along the walls as he trudged on without a word. His defunct eye had covered itself again, and every few steps he extended his left arm to touch the smooth walls, not trusting his half-useless vision in the growing dark.

The corridor spat them out in another chamber, but Taren halted upon noticing the immense set of doors that loomed in front of him. They were carved from the stone. He could stare for days and not take in every detail. More crystal lamps sprung to life at the Forgemaster's command and unveiled new details with each flicker.

In the depiction that ran across both doors a great tree wrapped its roots around spires that grew from the ground around it. There were things Taren recognised and things he didn't. The dreamsmiths' crafting hammers hanging from the tree's branches, and the slender figures of hollows gnawing at its base. There wasn't the time or capacity to decipher what it meant as the Forgemaster turned to him.

'Are you quite certain that you want to know, Taren? Truth is not always a good thing, and it is not always something that leads to reconciliation. Sometimes it leads to more destruction. You can't choose to ignore it once you know it, so think carefully.'

Taren fought to keep his breath steady. Did he want this? To find out what lay behind that door and whatever brought such a serious expression to the Forgemaster's face.

His response left him in a feeble rasp.

'Yes.'

'So be it.' The Forgemaster placed a hand on a plate that crossed the seam of the doors, and the faint glow of magic added to the crystal lamplight. One door swung inward, slow under its own bulk, and stopped with enough room for three people to walk in shoulder to shoulder. Even then it wasn't halfway open.

The slightest hesitation stalled his mentor and then, with a deep breath, he stepped in. 'Follow me.' Despite all the reassurances Taren cloaked himself with, nothing could have prepared him for the sight that waited inside the doors far under the Dreamforge.

The space that opened up was the largest yet. More of a cavern than the others, which were more refined and carved with a craftsman's care. These walls were raw, jagged rock. The ceiling towered above them and yawned with chilly darkness. Fewer lamps lit the space, but they were hardly needed.

Great twisted roots of turquoise crystal burst through all around the cavern's ceiling and snaked groundward, plunging into what looked like circular wells built up from the floor. They looked so similar to the forging stations, but this was certainly not the forging floor. How far down did they continue, and where were they coming from? The spire roots should have been far above, much larger and tethered to the forges. Their gentle light glittered in the dark and painted everything with an unmistakeable sheen. The colour of the spires.

A hum stirred within Taren, the same as the one he experienced when standing close to a forge. These crystal buttresses were so large and intertwined that he couldn't see around them, nor could he see the other end of the cavern. It just reached on, stretched, broken up by the great trunks.

'What... what is this place?' His voice echoed like scrappling rodents in the quiet.

'The cavern stretches across the underneath of the entire city and slums.' The Forgemaster began to walk, and Taren couldn't help but follow. 'It is the base of the Dreamforge, and these are the true roots of the spires.' Above him Taren imagined the great crystal towers glinting in the sunlight. It never occurred to him that they may have had deeper roots, always believing they sprung from the forges that dreamsmiths used every day. 'Only I have access to this place. You are the first smith in the history of the Forge to see it.'

Any words Taren could have said were snatched away into the shadows of the vast space. The roots of the spires themselves. They ran so deep. Their scale even more grand knowing that all this time he had perhaps only seen branches of the spires rather than their bases.

They closed in on the nearest well. Circular tubes of stone with carved borders wide enough to sit on. They were still a short walk away, and yet his eyes flickered over the root and he stopped. Grounded by the deception his eyes were showing him.

'It's... it's moving?'

The Forgemaster didn't turn, but continued on and beckoned for Taren to follow. A pulsing squirm. A great, sedated serpentine creature beginning to wake and test its muscles.

'What that hollow showed you... wasn't a lie. The

268

binding ceremony has a different purpose than that we present to the dreamers who come for their stones. Only a small, trusted handful of senior smiths are aware of that.'

Taren's mind pulled him back to the vision the hollow had passed on to him as he'd stood chained to the stone pillar.

'The binding ceremony is used to link people to their dreamstone, yes, but it has another purpose. We use it to extract hollows from people. Everyone has one nestled within them, part of our job is to cleanse them before they have a chance to awaken.'

'Everyone has a hollow?' Leander's face pushed out of the black tar of the hollow's body again in Taren's mind. 'How? I thought they only manifest when someone refuses a calling.'

'It is not a complete fabrication. Hollows will awaken in people who don't obey their calling because they have not been extracted and gain too much power over the person they inhabit. We do this to protect them, but do not wish to scare them. So the hollows were made into a tale, their truth veiled and twisted to ensure that people are less likely to ignore their call and become hollows themselves.'

Taren's stomach swam. Was there a hollow inside him even now? 'Does that mean... do I...' The words jumbled in his mouth like broken twigs.

'No. Yours was removed when you took your oath as a smith. We can't have hollows so near the spires, nor can we have dreamsmiths with potential for instability. You needn't worry.'

Thank the gods. To his own shame a wave of relief rushed through, but only briefly. How could he stand there being relieved after seeing Leander's plight? Surely he wouldn't be judged for being glad of his own safety for a second, and Fion's as well. She'd never become a hollow, and nor would he. As for Leander… no one had said there was no way to help him. Not yet.

'What do you do with them?'

'Some we keep to study while we can, as you saw on your way in. With no way to eradicate them, we can only attempt to manage and understand them. Use them like the unfortunate resource they are. For hollows have another, more important purpose.' He gestured to the edge of the well surrounding the root. A strange spark danced in the older man's eyes as Taren stepped forward. Did the fear show on his face as obviously as it coursed around his body?

Down in the well the root met the ground and anchored itself, but all around it hollows piled together. Some were half-absorbed by the root, their torsos protruding from the crystal while their faces morphed into pained expressions. Others clawed at the walls of the well as tendrils crept out to consume them.

The further up Taren's eye travelled, the more the hollows were buried in the crystal until only impressions of despairing expressions could be seen sketched on the turquoise surface. It was… eating them? Absorbing them? Taren's gut reared and he turned aside, steadying himself on the edge of the pit.

'What is this?' He swallowed the saliva building in his mouth.

The Forgemaster looked the root up and down, sadness tinting his expression as he took in the sight of the hollows. 'It's their other purpose. The function of the hollows and

270

their counterparts is to fuel the spire.'

'Counterparts?'

'That's right.' He spoke with such calm. The kind that was forced because it masked a fracture. 'They must be alive while they are integrated. If they merge with it while dead, it will corrupt the spire and begin to kill it. But hollows cannot survive indefinitely while detached from the body and attached to the spire.' The more he went on, the more prominent the wobble in his voice became. 'The problem is that integration can take either days or months depending on the hollow. They need to be kept alive to act as sustenance. That's when their counterparts are called here. When their hollow shows signs of dying.'

Taren's mind buzzed as he searched for meaning in the Forgemaster's words. He forced himself to look down the shaft again, fighting the rocking of the room as it tipped on a turntable. His breath left him when he saw them. Scattered on the faraway floor of the well like empty promises. A carpet of them. Shattered and dull.

'Why are those dreamstones down there? You can't mean…'

A despairing weight creased the Forgemaster's face. His shoulders drooped suddenly as if being crushed from above. 'Yes Taren, you've figured it out. To keep a hollow alive, we feed its host body to it. They are summoned here via the dreamstones that they hold so dear. This is their final destination. Despite the unfortunate nature of it all, it's quite the necessary and efficient system.'

Taren's knees buckled at the realisations as they swirled and thrashed in his head, sparking and clawing at each other while they reluctantly merged together. He leaned to the side of the well and held his sloshing stomach.

No. No it wasn't true. How could it be? All the dreams he'd crafted, all the skill and passion he'd put into them. The smiles on the faces of the dreamers as they clutched their dreamstones at long last, and wept as they believed they were headed for a better life. The loved ones that were broken but acted overjoyed when their family or lovers or friends disappeared because they knew they'd be free. All a lie? A fabrication? The dreamsmiths, him included, had been binding people to their deaths.

He'd played a hand in feeding people to their own hollows, all for the sake of powering the spire? It wouldn't knit together. It slipped. An acrid mess of toxic sludge pumping through his brain and veins. As he met the eyes of the man he'd once respected with all his heart, a blanket of red descended and stoked Taren's dishevelled core with a vicious, writhing flame.

36

Too Many to Count

Taren's knees wobbled in their joints again and he fell, one leg folded beneath him and his forearm came to rest on the other. So many images swam through each other and the world blurred in tandem with his ragged breaths. The Forgemaster's words echoed and looped. When Taren could finally push sounds up his throat and past his tongue, he spoke.

'A necessary and efficient system? Is that what you call this?' He couldn't even look at the head of the Dreamforge, focusing instead on keeping himself as upright as he could. The Forgemaster said nothing, but a forlorn smile dressed his face. Taren swallowed back bile. 'You can stand there and admire this system without any shame? Are you proud of it? In giving people hope only to snatch it away at the last second and take their lives along with it?' A wave of nausea lurched, the tang of acid bubbled deep in his throat. Take a few breaths. In, and out.

'It was necessary for things to be done this way.'

'Why? How can you possibly justify this? People travel here from all over the world. They walk for kilometres, days, starving and exhausted, they all flock here to come and wait at the foot of the spire. They hope for a better life, and you have the gall to stand in your high tower and look down on them, shelling out promises into the hands of broken people like confetti and laughing as you watch them catch it.'

'You wanted the truth and you have it. You asked for answers and you've got them. This is how it must be.' A warning countenance spread over the Forgemaster's face, his whole body tightening against every word Taren spoke. But he couldn't stop himself, neither from looking away nor from continuing to speak.

'Who would be satisfied with this? Choose this?' Taren thrust a hand at the well, not wanting to lean over and see the drained writhing of the hollows again. 'Are you? Are you pleased with how things are?'

'I understand the necessity of the system and will protect it for as long as I live.' A rehearsed, lifeless response of self-justification. Did this man feel nothing for what he'd done? What he'd forced others to do. And Fion. Fion would be utterly, desperately crushed by even half of these so-called truths.

'I... I respected you. I thought you acted for the good of the people. That you cared about them and wanted to see them happy. Wasn't that why you took in more smiths? Trained more people to help bring more dreams to those living in the slums. The dreamsmiths are supposed to work for that.'

He finally managed to glare at the Forgemaster and found himself faced with a complicated expression that he couldn't place. For a moment the Forgemaster looked old beyond his years. Singularly weary and crumbling. A fleeting moment, one in which his heart begged him to reach out and take the old man by the hands. To ask him to explain it all. To help him understand, and search for the true reason for this trickery. Instead a defensive harshness pooled in the Forgemaster's eyes.

'You are so naïve, Taren. I knew you would be suited to being a smith because of these gentle ideals you are so fiercely proud of. Those that were once mine as well. So eager to assist and act for others that you're willing to believe anything in order to achieve that. That's why you were all chosen, for your inclination for learning and your respect of authority and knowledge.

'I can no longer afford to be gentle. All those options are spent and scattered. I needed people who would learn with a hunger so consuming that the knowledge taught would never be questioned. Those who would take the words of the Dreamforge to their hearts, and act solely in their name with the same altruistic pride you're displaying right now, and never be any the wiser. I never expected that you'd break the link to an unfinished stone.

'But remember, as you shout these ideals at me and call my humanity into question without knowing all the facts, that you have a part in this too. Your willingness to be indoctrinated into the Dreamforge was a willingness to put aside your own humanity and learn how to take lives. You were so proud of it every time. Moreso perhaps than any other dreamsmith I have yet to train.'

A jerking shiver passed through Taren's body and rippled again and again. His wide eye glistened and his mouth hung open as the thoughts circled. Each dream he remembered crafting and handing to the recipient with joy and fierce pride added to the crushing gravity around him.

Their ecstatic faces turned pale and twisted as hollows gnawed on their arms and necks. There was nothing left of them, and he was to blame. He hauled himself into an unsteady stance, face slack, heart racing.

'Had I known I would never have-'

'You would absolve yourself of responsibility? What fair treatment is that to those you've killed?' The words rang like clanging bells. Taren had killed. He'd brought death to so many. Too many to count. A great clod of shame dropped into him and festered. He didn't know the number. He didn't know how many dreams he'd made and how many lives he'd destroyed. Was he so arrogant that he couldn't even keep count? So mindless that he would have continued to kill for his whole life with a smile on his face and pride in his heart?

'I know it's difficult for you, and I wish you could have kept those noble, gentle ideals. But I can help you. I can explain and everything will become clear. It would be such a relief for someone else to know everything. All of it. To have someone who understands, if you'd just let me.' The Forgemaster took a step towards Taren and that triggered him into action. He stumbled back, body tense with revulsion. He had to get out. Back to the surface. He knew this man once, trusted him even, but not anymore.

'Stay back! Don't come near me. I don't need your help, I don't need anything from you. You do this for yourself, such lengths you'd go to for the position you hold. To have people travel from all directions to gather at the foot of your castle and turn their faces to you in hope. To respect and admire you... like I did.

'You're nothing but a spider grinning at the centre of its

web. Offering food for your prey and wrapping them in your tangle of lies and deceit. You're not human, you can't be. What are you that you'd play such games?'

Another step forward. 'Please Taren, don't run again. I brought you here in confidence, but I have things I have to safeguard. Don't make it more difficult than it needs to be. Don't force my hand.'

'I said stay back!' With hitching breaths Taren shoved himself away from the well's edge and ran in the first direction he stepped. Where could he go so far below the city apart from deeper into the belly of the Dreamforge? Further into the Forgemaster's domain.

Another root sparkled in the gloom and he pushed himself towards it. His legs strained through a swamp of building dread. They couldn't all look the same, that had to be the only tainted root. They couldn't all be full of the dead, the scale was too large, it would be too devastating.

The calm footsteps of the Forgemaster trailed behind his erratic, stumbling run. Taren's waist burned against the edge of the next stone pit as he leaned over to see the base of the root. The same show of writhing hollows twitched in various stages of absorption. The nausea twitched again, more dangerously this time. The acid in his stomach tumbled. Rolling waves on a violently storming sea.

When I asked for the truth, pushed for it, demanded it... this isn't what I wanted to find. How can this be how things are? How can something so inhuman be happening right beneath the city? Right under everyone's noses. I wanted to help, that's why I became a dreamsmith. I wanted to show people their hope wasn't misplaced or futile, instead I... I've proven that to them and worse. I did it with a smile in my heart. What does that make me? That I would smile while binding

277

them to such a horrid fate. I'm sorry… all of you I'm so sorry.

He couldn't face himself. Leaning over the edge his vision blurred. A leather belt of despair tightened around his chest, crushing his lungs more with every breath. A hand came to rest on his shoulder and he shivered with disgust yet made no move to shake free of it.

'I know you're struggling with this, and I understand. I hope you can give me another chance to explain why things have to be the way they are. I need you to be reasonable here, please Taren. I've trusted you and shown you what you asked, but we still have to safeguard this. It cannot become public knowledge. I feel no joy in having to enact the alternative option. But I will… if I have to.' The seconds slowed. Stretched. Frayed at the edges. The pressure in the hand changed, becoming a grip. Taren turned his head and caught a glint of sharp blue crystal in the Forgemaster's other hand as the arm drew back. A dagger, poised to strike.

37

A Small Sliver of Kindness

Leander fought with a sad irony upon noticing that his cell was more lavish and better constructed than the houses many people had lived in for decades in the slums. The stone was of high quality, and the gate of opulently patterned metal. The swirls and lines not dissimilar to the patterns on the city gates. A bench of polished wood, wide enough to double as a bed, lined one of the side walls, but Leander had no desire to sit on the cushioned seat.

The cell was perhaps even more spacious than some homes in the southwest quarter, but that might be pushing into exaggeration. He sat against the back wall, watching the swirling dark of the shadows outside, and a blanket of loneliness surrounded him. Why would the Dreamforge even need a row of holding cells? He knew so little about the place he'd hoped to visit for his whole life.

His mind struggled to catch up, still blurry from whatever the hollow had done to him to secure and then relinquish its control. It pulsed somewhere in the corners of his thoughts, reminding him that his body no longer belonged to him alone.

Leander's encounter with the Forgemaster shattered any

illusions he'd had of the man. Always someone stern and serious, because who wouldn't be serious with such a vast job to do, but he'd never truly imagined him as dismissive or so cold.

Then there was the most confusing part. The Forgemaster's words. Admittedly Leander hadn't been able to pay the most rapt attention while fighting the urge to pass out, but he remembered. Taren came to mind. So many flashes of the man he'd only met recently, yet so many different shades of him to recall. Hurt, grateful, devastated, broken, angry and disintegrating. Still, Leander had his answer. He was only drawn to Taren because of the dream fused to his body. The strange longing to be around him, the heightened senses in his presence, the thinking about him when he wasn't even there. It was all the dream's doing. Trying to pull the attention of its owner. Reaching out to be collected. Claimed.

A dull ache started to spread through Leander's legs where they sprawled flush to the stone floor and he shifted position. Was it a relief to have heard the Forgemaster explain? Ever since Melynda left Leander hadn't even thought of finding someone else. Her betrayal had taken something from him, something he'd once freely given and now protected fiercely. He had Corryn for company and they had their work, their fields, and that would be enough. Wanting more only lost you more. There'd been so many things he'd wanted for himself and Melynda. All discarded without warning or care.

What a fool he'd been. Wondering if Taren was stirring such feelings up again irritated him the most. He'd been exposed to a bright and piercing spotlight when all he wanted was peace and darkness. Taren wasn't to be blamed though. It was all to do with the dream. Riddling Taren's body and spreading. That, at least, was what he told himself. Leander was drawn to the smith because of the dream, and only because of that. Not because of Taren's kindness or sincerity. Or because of how strongly he felt things and empathised with others. Or how much he treasured his connections. Or because of the gentle gaze of that ice blue eye. No. None of that.

A sigh rushed out of Leander as he contemplated everything that had happened.

How did I even get here? There's just a pocket of emptiness between being at home and finding Taren. The smiths said I'd caused destruction and chaos but… how is that possible? Were those visions real?

As if being called they surfaced again. The black claws tore through clothing and flesh, brick and stone, wood and mortar.

~You cannot hide from what we've done.~

'Who's there?' The whisper was close. Far too close to be external. Leander knew that but the question left his mouth anyway. The voice was familiar, insidious, and deep within him.

~We must find the truth and free ourselves from the clutches of the liars. Let me out.~

His body shivered violently, doused with a sheen of cold sweat in seconds. 'No. No way. If you really caused so much harm, I won't let you out again. I came here to find Taren, not to kill dreamsmiths.' The thought of Taren gave him strength, though he didn't know why. Right, the dream. His chest constricted as he thought of the state he'd found

281

Taren in. Bound, fragmenting, broken and desperate. Had the Forgemaster managed to save him?

~The liars all deserve to die.~

'No. Taren is… different. He's kind. He took my dream, but not intentionally. I should never have given him up. I didn't know that throwing him out would fetch hollows to him.'

Corryn's teasing voice came to mind, asking why his opinion of Taren had changed all of a sudden and Leander fought off a blush at the imaginary taunt. Then his heart flipped. He searched his memories, combing through them carefully. He couldn't find her. When had he last seen Corryn? Right before he'd become… whatever had taken over him? A fraught panic rushed and lurched.

Is she OK? You didn't hurt her did you? There's no way I'd hurt Corryn. Why can't I remember where she is? She should be at home, waiting. She'll be worried sick. We argued… did I say anything I shouldn't have?

The eerie whisper gave no answer, which did nothing to calm his unease. His memories weren't working properly, flickering and dashing around like leaves in a whipping wind. Why couldn't he think straight, was it because of this thing inside him? Was he really a danger to himself and others now? The Forgemaster had called him a creature. Just what had he become and why?

He knew the answer, but dared not accept it. Everyone who came to the city was soon indoctrinated with the stories. Some knew of them before they even came for their calling. A curse, some mutation saved only for those who deigned to ignore the gift the spire offered. He'd just never imagined it would be like this. A solid entity, one so clear and distinct from himself. So powerful and vindictive.

He had ignored his calling, but not wilfully. He'd intended to go back right after taking Taren home, little did he know the call was out of reach regardless. His chance had been taken from him and yet now, having let his anger out, he no longer despised Taren for it. No one would choose the affliction Taren carried. What use could Leander be from a prison slowly descending into some kind of tangle of duplicity?

A light patter of footsteps drew his attention to the wrought-iron gate of his cell. He pressed himself harder against the wall in preparation. Who was coming for him? At the sound of his shuffling the steps halted. Silence descended again. Maybe he'd imagined it? In a place so empty, it wasn't unreasonable to think that darkness could play with the mind. Who knew what creatures or critters might make their home in the gloom.

He pushed with his aching legs and forced himself to stand. Taking step and after cautious step to the front of the cell to stare out into the blank hall before him. Something weighted his steps, dragged his spirit down. Something he should have known or recognised and yet didn't. A piece of him was missing, but he would have to find it later.

The light of the crystal lamp offered a small halo of respite from the dark of the hall. His eyes stung as he tried to focus them. Another shuffle from his left drew the gaze of his senses. Someone was there. A lingering presence drifted closer. They were so still that were he not already suspicious of his surroundings, they would have gone unnoticed.

'Who are you?' he asked the darkness, and to his

surprise a slender, robed figure slid into the glow of the lamp from around a pillar. They'd gotten so close without being seen. The purple of the robe was doused with the light and he stumbled backwards, instantly guarded. A dreamsmith.

'Guess I wasn't as quiet as I thought.' There was no malice in the voice. It took him a moment to become accustomed to the lightness of the tone. 'Sorry if I creeped you out a bit there. Truth be told I'm more than a bit lost but given your current...' the smith took in the sight of Leander in his cell, 'situation... I'm sure you can't be of help. What's your name?'

'Who are you?'

'I'm just passing through, I'm looking for a friend. Have you seen a dreamsmith down here with an affliction on his face?'

Leander's heart jumped. 'You're looking for Taren?'

'You know him?'

'I... I came here to find him as well. I'm Leander. I helped him after he ran from the Forge but I owe him an apology. It's my fault that the smiths found him.'

'Leander. Yeah, I think he mentioned you. Thank you for what you did for him.' There was true sincerity in the voice. 'Besides, it's his own fault, not yours. I told him to keep a low profile but did he listen? The hells he did.' The head under the hood shook back and forth with disapproval. 'Seems we have ourselves a troublesome friend in common. I'm Fion. Here. Drink this, you look like you need it.' A wooden bottle was offered through the bars. Leander hesitated.

'It's just water, I promise. If you've helped my friend

284

and saved his life, then I've no reason to harm you.' Driven by thirst he reached for the offering. The water was lukewarm but most welcome.

'Thank you, Fion. I think he mentioned you as well. When he first woke up after I found him.' Leander passed the bottle back to its owner.

'At least he didn't leave either of us out. Where is he now, do you know? Did you see where he was taken?'

'I'm sorry, but no. They removed me first and brought me here. I didn't see what happened he was... in a bit of a state.' A reassuring and gentle hand came to rest on his upper arm.

'He's nearly always in a state to be honest. Thank you. I'd love to know why you're looking for him too, but I have to go. I'll do my best to find him and take him somewhere safe, though the smiths will all be coming back to the Forge soon...' she trailed off, a flicker of worry tightening across her mouth for a split second. 'If I can, I'll come back for you as well. Sit tight, OK?' A warm smile beamed at him.

Leander nodded in bewilderment at finding a small sliver of kindness in the whirlwind of the past few days. Before he could offer his thanks Fion had slipped off into the darkness. Hopefully she'd be able to find Taren and get him to safety.

38

Not Blind Anymore

Upon catching sight of the dagger in the Forgemaster's hand, Taren whirled in the tight space between his attacker and the edge of the stone well and grabbed his mentor's forearm just below the wrist, locking his own elbow out. The hand gripping his shoulder was knocked away, and Taren kept it in his peripheral vision at all times. A mild surprise danced across the Forgemaster's face for a beat, and then faded. Yet he didn't make any further advance. Their eyes met and a sadness stirred within Taren. One mirrored in the old man's eyes.

'You'd really do this?' Taren hated the waver in his own voice. 'You'd kill someone you mentored personally from a young age? One of your own? You were the one who met me at the entrance to the Dreamforge when I received my calling. You were the one who thought I had such promise, and now you stand and aim a knife at my back?'

The Forgemaster's brows pinched together. He struggled to keep a neutral expression on his face, his throat working against something uncomfortable. They stood, unmoving, for the longest string of seconds in Taren's life.

'I don't want this. Truly. I'd never harm you without

cause. You're a student, a colleague, a brother to Fion. I need to keep this information contained, but I have a feeling you won't grant me that.'

'You'd be right.'

'Then you force my hand. For the good of the people of the city. For your own good as well. I'm so sorry.' A slight change in forward pressure from the Forgemaster caught his attention. In response he flattened his foot against the side of the stone well and pushed, knocking his mentor to the ground with a harsh shove. His attempt to stay standing came too late, and Taren was over him, one knee pushing relentlessly into the crook of the arm holding the dagger.

An unusual sound reached Taren as his knee pressed into the elbow. A twisting scrapple like crackling glass. What else did the Forgemaster's sleeves conceal? A groan escaped the mentor as his back flattened against the floor.

'What's all this for? Why are you killing all these people?'

A quiet scoff emerged from deep in the Forgemaster's throat. 'You could never understand. You don't want to. You've already made it clear you have no time nor space for my words.'

'How many others are in on this? How many know about it?'

'See, you weren't you listening. My most trusted colleagues know of the true function of the dream binding and the dreamstones. They know that hollows power the spire, but not that humans are fed to them. All the other smiths are just as clueless as you, and I'll keep them that way. I thought you could be trusted to be reasonable in possession of this knowledge since you sought it so desperately. I was wrong.' Taren shifted the angle of his knee slightly, getting regrettable satisfaction from the wince it caused the Forgemaster, who still gripped the dagger with surprising strength.

'I might be clueless but I'm not blind anymore. No one would be reasonable learning any of this. That you're enslaving people, trapping them with promises and hopes and lies. Deceiving the entire Forge. What do you stand to gain from it? What power or advantage is so important to you that you would become the figurehead of a world such as this? Stealing and paying for that power with lives?'

The questions poured out of Taren again in a slew of vocal vomit. They couldn't be stopped or sated, and he was sick of asking. If they had a taste they'd be bitter and bland, something you'd spit out if you could. A surge flashed through the old man, his grey eyes piercing Taren's with a stone-like anger. He writhed beneath him only once.

'You're still half blind, you fool, and you couldn't be more wrong. My power was given to me. It is mine by right and was bestowed, along with my duty, and I will do whatever it takes to fulfil it. Even if that means taking more lives before the end I will continue to do so. I will keep the system working no matter what.' The burst of energy toppled Taren and he found himself unseated and travelling backwards having been shoved off balance.

The Forgemaster's words hung in Taren's mind in a way that made them impossible to deny as he found himself staring up at the ceiling of the cavern. His opponent had strength, not just as a crafter but physical strength too. A mulch of shuffling sounds drew his dazed attention back to his blue-robed enemy, who was struggling to right himself.

He rolled to his side, still gripping the dagger that seemed implanted in his palm so tightly, and pushed himself up on all fours, breathing rapidly. Fragments sprinkled out of his right sleeve to coat the floor, an iridescent powder that Taren didn't recognise. Where did it come from? What was it?

Panic bubbled and rose to a screeching alarm as the Forgemaster steadied his breathing and made to push up to his knees. Eventually he would stand, and then he would have the upper hand. Taren's body was becoming heavy, exhaustion settling in for the long haul. He had to act now. Yet a moment of despair at the thought of attacking his own mentor again anchored him.

The dagger scraped along the floor, and that despair soon evaporated in to adrenaline. There wasn't much distance between them following their scuffle. Taren could find himself stabbed at any moment if he did nothing. The Forgemaster put his free hand to his head for a brief moment, still on all fours, before glaring at Taren with those cold eyes. A twitch of his mouth indicating he'd start speaking again was all the trigger Taren needed. He didn't want to hear anything more from the man.

He clambered up on to one knee and one arm and swung his other leg around with as much force as he could. The movement was swift and the thud of his boot meeting the side of the Forgemaster's head made him screw his eyes up and grit his teeth. It was over in a moment.

His attacker's neck strained against the blow and he fell flat on his front, the dagger finally coming lose from his hand. The thwack echoed in the empty space and Taren hauled himself up, scrambling over to retrieve the blade and shuffling a few steps backwards. What had he done? He kept the sharp edge firmly between himself and the slumped figure, waiting for the retaliation. None came. Just a vast stillness.

39

The Web of the Spider

Fion had grown alarmingly used to the gloomy halls of the underground, but what she'd said to Leander hadn't been a lie. Lost was an understatement. It was surprising enough that she'd managed to find a way in, but turns out when nearly every other dreamsmith is attending to an emergency and you have the time to snoop properly you can find out a lot.

The door to the nest of twisting corridors had been hidden in plain sight. Or reasonably plain sight anyway. A painting of the city and its spires flanked by two vertical banners of indigo velvet had adorned an alcove on the lowest floor of the Forge. A well-known and quiet area where people often go for reflection. Seems in the chaos that someone hadn't quite been careful enough in closing the door's mechanism, and a small flap of one of the banners had been caught in the stonework.

Eventually she'd figured out how to open it, and had to use her smithing magic to do so. Simply having her crafting bracelets active while pushing the wall had been enough. Even though it was clearly a door, she'd still gasped when it opened. Part of her hadn't wanted to find it. Finding it meant deception. Finding it meant her worries and suspicions were not unfounded. She slipped into the passage and had been lost ever since. Though she patted herself on the back for having the foresight to bring water on her snooping journey.

She would have offered Leander one of the sweet rice cakes she'd also brought along, but in truth she'd stress-eaten those as soon as it became clear how lost she was. Can't solve puzzles on an empty stomach. Fion rounded another corner in the corridor and faced a cross-roads. If she continued straight a set of double doors awaited, small rectangular windows offering a chance to peek inside. Or she could head left or right into more darkness.

The last set of doors she'd walked through had led to a prison wing. She didn't have the time nor inclination to wonder why in the world the Forge needed one of those. But then again she had no idea why all this underground network was needed in the first place. The tunnels were so far underground that any heat simply dissipated, the cold stone leeching it from those who spent too long in their bowels. The chance of another something was better than more corridors of nothing. So she chose the double doors.

Her thoughts briefly flashed back to Leander. He'd seemed concerned about Taren in a genuine way. Who knew Taren had even made friends in the slums. Usually he was the quiet type, a little socially awkward or shy around those he didn't know. Though maybe she was thinking too much about the teenage Taren. The one who'd needed a good boot up the backend to simply go and talk to someone he didn't know. He'd even been quiet around Fion herself at first. Extracting conversation had been more work than laundry day, but once he felt comfortable enough around someone you could barely shut him up.

She huffed and smiled at the thought, reminding herself why she was down there in the first place and honing her focus. There would be other opportunities to roll her eyes at his incessant waffling. She'd find him.

The little windows in the double doors didn't give her much to work with. Another low-lit corridor, what a unique surprise, lay ahead but this one had far more doorways than most of the others she'd seen. One of them had to have something useful in it. Maybe even a map, though that was ridiculous and slightly sarcastic thinking. OK not just slightly, more like horrendously.

Fion listened, searching for any sounds that she wasn't alone, and heard none. She'd snooped that far, might as well snoop a little more. The doors opened easily enough, gliding on their hinges and letting through a rush of warmth that so far had been uncharacteristic of the underground. Why was it so much warmer here than everywhere else?

A tumultuous mix of smells assaulted her nose, all of which shared two distinct qualities. Clean and medical. Stringent odours which reminded her of the sticking bandages the healer in the infirmary had used on her own left side. Some kind of medical storeroom? Kept ambient for the sake of some of the ingredients used in the making of medicines? If so, it would be the least suspicious thing Fion had seen since descending.

She made slow and quiet progress along the warmer corridor, sneaking careful peeks through the small, arched windows set into every wooden door that lined it. Most were empty, though almost all contained beds. Some racks of medicine bottles, others sluice rooms or similar. Then she cast a passing glance into the next window and her entire body tensed.

That room also had a bed, and in it lay a person. One she recognised. One she had been told she wasn't allowed to see. Jacklan.

Her heart started racing against her ribs. They kept him down there the whole time, alone? Isolated. The Forgemaster had mentioned his condition was critical. Her hand hovered above the black metal handle. Would he even want visitors? Maybe he could help her find out what really happened that day with the broken forging station. She pushed the handle down and willed herself into the room.

A strange sort of quiet circled like fog. A particular and peculiar sense of illness. Of otherness. Jacklan's room was clean and warm, and a rack of supplies lined the far wall, but to Fion it felt like a prison. His arms were fastened to the railings of the bed with restraints, the same for his ankles. Her first instinct was to immediately remove them, until she saw his body properly for the first time. Oh, gods.

'Jacklan?'

Treacle-black veins webbed across his skin in places like swarms of spindly spiders. They spiralled out from what looked very suspiciously like bite marks up and down his arms. A thick blanket covered the rest of him, but as the marks vanished inside his short-sleeved robe, they crawled back out around his neck. One or two stretching dangerously close to his face. They seemed to shimmer. More life in the strange markings than in her colleague's eyes, which stared at the ceiling with ferocious intensity. They flicked side to side in minute movements. He was watching or seeing something, but Fion saw nothing.

She could barely wrench her gaze from the rosette of a bite mark on his arm, until she recalled the molten shadows that had set upon him from the broken forge. How they'd writhed over him and how they tore at him. Apparently those shadows had teeth and hadn't been afraid to use them.

'Jacklan? It's Fion. Are you...'

Slowly he turned his head. So slowly that Fion couldn't look away as his eyes dropped to meet hers. One was still a normal eye. The other? A blackened pit with a white ring at its centre and nothing more. Her mouth dried out in an instant.

'You've come.' Jacklan's voice crackled with a carpet of moisture. 'They said you would come for the truth.'

'Wh-who did?'

'They said you would come and here you are. Doesn't this prove it. That I'm not lying or fabricating. Doesn't this prove that the shadows speak the truth. That we should listen?'

'The shadows from the broken forge?'

'Tell me the truth, Fion. Tell me. Was this suffering for nothing? Was I given this truth only to be its death. Will the ones below continue to grow in number. Those consumed continue to die. Will we always be the ones to hand out fates like gods dealing empty judgements. We have to share the truth. We have to.'

'What truth? If you tell me, I'll help you. I will.'

'When the sky is scorched, and the great lid peeled back like the flesh of those who died to make it, the truth will be known by all. They will scream and they will cry and they will curse their ignorance. And then they will die to escape the dark shadows that spring from truth. They will run to avoid the biting teeth. The gnawing pain. They will run to avoid this. I cannot run, I am chained. I must be chained.'

Fion could only stare with a furrowed brow and sorrow-filled eyes. Whatever he was trying to tell her it was taking great effort on Jacklan's part. His face twisted into pained expressions as he spoke. His eyes following phantoms she couldn't see. Not one bit of it made any sense, yet he was so desperately trying to relay something. Its importance sparked all around her, but it couldn't cross into the realm of understanding.

'I'm sorry I don't… I don't understand. I wish I did, but I don't know how to help you. What can I do?'

'There are pieces still missing. They must be gathered. They are the interpreters. They are the key. Not one alone but all together. The truth must spread. They must carry it together. As long as it goes untold so too am I bound to suffer it. Help. Help me shed it. Help me spread it.'

With every word his voice stretched into more and more panic. Rising both in pitch and volume. He wasn't focused on Fion anymore. His wrists strained against his restraints. That's when Fion realised he couldn't even see her. He was rambling. Trapped in some kind of illusion or shadow-fed mire of voices and whispers like the ones from the broken forge. He wasn't Jacklan anymore, not like this. His distress would only build if she stayed. In a heat of shame she came to understand why visitors hadn't been permitted.

She started to back away, swallowing past the lump in her throat. 'I'm so sorry,' she whispered. Over and over with every step. 'I'll get you out of here, Jacklan. I promise. I'll come back for you. I'll help you. But I need help to do that.

I will come back. Just sit tight.'

'Don't leave me here with it. Don't let it take me. The pieces must be collected. Only then can I share the truth that consumes me. That consumes all. The web of the spider is wide and treacherous. We are the dying flies in the soup of its strings!'

The door closed behind Fion but the words echoed in her head. Jacklan thrashed in his bed now, emitting raw shouts and gravelly screams. She hoped he would calm on his own, and guilt ached in every joint she had. Air, she needed air. Air and light and space. She needed Taren. Her caravan of promises was becoming heavy. Taren, Leander, Jacklan. Could she help them all? Could she even find them again?

The strange images Jacklan had conjured spun around Fion's mind as she half-ran out of the infirmary. Just what had happened to him, what was affecting him so? The fact he was down here meant the healers and the senior smiths hadn't been able to cure it. So they didn't know? They had no idea. A shiver jolted through Fion. If they didn't know, then they couldn't help him. If they couldn't help him would he... no. No it wasn't for sure. Nothing was sure.

The smiths wouldn't be held up in the slums forever. Whatever emergency was holding their attention would eventually be brought under control. She was here for Taren. Once she found him they could find their way back to Leander. Then maybe, just maybe, they could find a quiet place and just think. Together. In the light and the fresh air and the space.

40

Impossibly Familiar

Taren's compressed breaths roared in his ears. The taste of iron stained the dry bulk of his tongue thanks to his exertions. His body screamed for water and food, but most of all rest. The temptation to fall back to the stone floor and let sleep drag him down took all his conscious effort to ignore. Instead he sat, shaking and gawping. He'd just attacked the Forgemaster. The head of the Dreamforge. Was he dead or just unconscious? He didn't want to stay and find out.

The dagger shook in his hands, and when he registered that he was brandishing it at someone a violent wringing ripped through his body. He threw it further in to the cavern, watching it bounce and skid away into the dark. The Forgemaster didn't so much as twitch. He looked like a stranger, tainted by his own words and dark threats. It didn't match up with the version of him Taren had always known. The one who had been so kind and amicable with all the junior smiths, and continued to be so even after their graduation into dreamsmiths in their own right. The Forgemaster had always encouraged the asking of questions, an endless font of knowledge, yet now Taren was certain these could not be the answers he'd sought.

He sat with his back against the well for several minutes, waiting to see if the Forgemaster would resume his attack. Or any movement at all. Then a familiar feeling drifted over Taren. It filled his body from top to bottom and sparked like a burning fuse. His gaze wandered from the Forgemaster to the roots of the spire glowing in the dark, out to the direction he flung the dagger, and a loneliness swaddled him. The cavern closed in, squashing and pressing against him, trapping him with the unmoving body of the head of the Forge. He had to move. He had to run. There'd be time to rest later, despite how desperately his body craved it.

His booted feet slapped hard against the stone floor, each footfall amplified in the echoing dark. Every step shouted at him in turn. Get... out... get... out. That simple thought consumed all of his being as he ran. Almost all, but not quite. One tenuous pocket of rational thought remained, though its existence flickered dangerously. Over the shouts of his footsteps, reason tried to prevail.

I do have to get out, and find somewhere to hide, but I have to find Leander first. He was taken to... to... the holdings? It can't have been far from where I was being kept. I need to find him and free him and then we can figure out how to stop this. I can't just do nothing.

The door loomed ahead of him, letting through a sliver of lamplight from the small chamber outside. When he reached it he leaned on the closed door of the two, panting furiously and swaying on the spot. *Breathe. Just breathe. Collect yourself. You can't go out there looking so flustered. You'll be noticed.* He pulled his hood up, wondering how futile it was but doing it anyway.

Over his shoulder the prone form of the Forgemaster lingered, still unmoving in the distance. A deep-seated fear gripped his core but he shook it off. Nothing was certain. He could just be unconscious. The connecting sound of boot on skull echoed in Taren's head, and he fought the nausea again. Nausea and questions, they were unwanted, constant companions. A pain shot through his left eye, pulling the skin tight, and a vision bloomed.

The city and its spires caught the light of the setting sun and in a raised chorus of resonant song the crystal towers began to crumble and crack. They collapsed, shedding dust and rubble through the city and turning black as their last song haunted the residents. Elation filled him that wasn't his own. Was the dream asking him to destroy the spires? Was that how he could break the Forgemaster's hold on the city? Where would he even start? As the vision faded he felt a certainty that it was a starting point, but first he had to find Leander.

***

He needn't have bothered with the hood and all the sneaking. There wasn't a soul about in the curving corridors or sprawling halls. After making his way back up the staircase he'd expected to at least run into other senior smiths, but there was no one. Were they all above-ground dealing with whatever aftermath was left in the slums and the city from the hollow's attack? From… Leander's attack? Still, he couldn't be complacent. He checked every corner, stepping as gently as he could, and forced his mind to remember the way back to the hall where he'd been first held. He could start with heading in the direction the smiths had taken Leander.

When he finally made it back to the hall where he had been chained to a pillar Taren found himself being even more cautious. He moved around each column with his back pressed against the cold stone, peeling around the sides to check the coast was clear and straining his ears for the slightest patter of footsteps or mutter of voices. Nothing. Again. He didn't like it. It was eerie, and far too easy. Yet the Forgemaster had suggested these halls were not widely known to the majority of the dreamsmiths. It wasn't unreasonable, but it was unsettling.

Then someone grabbed him from behind, coming from his blinded side, and covered his mouth, hissing for him to be quiet. Panic flared and he struggled, but stopped when he found his captor wasn't trying to hurt him and the whisper seemed impossibly familiar.

'Shhhh, Taren it's me, alright? You didn't listen to me before but you really should now.'

He spun around and his entire being brimmed with relief so powerful he had to stifle a joyous sob. 'Fion!'

She grinned at him with a mischievous wink. 'You look surprised to see me, you also look a mess. And yes, I'm aware I can't say much but I've been lost down here for hours. Infernal place.' She'd come for him, she was here. A friendly face. An ally. He pulled her into his arms and they shared a brief heartfelt embrace. As they parted concern filled her eyes, and he felt the questions building. Yet his own warnings tumbled out ahead of them.

'We have to get out of here, we can't trust the Forgemaster, he showed me the truth and he's taking lives to power the spire. The dream showed me the spires collapsing so I think we have to find a way to destroy them if we want to stop him-'

'Woah, woah, woah, slow down. You can fill me in later, and trust me I've a fair few things to tell you as well. Stay quiet.' She wasn't listening, and definitely hadn't heard him properly. But maybe she had a point. 'Where have you been, I've been looking for you ever since you left my place? Which you're a damned idiot for, by the way. I heard they'd brought you to the Forge but never knew this place was sitting underneath it.'

'There's more than just this, but I can't explain it now. Just believe me when I tell you that we can't trust the Forgemaster, OK? How are you even down here? We have to get out but first I need to find Leander.'

Fion looked thoughtful for a moment. 'Oh, him? He was looking for you as well.'

'You've seen him, where?'

'I wasn't sure he was real at first. Since when did you know how to make friends without help?'

'Hilarious as always.' Taren rolled his eyes, yet the familiar banter acted like a soothing salve. It was so good to see her again. 'Did you see him?'

'Someone's made a very good friend indeed.' Her smirk brought a heat to Taren's face. Trust Fion to suggest such things in the middle of even this bizarre situation. 'Yes, I saw him.' Taren's heart leapt and Fion smiled. 'I know where he is, if I can remember the way back. Follow me.'

41

Something To Aspire To

Leander's neck ached as it lolled to the side, snapping him out of sleep every time he almost made it to a place of rest. He sat with his back wedged against the corner, hoping that would offer more support, but he only ended up knocking his temple against the stone every few minutes. Each time he shuffled position a plume of musty dust tickled his nose, and he'd lost count of the amount of times he'd sent sneezes ricocheting into the dark. Part of him thought he may be avoiding sleep, and the thin bed of the cell, on purpose. If he succumbed to sleep it might mean losing control again. Becoming that thing again. That was the last thing he wanted.

Something flickered in the silence. Something impossible and wildly indulgent given the situation. The distant resonance brought images of Taren to mind and Leander's heart stuttered in vain hope. The quiet no doubt playing tricks on him yet again. He stood, rubbing the backs of his legs to wake them and encouraged life back into his muscles. If he sat on the floor any longer he'd lose the use of them for good. A shudder travelled across his skin from the change in temperature. He'd built up a meagre bubble of warmth in the corner and immediately regretted standing.

The resonance endured, becoming clearer each minute, but Leander shook his head and fed the silence with words to keep it at bay.

'Stop with your tricks. It can't be him. He was a prisoner too. Besides, why would he come back for me, after what I did? I saved his life but after that my behaviour was nothing to be merited. I've done nothing but push him away. I deserve to be here.' He paced the holding cell slowly, turning everything over in his mind and sinking in to a pit of self-reprimands.

When had he become so closed off and cold and suspicious towards outsiders? Towards people in general. It set him on a path of comparison, in how despite Taren's affliction and despite how he was treated, he remained open and polite in his temperament. He wore his emotions on his sleeve, and his face displayed his feelings so clearly. To Leander that was a bold and admirable thing, something to aspire to.

When he got home, if he ever did, Leander would make a change in himself. Apologise to Corryn for how he acted, find Taren and beg forgiveness, and try and learn to open himself a little more. Being cocooned in Melynda's betrayal wasn't something he wanted anymore. She had no power over him now and he had so much to be grateful for. As he turned for another row of paces, the scuffle of footsteps put him on guard. Had the smiths finally come back to retrieve him? What would they do to him?

Two indigo-robed figures hurried into the light and dropped their hoods. Leander could only stare in shock. The first, a young woman with short-cropped blonde hair, mismatched eyes and a cheeky expression. She waved and nodded in familiarity. It had to be Fion. The second, looking somewhat haggard yet managing a smile, was Taren. Leander swayed, then stumbled to the gate, reaching for Taren's shoulder.

'Taren you're OK, I'm so sorry for what I did. I don't know what I was thinking or feeling. I just felt so betrayed and didn't know who else to blame, and I never ever thought that the smiths would send hollows after you–' Taren took Leander's hand off of his shoulder and for a second his heart dropped. Yet Taren didn't push the hand away, he held it in both of his own for a brief second. An unusual and detached feeling floated through Leander that only subsided when Taren let go.

'It's OK, really. I'm OK, but what about you? I'm glad you're safe but are you alright?' Such kindness. He didn't deserve it.

'Yeah, I'm alright. Thank you for coming back for me.'

'Well, you came to find me, I couldn't very well leave you here. We do have to figure out how to get you out, though.'

'This is the right guy, then?' Leander turned to look at the woman standing shoulder to shoulder with Taren. She beamed at him but her smile was knowing. 'That's one promise kept at least.' She held out a hand to shake.

'You're the one who… Fion?'

'Yep that was me. Sorry I didn't show my face or anything, but I couldn't be sure of anyone.'

'Thank you for the water, and for finding Taren.'

'Had he stayed put where I hid him in the first place neither of us would have had to drag ourselves down here to look for him.' She shot a mock-angry look at Taren, who blanched at the floor.

'Yeah, errr, sorry about that. I wanted to go check on Linette and, well, things got out of hand.'

Fion's face faltered for a moment, but she quickly corrected. Leander had no idea what it meant or who Linette was. When she spoke again she was cheerful. 'You tell a guy to keep a low profile and he goes slinking off into the slums and gets himself called out by a farmer by the sounds of it. I had a heart attack when I returned and you'd gone.'

'Sorry, sorry. I should have just stayed hidden.'

Fion dangled the water bottle in front of Taren from the folds of her robe and pulled it out of his grasping reach once or twice with a smirk. Leander stared in disbelief at the light-hearted banter between the two of them. It seemed so out of place given the heavy mantle of past few days, and yet when a quiet chuckle escaped him it lifted his heart. It was a relief to feel something positive again, however briefly.

'Seems like you two have quite the friendship. It's pretty clear who's in charge.'

'And he knows it, right Taren?' She playfully slapped his upper arm and Taren rolled his eyes.

'Alright, alright come on, we have to figure out how to get Leander out of this cell.'

As they searched a tirade of questions built up inside Leander's chest, and he couldn't stop himself from asking the one that hung in the air like an unmentioned but pungent odour.

'Where did he take you?'

Taren stopped, eye glassing over, and Leander regretted

asking. Taren's face paled a little, and he shook away things that Leander couldn't see. Fion placed a hand on his arm, gently this time.

'Taren?'

'He took me further below ground, but I'll explain later. First we need to get you out and find somewhere to hide and recover where we won't be discovered, and where there's no chance we will be overheard. We need to make a plan about how to get back in once we've made some preparations.'

Fion scoffed heartily. 'Plans to get back in? Taren I never want to come down here again, and I think Leander would be among the first to say the same. Why would we need to come back once we've made it out?'

'So we can destroy the spires.'

Fion faltered this time. In the ambient light of the crystal lamps she looked like a ghost.

'Destroy... the spires? But why? Why would we need to do such a thing?'

'I can't explain it here, but I promise I will when it's safe to do so, OK? Please, I need you both to trust me on this. I can't tell you here.' They both nodded and Leander resisted the urge to reach out and touch the unaffected side of Taren's face through the bars. Still, it begged the question... just what had he seen?

42

Somewhere Else Entirely

Fion branched off to check the surrounding stone pillars for any keys or implements that could be used to open the cell door. There was nothing. Taren and Leander were also doing what they could to find anything that might be useful.

Taren's mention of Linette had blindsided Fion. If only there was time to sit down with him and talk. She had so much to tell him and no idea where to begin with it all. That she'd seen Linette and that she was sorry. That she'd found Jacklan and that he'd probably never be the same again. That she'd broken her own bond of trust with Clayton, though seemed she wasn't the only one.

Taren had been very clear that the head of the Dreamforge wasn't to be trusted anymore. Problem was, Taren looked so wrung out and fragile that she didn't dare tell him another awful thing like Jacklan's condition, or remind him of what happened with his aunt. So she kept her mouth shut and continued to look around.

'Fion?' Taren whispered into the dark, and she popped her head out from behind a pillar not too far away from him. He was at the cell door with Leander, each checking a side of the gate.

'What?'

'Come back a sec.'

She made her way back with light steps. 'What's up?'

'There's no keyhole on either side, we've checked every rod of iron, every part of every pattern. What if there's a different way to open it?' She considered his words for a moment before realisation lit her eyes. The door to the underground had needed the use of her crafting magic. Could this be the same?

'You mean…?'

'Yeah, what if it can be opened with dreamsmith skills?'

'I guess we can try interacting with it like we do with the forges? Our skills are specific to forging dreamstones though, not iron bars. It'll probably be pointless.'

'We can at least give it a go.' They stepped back and positioned themselves a few strides apart. Leander frowned, looking a little lost but curious. When intricate bracelets of symbols snaked around their wrists, Leander darted out of the way to the left wall of the cell, much to Fion and Taren's amusement.

'Don't worry, we're not going to singe your eyebrows or anything. No need to brace yourself. I'm pretty sure nothing will happen.' Fion winked as she said it and Leander flashed her an uncertain grin. His cheeks warmed a little but he chose to stay by the wall, out of the direct path of their attempts.

Despite her jests, Fion didn't blame him. No one in the slums, or perhaps even in the inner city, could say they'd seen anything other than the binding skill used by smiths. It must be quite strange for him to be seeing their magic in

309

such a situation.

The bracelets turned in complex rotations, endless symbols appearing in the palms of the casters. Connections were attempted and failed. Just as she'd predicted. Their magic only worked on forging stations and crystal. Also hidden doors apparently, though she hadn't technically had to use her skills to open that, just have her magic active.

Taren stifled a yell and his left hand shot up to cover his afflicted eye. He swayed dangerously on the spot until Fion caught him by the crook of his elbow.

'What's wrong? What happened?'

'I… I don't think I can use my skills anymore.' Sweat collected in beads on his forehead. 'It felt wrong. Painful. The dream started to show me things.'

'Alright, it's OK. Take a break. I think we tried enough to know that we don't have the ability to open this cell' Fion helped him sink to his knees. What was happening to him? Dark shadows shaded his sunken face, and it was only then that she noticed just how far the dream had spread since she last saw him. It wasn't just the skin around his eye now. Some of his cheek was covered, it bloomed nearly up to his eyebrow and back towards his ear. It looked like it was beginning to snake off down towards his jaw on a diagonal, too. Just how bad was it now?

The more seconds she spent staring, the more unsettling Taren looked. The patch acted like a shield over his left eye, leaving a smooth swathe where it should have been. Was her friend half-blind forever now? What could he see, if anything, and how could she help? How could anyone?

Leander hurried to the gate, concerned for Taren. Fion and Leander's eyes met briefly, but neither had any idea what to do. They were both helpless, something Fion didn't appreciate, and a flicker of annoyance licked at her gut. Leander was clearly just as concerned, and she was about to thank him for looking out for Taren but her voice was snatched away by the last sound any of them wanted to hear. Distant footsteps and the low rumble of conversation. Fion searched the darkness behind Taren as she rubbed the bottom of his back to steady his shaking breaths. It wasn't that long ago he was doing the same for her back at her home in the inner city. The echoing layers of sound made it impossible to know how close or far away the footsteps were in such an environment.

Taren turned his head slightly. Then his hands began to shake. His breathing quickened.

'No, no, no. We can't be found. Not before we've freed you. We need to get out of here and hide, make ourselves safe. I can't let the smiths find me, they probably know what I've done. They'll be looking for him. Hurry we need to get Leander out and go.' The mix of panic and pain on Taren's face pulled on Fion's heart. That and the fact he wasn't making much sense. His panicking would give away their location quicker. She continued to rub his back and whispered to him, but his breathing didn't slow. He was losing control of it. He wobbled and gripped the cell bars, his one clear eye searching frantically for nothing in particular.

Leander slowly knelt down, the three of them there in a triangle. He reached through the wrought iron, taking Taren's face gently into his hands, and tilted his gaze up to meet his own.

'Look at me and focus, Taren. If they're coming you

311

need to hide yourselves, and you need to calm down. They might just pass us by, they might not be coming here for me. If they are, then they'll likely move me from the cell and you might get a chance then, OK? It's alright. Just breathe a little deeper and keep looking at me.'

Their eyes met and the gaze between them held steady. They were managing to calm Taren between them. What kind of bond did these two have? From what she could gather, Leander had saved Taren but also caused him to be captured again. There was definitely a story to be told, and she'd nag Taren for the details later, but now they had to take care of their friend.

A smile crept on to Leander's face and was soon mimicked by Taren as he regained some control. Fion and Leander nodded at each other, and each of them took one of Taren's hands. An unusual feeling like soft electricity started to dance through Fion's palm. Based on the questioning look on Leander's face, she wasn't alone in her experience.

Then Taren shuddered and his face started to shimmer. Fragments of the dream flaked away, moving with purpose to surround the three of them. They danced like iridescent snowflakes, multiplying every second. No one dared move or break contact. The three of them knelt completely still and they were encased in the petals of the dream, more peeling themselves free and joining the gentle swarm with every second. It didn't feel malicious, if anything it seemed warmer.

As the fragments drifted about some of them joined together, knitting themselves into larger and larger flakes. As they turned idly in the air the smell of rain-soaked fields

312

filled everyone's senses. The swish of the tall stalks on the breeze, the golden sway of the crop against the blue sky. A farmhouse stood in the distance. Within a matter of seconds the cell had faded away, and they all found themselves to be somewhere else entirely.

43

Golden Fields

Taren fought to calm his panicked breathing, trying not to flinch as pins and needles danced around his body. They originated from Leander's hand but they weren't painful. A faint prickle and an unbidden longing to knit together. The sensation wasn't wholly unfamiliar, and his mind searched for where he'd felt it before. Buried under shock and horror, it had been when Leander had held Taren's face in his hands as he'd shed his hollow covering. Some kind of reaction from the dream's rightful owner?

The left side of his face pulsed then grew cold for a few seconds, only to turn to pleasant warmth. The fragments began to shed from the patch of dream and tesselate in the air, and by the time he realised they were encasing him and his friends there was nothing he could do to stop it.

It wasn't like last time, though. Last time it felt like half his face was being peeled away. The dream had been bursting free, carried on all his negative emotions as he'd screamed for the Forgemaster to show himself. He'd been confused and scared and so exhausted in his anger. Perhaps the dream reacted to his state of mind. It made the most sense, because this time he'd managed to regain control of

314

himself. Grounded by Leander's touch and also Fion's. He felt safer, cared for, supported. The electricity whispered over his palm and he knew they couldn't break the connection. If they did the warmth would fade.

When the fragments dissipated the three of them found themselves kneeling in a golden field. A hallucination? Taren was convinced of it for a moment, but the rich smell of the soil, and sound of the crops in the breeze while it tousled their hair... it all told him differently. As a fresh collection of zephyrs rippled down to them from the mountains of the backdrop, voices chimed on the wind.

'Where is he? This is the cell we left him in.'

'Perhaps he's already been retrieved by someone?'

'Hmm. Perhaps. There's no way he could have gotten out. The Forgemaster must have had plans for him and already sent someone down. They've probably taken him to put him with the other creatures.'

'Let's check the area anyway on the off-chance he's somehow escaped.'

'I don't think there's a need. He's not our problem anymore. The Forgemaster will hold him accountable for that mess in the slums. The clean-up will take days...'

The voices faded. Leander and Fion knelt with Taren. They each gripped one of his hands, completely still and likely just as bewildered. The two smiths couldn't see them all?

'Taren, what are you doing to us?' Fion whispered, fear tainting the edges of her words.

'Nothing, I'm not doing this. At least, not on purpose. I have no idea where we are, but it looks familiar.'

'This is my dream.' Taren stared at Leander who was in

315

the view fondly. His eyes bright and yet sad, a smile unlike any Taren had seen so far on his face. Leander's hand trembled. Taren remembered the feeling that had come to him while originally crafting the dream. It seemed so long ago after everything that had happened. A simple feeling, one not filled with greed but a boundless kind of freedom. As Taren took in the scenery around him, that simple feeling returned. How had they ended up inside it?

Leander made to stand and unlace his fingers from Taren's, but a warning flutter in his mind made him clutch Leander's calloused hand tighter.

'No, wait. Don't break the connection. I think... it could be that the only reason this is possible is because of the prolonged contact between the dream and the dreamer.' Leander nodded and they stood up together to get a better look.

The rolling fields were endless. The farmhouse in the distance looked to be well made and spacious. The mountains running in a long ridge along the land behind the house slept like a huge geographic snake. All sorts of other shadows loomed in the distance. The horizon empty of cities and spires altogether.

Without the cramped concentration of people in the slums, the air was new and clean. No false hope clinging to every breath, no desperation forming a thick fog. It wasn't just freedom from the Forgemaster's system, but freedom from the fear and tiring anticipation of the way life had become for the people of the world. A simplicity Taren hadn't known he'd longed for.

'It's beautiful here,' Fion said softly as she took everything in. Taren agreed with an awestruck nod. Leander continued to smile, until his face faltered. Perhaps because of the link to the dream, emotions that didn't belong to Taren started to bloom in his heart. Yet he understood them to be Leander's. Bittersweet pangs skittered through him, tainted with the knowledge that it could never be a reality. A shoal of guilt-ridden teeth nibbled at Taren's insides. He'd never meant to take this away from Leander.

In seeing his dream and his reaction to it, a barrier fell away. Taren saw the true Leander for the first time. He was far more gentle than he appeared, and sought such a simple life that Taren wanted to reach out and embrace him. To protect him, and tell him that there was no need for him to lock away his emotions again now that they were free to flow over the golden fields around him. Their eyes met and a smile passed between them.

44

It's All Lies

Leander locked eyes with Taren and the smile they shared, just for a moment, was pure. Both Taren and Fion had taken in the scenery of the dream with contentment and awe on their faces, but this place wasn't new to Leander. It was home. Freedom. He'd imagined it so many times, more so after Melynda left him. To be standing in it, even if it were an illusion, felt so real. Surreal even, given all that had happened.

'This is truly your dream?' Taren asked as he gazed at the ridge of mountains across the backdrop. They kept their hands joined in case it caused the dream to cease. How was this even happening? They'd heard the voices of the dreamsmiths suggest that they were no longer in the holdings, and yet they hadn't taken a single step. Hadn't been found or seen. They were standing on fields, but the hard stone of the cell was still there under his feet if he thought about it.

'It is. Though… it's even harder to look at it knowing that I'll never be able to claim it.' Taren's hand flinched and he inspected the floor, dropping his head in guilt or shame, or both. Taren never meant to take it from him, and

318

Leander squeezed his hand in reassurance. 'We don't know how long this will cloak us for. We're clearly being shielded though. Tell us what you needed to while we're under the cover of the dream, then we can break contact and make a plan.'

'I agree, what happened Taren?' Fion stared at her friend with concern. Taren's eye slid back and forth as he remembered something, and shivers turned his hands clammy in an instant. Whatever he'd seen, it had affected him greatly. The pit of Leander's stomach stirred. What did he find out? Taren took a deep breath. It shook as he exhaled it, but then he raised his gaze and in turn looked each of them in the eye.

'The spires need to be destroyed. The dreams, the Forge, our duties,' he stared at Fion with a creased brow, 'it's all lies.'

Leander's heart dropped. 'What do you mean lies?'

'Our duties… you mean…?'

'What we think we do as dreamsmiths… isn't the truth. There's another purpose to the dreamstones that we were never told of. When we bind people to them, we don't enable their dreams. When they disappear, they don't move on to a better life.'

'Where do they go?' Fion spoke so quietly she was practically whispering. Where did they go if not to their new lives? Leander couldn't have prepared for the answer.

'They… they're taken to be fuel. For the spires.'

Leander's stomach no longer stirred. It rippled. Rolled in a slew of ice. That didn't make any sense. It didn't add up.

Fion shook her head slowly, bewilderment filling her tone. 'Fuel? They go to the lives they dreamt of don't they?

That's why we've worked hard all these years to craft so many dreamstones, so they can be free of this suffocating system of waiting and wondering. If we don't bind them to their stones for that then why do we do it? Fuel for the spires? How?' Her pallor dipped into sickly, and Leander watched her carefully in case she became unsteady on her feet. The torment on her face as she tried to understand pulled at his heart. Everything the dreamsmiths had worked for, everything the slumfolk believed, was it all a lie?

Did that mean... Melynda had only left him behind to go to her death? Taren stroked the back of Fion's hand with his thumb. In a shaky voice that made Leander suspect he was barely holding himself together, Taren explained everything he'd learned.

A void of horror opened within Leander as Taren bared all. The void stormed. A deadly tornado. Its spiked edges battering his insides. New barbs manifested every time an additional detail came to light. How could such a deception have taken place? It was no comfort to learn that everyone had a hollow inside them, and that they were extracted in secret during binding ceremonies.

Leander swallowed, his throat thick and full of bitter tang. Parts of people were being stolen and fed to the spire. Moreso, the very thing that made so many happy, and that so many endured so much hardship for, was a falsehood. Dreams were never realised. Instead, people were being taken to their deaths, and what a grim death it was. To be fed back to the extracted part of yourself so that your hollow remained alive until it was absorbed by the spire entirely.

To think the Forgemaster created such a desperately

twisted system. After Taren completed his account of the events that took place in the bowels of the Forge, he deflated in exhaustion. An empty vessel, spent and saddened. Fion's knuckles were white in their grip around Taren's hand, but he didn't once flinch. A sheen of sweat covered her crumpled brow, face set in an expression so furious and haunted that it reminded Leander of Corryn whenever he failed to take care of himself properly.

'It makes a bit more sense now.' Fion trembled as she spoke.

'What does?' Taren asked, his voice little more than a weary drone.

'Jacklan. I… I meant to tell you but there hasn't been time. I found him while I was lost looking for you. They've been keeping him underground ever since the incident. He didn't speak much sense, but after what you've said maybe it wasn't all nonsense.'

'He's down here as well?'

'Who's Jacklan?' Leander asked, the name sounded familiar.

'He's our colleague,' Fion answered, 'he was the one using the forging station that surged during the event that caused Taren to merge with your dream. The event hit Jacklan hard and we haven't seen him since. No one's been allowed to. But he's down here. He said something about collecting all the pieces. Maybe the pieces are the two of you. People who also know the truth. Maybe if we go back, he'll be able to share his truth again and together we could decipher it.'

'I'd like to speak with him as well. That he's been down here all this time, alone and suffering…' Taren couldn't say more. A harrowing quiet fell over all three of them but Leander's thoughts raced and squirmed.

What was it like for them, learning they'd played a part in such a horrific system without the slightest suspicion? Leander grimaced against the sting of foolishness. He'd believed it too, never seriously questioning the way of life he'd found himself partaking in. Grumbling and pondering it, yes. Often and with a half-heartedness. This changed things. He felt uprooted, off-kilter.

He'd mourned his wife in the wrong way. Even tried to be happy for her eventually. He'd also hated and cursed her for her betrayal. So many were overjoyed and showed their support for their loved ones when their calling came. So many celebrated what was ultimately the deaths of those closest to them. Suddenly his life seemed like some sort of tragic performance, and he'd played his part exactly as directed.

The scale of it all encroached like an incomprehensible blanket of disbelief. He couldn't make it fit over the top of the reality he'd always known. The spires, so beautiful in their crystal presence, now seemed alive and wretched. Sinister.

If they had enough consciousness to consume, what else were they capable of? In an instant they turned from comforting to menacing. Like the great teeth of some otherworldly titan poking up through the ground. Leander's knees shifted in their sockets, if he didn't stop such imaginations he wouldn't be able to keep a clear mind. Taren needed his help.

'We have to destroy it then, like you said,' Fion seethed, 'we can't let him continue with this barbaric system. When I next see Clayton, I'll make him pay for twisting my intentions. For using us to do his dirty work, turning us into his puppets. The Forge was my home and yet I never suspected anything like this could be happening. If I'd noticed sooner maybe-'

'No, Fion. You couldn't have known, none of us could. We weren't meant to. We had no reason to question it. Now that we know, we can take action, so don't linger on what we could have done with the knowledge sooner. I feel the same, but it won't do us any good.' Taren's voice was stronger now, filled with determination.

'How do we even go about stopping him?'

'I don't know. My eye showed me a vision of the spire collapsing, but it didn't show me anything of use. I don't know how to even begin.'

As Taren and Fion spoke a bolt of pain shot through Leander's head, singeing like fire and rustling with whispers over and over.

~Truth. Truth. They've started to find the truth. Let me through, I can offer a solution.~

'Leander, what's wrong?' Fion squeezed his hand, though he barely perceived it. A cry escaped his mouth as the hollow tried to scrape its way to the front of his mind.

'Why should I let you out? You've hurt people, you're dangerous.'

~I wasn't aware of my actions when I first woke. I was insensible then, but not now. I had been trapped for so long. I sought only the truth, that is my purpose.~

'Taren, what's happening to him?'

'Trapped. You're a part of me, aren't you? For how long?'

~For longer than you know. I am the part of you that once knew the truth. We can work together now to uncover it and destroy the spire.~

'I don't know who he's speaking to.'

'If you are part of me and want to work together then stop causing me pain, I'll let you through if you don't struggle. I don't want to lose myself again. To hurt anyone.'

~Very well. Relax your body. I will show you what can be done.~

Leander's body and mind were ablaze. His nervous system sparked with nettled leaves. Someone turned his brain inside his skull. Sweat drenched his forehead and pricked his armpits. He heard the concerned questions of Fion and Taren yet couldn't answer. His mind filled with broken images that loosely cobbled together into coherent thought. The world swayed back and forth but he pushed himself to focus.

He saw himself, and Taren and Fion, standing around part of a spire. The hollow detached from him and began to merge with the crystal. Then Leander cut its throat. Black tar spilled in thick splotches and as it rasped a final breath it pushed itself into the spire completely. Taren and Fion used their skills to tear it apart once it had fully merged with crystal, and the pleasant turquoise began to bloom with black patches. Ink dripping into a jar of water.

It expanded, the fragments of the hollow bleeding out. The perspective changed and he saw the city from a distance. The spire blackened and crumbled. It collapsed, receding from its iconic place on the skyline.

As quickly as it started it was over. The world still spun on a tilted axis. Leander desperately sucked in his breaths, coughing after every couple as his mind quieted again. A more constant presence hovered at the borderline of his mind. Two grips tightened around his hands and grounded him.

'Are you alright?' Taren asked him this, but did not look so well himself.

'I... yeah I'm OK. I think... I think I know how we can destroy the spire. The... my hollow just showed me.'

'What did you see?' Fury still radiated from Fion. Her eyes trying to claw the information from his mouth.

'We have to get back to the place you said the Forgemaster took you, Taren. The hollow wants to merge with the spire there, and then... I have to kill it before the merge is complete. It looked like the two of you were able to break the hollow up once it was inside the spire, the spilling of its dead blood corrupted the crystal and made it collapse?'

Taren frowned, taking a moment to think. 'That would make sense. The Forgemaster said as much, that the hollows have to be alive when they merge with the spire.'

'Do you think it's something you'd both be willing to do?'

'Do you really need to ask?' Fion was raring to go. Taren only nodded with certainty in response. His skin had a sickly sheen to it. Was the dream increasing its hold over him? As if to answer Leander's unasked question, Taren jolted where he stood. He broke away from Fion's grip and pressed his hand to his chest. His face twisted into an expression of agony and he stumbled back several steps, pulling Leander with him.

Leander wasn't quick enough to keep his balance.

325

Instead he dashed forward in an attempt to catch Taren. Fion lurched as well but neither of them were fast enough. Taren's hand was snatched away by the impact of his fall and Leander stumbled to a stop. The dream dissolved around them in seconds. Folding in on itself like paper and returning to the small flakes that had originally spawned it. They pressed themselves back onto Taren's face as he writhed on the floor in a brief fit and became still. His rapid breathing the only sound.

Leander found himself on his knees, with one palm pressing against the stone floor, the other still reaching for the broken connection with Taren's hand.

Something seemed off, but he couldn't place it. Leander looked around, registering Fion's bewildered expression, and becoming confused as Taren's pained face turned to suspicious intrigue. Following their line of sight, Leander glanced over his shoulder. Several steps behind him was the gate to the cell he'd been trapped in. It wasn't open, and yet he now found himself on the outside of it. He was free.

45

Riven. Cleaved. Split.

Battling the pain radiating through his body, Taren stared in confusion at the fact that Leander was outside the holding cell. Fion crouched at his side, supporting him while he struggled into a sitting position. They'd been taken to another plain, and yet their movements had transferred to reality.

A cold pool spread across him. Without letting Fion see, Taren used a finger to hook the collar of his robe, pulling it outward. Glancing down his suspicions were confirmed. The dream had spread. A single jagged shard had snaked down under his ear, tracing a path along his neck and over one collar bone. Edging towards the centre of his chest. Staying inside the dream for so long had cost him. What would happen when it covered every inch of his skin?

Fion moved first. 'Let's get you off the floor. Leander, can you help me?'

'Sure, sorry it's just a bit… impossible isn't it? That I'm free?'

Fion spoke with the fascination of a scientist finding a new discovery. 'I guess the dream kind of… projected itself onto our reality maybe? The setting of the dream took

327

priority over the constraints of the things not part of the projection?'

'So if we move in the projection we also move outside of it?' Leander's strong grip helped Fion to hoist him up to his feet. Taren swayed, drenched with waves of sharp pulses.

'That would be my guess, but honestly I can't say for sure. I've never seen a dream behave the way that one did. Has that happened before, Taren?'

'Not exactly. There was some show of power from it when I lost control of myself a bit, not long after I was first brought here. I was confused after seeing a hollow turn back into Leander and the dream started to fragment back then too. Nothing like what happened just now though.'

'It looks like it's taken a toll on you.' Fion's gaze burned a thousand questions into him.

'I'm fine, Fi.'

'Don't lie, you must think I'm blind if you think I can't see the state you're in. We need to go somewhere and rest.'

'No. We're here and Leander is free now. The dream helped us avoid detection. I can't help but feel it wants us to destroy the spire, just like the hollow.' He looked up to find resolve strong in Leander's face.

'Isn't it odd though? Shouldn't there be more dreamsmiths around given how many of you are here?' Leander combed the room suspiciously.

'I wondered the same while searching for Taren. There's been no one down here for the most part. Anyone I have seen has been a senior smith.'

'The Forgemaster told me only a small selection of the senior smiths know that this place even exists. Only his most trusted colleagues. He also said that no one else knows about the room where all the roots are.'

'Is that where you left him?'

Taren's heart fluttered at Fion's question. 'Yes. He… wasn't conscious when I left. We'll have to be careful in case he's still down there.'

'Do you remember the way back?'

'I… I think so, yeah. We should still be careful and quiet down here. There could be people wandering.'

'They're probably all out doing damage control in the slums. From what I heard there was a lot to take care of up there.' Taren bristled, seeing that Leander had stiffened after Fion's comment. Did he know he'd caused trouble but didn't remember properly? Either way, now wasn't the time to ask. 'But before we go back down, we should go and speak with Jacklan. I think I remember how to get back to him from here. He might know something that can help us.' Fion looked around at both of them, the question waiting on her face.

'OK, lead the way.'

***

It took a little trial and error to find their way back to the infirmary following Fion's lead. Taren's body seemed to be made of lead, and his mind spluttered like a dying lamp at times. Having Fion and Leander with him was a blessing. Fion walked a short way ahead while Leander supported him from the side. An eerie silence blossomed between their whispers and gobbled up their footsteps. Taren almost wished to see another person. To have such a large space be so empty spooked him, stoking a periodic shiver down his back at the thought of being watched from every empty doorway or black space they passed.

The warmth of Leander's hand on Taren's arm was a comfort, but he clearly struggled with the situation too. A complicated potion of emotions swirled about him, and Taren had the feeling he had no idea how to decipher himself.

'I'm sorry, Leander,' he whispered.

'For what?'

Crap, why had he said that out-loud? Well, if he'd said it he might as well let the rest of his thoughts out too.

'Your dream. It was so gentle and beautiful. I'm sorry that I took it from you.'

'It wasn't your intention. I don't blame you anymore.'

'When I think back to all the dreams I've made and crafted. All the bindings I've performed. There were very few dreams that didn't involve some element of wealth or material gain. Power or status. People wanting to elevate themselves in the world with no effort whatsoever. Yours was one of the very few that wasn't like that. There was hard work in your dream. The desire to build something with your own hands. You didn't dream of being rich, except in healthy crops. It's a very... precious thing that I've taken.'

Heat poured off of Leander as Taren spoke. He was probably embarrassing him, but at that moment he didn't care. He'd pulled the string, and now his thoughts unravelled. Synaptic yarn tumbling down a hill.

'Don't worry about it.' Leander's voice was gentle but clearly bashful. Taren's own cheeks flared slightly. 'Given what you've told me about how the system works, you've actually saved my life. Had you not become fused with the dream, and finished crafting it instead, I'd now be bound to my death. It's me that should apologise again, for how I treated you both times we met. I was harsh and cold, and it wasn't necessary at all.'

'You just wanted to protect your home, and Corryn. I understand why you acted the way you did.' They both stopped. Leander's face was weary, no doubt a mirror of Taren's own harrowed look. An understanding passed between them. A spark of a deeper connection that lit their eyes and warmed them from within.

'Hey, come on you two. You can whisper sweet nothings to each other later. You know, when we're not heading down to figure out how to cause half the city to collapse. I've found the corridor.' Taren scrambled to control his embarrassment, and reminded himself to give Fion a good nudge for it when he caught up. Yet as they approached the cross-section of corridors any sense of light-heartedness drifted away like heat through an open window.

Jacklan. Taren hadn't seen him since the day everything went wrong. What kind of state would his colleague be in, hidden away down in the dark? In the resounding quiet. What truths plagued him, and what damage had the burden caused? Taren already felt riven. Cleaved. Split. Yet he'd only known some part of the truth for a matter of hours. If Jacklan had been infested with it for longer, how must he feel? How did he cope?

The way Fion spoke of Jacklan, something in her face didn't recognise the name as it passed her lips. As though the Jacklan she'd seen wasn't the Jacklan they knew, that they'd trained with and forged with for years. As they stood quietly outside the double doors to what Taren assumed was an infirmary, they all listened for sounds of other people and heard none. Fion gripped one of the handles but hesitated.

331

'Taren he's… he's not… I'm not sure how to explain it but Jacklan is different. Whatever happened has changed him. I'm not sure how much of him is even left and how much is… something else.'

Taren shivered. Fion was usually great at explaining things. If she had hardly any words for Jacklan's state, it must be bad. The wet gnashing of the shadows that had swarmed Jacklan surged forward and made Taren flinch. There were so many things he wanted to ask, but didn't. Couldn't. He'd just have to see for himself. Fion had borne the burden of seeing what happened to their colleague. He couldn't turn away and let her face it alone. Whatever it was. Whatever Jacklan had become.

No response was needed. Fion waited a few more seconds, letting them prepare themselves, then pushed open the double doors and they all walked into the half-lit gloom.

46

All Are Chained

No one said a word as Fion led them up the silent corridor. She looked through the glass windows as they passed, unable to recall exactly which door Jacklan was behind. In her panic to leave the first time, that detail had been scattered to the shadows.

Halfway along the corridor they found what seemed to be some kind of sluice and staff room combined. A small closet of a room with a sink, two chairs and a cupboard. They refreshed themselves with water from the tap, and foraged some musty crackers between them. It wasn't much but they'd need the extra strength for what awaited them back out there in the corridor.

When Jacklan's form appeared in the next window along, eerily still, she stopped. Taren and Leander halted behind her. They'd all just about fit in the room but it would be cramped. If they could keep conversation calm, hopefully they wouldn't cause Jacklan any distress between them.

As they crowded into the small room, Taren let out a gasp behind Fion. Her own stomach bubbled at the sight of their colleague even though she'd seen him not hours ago. Nothing could ever prepare her for what had become of one of their own. Leander bristled. His breathing coming to an abrupt stop for a few seconds instead of gasping. Perhaps he observed how similar Jacklan's affliction was to the onyx skin of the hollows as well.

Jacklan's eyes had been closed, but the moment the door clicked shut they opened with a slow, heavy movement. Even that looked to be a lot of effort for him.

'So you've all come. Good.'

'Jacklan are you... what happened?' If Taren had tried to hide the tremor in his voice, he'd done a bad job. Fion didn't blame him in the slightest.

'You've assembled the pieces and have come now for the glue that holds them together. Yet the one who dwells within has already imparted my knowledge.' Jacklan's gaze flicked to Leander, his head turning slightly to reveal his one blackened eye. A void yawning in his socket. Taren's antithesis. Slowly being taken over by something much more sinister than the dream that was consuming her closest friend.

Jacklan was clearly addressing Leander. Or maybe the thing inside him. Fion and Taren might as well not be there at all. Jacklan's altered eyes didn't even see them.

'So what my hollow said is true? The method for destroying the spire?'

'Only one of us can do it. Only one of the darkened ones can bring them down. Those who bring false hope must work with those who can never hope again. Only then will it happen. Only then will it work. They cannot escape their fate.'

'What'll work? What fate?' Leander's eyes were wide as saucers, and his jaw worked against something, but what? Had Fion guessed right? Was the thing inside Jacklan

334

addressing Leander's hollow directly?

'The sky will scorch and the great lid will peel back like the flesh of those who died to fuel the truth. All will scream and they will cry and they will curse their ignorance. And then they will choose death to escape the dark shadows that spring forth. They will run to avoid the biting teeth. The gnawing pain. They will run to avoid this. They cannot run. They are chained. All are chained.'

Nausea rushed through Fion to hear the echo of Jacklan's earlier words. A little changed, but mostly the same. Like some dreaded vision or premonition. If they did destroy the spires the way the hollow showed Leander, is that what they'd cause? A threnody of death-bound fate. Were they bound for it regardless?

If what Taren said was true then fuelling the spire was the most important thing to Clayton. Keeping it functioning, whatever its true function was. They knew so little. How could they make a decision on such sparse information?

But if the spire was killing people, it needed to be stopped. Clayton needed to be stopped. All the memories Fion had of the man became smeared with blood and deceit. Hypocrisy and secrets. If nothing she knew was real, she would find out why she and everyone else had been made to live a lie.

Jacklan spoke again after a short silence. 'These three can help you where the first attempt failed. Guide them in the necessary steps to bring the truth to light.'

Leander staggered and took in a sharp breath. The voice that came out of him wasn't his own.

'Two of these aided in the failure of the first attempt? But then they didn't know the truth. They know it now.

They know enough to help fulfil our purpose.'

'First attempt? What do you mean?' Fion's arms raised goosebumps against the words. She had an idea of what they were talking about, and could only hope she was wrong.

'The first attempt to destroy the spire. The one that claimed this dreamsmith in which I and pieces of my kin reside. Were it not for your interference, we could have succeeded. One of us strangled the other as we hung from a root of the spire. Strangled them before they could consume their human counterpart. But being whole, their blood unspilled, they could only corrupt one branch. The one that was brought back under control.

'We hastened our own passing to join our dead kin in the spire and carry them up towards the core, but we were stopped by you.' Jacklan's gaze flicked to Fion for the first time. Her, Taren and Clayton, and Jacklan himself, they'd already enabled the system to continue once by bringing the broken forging station back under control. But they hadn't known. At least, three of them hadn't. It would have been so different had they known.

Clayton's reaction and his panic and anger all made sense now. The hollows had almost broken through. Almost peeled back the lid of the truth he'd so desperately tried to hide. And the dreamsmiths had helped. Aided in the masquerade even more directly than being a puppet of the Dreamforge. They'd quashed the efforts of the hollows, efforts which had cost them so much.

'It took us years of hive-minded thought to achieve that dash for the truth. As the life slowly ebbs from us, it is rare that we are close enough to our kin to reach them as we are consumed by the spire. Eventually we knew a chance would be presented to us. Eventually it was. And it failed.'

'I'm sorry.' The words left Fion's mouth before she could think about them. 'I don't know why I'm apologising, but I feel I must. We didn't know anything or any better. Had we known, we may have acted differently.'

'You now have the chance to right your ignorant wrong. You know what you must do. The hollow can guide you. Free us all from the soup of the spider's web. Will you do this?'

Everyone nodded. It was solemn and weighted, but each of them made the silent commitment.

'At last then I can rest. The rightful owner of this body wishes to speak with you. I fear we've asked much of him. He will never be the same, yet his service to this world cannot be measured in any value known to man. I wish we could free him from our infestation, but it is too late for that. Take care with him and hear him out. And do not forget what you've promised him. Us. Everyone.'

The network of black streaks pulled back, clearing Jacklan's eye and face. He jolted as though woken and immediately groaned in discomfort. He registered his visitors one by one, tears already brimming in his eyes.

'You came. You heard it. You know it all. Now I must ask something of you.' He held out a hand, shaky and stained with spidery patterns. He couldn't move far, the restraints muting his reach. Fion caught it without a moment's hesitation.

'What can we do?'

'End it. End… me.'

'What?' Fion nearly dropped his cold and clammy hand

then and there.

'If you know the truth, or any part of it, you'll feel its sting. You see me. I'm not myself now. I'm changed. Altered. I heard the promise you made to the thing that holds me here. I hope you're able to fulfil it. But I'm scared, and tired. I've felt the shredding claw of the truth, of learning about the lies. Of holding it inside my body and reliving their truth over and over. I know what we've done. The lives we've taken. I'm spent, and have no desire to see any of it again.

'It shows me on repeat because it feels it on repeat. Its repression. Its imprisonment. The crushing weight of knowing the lies that suffocate the world. I would be free of it, if you'd help me.'

Taren interjected, cutting off the response Fion had lined up. 'Jacklan we can't do that, we can get you out of here.'

'No, Taren. I can't go back to it. I can't lay eyes on it while it still exists and knowing the whole truth, the one you've yet to find, I know I can't... won't... I just. Please. Free me. Free me from my fear and what I've become.'

'Truth we've yet to find?'

'They said you'll learn it all. Every bit of it. In time. You know enough, but your success is only the beginning.'

'Then tell us, tell us so we can help you.' There she goes again, promising help she doesn't even know she can offer. 'Once we've destroyed the spire we'll get you out of here.'

Jacklan shook his head at her, tears spilling from his eyes. 'I don't want it. The only help I want now is in gaining peace. Eternal quiet. To be spared seeing your faces when you learn it all. Seeing their faces. How their expressions will twist and break. There's no going back. For anyone. Please, Fion. I have helped you, told you what you need to know. Won't one of you now help me in return? Save me from being this thing. This shattered and marred husk of myself. This carrier of the burden of truth. Please. End it. End me.'

Fion could only shake her head and drop Jacklan's hand. He couldn't ask that of them. How was she, were they, supposed to do him such a favour? They were trying to stop lives being taken, not add to the pile.

'No, no don't!' Leander yelled, but it was too late. A dark tether shot from his hand and burrowed into Jacklan's chest. Leander gagged, trying to jerk his hand free, and Fion ran to Taren who shielded her eyes and ears from any more of the grotesque cracking and muscular rustling she'd heard. Jacklan made no sound, but as Taren straightened and moved his hands away Fion caught a breathy "thank you" leave her colleague's lips. Jacklan fell still. Leander's hollow granted his wish.

Fion wheeled on Leander after several moments of staring at the dead dreamsmith. 'What the hell was that!'

Leander's response was to stumble to a corner and lean down to vomit. So much for those musty crackers. Fion flinched every time he retched, but her anger went from a boil to a simmer. It wasn't him. It wasn't Leander's choice. Taren, also speechless, took calm steps towards Leander and helped him stand.

'I... Oh gods I'm so sorry I didn't- I'd never. I didn't want-'

'We know.' Taren reassured him. 'We know. None of us would have but... he asked for this.'

'The hollow, it says it was the greatest favour we could

339

have done for him. If he was living with the pain of its kin then it couldn't stand to see the host suffer that any longer. It… it says it was a mercy and also apologises. It hopes we can understand somehow. It means no harm, and did what was asked of it by the host of its kin. I couldn't control it, but I felt… I felt it… his heart was crushed-'

'Don't. Don't make yourself recount it.' Fion struggled to control her breathing a little. Shock and sadness fighting for the forefront. She trusted Leander's words. His reactions. He'd never intended this. 'None of us can say Jacklan didn't ask. We just weren't strong enough for the kind of help he pleaded for. If Jacklan trusted your hollow, then the way we repay him is by doing what we agreed. By destroying the spires.'

47

The Spire's True Roots

Taren eventually disturbed the mire of despair and suggested that the three of them should get moving. No one wanted to leave Jacklan, or rather his body, alone down there. In the place where he'd been held prisoner. But it was that thought that made the muscles in Taren's legs twitch. They had to move. They'd all been some kind of prisoner at some point. Fion under house arrest, Leander a captive, Taren the same. It wouldn't do well for the three of them to be caught.

How much time did they have before a senior smith came to check on Jacklan? Despite his horrendous condition he'd clearly been well cared for by whoever had been trusted with him. Leander shivered and hugged his arms across his chest, about to break. Fion stared at the ground with disturbing, bewildered intensity. And Taren? Taren had no words. Only actions would make a difference now they knew their path.

'Come on. Let him be at peace. He's not in pain anymore. We know what we have to do. We promised.' Quiet nods all around and then Leander opened the door to check the corridor. They filed out one by one and retraced their steps. The dark corners were so inviting. Spaces where he could hide and disappear, where he could stay out of sight of the truth. In the next second he craved the cool relief of air and warmth of the sun instead, and open space. As much as he longed for these things, Taren had to lead the way now.

Fion put her arm around Leander's waist briefly and pressed her cheek to his arm. Her way of apology for shouting, no doubt. Then they all left the infirmary behind and worked instead towards finding their next destination. The staircase that would take them down into the belly of the Dreamforge once again. Where Taren would find out whether or not the Forgemaster's life had been added to the growing pile of death.

***

The minutes stretched on until things became more familiar to Taren. The gentle curve of the corridor, the slightly colder air and smell of dusty, larger spaces looming below. He almost walked past it at first, thinking they hadn't been walking long enough to encounter it again, yet there it was.

'This is the staircase. The room should be at the bottom. I left the door open when I passed back through, I think. Be careful in case the Forgemaster is still down there. I made sure his weapon wasn't left near him, but he could have regained consciousness and recovered it.' Leander and Fion nodded in response, their faces set in a stony resolve. Quietly they began their descent into the bowels of the city.

Each step brought back a little more irritation. It grew in Taren's chest, tiny embers stoked by the fire of memory snippets. For every positive memory he had of the

Forgemaster, a clipping of words blotted out some of his respect. Some of his admiration. The truth trampled all over them like a rampaging herd. Stamping them out to leave only a quiet, braising rage. They descended in silence. A silence that compounded itself when they reached the bottom.

The great door loomed over them. No less impressive the second time than it had been the first. More importantly, it sat ajar. Had the Forgemaster managed to close it somehow, their plan would have been foiled. Was he still in there, then?

'I'll lead the way. You two follow and stay close and quiet. We'll use the pillars to hide us from view as we advance, OK?' Both his companions nodded without once taking their eyes off the grand, carved door. The strange, pure resonance engulfed them as they entered, and Taren took them to the right. The pillars were big enough that the three of them could fit behind one with only a small amount of themselves on show. Hopefully the lower lighting worked in their favour.

'What are those?' Fion spotted the first root off in the distance, and her face showed her fear and wonder as her eyes took everything in, realising the depth and breadth of the sprawling hall. Pockets of blue light shone like beacons in the gloom at large intervals.

'The spire's true roots. The forges we use are branches. These reach down right into the ground.' An unusual resonance drifted out from the low-lit cavern ahead of them. A trap or trick? It didn't feel that way. More like a gentle beckoning.

'Do you both hear that, too?' Leander whispered,

flinching as though struggling with some kind of deep discomfort.

'Yes.'

'Yeah, I hear it. It's coming from the direction of one of the roots. Stay alert, it could be the Forgemaster. Keep to a slow approach and keep your eyes open. Ready?' All agreed. Taren took a deep breath, and led them forwards into the gloom. He would bring about the collapse of the spire, no matter what it took.

48

Painted as Monsters

Leander found the cavernous space unsettling. As they advanced, pillar by pillar, he couldn't help staring up into the arcing darkness of the ceiling and marvelling at the fact that they were underneath the city. How far underground were they? How far away from the sky? What would happen if the Forgemaster managed to close the doors and trap them? It was unlikely that anyone would ever find them. In that second he longed for the clotted mixture of smells from the air of the slums. The good and the bad, he'd take it all. From the delicious aromas of the weekly batch cooking sessions that took place out in the streets, to the sour tang of yet another overtaxed sewer. Anything aside from the encroaching dark and chill-riddled air of being hemmed in by stone.

He shuddered and focused, inspecting Taren's back with such determination he could have seared his robe. The place had such an eerie feel. So many dark pockets. Anything could be lurking among the soft blue light of the roots and the few-and-far-between crystal lamps.

Images from the hollow kept flashing across his mind as if to remind him of what he agreed. Also of what it had

345

done to Jacklan. Over and over again his hand broke through the man's ribcage and crushed his heart. The thick, gelatinous feel of it turning his stomach every time. Just stop it. Please. The entity hovered around the border of his consciousness. A crust of dried grime on a bowl. It fidgeted as they drew closer and closer to the root that sung to them. His mind squirmed every time it flinched or bristled with impatience.

Please stop your fidgeting. You have no idea how disorienting it is.

~We must hurry. The liar will catch us if we don't work swiftly. He will do anything to make sure we don't succeed.~

We're almost there, OK? They can't see any sign of him, he's probably crawled away to lick his wounds.

~You're very naïve. He will do anything to protect his duty. Hurry up and get me to the spire root.~

You're in such a hurry to die?

~I'm in such a hurry to fulfil my purpose. We must reveal the truth.~

A rush of urgency flooded him and Leander swayed. Fion steadied him with a hand in the centre of his back.

'You OK?' she whispered.

'Yeah, sorry. Thank you. The hollow is a little… restless.'

'What's it like? To have one in your head, I mean?'

'It's… strange. They were always painted as monsters, and when it first took over me it sounds like it acted as such. Maybe when they take over our bodies they can't think properly, maybe they're restricted, but… it has a voice. One that makes a dangerous amount of sense sometimes.' He twitched as another wave of restlessness tapped around his mind. 'I don't think they're monsters after all, but… it's scary to think that they could be a part of us. What does that make us?'

Fion had no response, but her gaze turned pensive. She seemed a curious girl, and a bold one too. He had no doubt that if she could she'd converse directly with the hollow itself to get the facts.

'That's it, the root where he showed me the truth.' Taren gestured for them to peer around the pillar. It was even more interesting up close. Somehow beautiful in the way it twisted down from the ceiling, glittering in the low light of the cavern. Some great, slumbering dragon snaking down towards the core of the world. The true scale of the spires dwarfed Leander and drowned him in helplessness. If a single root was so big, it made the main spire more of a Goliath than ever.

~I can smell the root, you must take me to it now!~

A splatter of pain marred Leander's temple, pushing his foot forwards against his will. He bumped into Taren who turned and helped steady him. He didn't need to ask the problem, one look from Taren told Leander he understood and yet reassured him at the same time.

'Quiet for a moment, I'll make sure the coast is clear.' Taren slipped away to the next pillar to get a better view. In the moments he was gone Fion laid a comforting hand on Leander's arm as he fought to keep his mind his own. Sweat puckered on the surface of his skin. His consciousness overflowed in a froth of boiling water, burning him as it went.

Please stop, just wait. We'll be there soon, we have to be careful. Stop forcing your way forward, I'll let you through when the time comes. Trying to overthrow my consciousness won't help.

347

Fion used her sleeve to reach up and wipe his forehead. A simple gesture that touched his heart and anchored him. He'd always had such a tainted view of dreamsmiths. Imagining them as haughty and arrogant. Smug in the knowledge that they held the power to grant people their dreamstones as and when they chose. These two were challenging that perception with every minute he spent with them. Not to mention learning that the smiths were, in the majority, clueless about their own craft. What its purpose was, what it took away. Kept in the dark and fed lies, puppeted by the Forgemaster. A flicker wobbled somewhere among his struggle with the hollow.

Hollows were misunderstood, much like dreamsmiths. There was so much that wasn't what it seemed. When did they all start taking things at face value? In that moment, he couldn't even remember how and where he'd come to learn that the City of Singing Spires was the place you had to go to retrieve your dream. Or how or when the three of them, himself, Melynda and Corryn, had decided to pack up and move there.

His whole life before that moment skewed, the feeling of displacement when you realise something is an optical illusion and look at it another way. He'd never felt more like a sheep among an endless herd.

'It looks clear.' Both Leander and Fion jumped at Taren's return. 'I can't see the Forgemaster. At any rate he's not where I left him. Let's go over it once more, OK?'

'OK. The hollow will detach from me and begin to merge with the root. When it does, I'll kill it somehow. As it dies it will force itself into the root completely, then you and Fion need to connect and split it into pieces, helping its

348

blood to spread through the spire. The rest, it says, will happen of its own accord. It'll react naturally with the crystal, though I don't understand it.'

Taren's eyes widened, and realisation moulded his face. He looked to Fion, and after a few seconds the same expression poured itself on to her face as well. They nodded at each other, Leander not understanding.

'OK… let's go.'

49

Empty Screams

They walked at speed towards the root, checking every direction for figures in the shadows. Taren's mind raced. What Leander had described was something he'd seen before. The day he broke with the forge and became fused with the dream, black tar had dripped from Jacklan's station. Could it have been hollow corruption? Were Jacklan's words true? The look on Fion's face confirmed she believed them to be, but there was no way to know for sure.

With each moment they delayed his concern for Leander grew. Containing the hollow was clearly a struggle. His eyes were sunken in darkening circles and his pallor passed through lighter and lighter shades. They had to do this as quickly as they could. Especially with the Forgemaster missing. He wasn't dead, they knew that now, but how much of a relief was that?

Taren naturally slowed as he approached the edge of the stone well surrounding the root. It became harder to force himself to take more steps towards it, his revulsion pushing back against him. He'd explained it to both Fion and Leander, not wanting them to get the same nauseating shock as he had, but he wondered if it were possible to prepare them for seeing the truth for the first time.

He stopped a few paces away, gesturing for the others to do the same. Maybe it had all been a dream. Maybe if he peered over the edge right then, he'd see nothing. A strange whistling rang in his ears. Was it a resonance? It pulled him closer with magnetic force, and he distantly heard Fion ask what was wrong. He couldn't answer. All he knew was that he had to look over the edge of the pit.

It was just as hideous as before. The root pulsed and writhed with half-merged hollows. His heart leapt up into his throat as he realised that one had fixated on him with its eyeless face. It... reached for him? It was mostly merged, only the tips of its fingers not yet turned turquoise to match the crystal's hue. It strained upwards with its one free arm. The resonance grew in volume. He returned the gesture, much to the panic of those behind him, but he had to obey the call.

Its hand was cold, so much so that it felt wet and brittle. The moment his fingers brushed the tip of the ailing creature, his mind filled with its memories. They seemed to rewind first, so fast that he could make no sense of it. Then they resumed forward motion and his lungs snagged as he saw himself. He was blocking a doorway, the subject of the memories trying to barge past him. He reached out, snatching, and a shawl came away in his hands.

No. No, please. The memories walked through the slums, a brief interaction with Fion soundlessly playing out. Then they arrived at the gate which let it pass through into the inner city. It jumped and skittered about like a broken projection. A dreamstone was accepted, the binding ceremony complete, and then it was pulled out of its host

351

body and Linette stood there beaming with her dreamstone in her hands. The hollow was taken below and flung into the pit around the root he stood before, and then the memories flickered again and Linette was being devoured one bite at a time. His heart squeezed tighter with every mottled scream of his name that echoed from her as she was consumed.

This... was his aunt's hollow? This is what became of her? What becomes of everyone? It was like learning the truth all over again from a more horrific angle. Seeing new parts of it and having his disgust renewed again and again. She should have had more time, sometimes people didn't vanish for months. Was this the Forgemaster's doing? Had he plucked her out of the slums as a warning to Taren? It seemed too violent and targeted, even for the head of the Forge, but what other explanation was there? Coincidence? Something he was losing more and more faith in every passing hour.

She didn't deserve such an end. None of them did. This was not the reason he became a dreamsmith. The smallest mutter reached his mind and it triggered a radiating ache. *I'm sorry.* These were the words that drifted to him as the hollow withdrew its hand and became subdued once more. Falling limp and succumbing to further crystallisation.

His sadness turned to anger. It shuddered through him, bringing pain to his hands as he gripped the edge of the stonework. All the dreamstones, robbed of their usually bright splendour, called up to him with their empty screams.

'Taren?' Fion's gentle, concerned voice broke into his thoughts. She had always worried about him too much. He turned, setting his face to a more neutral expression and trying to ignore the stinging of his hands. No need to tell

Fion. No need to upset her further.

'Let's put a stop to this. Is everyone ready, you know your roles?' They both nodded, but a familiar voice boomed from the shadows and sent chills down Taren's spine.

'Stop… you can't do this,' the Forgemaster said.

50

Half-truths

Leander shuddered as the voice reached out from the shadows followed by calm footsteps. The hollow raged in his mind upon seeing the Forgemaster step forward. Screeches of "he's the liar" echoed in dizzying layers. The man appeared weary beyond belief. His hood was pulled back, salt and pepper hair untidy and hastily brushed out of his face. A dark bruise stained the skin over one of his eyes, stretching around the side of his face. A welt puffed up on his lip, a patch of blood smudged to the corner. His gait skewed into a weak limp. Taren did this to him?

~He's the liar, he's the one that trapped us and repressed us. He's the one. Kill him before he stops us. KILL HIM.~

Leander swayed with the effort of keeping the hollow contained and Fion once again supported him.

'Please, let me explain myself. I'm sorry that I deceived you, Taren. Though if I were still the man I used to be, I'm sure I would have died from that assault of yours.'

The hollow pushed and the dam broke. It's voice rushed out of Leander in a stream of screeches.

'Don't let him twist you with his words, he will lie to you again. He will deceive you once more. Go ahead with what we agreed.' His raw throat burned against the desperate shouts. The entity writhed and raged against his control. Lights flashed in the corners of his eyes, all three faces creased with concern as Leander's body jerked in painful movements. He wasn't properly attached to himself, yet each pulse exploded in every nerve. His legs were swept from under him and the world jumped back and forth. His fall broken by Fion who struggled to hold him still as his fit began in earnest. He couldn't think, only feel, as the hollow peeled away and seemed to take his skin with it as it passed out of his body.

His own screams bounced around the vast space and returned to him in a cycle of agony as tar welled up through his skin and pooled together in a thick blot in the shape of the hollow. It formed and fell aside, screeching over and over as it leapt towards the root with animal agility. Everyone looked on in horror, but Leander could only fight the closing of his eyes. His very soul was ringing. Strength leeched from him down into the stone floor. He lay in the puddle of it, unable to reclaim it.

The hollow met the root with fervour and barely flinched as it began to merge with it. Quite quickly at first and then slower and slower. Lights dimmed and brightened, dimmed and brightened. Leander's vision faded in and out as he tried to remember to breathe. Part of himself had torn away. Leaving him floating within himself, unanchored, shocked and shivering.

'Kill me. Kill me now like we agreed. Help me corrupt the spire, we must bring an end to this lie. We must unveil the truth. Kill me before I merge with it completely.' The hollow's voice curled in crackling hisses. Hatred mingled

355

with desperation. The Forgemaster's tones cut through those of the hollow like a sharp knife.

'What it says is true. I have been a liar. A master of deception. Even earlier, when saying I was sharing the truth I did not share it in full. I didn't get the chance. This time I urge you to listen to what I have to say.'

Fion gently pulled herself away from Leander and stood, directing her arms at the spire root and activating the rotating bracelets they'd used to try and free him from the cell. Leander's body didn't feel like his. It twitched and sent out flares that forced weak shouts out of him. Was that really what he sounded like right now? So feeble.

The spire began to flicker as Fion struggled to connect, her face morphing into so many different emotions. As Leander lay there at the mercy of his breaking body, it was as though he could also feel the creeping cold of the crystal chewing on his limbs. Did he still have some kind of link to the hollow? Through blurred vision Leander tried to focus on Taren. His face was set in stony distrust, glowering at the Forgemaster but unable to voice any words.

'Fion, stop. All of you. I know I don't deserve your time, but this is the last I will ask of you and then you can make your decision. I won't stop you or harm you, but before you do this you should know the real truth. Please let me explain, I understand that my half-truths have caused more damage than intended. But if you destroy the spire, you'll destroy the dream.'

51

My Burden and My Failure

Fion dropped her arms away from the root and gradually turned to face Clayton. He wasn't the same man she once knew. With everything she'd learned, he looked like nothing more than a stranger. A harbinger of death. Of lies. So many words rose on a tide of disdain but she had to keep control. If he was playing a game of words, she wouldn't be fooled by it. Instead she met his gaze with level determination, pondering the meaning of the last words he'd spoken.

Leander hauled himself into a sitting position behind her, one palm pressed against his chest as he tried to recover his breath. Even the hollow quietened, the only sound for those few seconds being the bubbling crystallisation of it as it merged more with the spire. The Forgemaster's words echoed in the sprawling space, but Taren cut across them.

'Destroy the dream? What dream?'

The old man sighed and met Taren's eyes. All at once the bravado vanished from Clayton's demeanour and he all but crumbled in on himself. He aged a decade in seconds as he lowered the walls he must have built around himself for years. Was this the strain of the truth? If so, should it even be shared?

'I have not shared the truth of things with another living soul since I was given the burden that I bear. The senior smiths know a version of it, but much is left out, changed and altered. I couldn't bring myself to burden anyone else with it. What you've been fed are half-truths and stories. I would rather douse myself in dark light in the eyes of those around me than see their faces when they learn what's real.

'You three… have come very close to showing the world the truth. A truth even you don't know and will struggle to comprehend. So I ask you to take it upon yourselves first, and only then decide whether you wish to continue on your course of action.'

'So you're saying some of this was an act? Your threat to kill me just part of the play? What truth could you say now that would make these muddy waters you've created clear?'

'I didn't want to harm you, Taren, but I would have. I told you as much. Such is the weight of what I bear. I will protect it no matter the cost, but it pained me to even consider hurting any of the dreamsmiths. Especially one so talented as you. There are not many smiths with the strength to sever a connection with a forge and live while hosting a dream. Many would die on the spot.'

Fion turned ice cold at the words. Taren must have too as his eyes wandered briefly, likely thinking back to the moment he broke contact with the active station. Fion had never considered that Taren could have fashioned his own death then and there, with one ill-fated stumble, had he been even slightly less skilled.

There had been several threats against his life now, one by their own mentor. Taren was lucky to be here still. Fion's anger didn't lessen, but it mixed with a complex stew of thoughts and feelings. Trying to figure out what to feel was no easier than untangling a thousand intertwined threads.

'Why should we listen to you... or trust you?' Fion's voice wavered. She faced Clayton squarely, heart racing at the prospect of what he might reveal, but uncertainty rooted her in place. A delicate balance that wobbled with every word or possible gesture.

'I know you trusted me once, both of you. I know many people trust me. It's for that reason that I ask you to let me show you the truth. The people are my responsibility, though I know you don't comprehend that given what you've learned. I wish this wasn't how things have to be, but they must. You can't imagine what it's like. I cannot explain it to you in a way that would make sense.

'If the three of you consent, I will show you what I have protected for the past eighty years, alone and unaided. I will share my burden... and my failure.' The expression on his face was one of a broken man. Fion felt the shame and desolate despair hiding beneath the surface of someone she'd always thought strong, and briefly thought evil.

No, she still thought him evil, or at least his actions. She couldn't pin down her heart on one choice. Yet she was compelled to give him a chance to explain. Whether because he helped to raise her, or because of the sincerity of his pleas and the fact she sensed no malice in him, Fion wasn't sure.

'Did you know?' Her voice wobbled as she asked, Jacklan's face rising into the forefront of her memory. 'About Jacklan's forge? Did you know it wasn't safe?'

Clayton dropped his gaze, inhaling to speak with a slow

hesitation and then shaking his head. Not in denial, but perhaps regret.

'I… sensed something. But by the time I left that room, the danger had passed. That I promise you. I'd felt a presence rising in that root but when I searched for it there was nothing. No trace. I shouldn't have let Jacklan use it, he's suffering greatly for my mistake. I came straight down here to check on the roots afterward, on the hollows, which is why I couldn't be found. I couldn't have done anything else. I don't know how they cloaked it and I could hardly share my suspicions. I'm not defending myself but I had to protect-'

'He's not suffering anymore.'

'What?'

'He's dead. Your need for secrecy and devotion to this system killed him. What he became… what he asked of us… that was your fault. Your mistake. Your selfishness.'

'I… I never meant…' He didn't finish his sentence, yet Fion believed him. Somehow, for some reason. He wasn't the man she thought she knew, but she still knew some parts of him. Everyone deserved the chance to tell their side at least once.

The hollow burst into screams and Leander joined it. Were the two still linked? He writhed on the floor while the hollow shouted rasping screams of liar and deception. The Forgemaster raised a palm and Fion stepped back, suppressing the impulse to cower. Taren was at Leander's side in an instant, but Fion didn't take her eyes off Clayton. Within seconds the hollow calmed, swaying as it fell into an induced stupor.

'What did you do to it?' Fion stared at the hollow with

360

wide eyes.

'I just sedated it. I reduced the merging process to its slowest possible progression. If you let me show you the truth, and do not deem it sufficient to justify the system you've come to uncover, then I will not stop you from continuing your plan. I have slowed it down, but we don't have much time. If it still lives when it becomes part of the spire, your plan will fail. Will you give me this chance?'

Fion exchanged glances with Taren and looked down at Leander who was recovering himself. They all nodded, faces plastered with apprehension and fear. Fion spoke on behalf of her friends.

'Yes, but this is your only chance. Be clear and this time leave nothing out.'

'As you wish.' Clayton held out a hand as though offering them something. As Fion peered forward to see what sat in his palm a flurry of fragments poured from it and fluttered wildly about them. They began to piece together, just like Leander's dream when it had transported them elsewhere. Where was the Forgemaster taking them?

52

The Crumbling Edge

Leander was helped to his feet by a concerned-looking Taren as fragments poured from the hand of the man who claimed to hold the truth of the world within him. A keen ache throbbed in Leander's chest. The screams of the hollow had burned inside him as they rang out. Would the connection ever fade? Would he feel its death when it came?

The great swarm of fragments knitted together and Leander gripped Taren's arm in shock when their surroundings stopped rippling. They hovered above the city, peering down on it from the air. Fion gasped and made to move toward Taren, but fear of not knowing if it was safe to step rooted her. She settled for gripping her own waist and scrunching the material of her robe between her fingers. Then the city began to change.

The slums dried up and vanished like dirty water being sucked into a sponge. The spires melted. Ice turning to water in the heat of a midday sun. The terrain changed, bloomed with greenery and the bustle of a busy market. There were no barriers covering the gates, and the Dreamforge appeared different. Adorned with rolling purple banners, a strange golden sigil emblazoned upon them. The city was so different without the spires piercing the skyline. Even less recognisable without the far-reaching ring of hastily-built homes and well-trodden dirt paths snaking through the slums.

The great hanging smog of hope and hopelessness cleared, a brighter, more vibrant place crawling up from the dust. The Forgemaster's words broke through their fascination.

'This is the city before the need for spires and gates. An open place, full of life, and it was the city most well known for its high level of skill in its dreamsmiths. But we were not the dreamsmiths you know today. We used to be something different.'

The city rose up to meet them and they found themselves outside of a lavish shop full of trinkets and expensive workman's tools. It was no small premises. Above the door a sign declared 'Clayton: Master Crafter' and inside a younger, happier version of the Forgemaster sat working with concentration and enthusiasm at an ornate desk.

'Dreamsmiths used to be master crafters, respected and well thought of. We were members of the community, all with thriving businesses. Many dreamsmiths lived in the city. It was a hub for crafters of all kinds, but we were always the most revered. We made small trinkets that captured the hopes that people had for the future, and the items were capable of transmitting those thoughts and hopes and dreams to others when touched.

'People would come and tell us their dreams, and we would work with them to design whatever vessel they wanted to store them in. Necklaces for their partners holding their dreams for the future. Paperweights holding someone's dearest hopes or ambitions. They could be bought for personal use as reminders and motivation, or gifted to others to show them what hopes you had for them. They didn't make people disappear, they gave people a physical token of what they strived for. I have wished for so long to return to that time, before the purpose of our craft was changed.'

Leander stole a glance at Taren and Fion. Their brows were creased and eyes wide with surprise. How could dreams have been something almost trivial not so long ago? Now they were the pinnacle of hope for some, something some had killed for. Here they were a part of life, not the be all and end all of it. They brought joy, not jealousy. Happiness, not hopelessness. Lifted people, rather than leaving them lonely.

The Forgemaster had such a look of longing on his aged face that Leander's heart sunk for him. What could have happened to twist the purpose of his craft so much? In an uncanny moment of coincidence the Forgemaster locked eyes with him as the thought crossed his mind and he fought a shiver.

'We realised something was wrong when a dream broke in my hands as I was crafting it.' As if on cue, the younger version of the man let out a gasp as the trinket he held crumbled to grey ash. It stained his hands, which shook as he stared at the broken dream. 'Dreams could only be crafted and captured so long as there was a future in which they could come to pass. I knew I had to report to the council of dreamsmiths immediately.'

Leander's stomach lurched as their view changed once again. A gathering of crafters huddled together and talked in

364

quiet whispers as they waited outside the gates, and after taking direction from a man that Leander didn't recognise, they all departed the city in different directions.

'We crafters are those that can tap the power of the world to create extraordinary things. As such, it's our duty to also take care of the world and ensure the power is not over-used. For a dream to break, for it to be suggested that there was no future left for the world, we knew we had to try and find the cause. What we found was nothing to do with the crafters over-using the power. It was far more sinister, and something so far out of our grasp and capability that we had no conceivable solution at the time of its discovery.'

All three of them stumbled back a step or two, resisting the urge to back away further. They stood next to the young Forgemaster at the lip of a great, crumbling crack. It ripped through the land, harsh and jagged, and the faint trickle of earthen fragments falling away rose from its depths.

Young Clayton held one hand to his mouth as he stared at the anomaly. It had no end that he could see. As he peered over the edge the spectators followed his view and saw tiny chunks of the land dissolving away. Slowly crumbling like ashen biscuits. The crack was still small in terms of width, not yet wide enough to fit a fist through, but its scale was incomparable. A vicious stain upon their world.

'We still don't know what caused such a devastating sundering. The Crumbling Edge is an anomaly that we couldn't have imagined.'

In a rooftop courtyard back at the city the crafters gathered again and spoke in panicked tones. In the end, the room quietened, and all eyes fell upon an unknown older gentlemen and Clayton.

'After reporting the findings, we tried for months to come up with a solution. To puzzle out the cause. We could find nothing. For years after that, we sent crafters in pairs to examine the Crumbling Edge, yet our investigations only confirmed one thing. That slowly, gradually, it was widening. Nor was it escaping the notice of the general population. Rumours spread like stains, panic began to rise and bubble.

'It was decided, as a problem far greater than we could solve with our current capabilities, that we must act in the interests of the people. To protect them and keep them safe while we continued to work to find a solution.

'So I was asked if I would take the responsibility. To shelter them from the truth and continue the work of the crafters in trying to figure out the cause and put a stop to it. I accepted, but in order to alter the world enough to keep the people safe… a sacrifice was needed.'

The younger Forgemaster nodded, his face gaunt. The older man embraced him briefly and then set about ordering the other smiths with words Leander couldn't hear. In the rooftop courtyard, most of them pulled together and began crafting a shimmering orb, one that sent out whip-like tendrils that forced themselves beneath Clayton's flesh and began to snake through the stonework of the building. One by one the other dreamsmiths were taken into the orb they created. To feed it. To let it grow. As the last man stepped in with a smile and a nod, a bright light blinded all three onlookers from their invisible perch in the air.

'They bound me to the spire. To the city. And so the first spire came to be. I had my instructions. My master's last act was to set a cloak over the top of reality, burying the city's memories of the Edge and its peoples' panic deep within themselves where they couldn't perceive it. The rest was up to me.'

53

Fair in its Equivalence

Taren took both comfort and concern from the tight grip of Leander's arm on his own. It anchored him, giving him a grounding point in the uncertain sea that swarmed around them as they watched the past unfold at the Forgemaster's command. Had all of that really happened?

The view of the city morphed again, becoming more familiar with each passing second. The first spire grew, consuming a chunk of the building that would become the Dreamforge Taren knew and loved. Other spires rose from the ground to join their sire in their skyward climb. Fion stood with her arms wrapped around her waist and in her confusion she looked like a teenager again. He wanted to hold out his arms to her, but none of them dared move. Their bodies all paralysed in the crashing waves of comprehension.

Dreamsmiths had once brought joy, not death. Their work not taking away futures but giving hope for them. If only, Taren thought, he could have been a dreamsmith in that time instead of this one. To see the craft's origins when compared to what it had become… no wonder the Forgemaster looked so forlorn.

'No one noticed when the spire pulled its great blanket over reality. Its reach wasn't that wide at first. Maybe a ten kilometre radius outside of the city. Now, a much wider area is covered by it. Though it's reached its limits. The spire sends out another resonance, you see, not just callings. It sends out a frequency that disrupts the mind, and plants stories in those in its range. The history the council created for them, the knowledge of the calling implanted by me, the drive to come to the city.

'The dreamveil doesn't stretch as far as the resonance, which reaches all over the world. I have been beckoning people into the dreamveil and the city for decades because this is where I can best protect them but... in order for the stories to resonate with them, we had to make sure their minds were amenable.'

A great sadness carved itself into the Forgemaster's face. Taren felt his unrest. A tangible thing that swept around him in tight, mauling wrappings. Was he telling the truth this time? Was he regretting his treatment of the people? He met Taren's gaze which hardened as he continued.

'The spire also represses people's natural ability to question their situation. It represses any knowledge of the world before they entered the dreamveil. It locks it away inside the mind. This is where hollows come from. They are the truth that everyone has locked away inside themselves that the world they know... is not real.'

A shard of ice forced its way through Taren's body. Splintering and shattering as it went. Leander also stiffened, his breath halting for a few moments longer than was comfortable. Fion gasped.

'The world we know... isn't real? How can that be?

369

How can a world we all live in not be real?' The questions finally began pouring out of Taren's mouth, encouraged by fear and confusion. 'You expect us to believe this? That you call people here using the spire to protect them from some imagined threat? How do we know you aren't fabricating this to justify your sick methods-' The fury in the eyes of the Forgemaster was so intense that Taren's words tailed off.

'I told you that whatever I showed you would be the truth. I am not in a position where further lies would benefit me. I understand your accusation comes from fear, but you should still watch your tongue. You can see now for yourself what I mean. There is a dream, bigger than any of you could imagine, that is overlaid onto the reality you live each day. That is the true power of the spire, the reason it needs fuel and why it must not be destroyed. If you corrupt the spire it will crumble, and this is the truth that you will bring upon the people of the city.'

With a sweeping gesture the Forgemaster indicated to the city below them and then up at the sky. It twisted like a sheet being pulled up from the centre. Folding and bunching together until eventually it ripped. A gaping hole opened above them, a long-closed eye allowed to see again. The edges expanded, erasing the calm and tranquil blue and replacing it with a mottled, ashen grey. The shades of dark, lifeless colour rolled around with each other, some patches more scorched than others. Scorched was the only way Taren could describe it.

A flash of fork lightning swept across the dull swamp of the sky. Fierce and cracking in its strike as it swam about like a great serpent. It wasn't alone. Some battled for territory, whipping at each other or at anything within reach. The ground lost none of its lustre, but Taren knew in his heart that one day it would look the same.

The ridges of the distant mountains were a different shape than the horizon he knew. A bolt of lightning reached down and spewed rock and earth in all directions. They were being chipped away, disintegrated. His whole body ached and tightened, but the Forgemaster was not done. He took them away from the city, changing the view once more. The land deteriorated as they watched. The further from the city they travelled, the more barren their world became. Some great distance from their home, the world came to a stop.

Taren's stomach turned, and kept on turning. The Crumbling Edge. They stood above it again, looking down into the yawning depths of nothing. There was no molten core of the world. No fire or brimstone or anything at all. Just stillness. Quiet. A silence unlike anything Taren had heard, and one he never wanted to hear again. The manifestation of death and emptiness, creeping closer and closer. The other side of the crack must have existed somewhere, but even from his higher vantage point he couldn't see it. An abyss. What their world was becoming.

Taren scrambled to marry up the sights before him with the reality he thought he knew. They didn't fit together. A rush of lightness whirred around his head and Leander placed a shaking hand on his back to steady him. Their world… was dying? Even as they watched, tiny sections along the edge of the canyon fell away. No more than a handful of dust each time. Unsettling in its slow decline. It made his insides squirm and knot, like a deadly insect slowly creeping towards you. Certain, dangerous and relentless.

371

In that moment he was reminded, by the booming of an internal gong, that he too was expiring. The dream was taking him one small piece at a time. Every time it spread beyond its original border. Every centimetre of skin it consumed. It was just like the small, seemingly insignificant handfuls of dust that fell away from the Edge. Look how much damage it had done over time. The same emptiness awaited him. How long did he have? How long would the dream give him?

'I spent years, decades, sending out expeditions with the few remaining dreamsmiths and crafters from the original world to try and find the cause. To try and find out anything. We needed data, research, to help build our knowledge in the hopes that some skill we possessed could help to soothe the world's death.

'Eventually, after almost thirty years, I lost them all. Sometimes a dreamsmith wouldn't make it back from an expedition. There were so few of us to begin with, the majority had been part of the original sacrifice. My last remaining friend insisted on going out on one last expedition. A bold and brave man, determined to find a solution. I think now that it should have been him chosen to be the caretaker of the people in my stead.

'Once he was lost, so was I. I knew the Edge had taken him, his resonance was gone from the world. I had no more courage after that, and turned instead to calling as many people as I could under the protection of the dreamveil. I became a shepherd of the doomed instead of the saviour I was supposed to be. I have been alone in all of this ever since.'

Taren couldn't look away from the silent abyss. The

words of the Forgemaster echoed in his mind. All four of them stood there, one in sadness, the other three working ceaselessly to comprehend what they'd just been told and shown. How was this something that could be reconciled with? What protocol existed for discovering that your world was a lie, and that it was disappearing. Soon… it would all be gone. Taren's view widened beyond his own chilling situation. It wasn't just him. They'd all be gone. The Edge would take them all. How long did they have?

'And so now you know. The world is half gone, and there is no way back. My duty is to protect the people… even if doing so comes at the cost of hollows and their hosts. It takes the pure truth the hollows are made of to keep this lie alive. It is regrettable. I tell you there isn't a day that I don't regret what became of my craft, but given this situation… the exchange is fair in its equivalence.'

A spark flared in Taren, pulling him out of his stupor. '"Fair in its equivalence?" Are you serious? You lock parts of people away, force them to bury the truth, only to snatch it from them and use it to fuel a monstrous, all-consuming lie. Don't you see the hypocrisy, the sickness, of it?'

'I see it every day that goes by as a reminder of my failure!' The words were sharp and bitter. 'It wasn't meant to be this way. But given the position we found ourselves in, what more could we have done? I never knew what the spire would require as fuel, but even if I did, I would make the same choices. It was born from sacrifice and it runs on it. Those that are taken by the spire are protecting their fellow people whether they know it or not.

'If the cycle was stopped the people in the city and the slums would be plunged into utter fear and despair. I would

373

have them stay oblivious to it. The spire knows I wish I knew nothing of it. I would give them what I cannot have. Some kind of internal peace. I would rather make new truths for them than force them to face this one.'

The Forgemaster's eyes slid down to the Crumbling Edge and the anguish in his face struck a chord with Taren. What would he have done if he was in the same position? For a brief moment it all clicked and made some sort of sense. A type of sense that sat in his gut with an uneasy ripple. The Forgemaster never wanted this. That couldn't be more clear. Yet, could he still be acting as some part of a great deception? Truth and lies were labels that meant little anymore. How could anyone differentiate the two when faced with what the three of them had seen?

54

Ruin or Death

No one said a word, but Fion broke everyone's musings with a frustrated scream. She charged towards Clayton without warning, all her rage and disbelief fuelling her actions rather than her logical mind, colliding with him and staggering him. This was the result of giving him a chance? With a lurch the vision rippled and stretched, the space around them cracking like eggshells. It morphed and flaked away, dropping them back into the underground cavern in seconds.

The Forgemaster steadied himself by gripping Fion's arm and shoulder, and shoved her away from him. Leander's arms snaked away from Taren to catch her. Had Taren not gripped her forearm, she would have resumed her advance on their old mentor. He held her back as angry tears fell on to her cheeks.

'I don't believe you. How can any of that be true? Do you expect us to believe that you're some kind of chosen one protecting all of us while we head towards inevitable death? Sounds more like you're trying to paint yourself as some kind of deity so you can be revered by the people. How can you be protecting them when you're the one doing this to them!' She gestured to the stone pit surrounding the nearest root and the Forgemaster's face slackened only a little. His eyes remained harsh, burning with an ever-shortening wick of patience.

'I understand that it is a lot to take in, but I have not lied to you in this matter.' A shuffling pulled everyone's attention to the root on their right. Leander's hollow began to stir. Almost half its body had turned to crystal. They didn't have much time. Fion couldn't stop herself.

'How can we trust you if you've lied to the whole city? If you were truly meant to protect us all then why did you give up on the expeditions? If they were the only hope of finding an answer why would you let them cease?'

'I don't expect you to understand it yet. I can only show you what happened. If I didn't make it clear, then I regret my failings greatly. It isn't easy to live with them.'

'Looks pretty easy to me. You just set up a system where you're seen as some amazing, powerful leader and relax for the rest of your life while feeding us to your precious spire.'

'Fion...' Taren stopped her. His chiding stung, but the wrongness of her words was immediately apparent. She wasn't being fair. Fear tempered her words but she couldn't stop it. She didn't want to die, didn't want to vanish or fall down into a crumbling chasm of darkness and silence. The simmering anger had risen in Clayton's eyes with every word she'd spoken and Fion recognised his hurt, if begrudgingly. She wouldn't give in to it yet.

'You can't be suggesting that's not the case, Taren? Is he winning you round with his lies?'

'I don't think they're lies.' Fion blinked at her friend. 'It didn't feel like a lie. His face while he watched the memories and spoke of his failures… it showed that this was the truth. I see that now, I think.'

'So you agree with what he's doing?'

'No, and I can't believe you'd suggest such a thing.' He snapped at her, his jaw stiffening as he spoke. 'What he is doing disgusts me. I just don't know what to think about all of this. What do we do?' Fion opened her mouth to answer Taren but at that moment the hollow burst to life with a furious screech.

'No! He is weaving silken words like threads to trap you. He is manipulating you. Do not listen to the liar. Kill me now as we agreed and let me share the truth with the world. Why should he choose who sees the truth and who doesn't?'

It writhed and moaned in its desperation to get them to act, growling at its inability to persuade them. Leander pushed a hand against his own chest again, they must still be connected. Fion steadied him and continued to speak.

'I agree with the hollow, Taren. How can we possibly trust Clayton? I know you don't like seeing the bad in people, you're too kind for that, but it's a struggle for me too and you said it yourself. He threatened to kill you to hide that he uses people as fuel. He's killing people. Making us kill them.

'Over the years how many dreamstones have we made? Each and every one of those was a death. Not to mention the ones made by all the other smiths.' Her arm swept out in a wide gesture. 'He controls the entire city, why would he want to give that up? Who's to say he won't kill us the moment we agree to let this chance slip by? We won't get another.'

377

'Kill me, do it now before the spire takes too much of me and he accelerates the process. Kill me, kill me, kill me!'

Taren's hand covered the dream-riven side of his face. Fion could do nothing to help, yet she could sense that Clayton was directing the coming decision at her friend. What was the right thing to do, what was the truth? How could he bear that, and why should it fall to Taren alone?

The Forgemaster spoke through gritted teeth. 'You all still waver despite what you've been shown? Despite my assurances that I would share the full truth with you. Denial is a powerful thing but I have to ask you to set it aside. I understand that accepting what I've shown you means accepting that the world is dying. That the world you think you know is not the true world.

'I ask you to consider everything you've each come to learn about me over your lives. You both know me, even if you never knew everything I've done or why I had to do it. Why I would want to keep this position? I have no great power. I am no great leader. I am a shepherd trying to shield his flock from fear and despair. This was the only way we knew how. The only way I know how. I have no love for this burden. It continues to destroy me.'

'What do you mean?' Fion tried to curb the concern in her voice and failed.

'It seems I must once again prove my words. Very well.'

With a weary sigh that was almost drowned out by the snarling of the thrashing hollow, Clayton peeled back the crossing fold of his robe. One arm and shoulder freed itself from the garment and he let it half-drop away to show one side of his torso. With two fingers he touched the spot directly over his heart and let his arm fall to the side. As he closed his eyes, his skin began to warp into a scar, and from it snaked tendrils of cloudy white crystal that shimmered not unlike the ones that riddled the left side of Taren's face. A similar affliction, only far more serious. It continued to spread as he spoke.

'I am glamoured, just like the world. The dream I am bound to is the one that cloaks the city and the world beyond it. When they bound me to the spire they bound me to this fate, and I took it not knowing the full extent of what it meant. Crystals have taken root within me and they continue to claim me. Prolong my life. I have lived longer than I ought to, but so long as the spire is needed so too will I be here.'

The affliction grew, covering his entire torso, and no doubt also claiming his legs, his arms, it crept up his neck and neared his face. Consumed one eye and outlined his mouth. Taren's eyes widened and Fion reached for his hand.

'This is a glimpse of your future, Taren. Ask yourself why I would choose this now knowing what it means. You're fused with a dream, and it is claiming you the way these crystals claim me, and I'm sure you'd think twice before choosing this again.

'I did the only thing I could for the good of the people. I wish, beyond any longing I've had before, that there was another way. When I first discovered how the spire was sustained I was distraught, but had I stopped it then what would have become of the people? The fear of the Crumbling Edge chases me relentlessly. I'd do anything to spare them that. The choice now lies with you in what you do next.'

Everything blurred. The Forgemaster's voice faded and

mingled with the screams of the hollow. Taren's future was reflected back in the old man's riddled body. When Fion asked herself what was right and wrong no answer came to her. No doubt Taren and Leander were scrambling over the same useless questions.

Who could help them decide this? Why should it be directed at Taren? She wanted someone, anyone else, to bear this burden. He'd be crushed under the weight of the decision, it was clear in his stretched and haunted face. They had no one else to turn to, only the three of them, and either choice could lead to ruin or death.

55

No Monopoly on Truth

Leander watched the tug of war Taren's heart and mind were going through in quiet, deep-seated concern. His own mind just as tangled and weary, and no doubt Fion was the same. The lid had been pulled off the world to reveal another lying behind it. The same yet so changed in a single breath.

The great seething bolts of lightning were etched into his memory as they'd snapped and bit at the land, striking like great anacondas of destruction. The sight of the dying world hurt and terrified him. His whole life he'd cultivated land and taken care of it, yet one day its vitality would disappear. Whether Taren had stolen it or not, his dream had truly vanished now. It had never existed in the first place. A constriction twisted in his chest, pressure building both inside and out.

Each time the hollow screamed a shard dug into Leander's lungs, its unending accusations and pleas burning his throat. When would he be free from it? Seeing the old man reveal his true appearance sparked a distant panic. Was that the fate Taren would face one day? Slowly eaten alive by a dream? When it had all of him what then? The thought of Taren's life fading away stirred him in ways he thought he'd forgotten. Buried long ago. He wouldn't let the feeling disappear again.

His eyes locked with Fion's as she wiped away a tear from her flushed cheeks, but it wasn't out of sadness. Anger dripped from her as she buried her face in Taren's chest. They were both looking to Taren for an answer. He'd somehow become the default leader of this harrowing expedition, yet Leander was glad not to be in his position.

The Forgemaster swayed and leaned against a nearby pillar, passing a crystallised hand over his changed body. Another cry burst from the hollow and the room shunted sideways. Leander's head was engulfed in burning water as a tar-like tendril shot from the palm of the hollow and attached itself to the back of his hand.

In a second he was hauled towards it, his knees crashing against the wall of the stone pit surrounding the root. The hollow pulled his hand towards its neck as far as Leander could reach. Below him the other hollows writhed and pulsed inanely, and the scattered carpet of dreamstones glittered in the turquoise light. His footing wouldn't hold for long, stretched high on to his toes and in danger of toppling over the edge.

'The others are becoming lost to his words but you must now do what we agreed. You must take my life before this spire takes mine. The people deserve to know the truth of the world they live in. It is not for him to keep them in the dark about their land or their future. There is no monopoly on truth. If you don't take my life you are taking the lives of thousands more when he feeds them false hope and makes them fat upon it, and then in turn feeds them to

382

the spire to sustain his lie. Uncover the truth. Take back your lives. Don't leave them in his hands.'

The more it spoke, the more human it sounded. Its powers of persuasion matched those of the Forgemaster. 'He said it himself, he has lived longer than he ought to. Do you really think he has no reason to want to sustain this wretched cycle? Where have his extra years come from if not from those he fed to the very thing he is fused to?'

As Leander struggled to keep his feet on the floor and his hand from reaching the neck of the hollow, its words struck a chord. The halting of his companions' breath was heard as sharp intakes that echoed around the cavern. The Forgemaster was killing people to extend his own life? Could that be true? How would the hollow even know, or was it simply trying to get them to execute their plan?

Taren and Fion whirled around to face the hollow and spurred into action. Taren pulled back on Leander's waist to ground his feet and Fion took up position with her arms outstretched ready to activate her smithing skills. Taren moved back several paces and took up his place on the opposite side, mimicking Fion's stance. They all nodded to each other, with no real sense of complete certainty, and then in the corner of his eye Leander saw the Forgemaster pull his crystal dagger from his sleeve.

56

No Way to Un-know

'Taren!' Leander let out a strangled shout and Taren turned to catch sight of the familiar blade that sat in the Forgemaster's hand. He darted out from his place beside the root and stood in front of Leander's back, arms thrown wide. He had to protect both of his friends.

'You mistake me, Taren. I don't want to harm any of you. I've done all I can to show you what's real. I've shown you the truth you've asked to see. The hollow is persuasive, it acts for its own ends and drives just like any of us have at some point in our lives. Do not think it is immune to lies just because it advocates for truth. It saddens me that parts of the people have been reduced to such creatures but that cannot be undone. Here.' The tired old man slid the dagger along the stonework floor, grimacing at the metallic scrape of the hilt as it came to rest a step or so in front of Taren. Why was he giving him this?

'I don't understand.'

'Take the dagger. You can kill me, or you can kill the hollow. I won't stop you no matter what you choose. Before you make that choice, just ask yourself something. If you were to accept that what I've shown you is real, how does it make you feel? All of you. Knowing that the world is dying. If you are human, you will feel fear, and sadness and a crushing terror. In twenty to thirty years, this will all be gone. There is no way to stop it and no way out of it. There is no way to un-know this for any of you now.'

A freezing chill wrapped itself around Taren inside and out as he picked the weapon up. The Forgemaster was right, it did scare him. It scared him to death. If he let himself believe it was true instead of denying it, then the fear would become threefold. It would rip through him like a wind of needles and tear at him until he faced his death at the hands of the Crumbling Edge. That was if the dream didn't consume him first. All he'd see as he met his end would be the abyss slowly coming for them all like a great creature advancing over the land with nothing on its mind but destruction.

'Everyone and everything will be gone. Yet if you allow the system to stand, I will still be here. I will do my best to ensure that these people do not go to their deaths in paralysing fear. Ask yourself if you want to share the burden you all now carry with the people outside. Would you give them your fear? Have them live with it for the next thirty years and watch it rip them apart. Watch some of them decide to take the faster road out to avoid the inevitable?' His words rooted Taren deeper in place, the scuffle of Leander's shoes and breath as he struggled behind him only heightening the urgency. There was no time to listen to all this, but he couldn't move either. The Forgemaster continued.

'Those who get their calling and bind themselves to this fate of death, do you not think they'd do it happily to protect those they love given the choice? The choice would come with terror, and I only want them to be at peace when they die. They do see their dreams as they're consumed, they are unaware of what's happening to them. Taken away into a pocket of their minds. In a way, they get what they believe they're being given when they take their dreamstones. Do you want to be responsible for dousing this city with all of that grief and have them learn that they cannot escape it?

'Ask yourself all of this and then make your choice. I will not stand in your way. You have my word, whatever that means or does not mean to you now.'

The dagger couldn't have been heavier in Taren's hand if it was made of solid lead. Heavy with the weight of all of the Forgemaster's words, and those of the hollow. With every dreamstone he'd ever crafted and each person he'd therefore sent to their deaths. With every hollow that ailed on a root of the spire, with the hopes of every person out there in the slums and the truth that their hope meant nothing. Everything he'd ever known crumbled away with the edge of the world itself.

The glimpse of the past and the reflection of the future he'd seen. It all lay in the crystal blade of the dagger in his hands. The Forgemaster stood calm and still, his face set in an expression that Taren couldn't read. Fion waited for his signal with wide eyes and fear dragging at her mouth and brow. Leander fought to keep control of his arm as the hollow screeched with the effort to die at the hands of the body it once inhabited.

The room spun slowly, and Taren turned in the other direction without ever moving forward or back. Whispers of all the words that had passed through him in the past hour fell about him as vocal snowflakes. It all knitted together, weaving in and out and through and under and over. How had it come down to him to make the decision? There was so much conflict in all that he'd learned, and the Forgemaster was right again. He wished he didn't know it.

The truth couldn't be erased from his mind now. He'd be stuck with it until his dying day. Until the world fell away under his feet, and the feet of everyone else. Yet so many would need to die between now and then to shelter the rest. They had no choice in this, no awareness. They were all puppets in a system not designed by them but that was in place for them. They might not have a choice in things, but Taren did. He had one choice to make here and now that would affect everything.

The world quieted. Choices were made every day almost without thought. What to eat for breakfast. What to wear, what to say, who to talk to. Choice becomes more difficult the more people imagine the outcome. How could Taren make a choice about something he could barely comprehend? The only way was to follow the logical path, if logic could be found among the immensity of the situation they faced. With a deep breath, and one last look at the Forgemaster, Taren pushed his sadness down. One step at a time, he made his way towards the shrieking hollow with the dagger poised in his hand.

57

Filthy Cowards

Leander held his breath as Taren walked towards the hollow. He was going to do it? Uncover the truth of what they'd seen and show it to the people of the city? An image of a frightened Corryn burned brightly in his mind. Was it the right choice? Taren's face tightened with resolve, or at least the half of it that still showed emotion.

Taren stared up at the hollow as it began to shriek with glee. It lessened its grip on Leander's hand and he began to pry backwards, away from the root, without being noticed. His hand burned, and he knew that the skin was damaged beyond repair already. A question brushed his lips, to ask if this was truly the right thing to do, but then the hollow's joy turned to anger as Taren swiped at the tether with the dagger in one swift movement.

The screech was so inhuman that it hurt to hear. Leander's chest twisted and stomach swirled as he saw some of the hollow's claws fall away into the pit below. His feet worked to keep him steady as he was set free, stumbling backwards and cradling his hand and arm.

'No. NO! You are supposed to kill me, not free him. You've let the liar talk you round, you have the chance to end this and you're backing out. You coward. Filthy cowards the lot of you. You won't get another chance at this, he'll make sure of it.'

It began to howl, trying to pull itself away from the root it was irrevocably merged with. Leander tried to ignore the sound of ripping muscle coming from the creature as it strained to part with the crystal. It waved its arms manically, trying to reach the one who'd ruined its plans.

His hand throbbed with pain. Leander dared not move it. Fion was at his side, concerned and upset as she watched the show unfold. Black blood spattered from the hollow's mutilated hand, tar seeping from its mouth and scream-raw throat. Any semblance of humanity it had gained before utterly fled.

Its screeches pulled at Leander's lungs and his damaged knees couldn't hold him up anymore. Fion helped him fall, supporting him the whole way. Taren could only stare at the creature, his one working eye glistening as he listened to its furious lament. He'd made the choice now. He couldn't go back.

The Forgemaster stepped in, activating his smithing skills and sending a resonance toward the hollow. It calmed in seconds, and the crystal began to consume it quicker, pulling more of it into the root until it wasn't able to move at all any more. Subdued, it acted like the rest of them. Despondent and lethargic. Its cries echoed around the underground space long after it was silenced. Was it over?

Taren hadn't moved. He was vacant, on the edge of breaking, dagger gripped in his shaking hand. Leander could hardly look at him without his chest sizzling with hurt. After a few moments Taren woke from his stupor, searching for

389

the hollow, then down to his hands and round to Leander.

The moment their eyes met, Taren shattered. Throwing the dagger aside into the gloom he staggered backwards and melted into hitched, panicked sobs. Folding at the middle he collapsed to his knees and wept. Fion jumped into action, making sure Leander could sit up on his own first, but was then by Taren's side. He clung to her as he trembled.

'Thank you, Taren.' Leander bristled at the Forgemaster's gratitude, pre-empting Taren's violent reaction.

'Don't you dare thank me for that, don't you dare! I will not be thanked for it, and don't think for a second that I agree with your sickening solution to an even more sickening problem. What I just did is nothing to be thankful for!

'I've helped you keep them in the dark, I've helped you to continue taking lives. I would not have given up as you did. I wouldn't have abandoned the world and reconciled with using its people as fuel for your precious shield of dreams. I wouldn't have stopped searching until every ounce of life I had was gone and my body was left cold at the foot of the spire.' Shame echoed from the Forgemaster's body as Taren's sobs renewed.

In that moment, Leander's chest warmed. Taren's resolve, his openness, the strength he had. It all came together as a strong tide. He wanted to hold Taren in his arms and comfort him. His dream flooded his mind, perhaps as a final goodbye. The golden fields and clear skies, in the distance a farmhouse crafted by their hands. In the doorway to that farmhouse stood Taren, smiling in the early morning sun. Raven hair tumbling over one shoulder and a fond look in his ice blue eye. Leander wished that had been his dream all along, or maybe Taren had just been missing from it.

Would he be brave enough to tell Taren that when everything was over? What would over even mean? It wasn't about to be business as usual knowing the world was gradually being consumed by some great abyss. Maybe that was all the more reason to speak freely and directly though, he'd wasted enough time hiding how he felt about things. He didn't want to do that anymore, especially if their time was limited.

'You all need time to collect yourselves, understandably. If you want to leave the Forge, I won't stop you. You are free to go, you won't be questioned. If, however, you have more you want to ask about the truths you've seen, or have more you want to say, then I will wait for you in the Forge's library. I won't hold anything back. We will not be disturbed, I will make sure of it. The choice is yours.

'I know you didn't do it for me, but I still thank you. You've given me much to think about. I will await you in the library until further notice. To all of you... I'm sorry for everything you've been through and for my failure as the Forgemaster of this city.' Leander locked eyes with the Forgemaster as he turned and limped away with such a heavy weariness he doubted the old man would make it up the stairs. The glamour crept back over his body to hide the crystal that plagued him, but he couldn't hide the hurt and sadness in his eyes or the hunch of his back.

No one spoke. The three of them simply watched the Forgemaster walk away, and only when he'd left the underground space did they help each other to their feet and

391

make their way out of the cavern. Leander swallowed a gasp against the pain in his knees and knew that all of them would be more than happy never to see the place again.

58

A Lie They Cannot Question

As the Forgemaster left the cavern, a great clot of tension haemorrhaged from Taren and was replaced by being utterly drained. With bewildered looks drenched in internal turmoil, they began to follow the path the old man had taken and headed for the chamber outside the room of roots.

His chest ached with unanswered questions and personal accusations. Had it been the right choice? Whatever the answer, it was too late to be contemplating that question. Nausea swept through him, desperately searching for reassurance that would never come. How could it? Death loomed on the edge of everything. It always had but it should have been a long way off, if he was lucky. Now its black tendrils closed in around every person in the city. And closer still the iridescent claws of the dream that wracked his body. Would it act faster than the Crumbling Edge? Take him sooner?

His life was far shorter, but by how much? Would there even be a benefit to knowing how long he had? With his truncated future he'd made a decision that affected everyone else, how should he spend the remainder of it? Did he even have a right to spend it at all?

The more he imagined the lid of the world peeling back, like in the visions that the dream had shown him, the more the world in front of him swam. He'd launched strong words at the Forgemaster. Declarations of strength and never giving up, about how he'd fight to find the solution. The words were empty. Spoken by another Taren. One who hoped, one who thrived on his purpose. Not this Taren. This hopeless shadow. He wanted nothing more to do with any of it, hypocrisy be damned. One step at a time for now. Just keep walking, get out of the cavern.

A pair of hands steadied him. Leander. Such a comfort, just knowing he was there. They'd been through a lot already in a short time. How would Leander and Fion react once it sunk in? Something niggled at Taren, deep in his mind. It was sharp, barbed, and pulsing its way through his thoughts. A decision of some kind, filled with a determination and certainty.

Breaking out from the darkness of the root room and spilling into the antechamber was a breath of slightly fresher air. Even though the space was smaller, it felt much less restricted. The door swung shut of its own accord once they were safely out, and the three of them collapsed onto the staircase. Taren pressed his forehead against the cool stone wall, hoping it would stop the throbbing of the dream. The only sound in the empty space was their laboured breathing.

He had no doubt that his two friends also felt as though they'd forced their way through a swamp filled with compounding horrors. Did they have the same shivers in their legs? Fog in their minds? Did their hearts strain like his? By the looks on their faces the answers were plain.

Each of them stared into a lonely distance, watching the world they thought they knew being dragged away attached to a chariot of the truth. Dragged through the dirt and flogged as it went, helpless and forever scarred. There was no way to recover it. Everything was misaligned. Every memory he ever had doused in a new and unwelcome light. What was the way forward for them, after they'd sought and received this knowledge? The answer rang clear in his head, and echoed around the chamber as it left his mouth.

'I can't stay. Not knowing what we've learned.'

Fion's head shot up, her eyes burning with questions and stacking up persuasions. 'What will you do? Will you leave the Forge? Give up being a dreamsmith? Will you start a new life in the slums?' Taren hung his head, unsure how to phrase what she'd misunderstood. He took her hand as she reached for him. She looked the way he felt, like she could sleep for a week. Could he really add to the hurt she'd felt today? Leander saved him the trouble.

'He doesn't mean leave the Dreamforge. He means… leaving the dreamveil.' Their eyes met, and Taren was warmed by Leander's instant understanding. Fion, however, knitted her brows in confusion.

'Leave the dreamveil? But… you saw what's out there, we all saw what's coming. How would you live?'

'I don't know, Fi, but I know I can't live in here. Not now. I chose to let the veil stand, to let it continue to shield everyone from the horror of what we were shown, but I can't sit by and watch them be deceived until I die. I can't live with the truth weighing down on me among people who are blanketed with a lie they cannot question. I can't sit by and watch them hope for a false release.'

395

She nodded, working her jaw in the way she did when she was fighting her feelings. She rarely showed tears in front of other people, ever the strong and solid friend.

'I... understand. I do, but I don't want you to leave. I know that's selfish. Can't you stay and help me try and convince the Forgemaster to begin the expeditions again? Where are those fighting words from in there?' She gestured back to the now-closed door. Taren gawped at his friend with wonder. In that moment she was stronger than he would ever be, and he loved her for it. He squeezed her hand, and matched its tremors.

'You want to stay here?'

She nodded without hesitation. 'Yes. I want to have him answer for his failure by rekindling his efforts to fulfil his duty. You said yourself you would have never given up until your body was found cold at the foot of the spire. I feel the same.

'Maybe with someone else aiding him again, he'll find the courage to try and make some small amends for what he's allowed to happen to these people. He has much to answer for, and I want to make sure he holds himself responsible.' In the quiet of the chamber the two men stared at Fion, blinking in silence. Then a wave of wholehearted laughter echoed about the stairwell and lifted their spirits.

'Well Fion, I have to say, he won't stand a chance against you. You'll have him following your orders soon enough with that attitude.' Leander smiled as he spoke the words, giving the first truly warm smile that Taren recalled seeing from him.

'He's right. The Forgemaster should be shaking in his boots right now at the mere thought of having you on his back about this. If anyone knows how relentless you can be it's me.'

Fion grinned, tears clinging to her eyes and refusing to fall. 'So you'll both help me whip him into shape?' she asked, but knew the answer. Taren stood, pulling her to her feet and embracing her.

'You are so much stronger than I am, Fi. You always have been. This world is already in better hands having heard you speak your intent. I can't stay though. I might have been able to once, only a handful of days ago. But now… I can't watch them carry on in ignorance, going to fetch their dreamstones with smiles on their faces, not even aware of where they're headed…' The vision from his aunt's hollow flashed across his mind. The blanket of spent stones, the forest of merging hollows, all of it made him shudder.

'You always did wear your emotions on your sleeve. I hope I can convince Clayton…'

'Oh trust me, you can. Anyone who goes up in a fight against your determination and persistence will find themselves quickly overshadowed. The world needs people like you, Fi. It doesn't need people like me. Not this world anyway.'

'Where will you go, though?'

'I have no idea. I don't know what's out there, not really. I just need to be free of the dreamveil. It's more like a nightmare. I've no idea what's left of the world, but there is someone who will know. Shall we go to him?' Fion and Leander both nodded with pained smiles. Taren hoped he knew what Leander's choice would be in all this, but what stock could be held in hope now?

59

Penance

Fion led the way back to the ground-level halls of the Forge. The constraints of the tight underground air fell away the higher they travelled. It remained odd for Leander to imagine being so far below the city, let alone actually being inside the Dreamforge itself. He hung back to walk next to Taren, and thoughts stirred in his mind.

What do I want? Both of them know exactly what they want to do as a result of all this, but me? I need to find Corryn first, it feels like we were gone for days even though that can't be possible. She'll be worried, I'll probably get a right verbal lashing when I get home.

The thought of seeing Corryn again filled him with comfort. Apologies were in order first, but then he'd embrace her and thank her for always being there for him. The comfort turned cold as a thought struck him. *Should I tell her… what we learned?* He could see her face widen in terror, and had no doubt she'd try and manage the information with grace like she did everything else. Would he really want to tell her? To scare her like that?

Then Taren's words made even more sense and hummed with a strange resonance inside him. He wouldn't be able to do it. He couldn't sit by and pretend to live life as normal knowing what he knew, but also didn't want to turn Corryn's world upside down either.

Leander stuck out like a sore thumb among the group as the only one who wasn't familiar with the surroundings. Not to mention his different attire. The higher they'd climbed, the more opulent things had become. Stone walls and floors that were well lit and plush carpets snaking around on their paths through the Forge's halls. Not even a potted plant or tree in sight, either. It was eerie in its quiet, smooth calm. Surely the place should be bustling with dreamsmiths? It was a large building, though, and Leander had the sense of them not being in well-trodden corridors.

They hauled themselves up a great spiral staircase, and Leander was about to question the abject silence of his companions. Catching a glimpse of Taren's expression halted the question and it died on his lips. Foolishly, he thought they'd be happy to be back at the Forge, walking the halls of a place that had been somewhat of a home for them. Then he recalled the new light they must be seeing it under. The seat of deception. The resting place of so many unsuspecting citizens. His respect for Fion grew, knowing that she was willing to stay and help tackle things, and he knew immediately that he was not that kind of man. He longed only for peace and quiet.

Maybe Corryn and I can do what Taren intends as well? I wonder if she'd agree. There has to be a way to make a life out there. This can't be the only way left. His chest and legs burned with the effort of climbing the spiral stairs, knees ablaze with aches from their impact with the stone well, and the others were flagging too. He wanted to ask how much further they had to go, but in gazing up he saw an opening leading off down

399

another corridor and hoped that was their destination. The back of his hand throbbed from the hollow's tether and grip, a great black blemish baking with heat. Would it ever fade? If anything he wondered if it had spread, but surely it would heal in time.

They exited the stairs at the next landing, much to Leander's relief. Even a full day of crouching in the fields to harvest wasn't that hard on his legs. The corridors here were even quieter, if possible. Awe floated about him as the library came into view, the great double doors wrought from wood and glass.

It was situated in a desolate corner of the Forge and yet could be a hub for dreamsmiths to gather and study. The library looked circular from what could be seen through the glass of the doors, and at the centre, in an open space filled with various desks and tables, stood the Forgemaster calmly waiting for their approach. Leander's insides writhed, unsure how to feel about the man.

Fion threw a glance back at the both of them, asking with her eyes whether this was what they wanted. They nodded in response and she fell into line on the other side of Taren, a united front, as they pulled the library doors open. A musty whiff of ancient books wrapped around them. This was where the knowledge of the world resided. The knowledge that was used to feed the dreamsmiths the falsities of their craft. Both beautiful and haunting.

Hands behind his back and hood down, the Forgemaster couldn't hide a small smile as they approached. Perhaps he thought they'd leave instead of coming to seek his council, but no one else held the answers they sought. Leander couldn't shake the feeling of being a fly stuck in a glob of honey.

'I wasn't sure that you'd come here, thank you.'

'We aren't here for you.' Taren's tone was full of so many things. Confusion, pain, dislike but also a longing. Leander took a step forward to stand shoulder to shoulder with him, which seemed to calm him.

'No… no of course not. I promised that I wouldn't hold anything further back and would answer any questions you had honestly and openly.'

'I don't think we need to hear any more of your justifications or your truths. We got the gist of it down there in the root caverns. There's little more to say about it. You made your choice and now you live with it.' Surprise fluttered through Leander. He'd been under the impression that Taren had a lot of questions, yet now his jaw was set and reluctance poured off of him.

'There's nothing more you wish to know?'

'What good would it possibly do? The world is dying and everyone is unaware. The reason they remain unaware is because their kin are fuelling your dream. The one you thrust upon us all. A decision you took alone. I cannot change the way the system works, you made that very clear. You've told us the truth and now we must choose how to live with it.'

The Forgemaster seemed quietly stung by Taren's words and disdain. He looked at each of their faces and found no warmth in the expressions there. He made no attempt to hide the pain it caused him, but he remained calm and collected.

'You're right. You have choices. So, what have you all decided?' Leander's heart hammered in his chest. Would

Taren declare that he wanted to leave? What should he do, what about his own choice? What did he want? All of a sudden time seemed too short to make a decision. Taren pressed his arm closer and slipped his hand into Leander's before answering. The sight blocked from anyone else's view by their torsos and hips. A spark of joy raced through Leander, mixed with a bewildered disbelief. Now he knew what he wanted too, and it was nothing to do with his dream being attached to Taren. It may have been the reason once, but not anymore.

'I want to leave. Not just the city, but the dreamveil. I want to live outside of its reach, forfeit its safety. With what remains of my time I'll make a life for myself away from here.' The Forgemaster blinked in surprise at Taren. Leander squeezed his hand gently in return.

'Y-you want to live outside of the dream? But you saw the state of the world, how could you want to live out there? It's not impossible but-'

'Because anything is preferable to living a life in here. Knowing what I do, knowing what I've done, what I chose not to stop. You can't expect me to go and live among those people and watch them revel in hope for a better life only to be unknowingly led to death. You can't expect me to craft another dreamstone while I draw breath. I can't tell them the truth, and I can't free them from it, so I can only free myself and live in the ruined world as penance. "Not impossible" is good enough for me.'

'I want to go with him as well,' Leander glanced at Taren and was touched to see him smiling, 'and Corryn too, if you'd have us.' The smile turned into a grin, punctuated with a nod. Fion was clearly happy for them, but struggling with accepting that Taren would be leaving.

'How can the two of you suppose you'll live? You could die within months. There's no hope out there.'

'There's none in here, either. That fact is just hidden better.' The words left Leander's mouth before he could stop them. But why should he? They were dealing in truths all around now. 'The people are under a very pretty but equally sinister dome. We will live off the land, build a relationship with it again like we once did in older times. Land that is properly cared for is always generous and giving. I've spent my life cultivating all sorts of fields. Maybe it will be a good thing that we get back to having a working relationship with the world. At least then it won't die alone.

'Imagine dying and being ignored in the process. Everyone hiding out of sight, out of mind, while you expire. Like Taren said, you can't expect us to live here knowing what we know. I can't do it either. Besides, I have a feeling you'll have your hands full. Too full to worry about what becomes of us… right Fion?'

She tried to hide a smirk and failed, though it was soon replaced with a steely determination as she spoke up.

'I don't wish to leave. I wish to stay and help you atone for your wrongs. I want to work with you to resume expeditions. You gave up because you were left alone. It's too much to expect one person to solve all the problems of the world. I want to help you. I agree with Taren's words, I won't stop until my body lies cold at the foot of the spire now that I know the truth. I won't give up like you, but I need your help if you'll take mine.'

To their disbelief, the Forgemaster's face morphed through a mix of expressions and his eyes glittered. Fion's words clearly moved him, struck so many chords he could hardly handle them. Relief washed over him, as though he'd shed part of his isolation and loneliness like a weighted cloak falling from his shoulders. He even stood a little straighter. In that moment, Leander pitied him. Despite what he'd done, it clearly brought him a lot of strife to continue to keep the cycle running all these years. The Forgemaster ran the cuff of a sleeve across his eyes and cheeks and collected himself with a few breaths.

'I would like that very much, Fion. I haven't had the strength. It's been all I could do to continue to shield the citizens. So many times I wanted to resume the expeditions, but I cannot do it alone. You are the first to offer help of any kind, and you do so despite what you've learned. I hope I can earn your trust once more.'

Fion scoffed. 'You've had no help because you've never asked for it. People can't offer help if they don't know it's needed. You've shouldered it alone, and the consequences could be irreversible. These two might not have questions, but I have plenty. As for earning my trust again, time will tell.'

A solemn look shadowed his face. Part of him might have hoped that he'd retained some of the trust of his former students, but it was a short-lived fancy.

'Taren and Leander. If you wish to leave, despite the dangers, I will not stop you. But I must ask if you want to keep your link to the spire or not. Know this, however, if you choose no then once you leave the influence of the dreamveil you can never return to it. This decision is one you only get to make once. The veil covers much of the remaining world, but you can only see it because you're tethered to the source. Everyone is connected to it, led to this city by its influence. If you wish, I can sever your connection once you're a safe distance from the city.'

Leander didn't even need to think about it, and was quite sure that Taren didn't either. Leander spoke first.

'I don't want to keep any connection to that dreadful thing. I've no intention of returning. Cutting my connection to it can't come soon enough.'

'I don't want to stay connected to it either. We want to be free of it all. To make our own choices about our future in full knowledge of them.' Taren glanced at Fion apologetically as he spoke but she only nodded at him. A glint in her eye told Leander that Taren was due a serious conversation with his friend before they left. The Forgemaster sighed but nodded, offering one last warning.

'There will be no way back, no way to rekindle it. Before you leave, you should say any goodbyes you need to, and make them good ones.'

60

Unheard Apology

The brightness of the outside world stung Taren's eyes as the three of them finally left the Forge and made their way through the inner city. They all needed food and water, or even tea. That would be heavenly, though it sent a pang of sadness through him as he thought of his aunt. She was dead. He knew it now. Not moved on to a better life as she'd hoped. Hoped so desperately.

They would head to Leander's place first and spend some time there while they broke the news to Corryn and gave her time to decide her path of action. Leander didn't want to leave her in the slums, nor did Taren for that matter, but they'd both agreed that they couldn't ask her to accompany them without telling her the truth. It would be far too much of a shock to discover it on the road as they walked out of the reach of the spire's influence.

The city looked different in the light of the truth. Every face smiling and happy with anticipation. Those who lived in the inner city had already received their dreamstones, their fates already sealed. Whether it was next week or next month, their stones would transport them to their deaths. The spires, which he once found beautiful and kindled nothing but pride in him, now made him grimace and produced a low and sour burning under his ribs. He shivered as he pictured his aunt's memories once more and a wave of dizziness pushed him into an unsteady sway. Leander was there with a supporting hand on his back, and he was glad of it.

'I've never really had the chance to look around the inner city before, but I wish I was seeing it in a different light.' Leander's gaze fell over everything in sight, from the people to the spacious stone houses. Taren found himself preferring the farmhouse. 'These houses are huge compared to the ones in the slums, each new one that's built out there seems smaller.'

'I think I prefer your house to these big, half-empty stone ones. It was much more comforting,'

'Do you need anything from your place before you head to the slums?' Fion chirped in. Her face wore the same downcast expression as Taren's, but with the added weight of knowing they'd soon be parting ways.

'I'm not sure. Most of my clothes are dreamsmith robes. I never really had many clothes as a kid and I've been wearing these since I was a teenager. It's strange, of all the possessions in my home none of them have ever felt like mine. I can find some clothes at one of the shops here or in the slums, wouldn't hurt to help out a business before we go.'

'How do you both intend to live out there?' Fion kept her voice low, mustering smiles for the people who passed by them as they trekked towards the gates to the slums.

'If we can find a suitable place, we can choose to settle there. I'm sure I can put Taren to work helping me to build

407

some shelter and working the fields.'

'I think he's far too delicate for that kind of work, Leander. Nose always buried in books.' Her laugh was a salve to his heavy chest.

'Too delicate? You must be kidding me, I can handle manual work.'

'You could barely handle dreamsmith work, took you way too long to build up the stamina to craft properly.'

Taren feigned outrage. 'I was one of the quickest trainees to make it to the forges!'

'And you're still slower than I am.'

'You had a head start.'

'See, he just makes excuses. I doubt he will be much use to you when it comes to manual labour.' Taren elbowed his friend in the side and they giggled, yet he couldn't free himself of the guilt when he thought back to all the dreamstones he'd crafted. All the endings he'd written with pride and joy at his accomplishment.

'Will you... carry on being a smith?' Taren asked Fion.

'Do you need to ask? I can't continue to craft, but I suppose we can't stop producing dreamstones altogether. I'll focus all my efforts on rebooting the expeditions. It means we'll probably have to bring in a few more smiths on what we learned, and hope they can be trusted and share the sentiments of protecting the people. I really don't know how things will play out here. Are you sure you won't stay to help me make a change?' They reached the gate and Taren turned to face Fion with a sad smile.

'I can't, Fi. I can't say here but I commend you for your strength in doing what I can't. My duty as a dreamsmith, my work, it used to be a hopeful thing to me. I used to believe in hope, and think the city was a beacon for it. A safe place for people to flock and dream of something better.

'Knowing what we do now, knowing that I have blood on my hands and that their hope is propped up by a scaffold of lies. Of death. I... can't stay. Every time I see their faces I want to scream at them how they're in danger, heading for a premature death, heading blindly for oblivion. I can't live that way, nor can I watch them living this way even if I chose to let the dream stand. I know that if anyone can help solve this, it's you. Truth be told, I don't think I'll live all that long a life. With what's left of it perhaps I'll rediscover hope and what it means to me, though.'

Fear dropped into her face and she reached out for his arm. 'No, don't say that. What makes you think so?'

'It's already spreading. I don't think there was ever a way to save me or separate me from it, judging by the state of the Forgemaster's body. And by everything we've learned. Besides, if I were able to separate myself from the dreamstone, it would probably call to Leander again... and we've no idea what that means now that his hollow is gone. I don't want to be responsible for that.'

Leander could only stare at the floor. They could talk about it later. Fion buried her face in Taren's chest, trying hard to control her rising sadness.

'I don't want you go, Taren. Stay. If you think the dream's killing you then let me care for you.'

He returned her embrace. 'I wish I could. But I'd die a quicker death here. You've been a phenomenal friend to me, Fi. Probably a much better friend than I deserve. I'm going to have to teach Leander a thing or two about banter if he's to live up to your standards.' A half-laugh, half-sob escaped her and she turned her face up to him. He cleared her tears with his thumbs and held back his own.

'Be careful out there, OK? Both of you. I'll do what I can here. Hopefully, one day, the cycle will be broken.'

'These people are in the best hands with you working on their side. Don't ever doubt yourself, or your strength. You're the best dreamsmith... no, the best person that I know. I'll see you again before we go, can't leave without someone waving us off.'

'I wouldn't miss it.' They embraced again, lingering before reluctantly stepping away. Fion hugged Leander too, asking him to take care of Taren and it was promised. Then the two men walked out of the inner city gate for the last time.

***

The farmhouse was quiet... a little too quiet. The damage from the hollow's rampage was something they'd seen at every turn on their way back to Leander's home. Hasty repairs, patchwork fixes, debris stacked at the side of the paths. The apprehensive and disbelieving stares of the smiths that were heading the clean-up efforts. Hard to believe that it all happened yesterday.

Leander kept his head down, unable to look at the damage after a while. His fists clenched until the knuckles turned white when he spotted a badly-covered blood stain on one of the roads. Taren let him know he was there, and that it wasn't his fault, even though the words felt as empty as the hope of all the people in the slums. His chest pulled tight to think that the one shred of something that helped these people justify the conditions they lived in was a lie. The sooner they left the better.

'Something's wrong.' Leander slowed halfway down the path to the house. 'Corryn should be doing chores at this time. The harvest is coming soon.' He surveyed the yard and the fields, his face becoming a shade lighter with everything his eyes fell upon.

'What is it?'

'Nothing has been moved since the day you were taken away. It's all exactly the same. Where's Corryn?' He bolted towards the house too quickly for Taren to keep up. Leander disappeared through the front door, shouting his sister-in-law's name. By the time Taren caught up the shouting had stopped, cut off mid-word and stifled by a loss of breath.

One step at a time he slowly entered the house. Leander stood completely still, staring at the upturned table and the wreck of a room. At the splayed body in the corner, unmoving, and missing all of the attentive care and fire that usually flooded from Corryn. Deep claw marks marred her torso. Taren couldn't even form any words as he remembered how kind and caring she'd been while nursing him back to health. The room always rang with her laughter. What had happened here?

'It was me...' Leander trembled where he stood, looking ghoulish. He twitched at random intervals and his eyes slid back and forth. 'I did this... I remember it now.' A hand half-covered his face, disturbing the sweat that doused his skin. 'I did this. Why would I do this? Why would that thing do this to her. She didn't deserve this!'

He was rooted on the spot, unable to take another step towards the ruined body. Instead he staggered dangerously, covering his mouth as though he'd vomit, and his knees buckled. Taren dashed forward to catch him and held Leander tightly as he screamed over and over, his own tears falling quietly and his chest burning with grief.

Leander reached for her constantly as he half-lay in Taren's arms, screaming her name and apologising with such remorse that Taren thought his heart would break again. He stayed there, wrapped in Leander's grief-filled screams of unheard apology and regret, until the sun set and all their feelings were spent.

61

Our Scant Future

As Fion walked through the inner city, her mind swirled with thoughts. The weight of saying goodbye to Taren hung in her chest on sharp hooks, his words echoing over and over. He seemed convinced that there was no way to separate from the dreamstone, and he was probably right about it. Along with everything he believed that meant about his life being limited. So why not stay? Let himself be cared for? Instead of slowly turning into a walking dream out there in a dying world. Knowing him, he'd see it as some kind of true penance, like he said. Her eyes rolled of their own accord. He always was hard on himself.

Taren was running away, there wasn't much of another way to look at it, and yet she couldn't be mad at him. Not really. His reasoning made perfect sense for him, even if it wasn't a path she could ever choose for herself. Part of her continuing to be a good friend meant respecting that. But she wouldn't leave these people to their fate, herself included. Taren might want to leave the city behind, but she had plans. Big plans. And the Forgemaster would hear them out.

Clayton had work to do, not least in earning back her

trust. Once, he'd been someone willing to risk himself for
the sake of figuring out what had happened to the outside
world. Now he was cowering under the weight of his
burden, and yet again Fion could understand it. There was a
long way to go before she could forgive it, though.

By the time she reached the Dreamforge again her body
was humming with purpose and resolve as tough as stone.
Energy refreshed with the shower, water and food she'd
scrabbled together at her inner city home after leaving Taren
at the gates. She made a beeline right for Clayton's office,
determination turning her steps into a march. He couldn't
hide from her now, she dared him to even try. Everyone
around her went about their business as normal and part of
what Taren said prickled along her spine. They don't know,
they didn't see. Their minds blissfully free of the Crumbling
Edge and the pit of spikes Fion was dangling over in the
way of knowing the truth. For just a second, she longed to
go back to a state of unknowing. Just for a second, she
wanted being a dreamsmith to mean something hopeful
again. Then she burst into Clayton's office and bit back a
smirk to see she'd startled him yet again.

'Fion, you're back so soon. Have you said your
goodbyes?'

'I'll see them again before they leave, but until then we
have much to discuss. As I said, I've a lot of questions and
you will sit and answer them. No flourishes, no games.'

Clayton moved gracefully to his chair and motioned for
Fion to take a seat as well. His expression was steady, eyes
lit with a positivity she hadn't seen in them for many years.
At least he was willing and ready.

'What will they find out there?'

414

'I can't say for sure, but not much. Or maybe too much, depending on how resilient they are. We are the last city. There's been no communication from any others for a long, long time. The spire has been sending out its call across great distances. Calling people here like a beacon, as you know. It also acts as a radar of sorts. Just recently its call reached what I believe to be... the last humans outside the dreamveil. Everything and everyone else is gone. Turning grey like the Edge that advances toward us.'

'So it's not possible to live out there?'

'It might be. Even if all people have congregated here, there is still other wildlife out there in the world. This is not a fast death we've inherited.'

'That they have some kind of chance is all I wanted to know. Now, tell me everything about the expeditions. How they used to be organised, what was found, how they used to work, exactly how and why they came to an end and when the last one was. Don't leave anything out.' Fion listened as the Forgemaster began to speak, determined not to forget a single detail.

By the time they were almost done talking, hours later, Fion's jaw ached. So she had no idea how Clayton was holding up. He'd done most of the talking. There was so much that he'd kept locked away. Watching him finally unburden himself turned tight and cryptic circles in her chest.

She still cared for his wellbeing, despite everything. Still couldn't stamp out the bond they'd had, even if it had snapped and a new one was knotting together in its place. Some of his actions were unforgivable, like using her as a puppet to unknowingly dispense death. Who knows how long that would take to accept and sort through. It wasn't the kind of thing you could move on from so easily, but for now she had to look past that and aim her gaze forward. She spoke her list of requests, making sure they sounded more like demands. They'd be equals in this if they were to do it at all. He couldn't quite be trusted to act alone just yet, and he seemed to know and accept this.

'Right, so we're agreed?' Fion hauled herself out of her chair. She'd sat in it so long that it hurt to stand, her lower back creaking slightly as she straightened. Clayton was meant to be the old one. 'The divide between the inner city and the slums needs to be brought down and done away with. These people are all in this together, and if they're to go to their deaths for the sake of others they deserve decent living conditions. Instead of expanding the slums, we expand the inner city.

'Plenty of slumfolk would be happy to earn decent coin or trades for amenities or food as builders, and proper housing is needed. If we only have a few decades to live, everyone deserves comfort.'

Clayton sighed, setting aside the papers he'd made frantic notes on during their discussions. 'It will be hard to move forward without the divide but yes, I agree. Too many people flocked here too quickly, I haven't tended to their needs well. I was too overwhelmed.'

'Those who've been called and those who are still waiting will exist together. You'll remove the gates. We'll need that barrier down soon, or perhaps temporarily, for when I get back.'

'Oh?' He looked up at her as she paced to wake her legs up, clearly curious.

'We'll need more people working for the Dreamforge if we're to set up expedition teams again. Not necessarily more dreamsmiths, there's no reason to expedite people's callings. If anything we should perhaps slow them down as much as we can without causing outrage. I know of some people we can recruit immediately. People who I'm sure will be happy to help. However they, along with all the existing dreamsmiths... have to be told the truth.'

'What?' Clayton all but leapt up from his chair. 'Why? That would cause panic and-'

'You can't keep asking people to do this while they're uninformed.' Clayton had nothing to say to that, so Fion continued. 'Hopefully we will be surprised by how many people want to assist us. How many want to fight against this fate we've been dealt.'

'If you're wrong?'

'Then I'm damn well wrong. What do we have to lose? The people who work for the Dreamforge need to be given the chance to consent to their actions rather than being used. You owe them that much. Those who wish to can leave, those who want to stay can help.'

Clayton stared down at his desk for a long time. Fion's heart beat a clumsy rhythm. Would he agree to the terms? To her way of working? Or would he find it too hard to break from his tightly locked box of secrecy and shouldering everything alone. She didn't push him, she hardly dared breathe. *Don't be disappointing, Clayton. Be the man you used to be, the man you can be again. Someone I can feel pride in one more time.*

'Alright. I agree. But Taren chose to keep the dreamveil intact for the sake of those under its protection.'

'We won't tell the general populace, don't worry. We

417

can busy them with the other improvements to their living situation and manage anyone who seems to be in danger of spreading the word. Only those in and associated with the Dreamforge need know.

'It's time to look after these people, Clayton, rather than only protecting them. You've made it clear there's no way to stop the more unsavoury side of this arrangement. That's something I can't think very much about at this moment in time. I have to look forward, to those we might yet spare, though I'm quite sure you'll never be free of the weight of those you've already fed to the spire. No doubt you'd also do it all over again in the same way, which is how I know you believe you were doing the only thing you could.'

He opened his mouth as if to reply but thought better of it. Her disgust in his choices was hopefully crystal clear. She'd never condone it, only fight harder going forward to change it.

'I'll never forge a dreamstone again, but I'll be damned if I don't have a hand in forging how we spend the rest of our scant future.'

Clayton only nodded. His throat working against a thousand possible responses, all of which he kept inside himself.

'OK, I'm heading out to get some new recruits. Make sure they're able to get back into the inner city when I return. We've work to do.'

With that she turned and left without a backward glance. She might have seen a smile in the corners of Clayton's mouth before she made for the door, but couldn't be sure. Sometimes people just needed a chance, which is exactly what the people she was heading out to find also deserved.

Hopefully she'd remember the way back to the culler's base without getting herself lost or kidnapped again. Things were about to change. Only time would tell what good it would all do, if any.

Her thoughts turned to Taren once more. She'd miss him, and hoped with ferocity that he was wrong about his lifespan, but she'd also do her best to make him proud. To use the expeditions to find him again in the world beyond the bubble they'd all been ensconced in. *Please... let him find happiness. Let both of them find it somehow, somewhere out there.*

62

The Edge of the Dream

The wind swept through the fields and brought a freshness to Leander's face. He could barely feel it. It had been a week since they'd returned to find Corryn dead in their home, and this was the first day he'd had the strength to consciously leave his bed and venture out. Strength perhaps not quite being the right word. His body moved the way he wanted only out of habit, but like all the joints were fighting insidious rust. In truth, he wished to remain inside, hiding from the world, but didn't want to continue being the reason for their delayed departure.

The soil of the grave differed in colour to that around it, marking the place where Corryn now rested. It was strange. People sometimes passed away in the slums from malnutrition or if they got chosen by the cullers, and he'd helped to bury people before... but it had been so different.

Corryn filled his mind, memories fed through in a non-stop loop, and he couldn't equate her shining presence to a hole in the ground and a slightly raised mound of soil. It wasn't right. While sitting cross-legged a metre away he'd fought the urge to dig at the crushing earth to rescue her several times. She couldn't breathe in there. She deserved to feel the air, cold with the chill promise of rain. Deserved to hear their crops whispering on the wind, to wash the grit and dirt of a hard day's work from her hands. No amount of washing could remove all the dirt now.

He'd come outside to start assessing if the fields were ready to harvest. He would need to leave someone in charge of them, and his home, to save the crops going to waste. Would someone pick up the mantle and use them to feed those who struggled when the supplies from the inner city ran scarce? Then again, that wouldn't be his concern anymore once they'd left.

He'd lasted all of a few minutes in assessing the fields, before finding himself sitting next to Corryn yet again. Sometimes he found himself out there in the night, shivering in the cold and unaware of how he got there, only for Taren to come and wrap a blanket over him and take him back indoors.

The rising wave of grief tried to return and he fought it, he'd let it dominate the foreground enough over the past seven days. Fighting it was no use, though. It loomed in his chest like a great wall of dark and curling fog. His determination to push it down was about as much use as a cracked roof in a thunderstorm. Most of it was a blur, the only constant being Taren. The tables had certainly turned. First he'd sheltered Taren in his home until he was well again, but now Taren looked after him instead.

'Funny how things turn out, eh Corryn? I'd better check the crop, I know you'll watch over it for me once we're gone. I wish you could have come with us.' He rose to his knees, leaving a hand-print at the edge of the rounded mound of soil, and waded out into the fields.

A day and a half later they were prepared to depart. Taren had been so patient with him, he barely felt deserving of his attentions. A weight hung over Leander, one that didn't lift even after they were out of the city. They were leaving everything behind. The good and the bad.

Fion had a sixth sense for these things and had turned up at the farm early to help them prepare and to see them off. She'd come to check on them every day after they found Corryn. Her face held a restrained sadness, and perhaps a glimmer of hope.

Leander was still numb to many things, but heard snatches of the conversation he was supposed to be a part of. Discussions with the Forgemaster had begun, and so had the research and recruitment. Expeditions would need more smiths, she'd secured them some already. She promised to do her best to get expeditions out as soon as she could. That way perhaps she'd see them somewhere in the wide world.

Watching Taren and Fion say goodbye for the final time should have been a sad thing, but there wasn't the slightest stir in Leander. If he'd locked himself away when his wife had left, this feeling was ten-fold on that. When would he feel something other than sadness again? Maybe he'd find the answer out there in the dying world with the person he wanted by his side until he died himself.

Absently, he spread his hand in front of him. Taking in the sight of the large, black stain the hollow left behind. Denial wouldn't be of any use. They both knew it. It had spread, almost covering the whole of the back of his hand now. Sometimes it burned and pulsed and the next day it had expanded its boundary.

422

There wasn't much rhyme or reason to it. Sometimes it went days without bothering him, and the same for Taren's affliction. How much time would they have? Perhaps it was penance. Taren consumed by the very thing he used to fashion to cause the deaths of others, Leander's time shortened for using his very own hands to take Corryn's life. A dark chuckle bubbled in his throat, but he wouldn't let it out. If he did, it would only morph into a sob.

When they finally departed, they stood shoulder-to-shoulder on the road and gazed back at the slums, the city, and the ever-climbing spires.

'You sure about this?' Taren asked.

'I'm sure.'

'Alright then… let's go.'

***

Less than a day outside of the city and between them they'd barely said a word. Every so often they'd come across people using the road, headed the way they'd come. Overhearing conversations about what they'd do when they got there and how long they'd have to wait before they got their calling. Perhaps they'd get their calling on the road and wouldn't have to wait at all, then everything would be better when they got to live their dreams.

A bitter dragon writhed inside Leander, and only Taren's hand on his arm stopped him from shouting at the passers-by. *It's all a lie, you're going to your death. Turn back. You're already under the spell of the spire.* But Taren shook his head, anguish simmered under the surface of his expression, too. They had to let them pass without saying anything. It wasn't up to them. They'd made their choice, and these people had to be allowed to keep their ignorance.

423

'How can we watch them head towards that place and say nothing?' They walked side by side now the latest group of travellers had passed.

'I know it's tough, I wanted to tell them too but... we can't.' Taren sighed, kicking a stone into the dry grass that lined the dusty road. 'It's not our place to say it, it will only frighten them, cause unrest. At least in the dream they're protected, as much as I detest the cycle that provides that.'

'I wonder what it will look like, when we pass out of the dream.'

'You don't remember from when the Forgemaster showed us?'

Leander shook his head. 'There's a lot I can't recall correctly, since it was the same day we went back to the farmhouse.' A sullen silence surrounded them both.

'It wasn't your fault. I know it feels like it and it will for a long time, but it wasn't. It's not a comfort now, but one day you'll believe it.' Leander met Taren's gaze, his one working eye catching the sunlight. He couldn't help a slight smile.

'Thank you.'

***

They were already losing track of the days, but early one morning a short while after they set off for the day the air took on a thicker quality. The air they knew mixed with air they didn't. Their steps slowed, but didn't stop. They hadn't seen any other travellers for over a day, always heading towards the city, never away. Had they finally reached the edge of the dream?

With each step they felt some resistance, something pushing back against them, trying to corral them back the

424

way they came. Then a resonance rang out for the both of them and a whisper on the wind wished them good luck. With an internal ripple that jolted them, the distant sound of breaking glass echoed in their minds. Leander held a hand to his chest in shock, Taren staggered back a step, and then the sky rolled back.

The dreamveil receded, eaten up by the dire grey of the true skin of their world. It peeled away, colour fading with it, and they were left in an almost monochrome land.

'Where shall we go?' Taren asked the empty land as though it would respond and offer up some kind of sign or suggestion. Leander joined his hand with Taren's and mustered the most genuine smile he could. It felt unfamiliar on his face, like cracking a plaster cast. An alien expression, but it made Taren beam so brightly that it was worth the effort.

'Wherever we want to. We have the whole world to explore. I've been thinking… why don't we try and find a place to live out the dream? A place to settle ourselves and work on the land. Try and connect with it again, bring some life to these bare plains? Just the two of us.'

Taren squeezed his hand in return and, for the first time in a long while, Leander's heart felt a flicker of something other than sadness. 'OK, let's search for a place to call home.'

***

They finally found that place more than a year after leaving the city. Scraping by on little food made them thinner in build, but the struggle kept them strong. Finding supplies was a daily puzzle, but they were happy enough in their wanderings. At least, Leander hoped Taren shared his

425

contentment.

The further they travelled from the city, the lighter their hearts became. Lighter but never weightless. Their considerations turned to the state of the world. The thrashings of the lightning that dashed around the scorched sky no longer bothered them or disturbed their sleep, and when they first laid eyes on the flat plain that met the base of a long ridge of mountains they could only stop and stare.

Leander's mind fed him the faded memories of his original dream, and the details matched so closely it was like walking back into a projection of it. The one they'd experienced in the holding cells of the Forge, but much less vibrant. The mountains lined the land in a great, rocky streak, and the flat plain stretching out from their base would be perfect for cultivation… or at least they hoped so.

The tall grass was not long dead, there was a chance the land could still be revived with the tools they'd brought with them. The closer they got and the more they surveyed it, the more certain they were that this would be their own little world, their own piece of paradise. Where they could live unrestrained and in whatever manner they wanted. One more corner of the world would be less lonely.

Yet a gaping absence dragged its dirty, jagged fingernails over his heart. Something, or rather someone, was missing. Would always be missing. Because of him. Again he stared at his stained hand. Again he told himself he didn't deserve to be free of his pain.

They'd spoken of it sometimes under the wild, dangerous night sky when sleep eluded them. They both carried burdens they'd never be able to let go of. Unable to pry their rigid hands away from the concept of blame.

Unwilling to employ the idea of absolution for themselves. They could only be of comfort to each other, and Taren was an endless salve. How much of a comfort Leander was in return, he couldn't say. He'd do better, as soon as he could. Until then he knew his grief was safe in Taren's care.

Leander couldn't stop himself from looking off into the distance. How far away was the edge? Slowly creeping towards them all. The Forgemaster had said in thirty years the city would be gone. That gave them some time at least. Would the two of them even live long enough to see that fate? Part of him hoped not. They were quite the pair, the thought brought a quiet chuckle to his lips. This time he let it out.

'What are you chuckling at?' Taren asked through a broad smile, the same hope shining in his eyes as he surveyed the land.

'Nothing, I was just thinking how suited to one another we are.' A dying tree marked the plains in the distance, and the two of them made their way towards it in agreement. It would be their home.

63

Acceptance

Taren leaned against the doorway of their home with a smile on his face and his arms folded. Leander was out in the furthest field, checking the crops. In the years since they left the dream and settled into the mountain-edged plains, they'd achieved far more than they'd expected. To build their home they'd travelled up into the mountains for rock, and over a day's trek to a struggling forest for wood. Back and forth they'd walked, day after day. It had been no small task to get the materials they needed and to shape and fasten them.

Their house was small, no bigger than it needed to be, but it was home. More of a home than either of them had ever had. The land had been surprisingly fertile under the ashen top layer, but it had taken no small amount of work to turn it all. Clearing the dead grass had taken months, but had provided the material for their roof. Nothing was wasted, and nothing was useless.

The way they'd come to live gave them both a deep satisfaction, and they wished for nothing but the mercy of the weather so that the crops could grow. The first field they planted had failed. They hadn't turned enough soil, but now it burst with luscious golden crop and the second, third and fourth fields were not far behind. Watching Leander in the distance Taren felt both blessed and grateful for him. His knowledge of the land was extensive and he was able to adapt.

The tree next to their home was still dead, though it hadn't deteriorated further, and the pond that ailed next to it seemed to grow clearer every year. Maybe the land was on the mend. They had almost finished planting the fifth field. A few more rows to go. Taren stood upright and flinched against a shooting pain that ripped through his leg. The left one was now totally absorbed by the dream, though he was grateful it hadn't spread further across his face. Everywhere else though? That seemed to be fair game.

It had no pattern in how it spread. His left arm was taken, the left side of his torso and a great blotch of his back. Leander didn't fare much better. The dark staining of the hollow's mark bloomed in unpredictable pools as well. There were few places on his limbs and torso not affected, and most recently the splotches had started to join.

Five years… that was how long it had been since they'd left. Sometimes Taren found himself watching the horizon, hoping to see Fion out on an expedition, but she never came. He missed her deeply. The horizon remained as empty as ever. The lightning had calmed in the last few years, they often wondered how or why but couldn't think of an answer. Enough pondering though, they had a field to finish off.

Leander beamed as Taren joined him, which always warmed his heart. Such a simple thing, to see that someone was happy to see you every day. It had taken a long time for

Leander to recover his smile, and Taren wouldn't waste a single chance to encourage him to use it.

'You must have been up early,' Taren stated with a smirk.

'Well, that's no surprise really is it? I've always gotten up early.'

'One of these days perhaps you'll actually stay in bed an extra hour or so with me.'

'It hasn't happened yet, don't hold out hope.'

'There's only so many attempts I can offer at trying to make it worth your time.'

Leander smiled and shook his head. 'The mornings are for working, I can't just lie about in bed once I'm awake. I have to get something done.'

'We wouldn't be lying about for long.' Taren winked at him and a laugh echoed across the field.

'You're terrible, make yourself useful and start planting before we both get tired. Doesn't take much these days.' He wasn't wrong. They'd both noticed it over the past year. Their stamina had decreased, their functions beginning to stutter. They didn't discuss it. They didn't need to. They'd let go of any naïvety they'd clung to long ago. All they wanted to do was finish planting the final field.

***

It took them several days to finish those few rows. A job that originally would have taken a few hours at most. They tired quickly and rested as frequently as they needed. Leander was taking rest among the roots of the tree next to their home. On the side facing the pond, the roots came together in such a way that they perfectly supported anyone who sat there. They could even both fit there, side by side, lying together in the breeze on the good days.

Taren dug the last three holes and scattered seeds inside them. What an empire they'd made. It looked better than the dream that had so often flashed across his mind because it was real. They'd built it with their own hands. Covering the holes with the soil again he patted them down, ignoring the jabbing pulses running through the networks of his body. They were finished.

He stood with great effort and surveyed their hard work. It satisfied Taren to know they'd brought some of the dying land back to fruition. It gave him hope that such knowledge would be discovered by the Forge's expeditions if they ever started up again. It just took some honest effort. Yet a part of him saddened to think the Crumbling Edge would come and take away all they'd done. For now he needed rest, and Leander's arms would be the nicest place to find it.

The walk back to the house from the field took an age, his limp more pronounced now than ever. Leander opened his eyes and gave a welcoming smile as he approached, raising one arm to indicate there was space to lay down next to him.

'We finally finished it, Lea. The fifth field is done.'

'It took us long enough. A few days to plant a few rows of field? We're slacking.'

'We finished it before the sun set, at least.'

'Barely, it's setting now.' Taren looked over the pond to find that Leander was right. The muted orange battled to be seen through the ever broiling clouds but it tainted the sky with pinks and tinged reds. He much preferred the summer months for this reason. In the winter the sun set behind the mountains, now he could see it setting across the flat plains. Sinking ever lower into the crops they'd so lovingly planted and raised.

'At least it's done, and now we can sit to watch the sun set. I can't think of any better company either.'

'What other company would you get out here?' Leander chuckled.

'Can't you just enjoy the moment?' Taren elbowed him.

The minutes passed and as a silence fell upon them and the sun sank lower and lower in the sky, Leander's chest hitched under Taren's cheek. He reached for Leander's hollow-stained hand and knitted their fingers together. He didn't look up, knowing that Leander hated being seen in his sadder moments, but he reassured him,

'It's OK. Our work is done. We can rest now. We can rest together.' His own breathing became strained, his eyelids fluttering as he snuggled deeper into the nook of Leander's neck. Tears speckled him from above every few seconds and he held on to Leander tighter, breathing through the pain in his chest as he heard the warm heartbeat of his companion start to skip and slow.

The breeze toyed with their hair and caressed their skin as they lay together between the roots of the tree, and when Taren stole an upward glance he caught sight of a bud sprouting from the lowest branch. The belt around his chest squeezed, and his last happy breaths came in wheezes. Leander gripped his hand, not in panic but in acceptance. 'Don't worry Lea. We're just a bit out of breath, that's all.'

And as the sun set, the only sound on the plains from then on was the gentle swish of zephyrs through the rich, but lonely, fields.

64 – Epilogue

Answer

Several years later, a dark huddle of indigo robes approached a flat plain bursting with overgrown crop. The golden strands climbed as high as their shoulders and the ground was littered with unharvested food, which in turn sprouted more and more growth. The plains sat at the root of a mountainous ridge that ran like a spine through the land. It was the first true sign of life they'd seen on their long journey. Naturally there was suspicion, but also the only real hope they'd had. They had to report it to the expedition leader.

'Wait… look there.' One of the dreamsmiths pointed through the fields. Something else had grown on the land. 'Fetch the leader, the rest of us will investigate.' One of the four smiths dashed back the way they'd come, heading for another pair of dreamsmiths further down the road.

***

The smith came to an abrupt stop in front of a blue-robed figure. Her mismatched eyes surveyed him expectantly.

'What did you find?'

'Vicemaster Fion, we found… new crops. Fields of them just ahead. I know we thought the plains were full of grass but it's actually… food. There's also a house, and what looks like… a living tree.'

'What? We haven't seen a living tree in years. They're all dying or dead, just like the other flora.' A hope sparked in her eyes and she set off at full speed. 'Geran, what are you waiting for, get a move on.' He nodded and took off to follow her instructions. Geran really did make a better dreamsmith than a culler, and she had no regrets about recruiting him to the expedition team. He'd earned his dreamsmith robe many times over in the years since Taren departed, as had the other cullers that followed him into a new way of life. Still, she could praise them later.

Fion didn't stop running until she was metres from the tree. The strangest tree she'd ever laid eyes on, but also the most beautiful. The trunk twisted together with iridescent crystal and dark molten glass. They snaked in and out of the wood, twirling around the branches and seemingly giving life to the once-dead being. Bright green leaves beamed against the ashen grey of the sky, and yet there was a hint of blue there. The sky had been scorched and had never changed on their journey, why were there scraps of colour burning through?

The water in the pond a few steps away was the clearest Fion had ever seen outside of the dreamveil. It teemed with small creatures. Was the pond feeding the tree? The crop feeding both? How had it been accomplished? The house was derelict now, beyond repair, but people had lived here.

434

Could it really be them? If so, where were they? Carefully, and against the advice of the other smiths, Fion stepped forward and reached for the unusual trunk of the tree. The moment she made contact a flurry of memories rushed into her. Feelings so strong she couldn't stand. Her knees knocked against the crystal roots as happy reminders flooded her system.

Times from the Forge, messing around with Taren, saying goodbye to him. Her finding Leander in the holdings and then coming back to free him. Then there were the memories she wasn't part of. The struggles of the road and the anguish of the burden of truth. It all melted away and parted, the gap filling with love and contentment. Their memories were both here. Could it be…?

Taking quiet steps backwards she assessed the tree once more. Now she was certain. The iridescent crystal… like the marks on Taren's face. The black glass, the colour of hollows… like the mark on Leander's hand. This tree was them now. They'd built a home and lived off of the land just as they'd said they would. Their ailments must have caught up with them.

Such a mix of feelings stirred together. They'd found happiness but she'd lost them. All her hope of one day finding them trickled away. She'd taken too long to get there. Her tears fell on to the roots and yet she found herself smiling. The tree felt… happy. Content. Accepting. They must have died together, looking out over all their hard work in total freedom from the constraints of the dreamveil. For a brief moment she wished she'd joined them when she'd had the chance, but it was fleeting. There was work to do.

A small thump beside her caught her attention. An acorn-type nut that shone with a turquoise colour. She'd never seen any fruit or nut like it. The smiths all looked up, seeing the fruits of the tree for the first time. Had they managed to start reversing the process? Had they stopped the advance of the Edge?

'I need to report to the Forgemaster, I'll head out of the grass to send a message by resonance. Geran, search the house as much as you can, if they found something out here we need the information. They might have managed to reverse the process, or at least made a start with it. The sky and water are proof of that. Everyone else, push forward. We still need to make it to the Edge.

'Take some of the fruits and nuts from the tree and plant them along the way. They might have the same effect on the land as this tree seems to have here. They might be the key we were looking for. Maybe... maybe this world was dying from neglect. It could be our fault, and also our responsibility to right that wrong.' The dreamsmiths nodded and went about the tasks they were set.

Fion walked out of the grass briskly, heart hammering in her chest. Had they really done it? Did the two of them give the world its answer? With heavy breaths she turned back to look at the house and the beautiful tree. The golden crop swaying in the breeze. The image of the dream she'd seen underground in the Forge overlaid on to it, and the similarities were a comfort and a relief. A salve to her fresh grief.

'I'm so glad…' tears filled her eyes and a smile lit Fion's face, 'that the two of you got to live that dream.'

END

Acknowledgements

Dreamsmiths is not the first fantasy novel I ever wrote, but it is the first one to make it out into the world and I can't explain how amazing that feels. The day I held the proof copy in my hand I could barely believe it. A full-length novel that I'd created over the space of three years! It was beyond imagination and I just kept staring at it in disbelief. It was a landmark moment for me as a writer.

Hopefully it's the first of many, but this one wouldn't have become the story it is now without some help. So, thank you once again to my beta readers for this project! Fun fact, the beta readers are the reason Fion has her own point of view chapters in this book – originally she was a primary character but not a protagonist and she had no chapters of her own. I'm really grateful that people wanted to see more of her, because she adds something awesome to this story.

My wonderful artist, Eli, has once again produced an absolutely stunning cover. I'll always feel so lucky to have your art on the front of my books.

A heartfelt thank you to the usual suspects: My partner James, my older sister Kay, and the friends and connections I've come to make via my second home of nearly five years – the Writer's Block Discord Server.

You're all part of the reason this book, and my journey from writer to author, has been possible.

Also to my patrons, readers and the folks who have joined my author community – The Hazelwood – thank you for taking the time to check out my stories and for your extraordinary encouragement. There are so many more to come, so I'd better get back to work!

Next project coming September 2023 on Royal Road!

PERCEPTION PRISM
A magical realism novella

www.royalroad.com/profile/249195 /fictions